Two Civil Wars

RODGER CARLYLE

This is a work of fiction. The names, characters, organizations and events are products of the author's imagination and bear no relation to any living person or are used fictitiously.

TWO CIVIL WARS. Copyright © 2022 by Rodger Carlyle. All rights reserved.

Published in the United States by Verity Books, an imprint of Comsult, LLC.

All rights reserved. Except for brief passages except quoted in newspaper, magazine, radio, television or online reviews, no portion of this book may be reproduced, distributed, or transmitted in any form or by any means, electronic or mechanical including photocopying, recording, or information storage or retrieval systems without the prior written permission of the author and/or Comsult, LLC.

First published in 2023.

ISBN 978-1-7379497-8-7 (paperback)
ISBN 978-1-7379497-7-0 (hardback)

Cover design and formatting: Damonza

1
THE AMERICAN CIVIL WAR, 1863

The Waters of England and Richmond, Virginia

THE CAPTAIN OF the Confederate States of America ship *SUMTER* sent a messenger, ordering the engineer to increase power. The rattle of the steam engine and vibration from the rocking beam was new to a captain who grew up under sail. He'd used the bell signal cord at the helm to send the same message five minutes before but sensed no increase in speed.

"I don't think I have ever seen as many sails out here as this morning," he commented to the young quartermaster at the ship's wheel.

"Tis not often, Sir, that the shipyard sends off three new ships at the same time. Them sails most likely just curious folks, come to see three steam-sail military raiders all lined up like in a parade."

Six men had managed to get the *SUMTER* out of the becalmed Southampton Harbor, using the ship's modern engine. Once freed from the harbor, the breezes steadily increased, a half-hour before the rest of the ship's company came aboard, battling large waves as they shuttled from a merchant ship that had carried them from Mobile, Alabama. The *SUMTER* had waited hours while the two ships in front of them transferred their crews from the same vessel.

On the deck, officers were organizing the new crew into work teams. The Captain wouldn't know the quality of his green crew until they'd drilled for days. He'd ordered that the first organization was to select gun crews for the British built cannons. He smiled as he watched the other two Confederate ships begin to run up sails. Obviously, their captains had different priorities.

"Yup, those must just be gawkers," commented the young quartermaster, "they all just want to get closer where they can get a better look."

As the Captain shifted his eyes from the deck to the ships in front of him, an uneasy feeling came over him. Eight ships were maneuvering to form an L shape, some moving across the bows of the two ships now under sail, the others slowly forming a line paralleling the Confederate ships. He turned to a young ensign at the chart table. "Sound battle stations," he ordered, as cannon fire echoed over the water.

He watched his befuddled crew staring at confused officers. The deck resembled a pen outside a dairy barn as a herd of cows was gathered for milking. The Captain pointed, swinging his arm at multiple points on the horizon where the flash of cannons was erupting.

"Sir," called the quartermaster. The young man pointed to their left where two ships were bearing down on them. Two more were on a course to cut off any retreat back toward England.

The ship's second in command raced up the stairs from the deck below. "Oh my God," he whispered. "Must be a least a dozen of the bastards, and they have the wind." He extended the telescope he was carrying. "They are flying the stars and stripes." He swung the telescope to the two Confederate ships.

"Our sister ships are both turning with the wind and running," continued the officer who had only been aboard an hour.

"How long will it take to get a full set of canvas set?" asked the Captain. "On steam power alone, we can't outrun our enemy, not in this wind."

"Honestly, Sir, it might take a day. On the way from Mobile we drew lots for crewmen for each ship. I only ended up with three men who have any experience under sail. Most of our crew are brown-water sailors, almost all from river steamers. But we got lucky, we have four experienced artillerymen."

The Captain stood quietly for a full minute. "Get below and get the gun crews to their stations. I'm going to sail straight into the enemy. Maybe the other two ships can get away."

The new officer stood frozen. "I mean now," screamed the Captain, as he tugged the bell cord ordering full speed.

Next to the ship a shell splashed harmlessly into the water, then two more. To the left of the *SUMPTER* the first Yankee ship had turned, paralleling the ship. As the Captain watched, four more of that ship's cannons fired, throwing huge geysers of water in front of his ship. The Captain leaned over the rail trying to be heard over the bedlam on the deck below. "Pick any target and fire at will."

The second enemy ship turned onto their course, unleashing a well-timed stream of fire from eight guns. The final shell slammed the *SUMTER* at the bow, the heavy shell scattering splinters as it crashed in one side of the metal clad wooden hull and out the other. The sound of one of their own cannons firing drowned out the screams of wounded men.

On the horizon, the other two Confederate commerce raiders had managed a turn away from the Yankee ships along their port side. The maneuver turned the ships across the broadside of the three Yankee warships that had crossed their bow. He watched as each of the Confederate ships was hit, but both were pulling away from their attackers. The combination of steam engines and sail made them faster than the pursuers.

As the Confederate ships ran, two more of their enemies gave up and turned toward the *SUMTER*. Below, a second gun fired and then a third. The Captain watched as one of his own shells shattered a mast of one of the Yankee ships to his left. The damaged Yankee fired all eight of its guns as it turned away from the fight. Two Yankee shells slammed the side of his ship, blasting two of the *SUMTER*'s guns from their mounts. Pieces of men, arms and heads scattered across the deck. Other men staggered away from the carnage clutching gaping wounds.

He was proud as another of his own guns fired, blasting away the quarterdeck of a second enemy ship. Below, a rebel yell like that heard on the battlefields of Maryland or Pennsylvania rose from those still able to fight. The yell was drowned out by the sound of two more shells slamming their hull and then an explosion as one of the shells pierced the five pressure tanks of their steam engine. Every opening to the lower decks erupted with scalding steam, the hiss mixed with the screams of men being boiled alive.

The ship rolled onto its port side, the explosion ripping a massive hole in that side of the hull opening to tons of water. The bow dove into the next wave. Thousands of pounds of water over the bow broke the back of the weakened ship. The *SUMPTER* began to fold in the center, just as another shell exploded just below the quarterdeck, turning what little was left of the captain and quartermaster into crab food.

The office of the President of the Confederate States of America was cramped, stifling; most of the men stripped their ties and unbuttoned their jackets. Only three defied common sense, President Jefferson Davis, a portly navy captain by the name of Peterson, and in the back of the room a man who looked like he should be sitting on the sidewalk, a tin cup in his hand. Davis reread the label of the folder on his desk, **STRATEGY TO DISRUPT NORTHERN**

MARINE COMMERCE, (use of commerce raiders to disrupt Yankee shipping).

"The *MOBILE STAR* brought the news of a fight, Sir," said Peterson. "She ran the Union blockade into Beaufort three days ago. The armed ships we ordered from the British were delivered on time. All three raiders slipped out of Southampton together. They pulled down the Union Jacks and ran up our flag. Transfer of men from the *MOBILE STAR* to fill out the three crews went smoothly in spite of strong winds."

President Davis dabbed at sweat on his lip. "So, all three of our new ships were delivered per our contract with the English?"

"They were, and all three were armed, with a full crew. But Sir, not one of them had ever drilled with their ship's new long-range cannons. Hell, Sir, not one of the crews had ever loaded or fired a shot. When the captain of the *MOBILE STAR* heard firing at sea only miles from the rendezvous, he assumed the three battle cruisers were testing their big guns. It was only when his lookout scrambled to the deck to report muzzle flashes from a dozen different points on the horizon did the *STAR'S* captain begin to worry. The sound of heavy guns only lasted about fifteen minutes."

"The *MOBILE STAR* waited for a half hour and then sailed out to where they had seen the flashes," interjected an admiral, reading from a report. "They found a small boat with six men pulling hard for the English coast. Beyond them they could see two Yankee ships out where there might be more survivors. The *MOBILE STAR* picked up six survivors of the newly commissioned *SUMTER,* including one officer."

The Confederate President dabbed at the sweat on his face with a huge blue handkerchief. The perfume of magnolias added a sickly-sweet layer to the heat. "Do we know how many survivors the Yankees picked up? Do we know what happened to the other two ships?"

"No, Mr. President," continued Peterson. "The men picked up

by the *MOBILE STAR* said their captain sailed directly into the encirclement of Yankee frigates so that the other two ships had a chance to get away. The *SUMTER* was running on his new steam engine, so he was slower than molasses in Maine. The other two were already under sail. The last our boys saw of them, one was on a dead run, slugging it out with two Yankees. The other was leading three more on a chase before a strong north wind."

"Why didn't the Yankee's go after the *MOBILE STAR*?"

"That's what got me to thinkin'," offered the man in a worn canvas coat in the back of the room. That's why we are here."

"I wondered why the head of Naval Intelligence was sitting in my office dressed like a common dock worker," laughed Davis.

"Jeff, those Yankees were waiting for those three ships, only those ships. They knew how many, what they would look like and when they were coming. The *MOBILE STAR* was flying the English flag when she sailed right by those ships searching for more survivors. The Yanks never even looked at her," finished Clyde Holmes.

Holmes was the man in charge of intelligence, plotting tactics to defeat a Yankee navy many times the size of the Confederates.

"We may still have two of those new cruisers out there raising hell with Yankee commerce," offered an admiral sitting next to Holmes. "But, Mr. President, someone gave the Yanks precise information on those ships. It wasn't the ambassador, and it wasn't me. That means it was either your pal the Secretary of Treasury or Mead over in the Quartermaster Corps. He was the one who put together the contracts in England, the one who set the schedule."

"Remember Mr. President, that Colonel Mead was a Yankee officer," snarled Holmes.

"Clyde," laughed Jeff Davis, "you are the only man in this room who was not a Yankee officer. Still, I get your point. It couldn't have been the treasury secretary; the only thing he did was authorize our British allies to draw on our funds in the Bahamas.

There are, however, other possibilities, are there not? There must have been people on Mead's staff who knew what was going on."

"I am just an old police investigator. I am not one of you West Point boys, but even I know that some clerk forwarding a message isn't likely credible enough to put a dozen Naval Frigates off from the harbor in Southampton on that specific day. No, whoever leaked this has some real credibility with your old comrades up in D.C."

"Probably right." The President's face reflected the painful betrayal of an old friend. "I assume you are all here to get my blessing to arrest Colonel Mead. You have it but do it quietly. We don't want to alert the press that we allowed a Yankee spy to operate right under our noses."

"Most of us feel the same, we don't need to drag the government through the morass of a spy scandal. Do you know my son, Mr. President?" asked Captain Peterson. He pointed at a young officer in the back of the room."

A young army lieutenant rose and stepped forward, extending his hand toward the President of the Confederate States of America.

"William was a junior officer at West Point the last year Mead was there. Mead made William a rifle instructor. I suggest that we allow him to take a squad of men over to Mead's home tonight when there won't be a lot of prying eyes around. I think he can convince Mead that it is in his best interest to surrender peacefully."

"Bullshit," snarled Holmes. "The man's a spy. He is headed for a firing squad. I came in disguise. I have two more men waiting outside. He'll never see us coming. We'll walk right into his office and haul his butt out."

"No. Jefferson Davis shook his head. "Captain Peterson is right; this should be done as quietly as possible."

"Lieutanant Peterson, do you know Colonel Mead well enough to convince him to go silently?"

"The Colonel is a very smart man, Sir. If he is guilty of this, he knew the risks. He is also a proud man, not the kind of man that will want to be paraded through the streets under guard. I can get him out of his house without a fight, Sir."

Holmes shook his head, his shaggy brown hair whipping in front of his eyes. "I know when to shut up, Jeff, just like you did when I arrested you for that fight in the saloon while you were home from the academy. I understand trying to keep problems quiet just like you did when you knew that fight might get you thrown out of the Point. But I want to go on record as objecting to coddling this spy." He rose and headed toward the street, then stopped and turned. "You need to arrest him right away before he gets any inkling that he is compromised. We may be able to catch him if he tries to go north, but if he heads toward Mexico, he's gone."

Jefferson Davis laughed. "Hell Clyde, if the Juaristas find him they will shoot him for working with my government and if the Monarchists get a hold of him, they will shoot him for being part of Lincoln's support for Juarez."

2
THE MEXICAN CIVIL WAR, 1864

Fresnillo, Mexico

THE MOUNTAINOUS LANDS of north-central Mexico had been a barrier to attacks by the Juarista army, what the locals called "the army of the Little Indian President." Any army could be met by overwhelming force in a narrow battlefield defined by the steep, boulder-strewn terrain. But multiple Juarista armies attacking from different directions were turning the barriers into a trap.

The conservatives owned the land grant haciendas. They were families that worshiped in Catholic churches and supported the new Monarchy in Mexico. They owned the rich gold and silver mines. They used their wealth to crush the government of a man who they believed was not the legitimate president of Mexico, explaining that the Juarez government was inefficient and corrupt. It also was a government determined to suppress the historical power of the landed elites and their primary ally, the Catholic Church.

Benito Juarez became President when the liberal elected President resigned in disgrace. As Chief Justice of the Mexican Supreme Court, Juarez was selected as his successor. The conservatives seized on the moment to petition the European powers to send Mexico a pedigreed noble to become emperor. In 1862, Emperor Maximilian arrived from Austria with an army of French regulars and military units from Germany, Austria and other European powers, each nation owed millions of dollars from delinquent loans to Mexico.

In the north, after years of trying, two small armies of Juaristas had surprised and defeated units of French and Royalist troops who guarded the region. At a small village where three roads came together outside of Fresnillo, the hastily assembled Royalist militia waited behind overturned wagons and piles of earth thrown up by local miners loyal to the landowners. Behind them, the road into the city of Fresnillo, the regional capital, was unguarded.

"Major Shannon, is your artillery ready?" asked a graying man in his early fifties. He deliberately spoke English. Colonel Miguel Huerta brushed the dust of the trail from his perfectly tailored blue uniform. Huerta was a colonel in the Royalist army. Next to him, a young French lieutenant stood talking to two French sergeants.

"We have only six cannons left," replied Shannon, an Irish mining engineer who in another life had been an officer in the British army. "The rest were lost when our roadblocks fell to the forces of the Little President. I have placed them where they can cover the approaches."

Huerta paused, thinking about the disastrous attacks the previous days. "The peasants sent no more than twenty-five soldiers through the rocks on the hillsides to strike from the rear. That's all it took, twenty-five men attacking from behind our fortifications to rout ten times that many of our soldiers. In spite of our warning, the French officers expected stupid Juarista commanders to march single file against their positions. Our allies seem to have little respect for Mexicans on either side of this conflict."

Huerta turned to the French lieutenant exchanging words in

that officer's native tongue. He turned back to the Irishman and continued. "The scouts tell the Lieutenant that the commanders of the units that ran away have been captured by the Juaristas. The enemy may put those men at the front of their columns. We may have to fire on our own friends to save Fresnillo."

"Can the French bring up reinforcements from those guarding the other side of the city?" asked Shannon. "Once our enemy feels the wrath of our cannons at close range, they will retreat and figure out how to surround us. We won't hold very long with only two hundred soldiers." He turned to Huerta; his face drawn. "We need to know if we have reinforcements coming."

Huerta passed on the question in French to the allied officer at his side. It didn't take the French officer long to seize salvation. In minutes the horses of the lieutenant and the two French sergeants were fading in the distance.

Huerta turned back to the Irishman who stood waiting for orders. "Thank you, Mike, for your help. When I interviewed you for the position of mine manager, I took note of your experience as a British artillery officer, but I never dreamed that my country would ever put that experience to use. I hope you live through today. You may commence firing at the column on the western road at your discretion."

Shannon lowered his old telescope. The group of several hundred men winding their way toward the village was within range, but with only a hundred shells for the old brass cannons, Shannon held his fire. From the hillside above town, two Mexican lookouts stood in the open, signaling the approach of the second column on the northern road. That group would appear through a narrow gap any moment now. Shannon hated letting his enemy get within a quarter mile before engaging, but the twisting road they traveled hid them.

From the lower road a Juarista cannon crashed, and a shell flew harmlessly over their position. Shannon watched as the Juarista soldiers nudged more cannons into position to fire. "They only have captured artillery," called Shannon. "That means they only have grape shot or solid shot, no exploding ordinance." Shannon made the sign of the cross on his chest. "Thank you, Father, for small blessings."

Shannon's prayer was interrupted as a hundred Juarista soldiers charged from the north road. With the French gone, Shannon switched to Spanish, no longer worried about insulting soldiers of a country that had been an enemy of Britain for centuries. He screamed out a warning as he gave the order to fire. In front of him, the rocks, nails, and lead balls from the first shot tore through the attackers. A dozen men stumbled but many more continued the charge. The second cannon maimed more men, but the charge did not falter until the third shot had reduced the enemy number by half. The remaining Juaristas scattered to either side of the road looking for cover, firing their muskets.

Shannon's amateur gun crews fumbled through a reload. From the lower road, a half dozen cannons were now lobbing solid shot at the village, blasting holes in rock and adobe structures, but doing little damage. Shannon ordered one of his three cannons covering that road to return fire. There wasn't much chance of causing any real damage, but it might slow the coming attack.

Colonel Huerta smiled as he directed twenty of his meager reserve of infantry to the barricades next to the cannons on the north road. One of the men reloading the cannons collapsed; blood gushed from a hole in his back, as Juarista soldiers moved from rock to rock toward their position. From behind Huerta, his youngest officer, the sixteen-year-old son of the owner of the Bank of Fresnillo grabbed Shannon's arm and spun him around. From the road to Fresnillo, the French lieutenant and one of the sergeants galloped back toward the village. A horse with an empty saddle ran with them.

Shannon grabbed a replacement from the barricade, leading

the man through a load of the cannon. Before the reload was complete, a second group of Juaristas charged. This group got to within a hundred yards before shot from the cannons ended the attack. The enemy survivors joined their Juarista comrades firing into the barricades. They targeted those working to reload the cannons. Where the artillery had done its work, the road flowed red. More than fifty men lay, some unmoving, others crawling toward cover or just twisting and screaming.

The man next to Shannon dropped, one of the huge fifty-caliber bullets from a Juarista musket nearly decapitating him. A second man clutched his stomach, trying to contain his insides after a bullet sliced the front of his abdomen open. Bullets swarmed by Shannon, kicking up dirt as they slapped the earthen barricade and clinking from the cannons.

A whistle from Shannon's left forced him to change positions. Instead of charging across a mile of open road, the enemy infantry on the west road had begun working their way from rock to rock, the closest only three hundred yards away. Shannon waited until a dozen men were exposed. He tapped the gunner of the closest gun on the shoulder. The cannon sent a hail of steel into the rocks. The shot brought the attack to an end for a half-dozen soldiers, but a dozen more took their place. Around the cannoneers inexperienced Royalist draftee soldiers struggled to reload their muskets and return fire.

Behind him, Colonel Huerta called, starting Shannon toward the Monarchist Colonel, infuriated to see the French had returned. The French officer's horse lay dead at the side of the road. "Fuego a voluntad," screamed Shannon. He repeated the order in English: "Fire at will."

"A small group has slipped around behind us and have set up a roadblock only a mile down the road," said Huerta. "The lieutenant thinks it is no more than a dozen men. He wants enough men to take it out. I am giving them to him. It is our only escape if we cannot stop the enemy." In the background the crash of three of Shannon's cannons let the men know that the enemy was paying dearly.

Before Shannon could respond, the French lieutenant stumbled and groaned, then sank to his knees, his head folding forward, the top of his head resting on the ground. Red stained his back. The French sergeant knelt to help his officer then collapsed, a bullet hole in the middle of his chest. Huerta and Shannon looked up at the hillside behind the village. Dozens of enemy soldiers were working their way from the hilltop toward them. Shannon's two spotters stood, their hands in the air as their enemy crawled from rock to rock past them. With a pistol in one hand and a machete in the other, a huge man stood in front of Shannon's lookouts screaming. The man swung the machete, catching one of the spotters on the right collar, opening him like a melon all the way to his waist. His partner picked up his rifle and aimed it toward the Royalists and pulled the trigger. With the machete at his back, he began to reload.

Terrified Royalist soldiers abandoned the barricades. Behind them, Juarista soldiers swarmed over the piles of earth, bayonetting the men at the cannons as they came. Huerta called to the few men in his reserve and then to the men running. He grabbed at them as they fled. He pointed at the tiny church. Some turned to follow him, but most dropped their weapons, the rocky ravine below the village offering salvation.

Shannon found himself being dragged by the boy officer toward the church, followed by Huerta and two other officers. With them were a couple of dozen soldiers who in another life had worked for Huerta either at the hacienda or at the mine. Around them, the Juarista soldiers herded the remaining royalist soldiers toward the church, shooting or bayonetting anyone who didn't move quickly enough.

The church windows bristled with the rifle barrels of the men trapped inside. They could not shoot without killing men who they had fought next to only minutes before. Behind what was left of their own troops, the officers watched the cannons from their own barricades being rolled toward the church. Huerta slipped a silver case from his coat, picking a cigar from the case. He then passed the case to the four other officers. He said nothing as he struck a match and lit his cigar, then passed the matches to the others. The young son of the bank president began to gag as he tried to imitate the others as they drew the smoke into their mouths; the rich smoke covering the smell terrified men had when they lost control of their insides.

In front of the church a wall of captured Royalist soldiers divided as two cannons were pushed through the crowd. Next to each was a sergeant of their own troops, a lit punk in his hands, and a gun at his head. "Por favor perdóname, Senior Huerta," cried the man. The captured sergeants lowered the burning wands to the cannons. The rock wall of the church exploded as two heavy shells ripped into the church. Inside a dozen men lay moaning and bleeding. The young officer was ripped in half, one of the cannon balls hitting him in the chest.

"I must stop this," uttered Huerta as he rose from the floor, sweeping rock fragments and dirt from his uniform. He smiled at Shannon as he extracted a perfectly laundered and pressed white bandana from his pocket and tied it to a shattered piece of window frame.

Outside, two Juarista officers accepted Huerta's sword, and then forced the officers into chairs around a table carried from a nearby home. The Juarista officers produced a bottle of Tequila and four glasses, pouring each of the men at the table a drink. One at a time they were led away for a short interrogation and then returned to the table. Each man was given a piece of paper and a pen and ink to write a letter to his family.

"They're going to shoot us, Mike," whispered Huerta. "I am sorry that I got you into this."

"I am no braver man than most," replied Shannon. "But I am first a Catholic. I guess I will die for my faith. These heathens are making war on the Church."

When the men were finished writing, their hands were bound behind their backs. They were led to the sidewall of the church. Each was offered a blindfold. Huerta refused his, but the others allowed pieces of torn uniforms to be tied around their faces. They listened as their executioners were given their orders and then as the officer counted: uno, dos, tres.

A dozen rifles exploded. The moans of men torn by bullets filled the quiet, then stopped. Shannon stood in shocked silence. He couldn't believe how little pain came with death. A moment later his blindfold was removed, and he looked down at the bodies of his comrades.

"Mr. Shannon," said one of the Juarista officers, "this is not your war. Go home." Shannon smiled nervously at Antonio, Colonel Huerta's younger brother.

∽

Maria Huerta watched the small column of Juarista troops as they wound their way through the trees in front of the hacienda. Their appearance could only mean one thing.

Miguel had been a dotting, older, husband. She'd learned to deeply love him in the six years they had been married. She was not going to give the Juaristas the satisfaction of her tears.

A young officer dismounted and approached the door. Maria swung it open before he could knock. He said nothing as he handed Miguel's note then offered to leave her for a few minutes while she read.

"Está muerto mi esposo?" she asked firmly.

"Si, Señora Huerta."

Maria looked past the young lieutenant toward the Nationalist major waiting at the gate. Somehow, she wasn't shocked to see her brother-in-law, Antonio waiting on a horse that her late husband had given him for his twenty-first birthday.

The nationalist lieutenant handed Maria a second letter, giving her four hours to pack anything she wanted from the house. She could take her carriage and one wagon, and the horses needed to pull them. The hacienda was now the property of the government of Benito Juarez.

Antonio helped Maria into her elegant coach. "I will see to Miguel's funeral," he offered. "I tried to convince him that once the American president began aiding the nationalists that his cause was doomed. But that was months ago."

"Could you do nothing to save your own brother?" replied Maria, her face scarlet.

"His only salvation would have been for him to swear allegiance to Benito Juarez. I would have never asked it," replied Antonio and then added. "Maria, where will you go?"

"First to Agua Calientes, to your uncle's hacienda. From there, who knows," she finished, wiping tears from her eyes.

"Maria, it may take two or three years, but the Nationalists will reach Agua Calientes. Our uncle is hated by Benito Juarez. It will not be safe for you at the Hacienda de la Cruz. You will be moving from one battlefield to the next."

"Perhaps, but we are still family. Maybe cousin Denali can talk some sense into her father." She paused before continuing, "or someone will come along and help Emperor Maximillian and President Juarez realize that they both want the same thing." She tapped the side of the coach signaling her driver. Turning to Antonio, she continued, "If the Canadians could just find the same hatred that the Americans and Mexicans have found, the whole continent would be killing each other."

As she drove away, she reread the second letter. The letter granting her safe passage explained that it was only because her cousin, Denali de la Cruz, had nursed the general leading the attack on

Fresnillo back to life after he had been seriously wounded months before, that she was allowed to take anything with her. Maria wondered which side that general had been fighting for when he was wounded. For many, loyalty was a process in Mexico. For Miguel, however, everything was absolute. Now he was absolutely dead. She whispered a prayer.

Cousin Denali, I have always wondered how much trouble you could get yourself into and survive, she thought. *Today I thank you for whatever you did for the General. Gracias.*

3

THE SAME DAY THAT MARIA BEGINS HER JOURNEY TO AGUA CALIENTE

THE LIGHT IN the parlor of Mead's house disappeared and a minute later a new light appeared in an upstairs window. Peterson and his troop watched silently from the street. The simple, white two-story home looked almost empty, as the home of a confirmed bachelor should. Peterson knew that Mead even refused the servants a man of his stature would normally employ.

"Sergeant, please have your men rest easy out here on the street while you and I explain things to the Colonel and arrest him. I don't think you will need to handcuff him. He's not a combat soldier, just a glorified shopkeeper."

Their knock on the door brought the sounds of footsteps bounding down the stairs. The window next to the door reflected the light of a candle growing brighter as it moved toward the door.

"Lieutenant, what are you doing here this late at night?" asked Colonel Mead. The man in his nightshirt stood a bit over six feet tall, with hair clipped only a quarter inch from his scalp.

His brown eyes scanned Peterson's face and then that of the older sergeant next to him. The dozen men casually leaning against the fence at the edge of the yard brought a smile to Mead's face. "Won't you two come in while I dress?"

"Wait in the entry, Sergeant," ordered Peterson. "I will follow the Colonel upstairs and explain the situation."

The two men were gone only five minutes. Peterson held a pistol at the Colonel's back as the two men descended the stairs and walked into the parlor. "Sergeant, would you please come here?" called Peterson. "The Colonel has a box of files that we will want for his trial."

The sergeant stepped into the room. Mead stood with his hands over his head near the back door. Before the sergeant could comment, he felt the barrel of a pistol slip into his left ear. "Listen very carefully and you will live to see those grandchildren of yours."

Five minutes later, the sergeant was flat on his stomach with his hands and feet tied tightly together and drawn up behind him, his mouth stuffed with a dishrag that tasted of soap. Peterson pushed on the sergeant's feet, rocking him back and forth like a children's wooden horse.

"Sergeant, the Colonel and I are going to leave you here," whispered Peterson. "There is only one United States, and we are both headed north to help make sure it stays that way. Please tell my father that was what he expected when he sent me to the Point."

Mead and Peterson slipped quietly into the alley behind the house and walked calmly two blocks to where the noise of a rowdy saloon crowd celebrating Wednesday drew them. The two men walked past the front door to the hitching posts on the side of the building. Each picked a horse, leading the stolen animal a block from the saloon before swinging into the saddle. Mead turned his mount south and kicked the horse into a trot.

Peterson caught up in seconds. "Colonel, shouldn't we be headed toward Washington?"

"Bill, in about an hour all hell is going to break loose in Richmond. Every town and every Confederate unit and checkpoint will be looking for us all the way to the front lines. We can't outrun the telegraph. I'm betting it will take a couple of days for them to start to look west or south. I think our best chance is to get to the US picket ships in Charleston. If that route is blocked, we head for Mexico."

※

Exhausted, Mead and Peterson stepped down from their saddles at a small inn where the owner stood shaking his head. "You boys sure don't take very good care of your horses. Those mounts of yours look like they been ridden real hard. They could use some rest and more than the water in that trough out there."

"You are right of course. We are carrying a private message from President Davis to the Governor of North Carolina. The colonel here needs to get there and back in four days. The message is about some troop movements and the President isn't comfortable sending it by telegraph."

"If you will take care of them, I have a couple of saddle horses I can loan you. You can swap them back for your horses on your way back through. I'll have the boy at the stable brush your mounts down and feed 'em."

"That would be really helpful. How much to board our horses for four days or so?" Mead reached into a pocket.

"Jeb down at the livery won't take a thing for helping the army, but the boy comes from a poor family, so a dollar would really help him out."

Mead counted out five silver dollars. "Here, this is for breakfast, a tip for the boy and any trouble that the owner of the livery encounters."

In thirty minutes, the men were back on the road. "Maybe it's the grits. I never developed a taste for them," laughed Peterson. "And my wife always liked my blue uniform better than this gray. Anyway, it will be good to go back to soldering instead of hiding in dark corners." Mead wasn't in the mood for small talk, he just nodded.

The roadblock was at a bridge just outside of Raleigh. By the time the men realized the traffic on the turnpike was coming to a stop, they were within a hundred yards of the simple bar over the road and the soldiers who manned it. The rebs had chosen the location well. To the left a freshly plowed field stretched for a mile. To the right was an impassible swamp. Mead studied Peterson and smiled. He quietly drew his revolver, hiding it behind the horse's head. "Might as well work up toward that bar slowly. It will give the horses a blow before we really need them."

They crept forward until there were only four wagons ahead of them. "Now said Mead." The two men spurred their mounts. In seconds they were at the bar, which had just been lifted to allow a buggy through. A Confederate officer watching from under a tree down the road tugged at his pistol as the two men raced past the six soldiers manning the checkpoint. The officer raised his pistol and fired, then ran into the center of the road taking aim at the men galloping at him. The Confederate officer shot again before Mead's pistol replied. The officer folded at the waist, a crimson splotch on his shirt. He stumbled backward two steps before collapsing onto the road. He looked up, blood bubbling from his mouth as he tried to call out. The fugitives raced past him rounding the next bend.

Coming the other direction were two companies of Confederate infantry and two mounted officers. "There is a Yankee raiding party just around the corner," screamed Peterson as the men rode by.

A hundred yards beyond the foot soldiers, Mead and Peterson slowed their mounts to a trot. "I'm really happy that boy couldn't shoot straight," said Peterson. "Probably grew up on a plantation hunting quail. He must have been flock shooting. I watched his aim. He shot between us."

"Probably right. I didn't want to shoot, but he wasn't going to miss with us riding straight away from him. We have to get off this road. I suggest we head toward the ocean on the first crossroad."

Mead reached down to pat his horse on the neck. His hand came away bloody. He leaned down to examine the wound. A small bullet had cut a furrow along his horse's neck before punching a hole just in front of his saddle.

"I don't think the wound is too bad. Those .35 caliber pistols most of the Confederate officers carry can't do much to heavy muscle. If I don't have to run him hard, he should heal up just fine."

Peterson was watching behind them where two horsemen had just stopped next to the Confederate infantry, now in skirmish lines across the road. In seconds those two horsemen and the two infantry officers kicked their horses into a gallop.

"That, Colonel, is not how this is going to play out. We have four mounted men on our tail."

The union men spurred their horses into a run. At a fork in the twisting road, Mead turned east onto a smaller side road that followed a stream through a narrow valley. Ahead was a steep hill. At the top, the two men reigned in their horses, hiding behind trees at the side of the road. Below, four crows circled, screeching at two Confederate officers who were close behind the men.

"Time to change horses," ordered Mead.

The Confederate officers following them warily approached the top of the rise. Each pulled his carbine from its scabbard and laid it in his lap. "Drop those rifles and step down gentlemen," ordered Mead.

Turning toward his voice, both men raised their short rifles. The first carbine fired in the general direction of the voice. Mead fired, tumbling the shooter from his horse. The other Confederate officer swung his carbine toward Mead and fired back without raising it to his shoulder. Mead's horse collapsed behind him, the heavy bullet hitting him between the eyes. Peterson shot twice.

The Confederate officer slumped from the saddle. Neither of the Confederate officers well trained mounts moved.

"Your friend is dead," said Mead to the wounded officer. He tugged the man's heavy wool uniform open and examined the wound just below his shoulder. The shot had smashed the collarbone and the shoulder joint behind it. Tiny fragments of bone stuck from the wound, but there was little blood. Mead tugged a bandana from the wounded man's neck and pressed it against the wound. "You are going to live. I'm taking you with us until I find a place to leave you and a horse well off from the road. By the time you get over the shock and crawl back in the saddle, we will be long gone."

"Y'all are the Yankee spies they are looking for," snarled the wounded man. He spat in Mead's face.

Mead wiped the spit away with the sleeve of his coat. "Right now, son, I am just an officer in the American army trying to save your life."

"Don't do me no favors, Yankee."

After hiding the dead soldier, Mead and Peterson left the wounded man, his feet tied, under a tree a few hundred yards from the road. Mead tied the horse that Peterson had been riding to another tree.

That evening they took turns sleeping in a haystack next to an empty cabin in the mountains. They gorged themselves on canned peaches they'd found in a root cellar next to the cabin. They were on their way again at midnight, the light of a full moon filtering through overhanging tree branches.

The two men were recognized once more on their way to Charleston. They escaped by turning off the road and leading their horses across a railroad trestle into thick woods. The smell of the saltwater below the bridge led them to a slough and a shack with no road in or out. Mead and Petersen stopped to rest only feet from a tilted cabin that had never seen paint. A door screeched across the buckled porch and five tattered men with glaring eyes emerged. Behind the men, the slough opened into Charleston Harbor.

"We ain't been movin' contraband or moonshine, or whatever you think we been doin', officer," said the oldest man. "An' my boys here ain't been nowhere near the army. They ain't deserters." The man wore homespun cotton pants with suspenders over his naked chest. His graying hair surrounded his head like the mane of a lion, molding into his filthy beard.

"Take it easy, old timer," replied Mead. "I'm Thomas Mead and that's William Peterson. William and I ran into some highwaymen a few hours ago and took off through the woods. We got ourselves all turned around, being from Virginia and all; we don't know these parts."

The men spread out as the two fugitives dismounted. Next to the father, the smallest brother fidgeted. To his left, the second brother, slightly bigger and a bit older leaned on a long stick. The biggest brother stood smiling, all four front teeth missing. A fifth man stood behind the other four shaking his head.

"We are late to report into our new army unit. Probably be in a world of trouble if we don't get there by tonight," added Peterson. My daddy would skin me if I ever got crosswise with General Michael, especially after he went out on a limb to get me an officer's posting. Even Colonel Mead here couldn't get me out of that."

The end of the long stick whistled at Mead's head, as the middle brother threw everything he had into a swing. Mead sidestepped, the end of the stick slamming into the ground. Before the man could lift the stick, Mead slammed his left foot down on the shaft, breaking it. He leaned forward, grabbing the end that the man was trying to raise with his left arm. Mead pulled him forward, picking up the broken piece lying on the ground with his right. Before the man could reset, Mead slammed the stick across the side of the brother's head. The man dropped, his scalp spraying blood. Mead swung to his left as two of the man's brothers lunged for him.

Ducking the first fist, Mead swung the broken stick, cracking the biggest brother across the knees, folding him over just as another brother delivered a kick aimed at Mead's stomach. The heavy boot caught the folded man in the side of the head. Mead leaped over the falling man, smashing the third brother's nose with his left fist and then drove him into the ground with his shoulder. His head made the sound of someone rapping a ripe melon as it hit a rock.

Mead crawled to his feet just as Peterson cocked his pistol, aiming at the two remaining men who stood, shocked.

"I told them, Pa, that they shouldn't mess with no army officers."

The old man smiled, his rotten teeth taking any warmth from the gesture. "No need for the gun, sonny. My boys are just testing you a bit. Now what do you two want?"

Peterson stared at the three ragged men at Mead's feet. He doubted that any of them had seen the inside of a classroom or ever worn store-bought clothes. "We told you; we just need directions on how to reach Charleston by tonight."

"You ain't got a chance in hell of cutting through the woods and swamp by then."

Mead took a minute to catch his breath. "I have an idea. Down at that dock there are a couple of boats. What do you use them for?"

"We here are oystermen. That is all we do with those boats. See up on the dock we have oyster rakes and all," replied the old man, again nervous.

"William, I know you don't carry much money when you travel. If we can get to Charleston in time, could you wire for enough money to buy yourself a new mount? I know my banker would get me funds out real quick."

"Probably would work for me too, Colonel. Why do you ask?"

Mead pointed at the dock. "Our two horses are worth a lot more than that beat up old boat. I was thinking we could trade our mounts straight across for that skiff and sail straight into Charleston City.

The smile on the old man's face made it clear that he was no poker player. "You two got a deal if you really mean that, Colonel."

Mead stepped over the three men laid out on the ground and extended his hand.

It took only a half-hour to row the old boat out to where the triangular sail caught a fresh wind. They scooted across the bay, steering south until they could see the faint line of Union blockade ships to the east of the harbor. Haze over the water made distances difficult to estimate. The first hour of their run east went smoothly. The sun was tipping toward the horizon when Peterson noticed a small steam powered scow pull out from the line of Confederate picket boats blocking access to the inner harbor. Although the boat was two miles away, it was obvious that it was trying to intercept them. Their tiny sail left their speed about half that of the powered boat.

Within an hour, the Confederate boat had closed in enough for its crew to stand waving their arms. When Mead and Peterson didn't respond, they began signaling. In the other direction the two men could clearly see American flags of the blockade ships whipping in the breeze.

"We're going to make it, Bill," chuckled Mead. "The Confederate sailors chasing us are going to be about thirty minutes too late."

From the shore to their left, a cannon boomed, then another and another. Within a minute the waters around their tiny craft began to erupt with geysers as shells from Rebel shore batteries splashed around them. From the Union ships, signals flashed from ship to ship.

Aboard the closest Union ship, the ship's commanding officer pushed his finger into the chest of a tall man with coal black hair and dark blue eyes. Chad Gritt had surprised his family, taking a commission in the Navy. At twenty-six he was the oldest lieutenant aboard. "I'm still not sure what you are doing here, Mr. Gritt," said the commander. "You are from a wealthy shipping family. You could have avoided serving. As it is, you only have a few months left on your enlistment."

"Honestly, Sir, it was my duty. I thought it would be a hell of an adventure, you know the kind that you sit in a rocking chair and tell your grandchildren about."

"Well, Mr. Gritt, you have been griping about being bored, so here is your chance for a little action before your enlistment ends. Take the ready launch and go find out why the Confederate Navy is after that boat out there. Maybe you can go home a hero."

Chad Gritt whipped a salute to his commanding officer, and somehow landed his lanky frame in the boat at the bottom of the ladder after missing the first couple of steps in his excitement. The boat was always manned and its crew maintained steam in its tiny boiler.

"Where to, Lieutenant?"

"We are going to rescue whoever the rebs are chasing out there."

"You mean we are going to go out there where all those shells are landing?" asked a young seaman.

"We are and we will be quick about it," replied Chad. The glare from his blue eyes left no room for further discussion. The seaman opened the valve that drove the boat's propeller.

∽

A bullet fired by their pursuers kicked a splinter from the mast in the center of the oyster boat. "Someone is coming to get us," said Peterson as Mead loaded the carbine he had taken from the dead Confederate officer. Mead carefully squeezed the trigger at a range too great to allow accuracy for either predator or prey.

Before either man knew what happened, the center of their small boat exploded upward. Mead bobbed to the surface, surrounded by debris, to find Peterson face down in the water only a few feet away. He stroked to Peterson's side and pushed the man's upper body up onto what was left of the bow.

"Damn," he muttered as his push brought Peterson's legs to the surface. Both legs were crushed below the knee. The feet were still attached, but not by anything you could recognize, bone and muscle and skin all crushed together.

Blood from the wounds turned the water a milky pink. Mead pushed the unconscious man well up onto the broken bow. Mead striped the lace from a boot and knotted it around Peterson's left leg and then put a similar tourniquet on the other. Peterson securely in place, he chanced a glance toward the enemy.

The rebel picket boat was still coming. Mead dove under the broken bow and recovered a life ring that had come over on the Mayflower. He rolled Peterson onto the ring, grabbed the attached ten feet of rope and began to sidestroke away from the rebel boat, toward his own navy. He smiled as he realized that the Union ships were firing at the boat pursuing him. When he looked back, the rebel boat was retreating.

What should have been a good thing became bad as the Confederate shore cannons began firing again raising huge torrents of water. The Union launch slowed in front of them. "Grab this wounded man," called Mead.

The rescue boat stopped next to the life ring, and Union sailors pulled Peterson into the boat.

"I have the wounded man," screamed Lieutenant Gritt. "You're next." Mead began stroking toward the boat. "Let's get the hell out of here," yelled Gritt.

As he spoke, a rebel cannon shell splashed into the water almost on top of Mead turning the water scarlet. Gritt dove into the water grabbing Mead, pushing him to the side of the boat where eager hands pulled him aboard. In seconds the same hands snatched Gritt from the water and the boat turned toward the Union ships. Mead's lower arm and hand were gone.

Chad fought to control his shaking. He pulled his belt from his waist and tightened it around the stump of Mead's left arm. "Whoever you are, you will live."

"I'm Colonel Thomas Mead."

Chad looked at the man's tattered gray uniform. "Colonel, huh. Which army?"

"Both," replied Mead.

TWENTY MONTHS LATER

4
LINCOLN'S CLANDESTINE EXPLORATION OF ALASKA, 1865

Iliamna River Country, Alaska

THOMAS MEAD, THE expedition leader huddled his handful of men at the top of the steep slope. He repeated the warning offered by the chief of the village where his exploration team had spent the night. "Remember, none of the villagers have crossed the pass since the rainstorm a few days ago." The trail up Chinglegash Creek to the summit was icy, but the grade was fairly gentle. Mead looked at the sheer slope in front of him. "The villagers refuse to cross after rain on ten feet of snow. The avalanche danger is just too great. But we have to get to the Russian trading post on the bay below, so be careful and above everything else, be quiet."

Next to Mead, his second in command Nick Kadzof translated his warning into Russian, although after months of traveling together the party used both English and Russian interchangeably. Kadzof nodded toward the senior guide, the half Russian and half Athabascan, Peter.

Peter brushed the wet snow from his shoulders and started down the trail. The path embedded into the steep hillside was less than a foot wide. To his left, his shoulder almost brushed the mountain. To his right, the mountain fell away only slightly less than vertically. Fifty yards from where he started, the guide twisted his body. He turned, finally spotting those at the top through the swirling snow. He pulled off his red stocking cap and waived it, the signal to follow.

The leather boots that had replaced his sealskin mukluks for the last day of the journey began to slide on the icy trail. Peter leaned into the steep hillside, plunging his hands into the snow in a desperate attempt to stay on his feet. The motion doomed the Russian guide. Stunned, flat on his back, his hips slid from the trail onto the slope.

His body raced across the crusted snow toward the canyon floor. He could imagine what the granite rocks, in the streambed a quarter mile below, would do to his body. Below him he could see the first snow covered mound. He closed his eyes, seeking refuge in the crucifix around his neck.

The man's falling body was just a blur to Mead and Kadzof watching from above.

Peter smashed into the mound feet first. Instead of the bone-shattering boulders he anticipated, tree limbs pummeled his body. The bulging pack on his back snagged, jerking him to a stop. He had fallen into the lone patch of scraggly alders clinging to the barren hillside, wind-tortured trees bent over and covered by heavy snow.

Kadzof and Mead started down the trail, but lost sight of the falling man. "My God, I think he fell all the way to the bottom," whispered Kadzof.

Breathless, tangled in the branches of the dwarf trees, every move brought Peter pain. Still, he was alive. Huge flakes of soggy snow floated above, melting as they touched his face. Across the narrow canyon, gnarled peaks came and went as each flurry passed. Grasping the branches around him, he fought off his fear and rolled onto his stomach.

The guide gazed at the streak in the snow left by his body. His gasping slowed as his lungs filled with air. He tested his toes, then his feet and legs. He moved the fingers on each hand; finally, he swiveled his head. Reaching up with his right hand, now minus a mitten, he probed his face. Wherever he placed his hand he came away with small amounts of blood but found no deep cuts or broken bones. He lay back thanking Saint Peter for saving him.

Above, the falling snow blocked Kadzof's view. He cupped his hands in front of his mouth and called softly down the slope, praying for an answer from his friend.

Peter didn't know how long he lay tangled in the alders before he noticed Nick's voice, more a whisper than a yell.

He drew a deep breath and screamed out his answer. "I am here and alive." His call was answered by a loud crack and rumble. He looked up to see the snow in the narrow gully he had been crossing give-way above the trail. He was too stunned to be afraid as he watched a cascade of snow and rocks descending the line he had just fallen. He covered his head as the snow wall rolled over him.

5
ILIAMNA BAY, ALASKA

NICK DROPPED TO his knee, unlacing his slippery leather boots. "Peter has a family. I must find him."

"No man could survive that," answered Mead. He placed his hand on the younger man's shoulder. "I am sorry, Nick. We will leave instructions at the trading post, that in the spring a search party find his body and bury him."

"I'll find him, Thomas."

"Nick, he's dead." Mead pressed down, keeping Kadzof from rising.

Nick looked up. "No, I'll find him. I was the one who talked him into helping us."

Mead used his one arm to lift the younger man to his feet. He pulled Nick's face close to his own. "If we dig for a day, we may find his body, but more likely we would just waste a day. He's dead. When we get to the bottom, we will say a prayer for his soul. You lead the rest of us to the bottom."

Nick wiped a tear from his eye. Mead was right. *My God what am I going to say to his wife?* He bent down and retied his boot, then started across the gulley cleared of snow by the avalanche. Below faint traces of red stained the snow all the way to the bottom of the canyon.

An hour later, the seven remaining members of the team huddled silently brewing tea.

"Nick, you and Charles will lead," directed Mead. "We leave as soon as the tide begins to fall. We will follow the shoreline around the point on our right to a small beach. From there the trading post should be just across the bay. The village chief said to build a fire and wait for a boat from the post."

The shoreline went from mud that would suck the shoes from your feet to granite boulders, to a slope too steep to climb in twenty feet. Mountains that stretched more than three thousand feet from the salt water surrounded the narrow T-shaped bay.

As the snow finally stopped the air turned colder leaving the boulders covered in ice. Within minutes all seven men were rubbing away the pain from falls. For men who had just spent months exploring the Yukon and Tanana Rivers all the way from the Bering Sea, pain was part of the trip.

A trip, which on level ground would have taken thirty minutes, took an hour and a half, and by the time the men had a fire going it was dusk. They were gratified to see not one, but two boats pull away from the shore below the Russian Trading Post across the bay.

Mead huddled with Nick Kadzof. "At the risk of seeming calloused over the loss of our guide, do you know what he was carrying?"

"Cooking supplies, his personal gear, food, and the map of the Tanana country."

"He carried no pouches from our exploration then?" asked Mead.

"No, the samples and nuggets are divided only among the three Americans. Charles, you and I are each carrying three pouches."

"President Lincoln demanded secrecy. When they find his body, the map will compromise us."

"No one can pick out the sites where we prospected from the map detail," suggested Kadzof, "I have the legend in my head."

"Peter's experience with Lieutenant Zagoskin during the Russian officer's interior exploration made every difference in our venture. His memory of gold in the villages of the Indians pointed directly to our routing. I was proud to be his friend," added Mead.

"Thomas, before the boats arrive, we should decide what we could do for his family."

"What is customary?"

"The Russians would provide one year's supplies to his family. We should provide two years' supplies. It will make Peter's wife rich by village standards. Even if Peter's brother doesn't take her in, she will have her pick of new husbands."

"We don't want to create problems for our Russian hosts," replied Mead.

"We will plead ignorance. Word will get around and it will make it easier to recruit if we come back. Tonight, I will sketch our trip from memory; we can recreate the map aboard ship."

6
CAPTAIN COOK'S INLET, ALASKA

THE MANAGER OF the Russian trading post glared at the weary men. Behind him a girl no more than fifteen years old watched from the door to the manager's bedroom. "I'll send one of my Aleuts to Paul's Harbor. I'm told your company ship *KATARINA* is in harbor there. If the seas stay calm, my paddler will be there in three days; you will be on your way in a week." Even though the manager had been told to look out for the explorers, it was clear that he resented their presence.

Seven out of ten of the employees of the Russian Trading Company were Creoles; that is of mixed Russian and Native blood, mostly Aleut. The manager of the Iliamna Trading Post was the thirty-year old son of a Russian woodsman and a Kenaitze Indian mother. Unlike the Aleuts, who had been kidnaped from their ancestral home in the Aleutian Islands and enslaved in service to the Russians, the Kenaitze had come into contact with the Russians through trade. In the pecking order of Russian American society, creoles fell below white Russians but above natives. In the hierarchy of creoles, the non-Aleut creoles generally ranked higher than the far larger contingent with Aleut blood. The Kenaitze creole manager ruled the trading post with an iron first, and the Americans were a distraction he didn't need, especially the huge Indian man who the American officers treated as an equal.

The Aleut paddler departed at first light. The young man smiled as he took the first few strokes out onto the bay, his upper body covered by Aleut hooded rainwear made from seal intestines. To Mead, his tiny skin covered kayak seemed frail for the hundred-mile trip through some of the roughest passages in the world. At some point, he would have to cross Shelikof Strait, a twenty-mile open water crossing of the narrow passage that separates Kodiak Island from the Alaskan mainland. Even ship captains had a healthy fear of Shelikof Strait. The extraordinary seamanship of the Aleut paddler in his skin boat was evident when the sails of the *KATARINA* were spotted only five days later.

Mead's men were ready to leave. They had been pushing themselves for months. With little else to do, they were having a difficult time adjusting to long hours in the banya, and too much sleep. Pooling their resources, they had traded American silver dollars for cheap vodka.

"Welcome aboard gentlemen," offered Chad Gritt as Mead led his men over the rail of the anchored ship.

Mead extended his hand. "Thanks. This beats the hell out of the first time we met. It seems that you are always there when I wrap up one of my adventures."

"It's just my job," answered Gritt.

"Job maybe, but it always seems to be voluntary," replied Mead. "You never did tell me how you happened to be serving there in Charleston?"

"I just figured it was my turn. No one in my family was serving. My father arranged my commission. It was only for a year. Besides, until that day when I fished you out of Charleston Bay, I envisioned myself as some kind of hero."

"You were a hero that day."

"No, I was just the man who my commanding officer pointed at. I like this meeting a whole lot better," laughed Chad.

Chad kept the *KATARINA* at anchor only four hours. The lanky captain preferred to err on the side of caution. He knew the winds could explode, almost out of nowhere on Cook's Inlet. The day he'd rescued Mead had destroyed the young man's dreams of reckless bravery. Men like Mead were born heroes. *My job is to get the heroes home,* he thought.

The bitter wind stung his blue eyes as he watched his crew run up a full set of sails.

The evening sun highlighted the conical island mountain, St. Augustine volcano only ten miles from the trading post. As the ship pushed south, a line of huge, white, volcanic mountains, some steaming, stretched away north like beacons. "This land is powerful, frightening," said Mead to Captain Gritt as the two men stood at the stern of the ship. " It makes a man feel very insignificant."

"It does that," added Nick Kadzof joining the men. "Even the rivers are dark, and they go on forever. A beautiful little girl drowned while we were in one of the villages. Both Mr. Mead and I helped search the bitter water until we were blue, trying to find her. The villagers were still looking when we left. When we stopped there again two months later, they hadn't found the body."

"The villagers will remember your help forever in a dance or a story. It's nice to have my first officer back," responded Chad. "You both must give me a complete recap at dinner."

"I had forgotten what real food tastes like," sighed Mead. "After almost a year of camp cooking, Angelo is a magician."

"Angelo saved a full case of his best wine for your return," laughed Chad, "Have another glass and continue your story."

"When we arrived at Alekseek at the mouth of the Yukon River last spring, the river was still frozen. The manager of the Russian trading post could only arrange four sleds and teams and even that took several days."

"Which was fine with us," added Nick. "We were dead tired. That Russian freight ship we took from New Archangel was a miserable experience. She only had bunks for three. That meant that the Russian crew was double bunking without us. We had to sleep in the hold. We found two spots where we could sleep with our legs stretched out. When lying flat we had about twelve inches of space between our nose and the hatch cover. When it was wet, which was always, it dripped continuously. The eight of us switched off bunking every four hours."

"And the food," added Mead, "those Russians live a tough life. Breakfast is grain gruel with molasses. Lunch consisted of a piece of sausage and hardtack. Dinner was different grain gruel with dried salmon. The diet provided plenty of energy, but after fifteen days it was hardly welcome." Mead savored a piece of cooked carrot.

"After we unloaded our provisions and packed for the Yukon trip, we took long hikes trying to get our legs back. With eight men and only four sleds we had a long walk in front of us. We got as far as Ikogmiutor, what the locals call Russian Mission, by dogsled. The weather was clear about half of the way and blinding snowstorms the other half. The wind never stopped. How the Native mushers found their way was magic," added Mead.

"The navigation all the way from Paul's Harbor was impressive," interjected Nick. "When that Russian ship entered Unimak Pass, through the Aleutian Islands, there were five New England whalers at anchor. That Russian captain sailed right between them into a fog so thick you could cut it, in a wind that made the rigging sing. He navigated those reefs and islands with nothing but a compass and his ears. He seemed to know the sound of each breaking surf. We were through the pass by morning. I'll bet those whalers are still waiting for clear weather." Nick laughed as he refilled his wine glass.

"At Russian Mission we had to wait out the river breakup. It was humbling," added Mead. "The site of a mile-wide river full of ice blocks, some the size of houses, grinding and crashing, shakes you to the core. It took four days for the majority of the ice to pass.

The manager at Russian Mission helped arrange boats. Each was about eighteen feet long with three pairs of oars and a sail. He pressed us to leave immediately so that we could travel while the weather was still cool and before the snowmelt pushed the river to flood stage. We took four boats and the manager provided eight men to accompany us and help us row. In addition to our supplies, they took trading goods of their own to use in purchasing winter furs on their way back down river."

Nick stood, walking the three steps to the window in the crowded captain's cabin. At five feet eight, unlike the others, he didn't need to duck under the overhead beams. He ran his fingers through his black curly hair, staring out onto the endless whitecapped waves.

"I assume that your men helped and did their share, including rowing?" quizzed Chad.

"We did our share and more," responded Nick. "Peter and Charles were especially appreciated. Peter's experience growing up on the river helped us at every village. Charles was big medicine with everyone we met. At six feet five, he towered over everyone else. His Algonquin features made him familiar. The fact that he didn't speak to the villagers made him mysterious." Nick turned away from the window, reseating himself.

Chad studied the young officer. Whatever was bothering him seemed to pass.

Mead retrieved a bottle of port and three glasses from the wall locker next to the door. Smiling at Chad, he quipped, "I figured you had a bottle of the good stuff."

"Help yourself."

Setting a glass in front of each of the three men, he circled the small table filling each with the captain's port while continuing his story.

"Peter helped keep our course true; he remembered almost every river and stream. When we reached the mouth of the Tanana River, he purchased large canoes, and we pushed up the river on our own. We bought some dried fish and meat at the village. The three Creoles from New Archangel pitched in at every camp, hunting to stretch our supplies. We had spruce chicken and rabbit, then rabbit and spruce chicken, then more rabbit," laughed Mead.

"From the mouth of the Tanana," added Nick, "we pushed upriver about 200 miles to a series of small rivers that poured into the Tanana from the North. On the third river we found traces of gold and began serious exploration. Every side creek had color. Thomas took the three men from New Archangel and followed Peter on up the Tanana while Charles and I set up a sluice box operation which we moved from tributary to tributary as we worked up what we had named Gold Creek. We arranged to meet at the end of September back at the Nenana Village. Local villagers would stop by occasionally to stare at the crazy Boston men playing in the water.

In the three months that we worked the streams, we gathered almost twenty pounds of nuggets and dust. We had no means of smelting so we don't know how much actual gold we found, but it may be more than ten pounds. The three years Charles spent with gold fever in California made every difference in our success. His expertise paid off. He knew where to look and how. He earned his pay," finished Nick.

"We should have started back earlier," chimed in Mead. "By the time we started down the Tanana it was snowing. We spent two days at a hot spring a couple of days below Nenana, where we gave away our canoes and employed three packers."

"Peter recommended that we go cross country, south to the Kuskokwim River and the Russian Trading Post of Odinochka."

"We fought our way through early snows and were constantly wet from stream crossings. Peter was a good guide, but I was pleased that Nick here was able to use his sextant to take star sighting position fixes along the way. We had expected the crossing to take a week but spent two reaching the Kuskokwim River. The day we reached the river it started to freeze. We had to wait until the ice was thick enough to travel. We recorded the crossing on the map."

"Our map was fairly complete, but unfortunately it has been lost," sighed Nick. "We sat around drumming our fingers for weeks before the manager of the Russian Trading Post at Noyo Odinochka agreed to provide two supply boats and crews to take us along the coast. On our own, we crossed a huge peninsula to the mouth of the Kvichak River. The supply boat cost us five gold pieces paid directly to the manager, who by the way, was the only white Russian we met on the trip. You know about the rest of our journey from our discussion of the loss of Peter."

"Gentlemen," smiled Chad, raising his glass, "to a remarkable exploration. I suggest that each of you take the days before we reach New Archangel to independently recap this story. When we brief the Assistant Secretary of State you will have two reports. You should wait until we are California bound before briefing him." Gritt stared at the ceiling a moment. "That is, if after meeting him you brief him at all."

Gritt smiled at the puzzlement on his guest's faces. "Oh, and one more thing, you should brief your men. There will be no discussion of the gold, none. Are we agreed?"

"The men already know the rules," offered Mead. "All will be well rewarded. Only Peter had a family, the others all want to settle in California, that's all they talk about, Fort Ross, sunshine and water that isn't solid for half the year. You will have to make room for them on the leg to San Francisco."

"Besides the gold, we heard stories of copper and coal, what the natives call rocks that burn. The country is really rich, and we only saw a tiny fraction of it," closed Kadzof.

The *KATARINA* leaned away from a northern wind flowing from the face of the Malaspina Glacier for hours. Beyond the broken blue and white ice jumble rose Mt. Saint Elias, the jagged snow-covered pinnacle dividing British Canada from Russian America. The dark green of the forest was a pencil thin line between two hemispheres. Below the green line was the dark blue sea flecked with the foam of breaking waves. Above it, rose massive, rugged mountains torn by great valleys and fjords, blanketed by winter snows. The sky above was powder blue.

A bitter wind blew steady, except where stronger gales blew from bays and valleys rolling the ship to starboard even miles offshore.

Finishing a huge bowl of hot oat cereal, Nick Kadzof cinched up his wool pants and pulled on the heavy wool sweater he had been using to cushion the hard bench in the galley. Slipping on his spotted sealskin parka, he refilled his heavy mug with tea from the samovar and started up the ladder to the deck, joining the captain overlooking the shoreline. He raised the mug to his lips; the warm steam eased the sting of the biting wind.

"You know captain, I believe that the wind is colder at sea than on land."

"I doubt that," replied Chad. "The extra humidity just makes it feel that way."

"It may be that. On our overland trip we never got warm. We just adjusted to the cold. Traveling all day and sleeping in a tent, you never get warm except in July when the sun even scorched the mosquitos."

"I prefer this; at least you can go below and warm up once in a while," offered Chad.

"Agreed," said Nick. "When we travel through the tropics there is no place to get away from the heat."

"That is a price we will pay twice to get home," replied Chad.

TWO CIVIL WARS | 45

Nick took another swig from his tea already cooling in the wind. "Tell me about Mead."

"What do you mean?"

"He is more than a simple surveyor. He may be the toughest man I've ever met. You know, missing an arm and all. Still, there is nothing that he can't do. Nothing slows him."

"There is more to this trip than meets the eye," answered Chad.

"I can see that. It bothers me to be so secretive with the Russians, even with the crew."

"You know that Miles Standish Pierce is a direct representative of Secretary of State Seward. He claims his mission is to discuss greater trade opportunities in Russian America. The most recent Royal Charter to the Russian American Company was supposed to close trade with America. The simple logistics of survival here has made that impossible. American Trade is less than before, but still strong. Our company alone will make more than a dozen voyages here this year." Gritt looked up, studying something no one else would see in the ship's rigging.

"The War Between the States is winding down and American companies have millions of dollars available for investment. There are only so many good projects in the Oregon country and in the northern plains. Your mission was to survey opportunities, just as Mead said. Russian America may be a great place to make huge returns. Miles is to determine how receptive the Russians might be to further investment."

"I pretty much knew that Captain, it still doesn't explain Mead or his journals or private collections. Why is he here?"

"Mr. Kadzof, all I can give you is a list of Mead's background. Mead is a West Pointer and still carries the rank of Colonel. Originally from Virginia, he was sent south before the war as an intelligence officer, with the cover of a Union army supply officer. When the war broke out the Johnny Rebs readily accepted him in the same capacity."

Gritt moved his gaze to the second mast. "I met Mead while serving as a lieutenant in the navy blockading Charleston Harbor in 1863," continued Chad. "By then, a spy ring he organized was sending reports north through the lines to Washington. Mead tipped off the north about three ships the South was purchasing. The North arranged a hot reception the day they sailed from Southampton."

"I know about the *SHENANDOAH*," replied Nick. "I never heard of other Confederate raiders.

"Two of them got away. Mead got word that the South was investigating a leak about the ships. He and another Union spy barely escaped being arrested. They hightailed it toward the Union fleet at Charleston."

"That's when you met Mead?" asked Nick.

Chad nodded his head. "Mead found a boat and headed toward our ship, and I was ordered to take a cutter out to meet him. A Confederate shell blew their little boat out of the water. The Lieutenant and Mead were badly wounded. I will never forget the color of the blood in the water. Mead helped us get the other man into the boat before he would let me help him. We're close friends now, but just being around him makes me feel small."

"That's an amazing story Captain, but it doesn't explain his being here".

"I don't know his exact orders, but after he recuperated, he was summoned to the White House. President Lincoln personally thanked him for his contribution. From that day Mead has worked directly for the President. His orders came from President Lincoln himself." Gritt shook his head, still amazed by Mead's bravery.

"Well, whatever his orders are, the President and Secretary Seward picked the right man. He tied a strap to the end of his paddle, then looped it over the shoulder above his missing arm and used one arm to pull the paddle. He matched us two-arm paddlers stroke for stroke. Wait until he tells his story of saving one of the Aleuts by killing a bear with his knife."

TWO CIVIL WARS | 47

"From the way he describes the trip, he loved every minute of it."

"That he did Captain. The tougher it was, the bigger his smile became. And one other thing amazes me about Mead."

"What is that Mr. Kadzof?"

"He never misses a thing. He notices if a river has gone up or down an inch. He notices a difference in how the birds sing from day to day. He can describe the slightest change in the clouds or the color of the leaves. It's humorous to watch him spread his frame out on the wet tundra to study the smallest flower with that magnifying glass of his."

"I suppose that knowing those tiny details could keep you alive in the espionage business." Gritt turned his gaze to a rope in the top of the rigging that might be fraying, logging the observation for inspection when they were at anchor. "Now I am going below for some breakfast and to warm up. You have the deck, Mr. Kadzof."

7
THE GULF OF ALASKA

THE MORNING OF March fifth dawned threatening rain. Mount Edgecumbe volcano, the gateway landmark for the entrance to New Archangel, Capital of Russian America, was lost in the morning mist. The *KATARINA* had pounded past Cape Cross on Yakobi Island in the pre-dawn hours. The strong northwest wind pushed the ship towards a shoreline full of rocks like shark's teeth. The string of islands that made up this part of Russian America lay just three miles off from the starboard beam.

An inexperienced sailor would cringe at the thundering noise on the deck. Each of the hundred plus ropes and lines between the deck and the sails sang in a different pitch in the wind. The banging of the spars from the top square sails against the *KATARINA*'s three raked masts sent a vibration throughout the ship like a drum section of a marching band with every drummer pounding out a different beat. The creaking and grinding of the schooner's hull as it twisted in heavy seas alternated between the sound of someone dragging chains over rocks and the cry of an amorous bull. The sea, broken by the ship's hull, along with the sound of the six-foot waves folding upon themselves created a constant drone similar to a waterfall. The ship rose and plunged, twisted and shook.

To the captain, shouting to be heard, the sounds were of speed. Just after one in the afternoon, the ship rounded Cape Edgecumbe and turned east toward the largest town in Russian America. The boom of a cannon from the Russian fort high on the hill above the town announced their arrival.

"Mr. Smith, drop the top sails!" called Chad.

"Aye, aye Captain," snapped Ott Smith Junior. He slid down the ladder to relay the Captain's instructions. In less than a minute, twelve men scampered up rope ladders into the high rigging to furl the sets of double topsails. A mouthful of large white teeth glistened in Ott's black face. In less than ten minutes the sails were secured, and the men were working their way back to the deck. Ott, the son of a former slave, took great pride in the efficiency of "his" men. Of even greater pride was his record of more than eight years, three voyages, without a serious injury to one of them. He buttoned his heavy wool coat in the chill northern air.

"Mr. Smith, you will please secure all canvas on the mid mast!" shouted the Captain.

The family of the bosun and that of the Captain had been intertwined for more than forty years. His mother was a free woman. His father, once a slave, had emancipation papers purchased by his wife. Ott's sister had become the first negro professor in a New England college, while he had chosen the sea.

In less than an hour, the *KATARINA* slipped past the six other ships before New Archangel and dropped its anchor only two hundred feet from the beach.

"Did you notice, Captain," asked Nick, "that only one ship, the small coastal supply boat, is flying a Russian flag? One Britt, one French Naval ship, one flying the flag of Chile and two other American ships."

"And your point is, Mr. Kadzof?"

"Only that the Russians are losing their grip on Russian America."

"Your father predicted that decades ago." Chad laughed. "Once he had lived in Boston then returned here on the first voyage of the *PRISCILLA II*, he felt that either Britain or the United States would someday control Russian America. Like my mother, he dedicated his life to making sure that it was America."

"He always talked about coming back here to live," said Nick.

"And no doubt he would have," laughed Chad, "except a beautiful Italian girl half his age captured him, holding him in Boston."

"You make my mother sound like a mean-spirited jailer," said Nick.

"Certainly not a jailer" mused Chad. "A jailer would not have allowed him more trips to this wild place. It was Sergei who was in a hurry to get home. Without his influence here in New Archangel and my mother's influence with the Royal family, our contracts with the Russians would have been impossible. No other company has the freedom we enjoy here."

"Mr. Smith, you will please lower two boats," directed Chad. "After we re-provision and deliver the consignments from their posts to the Russian Trading Company you will assist Mr. deLaguera in re-anchoring further offshore and then you may release all but the watch crew for liberty. We expect to have our cargo loaded and be on our way home in three days."

Turning to a second officer, Patrick deLaguera, who had just arrived on deck, Chad repeated his instructions. "Mr. deLaguera, you have the ship. Mr. Kadzof will relieve you tomorrow."

"The governor sends his regrets at his absence, but your sudden arrival made it imperative that he complete his discussions with your government's representative Mr. Miles Standish Pierce," offered the governor's secretary as their boat reached the dock.

"As well he should," offered Chad. "I will buy the first round at Kuzanoff's at six o'clock. Until then, I will be at my mother's house taking a bath and shaving with real hot water."

The captain's parents, Chad Grittenberg Senior and Katarina, a distant relative of the Tsar, had built a one-story home on the outskirts of the town just above a crescent shaped gravel beach. Behind the house was a small log building straddling a stream, divided into two rooms. On the left was a traditional Russian banya with a tile-covered plaster stove in the corner and two benches. On the right was a New England-style bathroom with a cast iron stove complete with large water-heating tanks built into the top. To the left of the stove was a crowfoot bathtub and to the right a counter with a washbasin below an oval mirror.

"I see you ship come in bay and I come to light fires."

Before Chad even reached the front door, Sasha had stepped from the porch with a snifter of warm brandy for the Captain. She had been a friend of the family since the first visit of a company ship. The Gritts employed her to help with household chores and laundry since her husband had died in a hunting accident. Now, almost sixty, she had a son and son-in-law working for the company. Each year Gritt RusAm Trading posted a deposit at the Russian store; she could draw against it for food, clothing, or any other goods she needed.

"You not gone long?"

"No, only to Paul's Harbor and two other trading posts."

"Just like for your mama, I make house ready when I see your ship."

"Thank you, as always."

"You banya hot now, then water for shave and bath done. You not fall through door in floor where water bucket go to stream."

"You're worse than my own mother."

The woman turned to go, then stopped. She stared a Chad, a slight smile on her face.

"Oh yeah, I almost forgot," offered Chad with a smile, pulling a package wrapped in a bright red scarf from under his coat.

Unwrapping the package, her tan face glowing, "you bring two new books, one English, one Russian. Thank you, son of my best friend. I will read with spectacles you bring two years ago and then share. You want girl from village to help with banya and bath."

"No, not tonight" laughed Chad finishing his brandy. "I'm meeting some men at Kuzanoff's later."

Ten minutes in the banya was all he could take. Opening the trap door he lowered the tin bucket into the stream, lifted and poured the bucket of cold water over his head. Moving next door, he ladled a small amount of hot water into the washbasin and tempering it with water from the stream he shaved.

Folding his knees up under his chin he squeezed into the bathtub and soaped his body. Again, he rinsed with cold stream water. Wrapping himself in a towel, he walked out on the porch and sat down on a cedar log that served as a stool.

The cool moist breeze drifting off from the ocean lifted his spirit as it cooled his body. The woodsy perfume of hot cedar from the banya filled his nostrils. It mixed with the musty smell from the decaying leaves and fermenting berries of the late winter forest and the sharp salty sea air. A light falling mist and the gentle lap of tiny waves on the beach only a hundred feet away set a sleepy mood. The brandy and the heat from the bathhouse added to it.

Chad closed his eyes and leaned back against the wall of the bathhouse. He could hear the voices of his mother and father from years ago. Katarina, Chad's mother had used her influence to procure a supply and shipping contract with the Russian monopoly. The family had managed to stretch the contract into half a dozen ventures in areas where the Russians were uninterested and in ventures that needed outside capital. After three decades these ventures produced only a modest profit. Some did not even cover all of their expenses. *Maybe if we succeed at our current mission, that will all change. President Lincoln needs Mead's report.* He smiled as he began to replay Alaskan adventures of a young boy in his mind.

He jerked awake, not knowing how long he had been asleep. "*You have work to do*, he told himself. Willing himself to his feet, he walked the hundred steps to the house and dressed.

Sasha was uncovering the furniture as he closed the back door. He didn't have the courage to tell this woman who was more an aunt than an employee that he would only be there a couple more days.

8
NEW ARCHANGEL, RUSSIAN AMERICA

THE NEW ARCHANGEL Inn, better known as Kuzanoff's, had started as a small log inn with six tables, a bar stocked with four or five beverages, and one choice for each meal.

There were now a dozen tables and more than ten types of alcohol available, including a porter style beer imported from San Francisco. Above the restaurant were six small hotel rooms.

One thing had not changed. The menu board next to the door still listed only grilled sausage with fried potatoes and cabbage, written in Russian and English.

Lena, the owner's daughter, watched Chad Junior coming up the street. She handed him his usual warm brandy as he came through the door.

"Spaciba, Lena," said Chad, shaking out his rain slicker at the door, hanging it on a peg next to the kitchen.

Miles Standish Pierce, the Under Secretary of State for Trade, and his interpreter sat at the corner table overlooking the harbor. Pierce, at five foot five inches, never missed an opportunity to impress. After weeks at sea with Pierce, Chad knew his pitch by heart; direct descendant of Miles Standish; graduate of Harvard College; father an ambassador to France; richest family in Rhode Island; wife of Italian nobility. Pierce was thirty-three, sandy haired with dark brown eyes and permanent wrinkles at the end of his unsmiling mouth.

Alexi Kraus was a different sort altogether. At five foot six he was only slightly taller than Pierce but carried a portly body. His dark blue eyes sat behind bifocal glasses under a prematurely bald head. The same age as Pierce, it had taken Alexi six years to complete his course work at the University of Rhode Island, working a year then attending class for a year. Unlike Pierce, he was a second generation American, the son of Natalia, an immigrant from Russia and Pierre of mixed French and Spanish descent, and somewhere in his family history, German. Speaking fluent Russian, French, Spanish and English, he was following his ambition as a career diplomat. There was one other distinct difference between Pierce and Kraus; Chad liked Kraus.

"Good evening gentlemen," greeted Chad. "Have you seen either Nicholas or Thomas?" Pierce turned his head to gaze out the window allowing Kraus to respond.

"I believe they are still at the bathhouse."

"I hope they burn their clothes," added Pierce reaching for his wine glass. "They came in about an hour ago. They smelled like stable hands."

"As would you Pierce if you had just spent months trekking through the unknown."

"Captain Gritt, I know that your family is friends with Secretary Seward; still, I would appreciate you maintaining diplomatic decorum while we are in Russia. You will join us."

Seating himself at the table Chad smiled. "Mr. Secretary, those men have traveled two thousand difficult miles. They have not seen clean clothes in months."

"There is no excuse for their pungent disturbance."

"Secretary Pierce, it comes with the mission and I for one toast their accomplishment."

"As do I," offered Kraus raising his glass. "To a successful reconnaissance."

Chad extended his brandy tapping Kraus' beer stein. Reluctantly Pierce raised his glass an inch.

"I still would like to know what Mr. Mead's orders were," said Pierce. "I am sure that the Russians share my quandary. This adventure undermined my efforts at an expanded trade agreement."

"So, your negotiations did not go as well as planned?"

"The governor is a navy man, not a businessman. He simply could not grasp the value of expanded trade or investment. More than once he asked if Mr. Mead was part of Gritt RusAm Trading, didn't he Alexi?"

"Not exactly, Mr. Secretary. What he asked was whether any commercial opportunities identified by Mr. Kadzof and Mr. Mead could be developed under the existing trade agreement with the Captain's company."

Pierce scowled at his interpreter. "And I told him that I personally knew of a dozen companies that had stronger financial backing for new ventures."

"Secretary Pierce, as I explained more than once, all Governor Patrumier can do is recommend actions to his board of directors. The Russian American Company's five-year operating charter granted by the Russian Government ties even their hands. He cannot actually sign new trade agreements."

Pierce ignored the statement. "Captain Gritt, your small firm does not have the resources to do major development. I have friends who could invest millions in the right type of projects."

"Mr. Secretary," interjected Alexi, "Secretary Seward made it clear that your goal was to seek agreement to potentially joint venture viable projects with the Russian American Company. He said nothing about which American companies would be the partners.

If Gritt RusAm or the other companies with existing agreements can act as a go between, and this overrides the Governor's restrictions, we should pursue that course."

"You are so naive, Alexi. America's real capitalists will not trust their funds to a small trading company with only ten ships. These are the business elite whose factories and mills produce what it takes to put the Southern rabble in their place. They are building the telegraphs and railroads. They build the weapons that are crushing the Confederacy."

Redirecting a hard gaze at Chad, Pierce continued. "Beyond the obvious fishing and timber potential, have our trekkers uncovered other opportunities?"

"I believe so. As per Seward's request they are compiling written reports. I have asked them to hold those reports until we have cleared port."

"Captain Gritt, I still have a day to work. I didn't ask to make this trip to sweep up crumbs. Those reports could lead to a major trade deal. My industrialist colleagues could capitalize any new venture in months. How can I present a proposal to the Governor if we are already at sea?"

"Mr. Secretary, have you not heard one word of this conversation? The Governor cannot make a new agreement. He can recommend agreements to his board in Russia or authorize those companies with existing contracts to open new ventures."

"Your impertinence disgusts me Captain. I will ensure that your attitude is discussed with Secretary Seward. Now Alexi, will you find Mr. Mead and Mr. Kadzof and ask them to present their reports to me yet this evening."

"Mr. Secretary," whispered Kraus, "those men do not report to you."

Pierce's face, already red, turned scarlet.

Chad decided that it was time to diffuse the situation. "Mr. Secretary, the Russians are the world's best chess players. Since any new investment deal will have to be negotiated in St. Petersburg anyway, why would a man of your experience want to tip them off early? Your confidential report to the Secretary of State will form the basis of any negotiation."

"The Captain is correct, Mr. Secretary," added Kraus. "In all likelihood, you will be sent to Russia to negotiate. By playing our cards close today, it buys you time to discuss the findings with your rich friends and be prepared to propose concrete agreements."

Pierce responded by draining his wine glass.

His silence finally led to a question. "Captain, if we leave here the day after tomorrow, how long does it take to return to San Francisco? From what I have seen there is little of value in this frozen wasteland. America could better use its might and money elsewhere anyway."

"Mr. Secretary the *KATARINA* should carry us there in less than two weeks."

"Thank God, I look forward to a descent bed and meal."

An hour later Nick Kadzof shoveled a fork full of fried potatoes into his mouth.

"I feel sorry for Kraus," confided Chad to Kadzof and Mead. "He has shared every meal for seven months with Secretary Pierce. Thank you for rescuing me."

"I take it that Pierce is not your favorite traveling companion?" queried Nick.

"With good reason," spat Mead. "I have known Pierce for years and have never admitted it before just now. When we left a year ago, I didn't know that Secretary Seward was sending Pierce on our pick-up ship. Tell me Chad, why would Seward do that?"

"Pierce has powerful friends and allies in Congress. He has openly questioned the rumored Alaska purchase. If Seward or the President hopes to do anything in Alaska, they will want Pierce and those power brokers behind him. Pierce loves a deal, since he never puts up any of his own money and always gets his piece of the pie."

A pounding rain and steady wind from the northwest greeted the crew of the *KATARINA* on Friday morning. A shipment of cedar lumber filled the ship's center hold. Blocks of ice cut from local lakes and packed in sawdust filled the unheated forward hold, topped by kegs of salted salmon. In the rear hold, bales of beaver skins were stacked around a coal burning stove installed for the sole purpose of keeping mold and mildew out of the portion of the cargo that would travel all the way to Boston.

"Mr. Smith," commanded the Captain, "you may run up the main sails and one set only of top sails. Let us see if we can beat our northbound time on the way back to California."

"Aye, aye Captain. We will not let you down. Haste makes money."

"Beyond the obvious," asked Patrick deLaguera, "what is Ott referring to?"

"The ice, Mr. deLaguera," answered Chad. "Ott there has made this run three times. We lose two percent of the ice to melting every day we are at sea. In San Francisco the ice is worth more than the lumber."

"Ah, I would hate to think of California's best drinking warm champagne." deLaguera tucked his wool scarf into the front of his coat and paused. "Captain, what is going on?"

Chad had grown weary of the question. "Mr. deLaguera, our parents have been friends for forty years. When you gave up real estate speculation to follow your father to sea, he promised your mother it was safe, and my father backed him up. When you first sailed with me, my mother made me promise to look after you."

"Where is this speech leading?"

"It is just that if I tell you, Mead will have to kill you, so you see my dilemma. I could never go home again."

deLaguera laughed. "You could at least give me a hint, Captain." He tugged the wet felt hat from his head and ran his fingers through thick curly black hair.

"When the war ends, you might have to consider moving to San Francisco to take over your own ship."

"Hail Mary, my own ship and a captain's pay. You know I would prefer to live where it is hot, and a few people speak Spanish."

"There remains a great deal of hard analysis, then tough negotiations, but it could happen. Within two years you will be ready for command," offered Chad.

"Thank you for your confidence," smiled deLaguere.

"Until this trip I was not so sure."

"I have lived a life lacking in responsibility. But my life now belongs to the company." He stretched his long frame out, extending his arms and mimicked a matador taunting a bull with the invisible cape in his hands.

9
SAN FRANCISCO

THE MAN IN the felt slouch hat continued reading. "Surrendered to Grant April 11, 1865. Damn the news, the papers cannot be right." The man slammed his fist onto the table.

"Sit quiet, Carlton, do not raise your voice," answered Captain Barkston Jackson of the Confederate States Raider RETRIBUTION, now at anchor in San Francisco Bay, flying the enemy's flag.

"Damn it all Barkston, if Bobby Lee has surrendered, it is all over but the burial. Walker's boys upa' raidin' the Yankee transport trains between here and the Missisip' means nothing. Even if he makes it to our rendezvous on the Sea of Cortez, what do we do, tell him to go home?"

"Please, Carlton, lower your voice, we are surrounded by enemy ears. Walker will do his job as he sees fit, now we do ours."

"What job, the South is in its grave and that drunkard Grant is shoveling the earth's own blanket in on top of the corpse."

"Our job has not changed. Amy Winters sent word today. She and her husband hosted a dinner for the Yankee quartermaster officers last night; you know, to thank them for supporting the Northern railroad route."

"So what, Barkston, so what, it is over."

"You know, Carlton, you have always run your mouth when you're into the mash. Now shut up and let me finish."

"Finish then, but the men will never fight again. They can go home to their dirt farms, but what about the officers?"

"There is no dry eye aboard the *RETRIBUTION* this night. I have confined all but Marcus Bolton and Pedro Davis to the ship, so no one flaps his lips or worse."

"Or worse? We should burn this Yankee cesspool to the ground. With no evening wind to fill Yankee sails, our steam wheeler will have us out of the Golden Gate before the Yankees could even bring a cannon to bear."

"Carlton, shut up and listen. If President Davis is still in the fight, as the paper says, he's buying time for those dedicated to the cause to get away. They will run with nothing but their wives and children. Nowhere in the world will our paper money be good. Maybe a thousand families with no homes to go back to and empty pockets to run on."

"That's what I'm sayin',' Barkston, it's over," snapped Lee.

"Maybe for Bobby Lee and some others, but not for the crew of the *RETRIBUTION*. May I continue Carlton, or do I buy you a pail of beer to drown yourself in?"

"You have never spoken to me like this before, Captain Jackman."

"I have never seen you quit before, First officer Lee."

Lee wiped his brow. He took three deep breaths. "Alright, Barkston."

"As I was saying, Amy Winters held a dinner for the Yankee officers. Our man slipped her a note on the shipment of the gold. They have decided not to ship it overland, due to Walkers attacks. He's been cutting up the Yanks up more than they acknowledge.

It was only a matter of time before the Yanks figured out that the raids on their supply caravans were more than local thieves."

"So it goes by sea, just as we suspected," observed Lee.

"That's right, but instead of shipping it on the navy gunboat, anchored near us, they are slipping it secretly onto a fast ship traveling through from Russian America."

"Why would they risk millions of dollars' worth of gold on an unarmed vessel?"

"The U.S. Navy's *DUCATOR* has had nothing but trouble with its boilers. It's one thing to lose one navy ship to an accident and quite another to risk months of gold production."

"Do we know which ship has been selected?"

"That we do. She's the *KATARINA*, home ported in both New Archangel and Boston. What makes her attractive is her speed. She is a three-hundred-fifty mile per day, large canvas wind dancer."

"My God, we can never catch her, even with steam."

"Do not blaspheme in front of me, Carlton."

"I am sorry, but it really is over, nothin' is working out."

"We cannot fail, we simply will not. Don't you see how this plays out? That gold held someplace like Havana could be the bank for hundreds of men just like you and me, men starting over. Each million in gold could give one thousand men a thousand dollars each."

"But if the war is over, doesn't that make us pirates fitted for a noose if we are caught?"

"Perhaps, if we're caught and if the war is over, which as of today it is not. And there is one other bonus to consider. The *KATARINA* has two of William Seward's agents aboard, no doubt nigger lovers like him. And there is supposedly a secret cargo moving from Russian America to Washington."

"What do you mean, secret cargo?"

"The rumor is a small gold shipment from the workings of an exploration company. It would make a good going-home bonus for the crew. They get a stipend; we both receive an officer's share of the larger shipment and I finish the war with the scalps of two of Seward's lieutenants on my belt."

"For God's sake; I'm sorry, but the war's almost over, haven't you had your fill of killing?" Besides, the Yankee ship is too fast for us."

"Until I see that Jeff Davis has surrendered or been captured, my license to hunt Yankees is still valid. The damn Yankee war has cost me my home, burned to the ground. It's cost me my property, the niggers set free, and the shipyard in Maryland burned to keep it out of Yankee hands, and most of all my family. Jeb died at Gettysburg. Alan at Fredericksburg, my sweet Elaine gone of a broken heart and dysentery while my mother and father now support the Yankee cause from their summer home in Maine. Only my lovely daughter, Claire, is still with me. At least I think she is, I haven't heard from her in seven months."

"No one has paid more than you, Barkston, that's God's truth. But even if the Lord grants you revenge, we still can't catch a ship that's five knots faster. "

Barkston looked past his friend and first officer and waived to the barmaid. He held up two fingers on each hand ordering two more scotch whiskies and two more beers.

The din of the waterfront saloon, the roar of two hundred sailors, miners, businessmen and laborers, pounded in on him. Barkston closed his eyes and a vision of sitting in the silence of the southernwoods, a rifle on his lap, watching the trees where wild turkeys roosted, filled his head. The piano and song, the laughter and argument, the squeak of wooden chair legs on a wooden floor and the clank of glasses all combined to hide their presence and mask their conversation. Someday he would once again find a quiet place. His worn body demanded quiet but for now this place worked.

"We will bring her to us Carlton," smiled the Captain. "As soon as Bolton and Davis arrive, I'll brief all three of you."

∽

"I never heard what happened to the family name Mr. Gritt?"

"It's not much of a story, Mr. Winters," laughed Chad. "My grandfather shortened it from Von Grittenberg to Grittenberg, to lose the aristocratic entitlement. When my mother talked my father into traveling to St. Petersburg to repeat their wedding vows, they shortened it again. Evidently there was some sort of disagreement between the Prussian House of Von Grittenberg and the Russian Orthodox Church over the right to import tobacco."

"Your father was nothing if not a pragmatic young man," replied Grant Winters. "His trading ships were the foundation of my success. The mining supplies and practical goods your father sent from New England were the beginning of Winters Trading. I was proud to call Chad Grittenberg my friend."

"The grain and dried fruits and vegetables you arranged for the Russian American trade paid handsomely in New Archangel and stocked my mother's trading company," replied Chad. "And the Russian's payment in furs opened so many doors in China. My family owes the success of the California trade, first to your late friend Louise Argiello and his selection of a young Boston adventurer as his partner when the Stars and Stripes replaced the Mexican flag in California del Norte. I toast to your health and ongoing success, Grant," Chad raised his glass.

Chad Gritt, head of Gritt RusAm Trading arrived at the mansion of the firm's agent and principal trading partner in San Francisco precisely at four in the afternoon. Though Grittenberg Shipping and later successor RusAm Trading Ships had entered the bay for decades trading goods from New England for California's riches, and then sailing on to Russian America and China, Chad had never before met Grant Winters.

The Gritt family had developed a yearly trading schedule with the former Commandant of the Presidio de San Francisco, his

Excellency Louis Argiello, beginning in 1828. The trading company created by Argiello grew supporting primarily the Hacienda economy of Old Mexico as well as supplying the Mexican military. Argiello and Chad's father had become close friends and business associates. When the flood of American farmers, loggers and merchants began to reach California del Norte in the mid 1840's, Argiello had selected, at Chad Senior's recommendation, a young Boston businessman as a partner. They established a retail mercantile catering to the newly arriving Americans. The San Francisco store was an instant success and led to the establishment of a second store, catering to the loggers and farmers heading into the Sacramento area in 1848. The new store carried a more limited food and dry goods line than the original San Francisco mercantile. What it lacked in traditional goods it made up for in tools, logging equipment and farming supplies.

When gold was discovered at Sutter's Mill in 1849, the Sacramento mercantile had been first in the supply line, meeting the demands of the California Gold Rush.

Chad's father had arrived on the company ship *BARANOFF* just weeks after the gold discovery. Chad Senior, Argiello and Winters recognized the opportunity at once. The harbor was filling with ships abandoned by their crews, drawn to the Gold Rush. The three men provided a bonus, equal to a year's wages, to the crew of the *BARANOFF* to keep them from joining the gold seekers. Chad then purchased the fastest vessel at anchor and split his crew, sending the new vessel back to Boston to set up a shuttle to meet the exploding demand.

Argiello and Winters had become wealthy and when Argiello passed away, Grant purchased his share of the business from his sons, whose passion was for ranching, not manning a store counter.

Chad, who was studying while all of this was taking place, eventually apprenticed himself as a junior officer on a company ship to learn the family business. He had earned his captain's ticket and then spent much of the next five years tied to a desk followed by a short stint as a naval officer. This trip on the *KATARINA*, was only his third commercial voyage that decade.

"Wha' Grant, why don't you introduce me to the young gentleman?" sang a voice from behind Chad. He turned to find a tall, auburn-haired woman in her mid-twenties. Amy Winters wore a lavender silk gown that might have been painted on, not the kind of thing Chad expected until he watched Grant's face.

"Mr. Chad Gritt, my wife, the former Miss Amy Kittering, of Virginia."

"I am honored and pleased to make your acquaintance, Mrs. Winters."

"You will call me Amy and I shall call you Chad." Turning to Grant she continued, "You two gentlemen will have to move this business talk into the carriage, or we will be late for our dinner reservation."

Grant cinched up his tie and buttoned one button on his plain gray suit.

"Of course, my dear."

"Oh, and Grant, I hope you don't mind but I asked my old family friend Captain Jackman and another of his officers from the *RETRIBUTION*, to join us."

Grant's eyes flicked toward his wife as he tugged at the left end of his graying mustache. His face flushed. He buttoned a second button and started toward the door.

∽

McClenaghan's Wharf was two blocks back from the docks. A three-story wood building, fronted by two sets of double glass doors, it wouldn't stand out from the surrounding buildings, thrown up in the boom of the past fifteen years, except for the color. McClanahans was the only shamrock green building in San Francisco. Over the doors was a white sign that ran the full hundred feet across the front of the structure. "McClenaghan's Wharf Full Service Saloon" was stenciled over the white background in dark red letters.

Two officers from the *RETRIBUTION* stepped up onto the porch. Marcus Bolton was carried on the roster as the third officer. His lack of sailing skills was more than compensated for by his skill with weapons and his willingness to use them. He had trained as a soldier in his native Britain and honed his skills in India. His unpredictability and penchant for unconstrained brutality had ended his military career. He had worked his way home, as a jailer on a ship carrying military prisoners back to England and found he liked the work. Reports of beatings and the unexplained disappearance of two prisoners had led to an investigation when the ship docked in South Hampton. Bolton had immediately signed onto the crew of a ship in route to Charleston, South Carolina and fled without drawing his pay. In Charleston, he jumped ship again when offered an officer's billet on a slaver, a position that had earned him a modest tobacco farm. Now forty, he was three inches shy of six feet and a stocky one hundred ninety pounds. A white straw hat was pulled down over his shock of black hair. His face was round, childlike but in the way of the playground bully. In his belt and tucked into his brown felt jacket he carried three knives.

His companion was very different. Pedro Davis was the son of an English whaling captain and a Mexican mother. Of slight build and a full six feet tall, he had dark skin, dark hair and striking light blue eyes. His father had established the family home in Charleston when his new bride had found the wet, windy weather in England was not her cup of tea. He was well educated and over his mother's objections had followed his father to sea after college. Now twenty-eight years old he had signed on with Captain Jackman as an officer and navigator, after his father's death at Yankee hands while trying to run a naval blockade.

Carlton Lee picked out Bolton and Davis as they pushed

their way through the crowd looking for their captain. Standing, he waived with his right hand, catching their attention with a shrill whistle. With his left hand he motioned to the barmaid. She arrived to take the newcomers' order as they seated themselves.

"The plan, gentlemen, will be to lure the *KATARINA* across the Sea of Cortez and hopefully pin her into the bay at Teacapan. You, Mr. Davis, are the key. We must convince this Captain Gritt to take you aboard and stop at Teacapan in order for you to gather up your mother and sister. I have arranged for you and me to have dinner with the Captain and Amy and Grant Winters this evening. With God's blessing, Gritt can be appealed to in the name of reuniting a family torn apart by war."

"Captain Jackman," responded Pedro, "this war is over. Too many have died. Now some of the Yankee crew and maybe some of us will join them, for what? Even if we take the gold, the Confederacy is over. What good can it do?"

"Carlton and I discussed it earlier. The gold will give the crew and a lot of destitute Confederate supporters something with which to start over."

"I don't care captain. I am done with the war. When we heard the news about General Lee last night, we all agreed, it was time to go home. My mother and sister must be weary of the exile my father forced upon them. They went from one civil war to another. I'm sure they are ready to come home. No captain, I am done with this war."

"For me this war will never be over." Jackman wrapped two huge hands around his beer mug, squeezing it until his fingers turned white. "Lieutenant Davis, you are a serving officer in the Confederate Navy. Your duty is to follow orders, my orders!"

"I have followed your orders, even those I didn't agree with for years. Now what, will you threaten me because I am sick to death of blood?"

Barkston started to rise, but a hand on his forearm stopped him.

"Calm yourself Captain," whispered Carlton Lee. "You stopped me from making a scene." Turning to Pedro Davis he continued, "Lieutenant, no one will forget your bravery or your commitment. You have a very different situation than your fellow officers."

"Spit it out Carlton."

"Your family has retained its wealth and its heritage. Most of your father's holdings are in England. Your mother is from a wealthy land-owning family in Mexico. You have something to go home to, the means to move your life forward. Most of the South's officers have nothin'. Like the Captain here, they have lost it all."

"I understand that, Carlton. I simply cannot stomach more bloodshed. I reached my limit when we took the *PEREGRINE* of New Haven last month."

"You are treading dangerously," spat Jackman.

"Take it easy, Barkston," quieted Lee; "let him talk this out, just as you let me." Lee turned and nodded to Pedro.

"Well, Carlton, Captain," he responded turning to look Jackman in the eyes; "There was no justification, I mean she was becalmed, and we had steam power. We swept her decks with grapeshot. We boarded her and took everything of value even the jewelry of the three women. They had surrendered. There were only eleven able bodied men left to take care of the women and nine children. The *PEREGRINE* was no threat, yet you still ordered her fired, leaving them in three longboats a hundred miles from the coast of Peru."

"It was war," sneered Bolton, who had remained silent up until that time. "If they had gotten her underway and made it to California, our mission here would have been compromised; we could have been captured."

"Don't talk nonsense, Marcus. You slit her captain's throat. You cut off a woman's finger just to take her ring. You have been fighting and killing too long. You didn't even hear the cries of the children as they watched the ship burn, but I did. I will hear it in my sleep for as long as I live," whispered Davis.

"Pedro, we cannot do this without you. What do you want?" asked Jackman.

"Nothing, just passage home for me and my family."

"The *RETRIBUTION* is going to take that shipment, Lieutenant, even if we have to chase the *KATARINA* until she is becalmed. We may bypass the Sea of Cortez altogether. Now, what do you want? Your shipmates and a lot of very good men are counting on you."

The young officer sat staring at a dozen can-can dancers on the stage, seeing none of them. He drained his beer. He fixed his glare on Bolton. "All right, Captain, I will help under these conditions."

"Go on."

"First, no one dies, no one. Second, you do not destroy the ship. After you take the gold, we pick up my family. I will have them waiting."

"I agree to your terms Lieutenant, but I must insist, that we shred her sails so that we get a good head start. I would think, Carlton, that it will take at least five days to remake a set of sails. Do you agree?" asked Jackman.

"At least," answered Lee.

"The canvas only, no other damage and no bloodshed?" asked Pedro.

"You have my word, Lieutenant. Now, Carlton and Marcus, you stay here and stay sober. If I have further need of you tonight, I will send for you. Pedro, you and I will discuss our story on our walk to the restaurant. We will all meet aboard the ship at midnight. Now, Lieutenant, we should not be late."

"Please do tell, Captain Gritt, how many more days before you leave for home?" The creak of the springs and the clatter of the steel wheel rims along with the clip-clop of the horse's hooves over cobblestone streets made it difficult to hear Amy Winters' soft drawl.

"If, Mrs. Winters, you are asking how long we will be at your husband's docks, he knows far better than I."

"Your special cargo from Sacramento will be here tomorrow," responded Grant Winters. "The rifles and ammunition for our friends in Peru arrived today. We can load tomorrow. Have you made arrangements for the five marines who will be traveling with you?"

"We are rigging bunks in the center hold where the special cargo will be stowed. It won't be luxurious, but it certainly beats a hammock in the passageway," laughed Chad. "We are not equipped for passengers beyond the three government men who made the round trip to Russian America. As it is, Angelo will be feeding us in shifts."

From the Winters' palatial home, it was no more than a mile to the Napoleon Hotel and the finest French restaurant in the city. The carriage, however, had to travel more than two miles, zigzagging across the steep hillside. Jackman and Davis waited in the lobby.

Jackman stretched his blocky five-foot-eight-inch frame out of the leather chair and swept his billed Captain's cap from his gray flecked dark brown hair. "My dear Amy, my how you have grown from that spindly girl who graced my ship on her way to study in Connecticut."

"Why, Captain Jackman," replied Amy, "as I said the other night, you yourself have not aged one day in the last eight years. Captain Chad Gritt, this is my old family friend, Captain Barkston Jackson and his friend."

"This is our third officer, Pedro Davis, navigator extraordinaire, master of Spanish, French and English, and as good an officer as ever stood a watch," beamed Jackman, his cap tucked under his arm. Both Confederate officers wore ill-fitting blue suits taken from chests of clothes captured from the *RETRIBUTION's* victims.

"My father was working the southern whaling grounds for a season with only moderate success," laughed Pedro, as the waiter refilled their glasses with excellent Bordeaux. "He decided to move north. Just off from the Mexican town of Los Mochis he broke his leg in an accident. Pulling into port for medical attention he met my mother. The connection was immediate. His first officer took his ship north along the Baja Coast while my father "convalesced". By the time the ship returned for him, his new wife joined him in the Captain's cabin on her way to her new home in England. "Oh," laughed Pedro continuing "and my father, who had never been a religious man, held lay Catholic mass all the way back to South Hampton."

Dinner was ordered from a menu that offered more than a dozen entrees, from local beef, fish and shellfish, to salted cod and salmon from Russian America. They chose the house specialty, a roasted fatty goose, prepared from geese specially raised for the chef. Another bottle of wine appeared.

"Why, Mr. Davis, your mother sounds like a very special woman; from the hacienda life of Mexico to the isolation of a Captain's wife with small children in England to a socialite in Charleston. How, pray tell, did she end up back in western Mexico?"

"When the southern rebellion started, my father pulled the three family ships out of Charleston back to England. He convinced my mother to take my sister and return to her family, which owns land dating to a Spanish crown land grant not far from Acapprieta. He was certain that the harbor at Charleston would be the target of the North's vastly superior navy. Our family home sits right on the bay, between two points with heavy batteries of guns, an obvious target."

"And did it survive the war?" asked Amy.

"At last report the blockade of Charleston had not led to shelling of the shore installations to any degree. Our caretakers, a nice

Irish couple, report that the house still stands, but the docks and warehouse have been taken over by the Confederate Navy."

"Thank God," marveled Amy.

"And your family home, Mrs. Winters? You are obviously originally from the South. How did your family fare in this terrible war?" asked Chad.

Tears made words unnecessary.

"My wife's farm in southern Virginia was destroyed in one of the battles," answered Grant Winters. "Although her father supported the preservation of the Union, the family had stayed. Amy has not heard from her father or her mother in more than two years. We even held off our wedding for a year. I stayed in New York while she tried again and again to reach them."

A large tureen of cream of asparagus soup arrived at the table, followed by dinner and more conversation. While they waited for a chocolate torte, Amy Winters' favorite dessert, Chad turned uncomfortably to Pedro Davis.

"Mr. Davis, under any other circumstances I would be very pleased to help you gather your family and return you to your home, or at least to Annapolis, our next port of call, but all of our passenger cabins are occupied by government representatives returning from Russian America. I am sure that our navigator Patrick deLaguera, who also is our Spanish interpreter, would be happy to rig a hammock in his cabin, just to have your company. You share many experiences and have a similar background. Unfortunately, we have no place to put your mother and sister. We also have several unplanned mouths to feed as it is. Again, I am sorry."

Amy Winters, finally composed, looked up at Barkston Jackman and at Pedro Davis. "Captain Grittenberg will be carrying some special secret cargo for the government along with marine guards."

Chad felt the hair rise on the back of his neck.

"Amy, dear," snapped Grant, "that sort of gossip is dangerous during war time."

"Oh, ah am so sorry, Grant, we are among friends here and the war seems almost over."

"Do not fret, Amy," consoled Jackman, "there has been no damage done, I am sure."

After dessert the party retired to the lobby bar.

"Grant, dear, would you mind if we moved our small party to the club? You gentlemen can have your brandy and a cigar. I can join the other ladies in the piano room for a sherry. You know how I hate cigars."

"I would love to accompany you," interjected Chad, "but my ship's officers and the three government men are at The Golden Gate celebrating the birthdays of their Russian interpreter and our bosun. I should visit them. Our one Spanish speaking officer tends to get a bit rowdy if he drinks."

"Oh dear, Captain Gritt, will that party not allow you to join us for at least a short while?"

"It may, Mrs. Winters, it has the makings of an all-nighter," laughed Chad, "but not if I take an hour with you all before I join the party."

"And the gentlemen from the *RETRIBUTION*?" asked Amy.

"Pedro, you go on with our new friends," smiled Jackman. "Amy, I must pass," he apologized. "I must check on a cargo for the Sandwich Islands."

Chad stood and stretched his hand out to Jackman. "Perhaps we will have time later in the week for a glass and a cigar."

"I would welcome that," responded Jackman, "but we clear port day after tomorrow." Turning to Davis he continued, "Pedro, if we haven't found a berth for you by tomorrow evening, we will move you into the hotel here before we depart. I am sure that you can find a couple of paid staterooms within a week or two. I will prepay your wages and advance you a portion of your share of the expected profits."

Looking back at the others he added, "Grant, thank you for

dinner. You obviously are making my old friend's daughter very happy. Now, if you will excuse me."

As the rest of the party waited for the Winters' carriage, Jackman walked the six blocks back to McClenaghan's. He sat down at the table still occupied by Carlton Lee and Marcus Bolton. "Mr. Lee, please return to the ship and have Ivan Beletsky join Marcus at the Golden Gate within the hour."

"Barkston, why Ivan; if there is something that you need, I can do it."

"Carlton, don't question my orders, we haven't the time. Now hurry and after the longboat returns to the dock, please have the boat wait for us. Marcus and I are going for a walk."

It took about fifteen minutes for the two men to walk to the Golden Gate. "All right Marcus, just to make sure that there is no mistake, repeat the plan back to me," ordered Jackman.

"I use officer status to strike up a conversation with the *KATARINA*'s navigator and Ivan uses his Russian to do the same with their Russian interpreter. We buy all the drinks and talk them into moving to our favorite saloon."

"That's right, Marcus. They need to die quietly and, in a place, where their bodies will not be found within the week. No one can know that you belong to the *RETRIBUTION*."

"I understand Barkston, but why the Spanish speaker and the interpreter?"

"We need the Spaniard's job and the Russian's cabin."

"Can you explain why?" asked Bolton.

"Later. Now, Marcus, two more things; first make sure Ivan understands that no one ever learns about tonight's work. We can't let Ivan run his mouth.

"Aye aye, Captain," replied Boulton pulling his knives one at a time, checking their edge. Barkston Jackman disappeared into the night.

Ten minutes later Jackman pushed through the glass doors at

the Merchants Club. "Why Captain Jackman, I thought you were otherwise engaged for the balance of the evening," commented Winters as Jackman seated himself.

"We finished quickly," answered Jackman, "and I figured that if Captain Gritt could steal an additional hour with friends, I deserved no less.

10
SAN FRANCISCO

BOLTON AND THE Confederate crew's only Russian speaker stood, whispering as they watched the party of American crewmen become more boisterous.

"Ivan, the captain has ordered us to find out about the route that the American ship will be taking, nothing more." When Bolton smiled, he looked a lot like a barracuda.

Ivan looked down at the shorter Bolton. He didn't believe a word, but not enough to openly challenge a man he feared more than any he had ever known. "But why take them to an abandoned building?"

"The Captain wants the discussion to be private even if I have to use a little force. We think they are on a secret Yankee government mission. I doubt that they will volunteer any information."

Ivan felt his stomach tighten. "The war is over. If I just disappear into the crowd here, I can catch a train east and be home before the harvest season. Mr. Bolton, I just want to go home."

"I can get the Captain to advance you enough to get you home from the Yankee funds he stashes in his safe. But tonight, he needs you to get the interpreter to a place where we can interrogate him quietly. We will leave them tied up. This has to remain a secret."

"My Russian is rusty. My grandmother taught me her language, but my parents only spoke English around the farm."

"Ivan, do your best." Bolton wrapped his huge hand around the man's thin arm and squeezed until tears filled the Ivan's eyes. "You don't want to piss me off."

An hour later Ivan tugged at a disintegrating door partially torn from its hinges. Two half- drunk men stumbled into the collapsing warehouse at the end of a pier, trying to figure out why they were there.

"Stay here Ivan," ordered Bolton as he followed the men. He was back in less than a minute, wiping blood from a knife.

"What have you done Mr. Bolton?" Ivan stepped back. "You just murdered two men?"

Bolton grabbed Ivan by the front of his jacket and rammed the twelve-inch blade up under his ribcage, then rammed it a second time into his other lung. He dragged the heaving man into the building. Bolton looked into the dying man's eyes. "Three, Ivan."

11
SAN FRANCISCO

TWO SEA LIONS watched the activities on the dock near the streamlined ship with three raked masts.

"Sergeant, a word with you please," said Chad.

"One moment, Captain. My orders are to supervise the loading and securing of the cargo. The boys are not quite finished."

At precisely noon, four wagons arrived at the dock. Each carried boxes of tinned biscuit, crates of produce, barrels of water and other supplies needed for a three-month voyage to Maryland. Secreted in each wagon were boxes of gold bars on their way to the U.S. Treasury.

Three 'workmen' accompanied each wagon, a driver and two freight men. All were army soldiers in plain clothes, their weapons hidden.

Not far away, the *DUCATOR*, a navy gunboat, was tied to a dock. She had been moved to the dock adjacent to where the *KATARINA* was berthed the night before. First, she was to be a decoy. At that very moment, army wagons were unloading sixteen heavy boxes under the watchful eye of two companies of uniformed soldiers. Her second mission had been accomplished the night before when five of her crew, dressed in civilian clothing and carrying heavy sea bags, left the navy gunboat and boarded the *KATARINA*.

"Captain, you wanted to see me," said Sgt. Jack Mosby, stifling an urge to salute.

"About your troop's sergeant. Aren't your men a little young?"

"Too young if you are asking me sir. Two of em' are new recruits from here in California. Only one has combat experience."

"We were told that we would have a marine security detail to protect this shipment. No one asked us to be nursemaids."

"The Captain of the *DUCATOR* figured that with the war over and all, the only risk would be thievery. He figured that with around the clock watches, none of your boys would dip their fingers."

"Well sergeant, the war is not over; the morning papers report fighting in Texas and Alabama."

"I know that Captain, but for sixteen years I have followed orders. Besides, my commanding officer probably figures he doesn't need any more snot nosed kids to train."

"I assume, Sergeant, that you will train your men."

"My orders are to keep an eye on the shipment."

"Sergeant, your men will berth in the center hold with the shipment. Only you and I have a key for the lock."

"I see your drift, Captain."

"One of my officers will provide security while you drill," offered Chad.

"That should be alright, but one problem Captain."

"Yes?"

"My men were only issued antique navy side arms. I doubt they have been fired in years. None of the men even know how to load them. We have no rifles."

"Oh, great God," moaned Chad. "Is there anything else you need to do your job?"

"Don't blame me Captain Gritt, I'm just a followin' orders."

Sergeant, I will loan you rifles, new repeaters," offered Chad.

"You sound like a man expectin' trouble Captain," replied the sergeant.

"Sergeant, I am a man who always carries twenty feet of rope when fifteen will do."

Mosby smiled. "I will start a drillin' them boys as soon as we clear port."

All of the provisions were either loaded or on the dock by two in the afternoon. Weaving his way through the wagons and stacks of freight, Grant Winters parked his surrey, and bounded up the gangway out of breath. "Is the Captain aboard?"

"He is below, Mr. Winters, I will find him for you." Nick was back in less than a minute, Gritt following.

"Any luck, Grant?"

"Well, no and yes, and the yes is bad luck," answered Winters.

"Let's have it then."

"I have had the police and my own men canvasing the bars, brothels and hospitals since noon yesterday. There was no sign of either Mr. deLaguera or Mr. Kraus."

"Men do not simply disappear," said Nick to both Winters and Gritt.

"My thoughts as well. That's why this morning I sent my wife to all three stage lines. Two tickets were sold for the ferry to Vallejo with continuing passage to Sacramento, one in the name of P. deLaguera and the other in the name of A. Kraus. There is no way to tell if our friends actually took passage, but it appears that they got gold fever."

"God damn Patrick to hell," exploded Chad. "And to think I considered making him a ship's captain. The bastard was always unreliable."

"Patrick had his bad points, that's for sure," replied Nick, "but this does not make any sense."

"It sure as hell does," replied Chad.

"No argument intended, Captain, but all of the way from New Archangel, Pat talked about this big break and moving to California."

"It appears that he just did."

"But what about Mr. Kraus, he seemed reliable," observed Kadzof.

"I only know Alexi from this trip. He may have been an ax murderer before joining the government."

"I find this very suspicious, Captain," continued Kadzof.

"Enough," demanded Chad.

"Grant, would you please take Nick here and see if you can find that young navigator we met at dinner the other night, what's his name?"

"Pedro Davis," answered Winters.

"Tell him that if he still needs a berth, he can join us as third officer and navigator. He draws no pay, but we will make Mr. Kraus' cabin available for his family.

The two men made their way to Winters' surrey but were stopped by Chad's booming voice. "Tell him we weigh anchor on the morning tide."

Pedro came aboard only two hours later.

༄

"Mr. Kadzof" directed Chad "you will double check Mr. Davis' navigation until I tell you to stop."

"Mr. Davis, please do not take this as an insult, but we have never sailed together, and I have only your word and that of Captain Barkston for your skills."

"No offense taken and thank you."

"Just do your job mister and smile once in a while. You will be very unpleasant company with that scowl all of the way to Maryland."

"Aye aye, Captain, first port of call is Teacapan."

"You know, Captain, it was about a year ago that I last saw these bluffs," remarked Kadzof. "The *PRISCILLA II*, the ship that carried us to Alaska, was a couple of knots slower than the *KATARINA* but we seemed to always have the wind at our back."

To the east, the evening sun painted the bluffs of Point Sur a brilliant gold. Above, the hills were a mottled green of spring grasses, flowers and trees. Scattered randomly along the hillsides, patches of red or yellow, white or blue reflected the season.

"It is hard to imagine these hills all brown and gray," continued Nick. "They say that most of the year, this coast is drab and dry. The spring rains give life to the land."

"Even in the summer, there are oases of green in those hills," said Chad. "My mother tells a story about a picnic lunch with my father the day after they met. They borrowed horses and found a grassy glen with a clear spring under the shade of oak trees."

"I like this country," replied Nick. "If Patrick doesn't return, I would appreciate you considering me for a Pacific posting."

"If and when, you will have first opportunity for a Captain's berth out of San Francisco."

"What about Patrick?" asked Nick.

"Patrick has set his last sail. He will never work for us again."

"I still think that there is something wrong there, Captain."

"Perhaps, but it is no concern of mine. I am through with Patrick's antics."

"I agree with your decision; still, something in this queers my stomach."

Chad laughed. "Then go below and ask Angelo for a cup of his calendula tea. He claims that it settles the stomach, evaporates headache, alleviates cramps, cures the clap and regrows hair on your head. Just be quick about it. As soon as you are back on deck, I need to spend some time with Sergeant Mosby."

TWO CIVIL WARS | 85

"I picked up a Spencer Repeater from a wounded cavalry major last fall. He had no use for it, havin' lost an arm. Held seven rounds. Good close-in weapon, but I still prefer the Sharps for range," stated Mosby.

"To be honest Sergeant, I have never fired one of these Henry's. The .44 caliber bullet should do the trick, but each cartridge holds little powder. Like your Spencer, it is probably a close-in rifle," said Chad.

"Twelve, thirteen, fourteen, fifteen, the damn thing holds fifteen cartridges," smiled Mosby. "No wonders the Rebs call it the gun you load on Sunday and shoot all week."

"Did your Spencer make it aboard Sergeant?"

"Naw, my lieutenant offered me thirty dollars for it. I sold it."

"That is unfortunate, it would have been an interesting exercise to compare the two." Chad plucked a rifle from the open case at his feet. "You and your men unpack these five rifles, clean the grease out of them while I locate a case of shells for you."

"Yes sir, Captain. How do you come to be a carryin' these here Henry's?"

"Grant Winters sold a hundred rifles to the Army of Peru along with two hundred rounds of ammunition for each. I bought another hundred and ammunition from Winters. Once the Peruvian army sees the rifle, I figure they will want more. They are always feuding with Bolivia."

"We will be a givin' them a thorough test over the next few weeks," offered Mosby.

"You do that Sergeant, and once you have mastered the Henry, I would appreciate some instruction myself."

"Ma pleasure, Captain."

"Just out of curiosity, Sergeant," added Chad, "I detect a Southern drawl in your voice. How did you come to be in the Northern Navy?"

"Marines, not Navy, Captain, I am not a deck swabber."

"No insult intended, Sergeant; still, I am curious."

"Well, I was a raised up in Kentuck' till I was twenty when the wanderlust got hold of me. After four or five years I found myself in Providence earning my keep as a prizefighter. One night in a saloon I got into a fight over a pretty young thing and mosta' killed a man. Wake up next mornin' in bed with the gal. She sure looked like a keeper while I was drunk."

"But not in the morning?" laughed Chad. "Others have suffered that fate."

"So right you are. Well, she was a tellin' me how many children we were gonna' have and what kind of house she wanted when the constable knocked on the door."

"The constable, huh," remarked Chad.

"Yep, turns out the man I beat up was the mayor's son, so there I am in jail. Ma' beauty visits me every day till the trial. The judge gives me two choices. I can marry my beauty, join the church and pay off a big fine over the next year or I can volunteer for the Marines. I been a United States Marine since that week. It is my home. When the Johnny Rebs attacked Fort Sumter, they attacked my family."

"Have you no other home even today?" queried Chad.

"That I do. Still Providence. Went back after my first tour and married ma' beauty. Got four kids, all girls."

"I meant no insult with my earlier comment, Sergeant," offered Chad.

"None taken, Captain Gritt. Long as ma' beauty stays out of saloons I do not have to fret about lonely Marines. Took this assignment to get home faster. Still got my sights set on makin' a boy."

"I wish you luck on that mission, Sergeant. Now let me find the ammunition for the Henry's. By the way, if you do not like the Henry, the ship's small armory has four Sharps .45/90 rifles."

The *KATARINA* could cover more than three hundred miles per day with favorable wind; Chad planned two days to Mexican waters. Passing the harbor of San Diego, Grit's frustration was on full display. "Five damned days to cover three hundred miles," he snarled at the quartermaster. "At this pace we won't be home until Christmas."

The farther south they ran the warmer the days became. The routine of a sailing ship on a long journey took over. The crew was divided into six-hour watches. Men from another watch were called out if a major sail change was required. Mealtime was the highlight of each day.

Angelo Gasparetti was in charge of the ship's galley. The short and stocky 39 year-old wore the face of a cherub with dark brown eyes and a five o'clock shadow. His long, wavy, black hair was neatly pulled back and tied with hemp cord.

Angelo's uncle Pietro had made several voyages with the Captain's father before starting one of Boston's favorite Italian restaurants. Angelo had worked for his uncle as a chef's assistant until five years before, when he had followed Pietro's protégés in going to sea with Gritt RusAm Trading. Five or six years at sea could earn a cook enough to start his own restaurant.

Gritt RusAm had a reputation for sailing fine, well-maintained ships. Still, the thing that allowed Gritt RusAm to recruit the best sailors was its reputation for the best meals at sea.

Tonight, was no exception. Angelo had built a cold room below the galley. Against one wall, piled from floor to ceiling, were ice blocks from Alaska. Hanging next to the ice was a side of beef, the other half having been consumed over the previous six days. Tonight's meal started with a thirty-pound strip of steaks.

"Steak fried heavy with pepper, mashed potatoes with chives and sautéed peppers and squash, Captain," said Angelo. "The crew gets our normal Sunday double ration of the Rum citrus grog, but in honor of Mr. Davis' first Sunday aboard I have sacrificed one of my bottles of Cabernet for the officers."

"Thank you, you have outdone yourself," replied Chad. The captain knew that exceptional meals gave the crew something to look forward to, overcoming boredom.

The small chartroom next to the Captain's cabin served as the officer's mess aboard the ship. With the ship creeping along the west coast of Baja California, all three officers were below for the once-a-week dinner together. Thomas Mead joined them.

"Mr. Davis" smiled Chad raising his glass, "welcome aboard." Gritt, Davis, and Kadzof and Mead clinked their glasses.

"Tell me, Pedro," inquired Nick, "where is your father now?"

"Gone now, three years. The family business was doing poorly. When we moved to the States father sold his whalers and went into shipping. His ship was sunk attempting to run a union blockade, with a load of cotton for British mills."

"With your father dead at Union hands, how did you come to serve on a Union ship?"

The line of questioning wrenched Pedro's stomach. He hoped it didn't show as he wiped a bead of sweat from his brow. "Any fool can see that the North, with its endless manpower and industrial base is going to win the war," he answered truthfully. "My father was a merchant seaman not a rebel," he continued, also truthfully. "I do not hold the North responsible," he lied.

"And how did you come to serve on the *RETRIBUTION*?" asked Chad.

"Captain Jackman was running cargo between Wilmington and England. His third officer, a North Carolina man, jumped ship in England to join a Confederate ship in South Hampton. I had leased our two remaining ships to the British East India Company for the India trade and was available."

"So, you have served on the *RETRIBUTION* since 1863?" asked Nick.

"Correct, until she sailed after our dinner," replied Pedro.

"We see few ocean steamers making the run to California," commented Chad.

Pedro closed his eyes, visualizing the script given to him. "We were chartered to a company running mining equipment to northern Sinaloa state in Mexico, well away from the trouble."

"Now I see how a Spanish speaking officer, especially one with Mexican contacts, would be so valuable. I am sure that Jackman will miss you," mused Nick.

"Yes," answered Davis, "I suppose that he will, but there are others on the crew who speak Spanish. It was very considerate of Captain Jackman to let me take my family home." Pedro's stomach turned as he stared at the wine glass in front of him. "It's too bad your two men jumped ship, but I thank you for helping me out."

FROM THE FRYING PAN INTO THE FIRE

12
TEACAPAN BAY, MEXICO

IT TOOK THIRTEEN days pushing down the Pacific coast for the *RETRIBUTION* to reach the huge T-shaped bay on the Mexican coast. The small village of Teacapan sat at the end of a peninsula that extended from the north. Across the narrow bay entrance lay the northern tip of a much larger peninsula; one that ran more than seventy miles south. The shoreline was a combination of minuscule hills and low plateaus. The earth above the bleached white sand was a bland tan with drab gray rock. Scraggly trees, all with pale green or gray foliage somehow survived. Mixed in were occasional palms and along the shoreline mangroves typical of shallow lagoons. In the distance there might have been jungle. The haze obscured everything except mountaintops. The land appeared lifeless except for thousands of soaring birds.

The sea just offshore was anything but lifeless. Pods of dolphin followed huge schools of tuna to the surface. Everywhere swarms of seabirds feasted on tiny fish pushed to the surface. Great gray sharks swam leisurely out of the path of the ship's two huge paddle wheels mounted on either side of the hull amidships. Above, stubby masts offered the possibility of a few more knots of speed if her sails were offered favorable wind. Over the last ten days, not a single sail had been set.

"Mr. Lee," ordered Captain Jackman, "please go below and ask Mr. Piper to walk the engines down slowly, he will want to baby the boilers." The *RETRIBUTION* was a steamer with paddle wheels on either side of the ship. Unlike sailing ships designed with a propeller at the stern, where its use was only to provide movement when the sails were furled, the *RETRIBUTION's* design was built as a steamer first. In the right winds, adding sails to her two masts might add four or five knots of speed. With winds in her face, she was faster than any sailing ship.

"On my way Captain. Do you think we have the *KATARINA* at our stern?"

"Rest assured Carlton she is at least four days behind us. The southerly winds would have slowed her to a crawl."

The engine room of the British built paddle wheel steamer was only one step removed from hell. The thud, thud, thud, of the engine was deafening. The drone of the firebox and the hiss of steam added to the clamor. The four men in the engine room screamed at each other to be heard above the mechanical noise. The crunch of two shovels into the pile of coal was almost drowned out by the creak of the drive shafts turning in their bearings, driven by humming gear assemblies. Carlton Lee noticed almost no noise as he descended the ladder into the engine room.

The heat is what he noticed. The blistering sun in the clear Mexican sky left the temperature on the quarterdeck of the *RETRIBUTION* hovering at ninety degrees. But it was hot in the engine room. Hot that hit you like a club as you descended. The ship's engineer, his assistant and the two stokers were dripping from head to toe. Their uniforms consisted of a pair of canvas pants cut off at the knees and heavy leather boots, soaked through with perspiration.

"Mr. Piper," screamed Carlton Lee, "you can begin reducing your steam."

"Thank the Captain," bellowed Piper, "and tell him that we need to chat about our fuel situation. Tell him I will be up as soon as we bring down the fires."

Bringing the pressure down was a tedious process, monitoring pressure gauges for each boiler. It was more than forty minutes before Lieutenant Brandon Piper approached the quarterdeck pulling on a shirt in the ninety-degree heat. The ship's captain and first officer stood sweltering in shirts, ties and jackets.

"My compliments, Captain," said Piper, "you said we could make this run in two weeks and we cut a full day off from the schedule."

"We could not have done it without your black crew. You squeezed every knot out of your boilers" answered Jackman. "You will have the day you requested for maintenance."

"Thank you, Captain. We can use help from the daylight sailors, my crew is bone tired."

"You will have all of the labor you can use," replied the Captain, "anything else?"

"Only the coal problem, we do not have enough in the bunkers to make Conception. This hard run burned more coal than planned." Piper ran his hand over his bald bead, wiping the sweat onto the deck as he leaned forward. The moisture continued to drip from his carefully waxed mustache as he straightened to his full height of four inches plus six feet. His rail thin body shivered as if he were chilled. "We will have to stop in Acapulco to top off the coal as planned," he continued.

"The Captain and I were discussing that earlier," said Carlton Lee. "Once we take the *KATARINA* word will spread down the coast. It will be far too dangerous to make port in Southwest Mexico. Millions in gold would be too tempting a target to the

Juarista's. They could arm and outfit ten thousand more peasants against the French."

"We don't have to detour north to Puerto Penasco to fetch up Walker and his boys. We can make Acapulco in less than five days. It will take twice that long to reach Acapulco on horseback."

"You are correct of course Brandon," laughed Lee, "but only two days to Guadalajara where I am sure they have telegraph by now."

"Ain't the telegraph run by the government down here?" asked Piper.

"Probably," replied Jackman, "but which government? Much of the country still backs Benito Juarez. It is mostly the big landowners and the church that invited the French and their Emperor. It is a risk we cannot take."

"If we ration, we might be able to make Peru," offered the Engineer. "There is coal there. You might have to wait days to get delivery."

"That sounds pretty thin," answered Lee.

"That leaves wood. If we mix our remaining coal with wood and make steam for no more than five knots, we will make it."

"How much wood will you need," asked Jackman?

"At a cord a day, about fifteen cords."

"We have plenty of hold space with the cannons remounted," replied Lee. "The chart shows a river south of here, perhaps a hundred miles, the San Pedro. There should be timber there. With all of us working, we should be able to cut that much in two days."

"It won't be the first time we have had to burn wood," smiled Piper. "I can give you seven easy knots; that should get us there by morning."

"First, Mr. Piper, I want to put Mr. Bolton and two other men ashore on the point opposite the village along with canvas for shelter from this brutal sun, and water and food for three days. We will give them two rifles and two pistols each and the spare glass. They can keep an eye out for the *KATARINA*."

Jackman turned to his second in command. "Mr. Lee, please let Marcus know what we have in store for him and pick two more men. Also, since we may go into action immediately after he rejoins the ship, please have him use the next hour to recheck his six cannon. And tell the bosun to report to me."

"Aye aye, Captain."

Axel Forrest was young to be a bosun at only twenty-four. A distant relative of the famous Confederate General Nathan Bedford Forrest, he had hoped to join the cavalry, but at over two hundred fifty pounds he was too heavy. He was a competent director of the enlisted crew, when necessary, keeping them in line by instilling the fear of God and his own fists.

"Bosun, please work with Mr. Lee to draw supplies for a mission ashore, to be led by Ensign Bolton. Load them into the small boat and prepare to put the boat over the side.

Also, Mr. Piper will require men tomorrow chipping clinkers from the boilers and doing other maintenance. Give him your two best men, men who deserve light duty."

"Why would I ask my most worthy men to do that God forsaken job?"

"Because the rest of us will spend the day cutting wood. Now get a move on."

⁂

The morning dawned clear as had every morning for a week. By the time the sun actually climbed over the rugged hills ten miles to the east, the men were at work in a stand of large trees where a river touched the Pacific. Two peasant families living at the mouth of the river had fled up a narrow rocky trail as they came ashore.

Juan Bacon was just happy to be out of the engine room. Originally from Texas, the morning heat felt good. With shoulders and back like an ox from shoveling coal, he was manning one end of a crosscut saw when the Captain summoned him.

"Juan, you speak Spanish, correct?" asked Jackman.

"Si, Senior," replied Juan, a sly smile on his face.

Jackman forced a laugh. "What were those men yelling about as they fled?"

"They called us filthy Frenchmen, probably the ship, the officers in uniform and the commands in a language that wasn't Spanish."

"Why would they take their families? We wouldn't hurt them."

"They don't know that, Captain. Probably just scared."

By afternoon, six cords of wood had been cut and four cords had been ferried to the ship. There was no warning before the first bullet smacked the pile of wood, just missing Carlton Lee. In less than a minute, two more shots were fired from the trees upriver. Four marksmen who had been issued rifles began scanning the woods for whoever was shooting at them. Captain Jackman and First Officer Lee crouched behind a pile of firewood with pistols drawn, while the remainder of the work party tried to disappear into the ground.

One of the ship's boats was making its way empty from the ship. Another was unloading its final sling of wood onto the deck. Both of the other boats were drawn up to the beach no more than a hundred feet from the work party, one fully loaded with wood, and the other just starting to load.

"I don't see a damn thing," snapped Lee.

"Probably just a peasant or two from upriver," replied the Captain.

Three more shots in quick succession smacked into logs and piles of wood where the crew had taken cover. This time, one of the Confederate marksmen returned a shot.

"Carswell, what did you shoot at?"

"Man in a white shirt and straw hat about a hunnert' yads' out, Cap'n." Carswell Evis was the Sergeant of the guard aboard the *RETRIBUTION*. A forty-something family man from Tennessee, he had been a sharpshooter for Stonewall Jackson's Brigade before losing a leg to a Yankee artillery shell. All four of the men armed with rifles were from Tennessee or Kentucky, where they had grown up barking squirrels and heading grouse.

"Ah missed him, Cap'n," continued Evis, but if'n he pops up at the same place again he will meet his maker."

"Mr. Lee, make your way to the shore and have the loaded boat return to the ship and unload. Have them bring rifles and shells for four more men on their return. Tell them to row like lives depend on them."

"And the other boat, Captain?"

"Have them finish loading then make their round trip snappy."

"Are we going to make a fight of it Barkston?" asked Lee.

"There appear to be only three shooters out there, Carlton, with eight rifles and two pistols it should not take long to send them back where they came from. Now move."

Lee's dash toward the beach brought four rapid shots, one slapping the hat from his head. The shots were answered by two of the *RETRIBUTION's* sharpshooters.

"Three, then four, now three again Cap'n," yelled Evis. "Both young Axel an' me found that fella. They be a lightin' candles for him come Sunday."

The next round of shots came from not only their front, but from the tiny stick and mud walled farmhouse to their left. This time, seven bullets were sent to do them harm. The Captain could see flashes of movement in the trees as their assailants repositioned themselves.

"They are not skilled, Cap'n," yelled Evis. "It take em' most of a minute to reload. An they shoot like I crap, Cap'n, stinkin'."

A moment later, eight shots slapped the trees and ground around the cutting crew. All four sharpshooters returned fire.

"Seven, then eight, now seven again," measured Carswell. "They be addin' faster than me and my boys can subtract." His shout was answered by three shots from the far side of the river, one catching Evis in the right leg shattering his wooden leg and knocking him flat.

"They are multiplyin' like cottontails in a rich holler. If we don't move now, they are a gonna' flank us and lay fire on the boats," stammered the sergeant.

Captain Jackman turned to the beach. The next load of wood was just leaving shore. Two empty boats were on the way to the beach.

"Mr. Forrest," Jackman shouted to his bosun, "organize the men into groups of six and send them to the boats one group at a time. Tell them to take their tools with them. Any man who drops his ax or saw will be sent back to retrieve it. When I give the order send the first six and have them scatter and fly like a covey of Georgia quail."

It took twenty minutes to get the unarmed woodcutters to the beach and into boats. A ragged volley chased each group as they ran. One man was wounded, a leg wound.

The four marksmen returned fire, but their enemy was offering little to shoot at.

"Cap'n, Axel will be a helpin' me to the boat with my leg shot off and all. Benny and Chase will give cover, then run like they stole the melon."

"Go Sergeant, I have five shots in my revolver. I will stay and give you cover."

Evis, Jackman and the farm boy, Bo, and Axel Forrest, each fired at the unseen enemy and then struck out for the beach. Evis and Axel were doing their best imitation of a three-legged sack race. At six feet four, Axel wrapped his right arm across the shorter man's shoulder and under his right arm. Carswell extended his left arm around the big bosun and grabbed his belt tightly. Axel carried his rifle in his left hand; Carswell used his rifle as a crutch.

Jackman walked backward in a crouch behind the two men

raising his pistol to return shots with the Mexican skirmishers as he walked. The three men were fifty feet from the waiting boat when Benny and Chase came running toward them weaving from tree to tree for cover. Carlton Lee waited on the beach with his pistol pointed at a patch of black powder smoke from across the river.

"Get the hell in the boat and let's get off this beach" he yelled as Evis, Jackman and Axel Forest stumbled to the boat and dove over the bow, followed seconds later by the last two men. Lee emptied his pistol at the flashes of white shirts in the trees, and then began to push the boat from the beach. When the water reached his thighs he dove headfirst into the boat, his legs dangling over the side. The two men manning the oars, drowning in adrenaline, pulled the boat through the splashes of bullets hitting the water and in less than two minutes were out of range of the Mexican muskets.

Carlton twisted his legs into the boat and sat facing away from the shore. In the bottom of the boat lay Axel Forrest, blood pouring from his back, mixing with the seawater.

"I felt Axel get hit when he first picked me up," whispered Evis. "He never made a peep. He jus' lit out like a mule haulin' his load."

Axel's blue eyes were open, and a spot of blood dribbled from his mouth.

"Tell my mama," he said. He coughed, coughed again, each spasm lifting his body from the water in the boat's bottom. He twisted his face toward Jackman, his muscles rigid. He died stretched taught like a cable holding freight on a rail car.

"Damn, Damn, Damn" was all that the Captain could say. He reached down and pushed the young man's eyes closed with his index finger.

"It is a bad time, Captain, and I mean no disrespect to Axel here, but we only have a half of the wood we will need," said Lee.

"We will set an economy cruise back to Teacapan. It will take an extra day. Then we will burn the *KATARINA*. We will take her and cut her up and burn her.

13
TEACAPAN, MEXICO

THE SEVENTEENTH MORNING dawned as clear and warm as the previous sixteen. The *KATARINA*, gliding before a gentle breeze, rounded the southernmost point of the Baja Peninsula. The hills above the beach were dry and colorless. Scrub trees and cactus spattered the land. Rocks occupied even the washes and gullies.

"Have you ever seen more birds, Mr. Davis?" asked Nick. In every direction the sea churned with small fish frantic to escape being breakfast. Above the fish thousands of sea birds dropped like darts into the writhing masses. Long chains of graceful brown pelicans skimmed the water seeming to flap their wings so seldom that it was hard to believe they stayed airborne. Above the ship black and white frigate birds soared, their long, bent wings riding the faint breeze. One bird with wings over six feet between the pointed wing tips soared directly over the ship, a bright red sack under its chin. A hundred yards off from the port beam the frigate folded its wings and dove ripping a freshly caught fish from the beak of another bird. Suddenly, all of the birds abandoned their fishing, rising in clouds. The sardines that had made the water boil one minute disappeared the next.

"Pedro," called Nick, "would you look at this?" Below the ship and stretching in every direction was an endless school of sharks. The strange fish with their unusual T-shaped heads swam under and around the boat. Fish no more than four feet in length, shadowed monsters of fifteen feet.

"Truly amazing," replied Petro Davis. "Can you imagine the sheer amount of prey that it takes to feed this mass?"

"Care for a morning swim?" asked Nick.

"I believe that I will wait for Teacapan."

"How long a wait, when do we arrive?"

"Day after tomorrow, assuming the afternoon breeze continues."

"I will be happy to see us there and on our way again. The sharks are a bad omen."

"You are just homesick," replied Pedro hoping his nervousness didn't show. "But I will travel with haste. It is a full day's ride from Teacapan to Acaponeta where my mother and sister are staying. It will take them a day or two to prepare to travel, then one more day for the coach ride back to the ship. I estimate four days at Teacapan."

"I was not asking you to do the impossible," replied Nick. "Day after day with the wind in our face has made me impatient, and the miles of sharks make me nervous."

From Acaponeta, Pedro planned a return via the village of Tecuala, a much shorter route to the bay based on the map he'd drawn when he'd visited six months before. The Rebel ship *RETRIBUTION* would be waiting where the track from Tecuala reached the sea. The thievery would happen while he was away, leaving the Yankee ship without sails near the village of Teacapan.

The shoreline just to the north of Teacapan took shape out of the ocean haze at midmorning two days later. The crew, anticipating some time ashore to stretch their legs, filed slowly to the port beam of the ship watching the shore grow larger. No one paid any attention to the distant ship with smoky smudge above it, closing rapidly from the southwest.

"Mr. Smith," directed the Captain, "we will reduce canvases, drop top sails just off shore from the village. Please send young Kelley forward to take soundings as we close on the shoreline. I want one fifteen-fathom reading every five minutes."

Tom Kelley counted out fifteen knots in the sounding line as he positioned himself on the starboard side of the ship just behind the bow. Each knot represented six feet of line. At the end was a lead ball. Cradling the coiled line in his left hand, Kelley slowly twirled six feet of line from his right hand, reaching out to keep the whirling lead ball clear of the ship. The ball spun faster and faster until Kelley released the ball allowing the line to run from his left hand. The ball arched out past the bow then splashed into the water. Tom allowed the ball to sink until the line stretched straight down below the ship and then he began to retrieve it.

"Fifteen fathoms, no contact" he sung out.

Mr. Davis, if we have you ashore within the hour, can you reach your home yet tonight?"

"I believe so Captain." Pedro's heart raced. "If necessary, I will ride all night."

The Captain and Davis watched the shore grow larger.

"Fifteen fathoms, no contact," sang out Kelley.

"Will we be able to fill some empty water casks here?" asked Chad.

"I have never been in the village Captain, but they must have a well. I suggest that you offer to pay a small price for water. You may also be able to purchase chickens or pigs and even some vegetables."

"Will you have trouble finding a horse?"

"Fifteen fathoms, contact."

"This is Mexico, if there is a good horse in the village, all it takes is money."

"Mr. Kadzof, we will swing to the tip of the peninsula and then work back to the village," ordered Chad.

"Mr. Smith, you will drop the top sails as we come about" directed the Captain.

"Aye Aye, Sir."

"Fourteen fathoms, the bottom coming up," sang out Kelley.

"I will send our chef ashore along with Mr. Kadzof and a couple of men," said Chad. "He speaks a spec of Spanish and will know what food stuffs we need."

The Captain sent for Angelo.

"Thirteen fathoms, bottom coming up."

"Ott stand by to send your crew up the rigging," ordered the Captain.

With all hands watching the shore on the port beam it was young Thomas Kelley casting the sounding line on the starboard beam that sounded the warning. "Captain, that paddle wheel steamer is closing on us fast," called Kelley.

The entire quarterdeck turned as one. Raising his telescope, Chad surveyed the oncoming ship, now only two miles away. "I can see no flag, but her bow is straight on," said Chad to no one in particular. "She is churning up the sea in a hurry."

Pedro's heart began to pound. *This was not the plan.*

"I do not like this," continued Chad. "She mounts a large bore gun on the bow and there appears to be a gun crew making ready."

The bow of the steamer disappeared in a puff of smoke. A moment later a heavy shell whistled as it screamed over the ship punching a hole through one of the topsails.

There was to be no destruction, thought Pedro Davis.

"What the hell? That bastard can shoot. One shot from two miles and he is dead on."

The paddlewheel steamer was making ten knots, while the *KATARINA*, sailing before a light wind was slipping through the water at less than half of that.

"Twelve fathoms, bottom coming up."

At a range of a mile and a half the steamer turned north preparing to pass the *KATARINA* starboard beam to starboard beam. "Ott, belay the order to reduce top canvas," shouted Chad. "You will run up fore and aft sails; every bit of canvas she will take. Tell your men to pray for an early wind."

"Mr. Davis, please take the wheel and steer for the mouth of the bay."

"Brian," said Chad to the quartermaster just relinquishing the wheel to Pedro Davis, "Find Mr. Kadzof, Mr. Pierce, Mr. Mead and Sergeant Mosby and bring them here."

The steamer was passing the southbound *KATARINA*. Two puffs of smoke rose from the steamer's starboard beam. One shell smacked the water three hundred yards from the *KATARINA*'s beam while another struck just behind the ship.

"The bastard mounts heavy guns per side as well as the bow chaser," said Chad, studying the churning steamer from bow to stern through his glass. His eye froze at the stern of the steamer as it began a slow turn into the *KATARINA*.

"Ten fathoms, bottom coming up quickly."

"Brian, tell Kadzof and the others that she is flying the Confederate Cross-Bar flag."

"Aye Aye, Captain."

"Mr. Davis does Teacapan have any fortifications?" asked Chad.

"I doubt that it does. It is a fishing village."

"Nine fathoms, bottom coming up," shouted Kelley.

It took two minutes for the Second Officer, the Assistant Secretary of State, the President's Explorer and the Sergeant of the Marines to reach the quarterdeck.

"Brian, thank you. Now relieve Mr. Davis. Steer a course for the mouth of the bay."

The rebel ship had taken up station a mile and a half further offshore than the *KATARINA* and slightly behind. A puff of smoke from her bow precluded a splash directly between the *KATARINA* and the village.

"You must run for the village, Captain," squawked Miles Pierce. "You cannot allow the rebels to take this ship."

"Mr. Pierce," replied Nick, "that ship just sent us a clear message that we would never make the village."

"He is herding us like a lamb," said Mead. "What are our chances of outrunning that puffing dragon?"

"Not good." Chad surveyed the sails including the last four just set by Smith's deck crew. All sails carried wind, but the sea showed only ripples. "It takes fifteen knots of wind to put wind streaks on the water and twenty or more to create white caps. We need another ten knots of wind to outrun her."

"Eight fathoms, the bottom coming up."

"The Rebs are pushing us into the bay" added Nick. "Once we are in there we are trapped."

"I agree," replied Chad.

"Brian, give me a twenty degree turn to starboard."

The ship's turn was immediately answered by a shell, which threw up a geyser less than a hundred feet from the starboard beam. "I figured that would happen," said Chad just as a second shell hit even closer. "Brian, give me thirty degrees to port," we will take our chances in the bay."

"Seven fathoms, bottom coming up."

The bay at Teacapan is one hundred miles long. Teacapan, the village, sits at the southernmost point of the northern peninsula. The western shore of the bay is a long-rugged peninsula. The entrance to the bay, the gap between the peninsulas is less than ten miles wide. The *KATARINA* was closing on the entrance.

The five men huddled around the woefully inadequate chart of the West Coast of Mexico. The scale of the chart yielded a drawing of the bay only three inches long. The only notation on the southern arm read "shallow."

"Captain Gritt," yammered Pierce, "it must be the gold. The Rebs must be after the gold."

"What gold, Mr. Secretary?"

"Oh, come now Captain, everyone knows about the California gold shipment."

"Is that true, Thomas?" Chad asked.

"There was a rumor in San Francisco about a shipment; with a half dozen Marines aboard, the *KATARINA* has to be the ship," answered Mead.

"But the war is done," drawled Mosby.

"Perhaps they don't know that," answered Chad.

"We can tell them," whined Pierce.

"Do you think that they will believe you?" asked Nick.

"They may."

"Don't talk rubbish, Pierce," answered Mead. "If she has been prowling these waters, she would have no notice of the war's end."

"There are no reports of a Confederate raider in these waters," added Chad.

Pierce shifted from one foot to the other and back. "That is not completely accurate Captain," replied Pierce. "Last year there were a half dozen reports of a raider in the Pacific, three from ships that escaped and three from survivors. There were over a dozen ships that disappeared as well."

"I saw no notices to mariners."

"I did not want to disrupt trade over one rebel ship," answered Pierce.

"Dandy, just dandy, did it ever occur to you, Miles, that an adequate warning could save ships and lives?"

"My obligation is to maximize trade and customs duties. Besides, how can a simple notice protect unarmed merchant ships?"

"Vigilance, Pierce. Vigilance."

"If you gents are through throwin' high steppin' words at one another" said Sergeant Mosby, "we should conjure on how to defend ourselves."

"The Sergeant is right," added Mead."

"I have a plan, well not really a plan but a strategy" interjected Nick, "that is if anyone is interested."

"Let's hear it Mr. Kadzof."

"The chart has no detail, but it does offer information. The south arm of the bay is marked shallow and as you can see the bay has pockets along the inside shoreline, and then curves to the left. That steamer has to draw more water than the *KATARINA,* so let's suppose that they cannot make it behind one of the points. If we can get far enough into the side bay and hug the shore, the rebel gunboat could not bring her guns to bear."

Gritt looked up at the swell breaking over a long sandbar along the front of the bay. Maybe the Katarina might slip over the obstacle, but he doubted that the steamer could. He kept the thoughts to himself.

"That is your idea?" snapped Pierce. "We would be trapped. She could just wait us out."

"Hold on Mr. Secretary," spat Mead. "The Rebs are just as likely to send in a boarding party. They think we are unarmed. We have twenty-nine men aboard and a great equalizer."

"An equalizer?" asked Nick.

"You a' firen' to the Henry's, right Mr. Mead?" said Sergeant Mosby smiling.

"I am indeed."

"What is your plan, Thomas?" asked Chad.

"If the rebel ship wanted to sink us, we would be treading water already" commented Mead. "She wants to board us. With the wind freshening we should slowly pull away from her. The Rebs do not care; we are trapped. All they have to do is use their more maneuverable ship as a cork in the bottle."

Gritt watched as the swell carried his ship toward the sandbar.

He bit his lip until it bled, waiting for the ship to run aground. The relief of his ship crossing the bar with little trouble was tempered as he watched the rebel ship riding over the swell. "Not quite shallow enough," he muttered to no one.

"So, then we just wait for their boats to come along side and surprise them They ain't gonna like the taste of the Henry's," added Mosby.

"Not bad" commended Mead, "but I had in mind a more aggressive defense."

Three fathoms, bottom steady" called Kelley retrieving the sounding weight. He coiled the sounding rope at his feet, dropping the ball in the center. He plopped onto a storage locker at the bow, rubbing a shoulder strained by a full hour of casting the sounding ball.

"The problem is, gentlemen, that if the Rebs do not send a boarding party, and they decide to blockade us, it is only a matter of days before they figure out how to bring their guns to bear. Those British naval guns have a range of almost five miles."

"You seem to know a great deal about the rebel ship," commented Pedro Davis, speaking for the first time.

"I believe that our opponent is one of three British built raiders. In another life, years ago I tried to stop them before they got to sea. One was sunk, the second, we all know about. She has seized or sunk more Northern ships than the rest of the Confederate Navy combined. I believe that this is the third ship, the one that has been missing for more than two years. It is a long story, but before I tried to help sink her, I helped the Confederacy buy her."

"Ah' would love to hear yer' story someday, Mr. Mead, or whatever your title is."

"Until now, mister worked," replied Mead, "but for the next day or so Colonel Mead may be more appropriate, Sergeant."

"What's your plan, Colonel?"

"It will take us hours to reach the end of the bay. We use the time to load four-dozen Henry rifles plus food and water into two of the boats. We do it slowly and methodically, so we do not tip off the Rebs. When we make the turn into a side bay or if it stays deep enough to make a turn at the head of the bay, we need a good lead on the steamer."

"Two and a half fathoms." Kelley no longer threw the ball; he could see the bottom clearly through the clear water.

"We put two of our four boats loaded with provisions over the side the minute the rebel ship cannot see us. I will take eleven men ashore and hide. If the Rebs do not attack the *KATARINA* tonight or tomorrow, we will attack the rebel ship the second night. If we cannot sink her, we should at least be able to disable her by blowing up her paddle wheels or her rudder. Either way you have a chance to escape."

"I do not favor dividing our few men," replied Chad.

"Chad, I gave that some thought," answered Mead. "The key is the Henry rifle. With two loaded Henry rifles each, my dozen men can put down a volley of fire similar to a full company of men armed with single shot rifles; one hundred eighty rounds before we drop the first rifle and pick up the next. With each man carrying two weapons we should be able to sweep the Rebel ship without having to reload."

"I can see that," answered Chad.

Mead continued, "We will build some black powder charges with long fuses before we go in, and then designate three good swimmers to set the charges on the wheels and the rudder. With long fuses we can try to take the ship and still have time to cut them if we succeed. If we fail, the charges still disable the steamer."

"I see that too," said Chad.

"And with seventeen men still aboard the *KATARINA*, armed Henrys, no small boat will have a chance of getting boarders over your rail."

"That I can see as well."

"Then what am I missing, Chad? You pulled my butt out of the ocean once before when one of my plans failed."

"Maybe nothing, Thomas," replied Chad, "maybe everything. I don't want to give in to the rebs. More than that, I want to finish our mission for the President and get everybody home."

Mead nodded his head but said nothing.

"First, if you only disable the Reb ship, she still has long-range cannons. Unless the winds come around to the south, we will have to tow the *KATARINA* out of our hide with the two remaining long boats. The Rebel ship, even at anchor, will have hours to get our range. Second, once we do get past the cork in the bottle, we cannot turn around and come back for you and your men. Finally, if all of this does not work, we will need every man aboard to make it home safely. Mexico is also in the midst of a civil war, one with massed armies that take no prisoners. Twenty-nine well-armed men with a packet full of gold for buying help and bribing officials have a chance of getting back to the USA. Twenty-nine men each armed with several Henrys have a chance of talking instead of fighting. Any fewer men reduce our menace factor. Thomas, you are the military mind here. We will need you if we have to cross Mexico."

"You sometimes sell yourself short Chad, but what do you propose?"

"We adopt your plan; it gives us the best chance for coming out of this with the smallest losses. I would only add that we prepare as well as possible for an overland escape if it becomes necessary."

"That makes sense," said Mead. "It also means that my dozen men must succeed in taking the Reb ship. If we fail, those of us that survive will return to shore abeam the *KATARINA and* provide what cover we can for your evacuation. I'll try to stay alive."

"Colonel, Captain," interjected Pedro Davis, "you should not underestimate your enemy. So far, the rebel ship has played a careful game. She clearly is after our cargo, not our lives."

"What do you mean?" asked Mead.

"It is just that the rebels clearly have a plan to force our surrender. They intend to run us aground or damage us so that they can take us. They have been cautiously following a plan."

"What is your point, Mr. Davis?" responded Nick Kadzof.

"Just that our lives are more important than your cargo."

"We will not give up without a fight Mr. Davis," said Chad, surprising himself.

"Just a minute Captain," interjected Pierce. "Maybe we should consider Pedro's comments. No one needs to die with the war virtually over."

"Mr. Secretary, we fly the flag, and we fight the fight. Besides, with the war lost do you really think the Confederates will be at all concerned about our lives?" Mead shook his head.

"They probably just want to go home just like us," added Pedro.

"Bottom coming up."

"Enough, we need to get moving," cut off the Captain.

The next two hours were spent preparing for two scenarios. Two of the boats were prepared for Mead's men. The ten men selected included three Marines, Corporal Bush being assigned by Mosby to keep an eye on the unopened boxes of gold. One box sat in the carpenter's shop where the ship's carpenter Sig Belson and two assistants worked feverishly sawing gold bars into smaller pieces, then beating them into flat strips. As the strips were finished, each was sewn into a pocket of one of ten vests quickly stitched from sailcloth. The goal was to divide one hundred pounds of gold among ten of the men to be used in case the crew was forced ashore. Nick Kadzof, who had spent months traveling Alaska with Mead volunteered to lead six other men selected from the crew to fill out Mead's party.

Each man was issued two Henry rifles and fifty rounds of ammunition. Strips of sailcloth were prepared as crude rifle slings. It would be awkward, but each man could sling a rifle over his back, leaving his hands free to climb over the rail of the enemy vessel. Two pistols came from the marines. Thomas Mead tied long cords to each and practiced drawing them from his belt one at a time. With only one arm, the pistols would be easier to use.

"Two and a half fathoms, the bottom coming up" called Kelley.

Gritt trained his telescope on the enemy ship. *Maybe Pierce is right,* he thought. Still, they hadn't suffered any casualties. "Time is on our side," he announced.

The ship now had a four-mile Lead over the Confederate steamer, which had stopped to pick up some men from the beach once the *KATARINA* had committed to the Southern bay. With only a few feet of water under the keel, the *KATARINA* slowed, looking for the deep channel, which didn't exist. She hugged the bank as closely as water depth could allow and at four-thirty in the afternoon, she rounded a point and was concealed from the following ship.

In minutes, two prepared long boats were over the side and Colonel Mead, First Officer Kadzof and Sergeant Mosby led their men around the bow of the *KATARINA* and toward the eastern shore of the bay. The party had reached the shore and secreted themselves in a tiny cove that hid them from searching eyes in the west.

The *KATARINA* continued to the east another mile before Kelley's call of shallow water brought their progress to an end. The lightly loaded ship drew thirteen feet of water at the keel, which meant that inches of water separated the ship from the rocky bottom.

"Mr. Smith, you will furl all sails after the anchor bites" ordered Chad. From the quarterdeck Chad trained his brass telescope at the point that they had rounded only minutes before. "The smoke over the point gives us some idea of where the rebel ship lies," observed Chad. "Mr. Secretary, would you please remain here and make sure that the Rebels do not round that point?"

"I will," replied Pierce. "But if she does, I say we give her the gold rather than die."

"If it comes to that choice, you have my word, Mr. Pierce."

"Now, Mr. Davis, will you please join me in preparing the other two boats for an escape should one become necessary."

"Aye Aye, Captain," replied Pedro, "but with only an hour or two of light left, I think we can sleep tonight. The morning will be another matter entirely. Pedro could only imagine the fury of Captain Gritt when he learned who was on the rebel boat.

"Once we get the boats outfitted and ready for water we can break for dinner. We will use the dark to ready ourselves to repel boarders in the dawn," replied Chad.

"You are a stubborn man, Captain."

"I take after my mother, Mr. Davis."

As the dark descended the enemy ship held station just around the point and just out of sight. Every few minutes, a streak of sparks rose into the still evening air marking its exact position no more than three miles away.

"She hasn't moved in an hour," said Gritt. "Maybe she's run aground."

"Any decent captain would anchor before that," stated Davis. "That ship is burning wood; coal does not throw off sparks."

14
TEACAPAN, MEXICO

ANGELO, THE SHIP'S cook, took his job very seriously. Crossing the deck he arrived at his secret, a small low greenhouse built along the ship's stern. He snipped four large stalks of dill from his herb box then moved to the next box. He would take most of his lettuce and radishes for the meal.

"Dinner in one hour Captain, Doctor," he announced. "I will serve half at seven o'clock and the rest of the crew a half hour later."

"What is the special occasion, Angelo?" asked Christopher Parker the ship's business manager, selected by Chad because of his training as a doctor.

"I took you at your word, Mr. Parker" replied the cook. "With the possibility of a fight tomorrow we will serve well tonight and poorly in the morning."

"Very good Angelo, bread and tea only for breakfast."

"We make up for it tonight, baked Dorado fish with dill, cornbread, a real green salad, and chocolate cake. Citrus rum punch to wash it all down for one and all."

"I have not seen my wife in a year, Angelo, but I will not be rushing home thinking about her cooking."

"Ha, Mr. Parker, when you get close to home your thinking will not be done with your stomach or your head."

"I can see why you were called to the kitchen instead of the pulpit." Parker smiled.

"I opened two bottles of nice wine for the officer's table; pour yourself a glass while I whistle up my customers."

"No working ship serves food like this," commented Pedro Davis, his mind working overtime to come up with a solution to the trap he was in.

"It is a tradition on Gritt ships," answered Chad. "Angelo's uncle sailed with my father in '20 and started the tradition."

"It surely beats the average rubbish, bacon and beans day after day." Pedro had gotten to know Gritt well enough to realize that the minute the Captain knew who their opponent was, he was a dead man.

"That it does," laughed Parker.

"Back to business gentlemen," interjected Chad. "In each of the boats we load five of the gold vests, two Henry rifles for each man, ammunition, thirty bottles of wine, and the food Angelo has set out. We will also need blankets and enough sailcloth to make shelters. I also want four of the long-range sharps rifles, and whatever Angelo will need to cook. We balance the load between the two boats and put the boats in the water on the side away from the rebel ship."

"I understand everything except the wine," replied Ott Smith who had joined the officer's table after supper with his men. "I do not want my men stupid with drink."

"Agreed, Ott," answered Chad. "The key is the bottles, if we have to strike out over land, we will not want to lug three-hundred-pound water casks. The wine bottles with their corks will make serviceable canteens."

The men concluded with their plans to defend the ship. They would pre-position loaded rifles throughout the ship and set up Doc Parker in the Galley to treat any injured.

"And Mr. Smith, I want one of us plus three of your crew on lookout all night. Relieve the watch every two hours. That should get all of us five or six hours of rest."

Preparations were completed by sunset, and the first watch was posted. Four watches came and went, nothing happened.

"Your men are grumbling," said Pierce. "Two slices of bread and a mug of tea is not a breakfast, Captain."

"My men grumbling or your stomach, Mr. Secretary?"

"I admit my hunger. Angelo knows that I do not like fish and the piece of hard Russian sausage that I scrounged did not set well. You cannot expect your men or me to fight on an empty stomach."

"Mr. Pierce, the meal strategy came directly from Doc Parker."

"Parker may not need to eat but I do."

"Did you know that Parker got that eye patch during the war? How he got it is a funny story."

"I don't care."

The captain looked away in disgust. "Chris was the regimental surgeon for the Fourth Vermont. He saw hundreds of men on his operating table in two years of war. He lost every man who reached him with a full stomach and a stomach wound. When Doc Parker says no food this morning his word is gospel."

"You seem to attract damaged goods, Captain."

"Pierce, you above all others, know how many men have served in this brutal war."

"Do not lecture me, Captain Gritt. I chose to serve in the government while you were playing at military then went back to your business. You profited from the war."

Mead replaced the sentry on the other side of the peninsula. In the distance, sparks from the Confederate ship marked its location. The occasional flash of light appeared where someone opened a door. The sentry could barely keep his eyes open, still he took the time to brief the colonel.

"I swear I heard voices from down near the end of the peninsula about an hour ago sir. It's just too damned dark to see anything yet but keep an eye that direction."

"Thanks, go get some rest. I thought the Rebs would try to take the ship last night, but with full light in an hour, I think we are fine until tonight. Get some sleep."

Mead found a small outcropping of boulders just above the sandy beach and settled in to watch. A slight breeze from the south felt good after a night trying to sleep on the hot sand in the middle of the peninsula. Mead reached for his pipe and a pouch of tobacco, then thought better of the idea. Still the joy of a smoke overlooking the peaceful bay stuck in his mind.

His eyes clicked wide open as he figured out the sudden tobacco craving. A wisp of smoke found his nose from his left. He turned to study the beach in that direction. A quarter mile away he caught the glow of someone drawing on a cigarette. As he watched the glow drew closer.

Mead drew both pistols and laid them on the flat rock in front of him just as the sound of men whispering reached his ears. Against the glow of faint morning light on the water, he counted four men creeping toward him. He cocked one of the pistols and waited.

Walking only feet apart, all four men stopped in front of where he hid. Mead rested the pistol on the rock. "Drop those rifles."

All four men swung toward where he hid. They searched for the man behind the voice. Glare from the rising sun creeping over the mountains behind him made him invisible. "I said drop those rifles, or me and my men are going to open fire."

"I think there is just one of them," came a voice in front of Mead. "We can take one sentry." All four men began to raise their weapons.

Mead squeezed off two rounds at the man closest to him and then switched targets and fired twice. The first man was down and the second was staggering, his arm hanging at his side. The fifth shot misfired, sending a tiny puff of sparks out toward the patrol.

"Get that son of a bitch," screamed the man now cradling his arm. "His pistol is empty."

The two remaining rebels raised their rifles and fired at the flash of Meads pistol.

Mead was already moving, the second pistol in his hand. He reached up over a rock in front of him and fired again. With only one hand, reloading the other pistol was impossible. The odds were now against him. There were still armed men out there and he only had four shots left. *If you are going to run a bluff, it had better be believable,* he thought. He shot another rebel sailor in the shoulder.

"Pick up your wounded men and get moving," he screamed. "Leave the rifles in the sand. When you get back to your ship tell your captain that this is what awaits any attempt to take the KATARINA. Tell him to weigh his anchor and get the hell out of here. The war is over."

Mead slipped past the rock where he hid. The man cradling his arm pointed at the man collapsed on the beach. Mead nodded. The sailor with the wounded shoulder helped the unwounded man lift the body of his dead companion, dragging it the direction they came from.

"I will deliver your message, whoever you are. But I don't think my captain is going to believe ya'll."

Mead watched as the men struggled back the direction they had come from. He walked out onto the sand to where four rifles lay. Thirty yards down the beach the man cradling his arm turned to face him. Mead squeezed off two carefully aimed shots. Sand flew from either side of the man. The wounded man turned again, joining his men dragging the body toward a small boat. Mead watched as the boat pulled away from the shore.

He used his foot to dig a small trench next to each rifle and then buried them. The pool of blood where the first man he shot had fallen told Mead that both shots had been kill shots.

※

The noise of shots raised dozens of birds and sent them scurrying out to sea. Chad checked his watch. The sun cast a glow around the hills to the east and reflected yellow and red on the ripples just stirring the glassy bay.

"It would appear that Mead has been discovered," commented Chad.

"His men were probably just hunting," said Pierce.

Chad shook his head. "There were two types of weapons. The first four shots were either a pistol or one of the Henrys. The next two were heavy rifles. The last three were again lighter weapons. My guess is that the Rebs put a patrol ashore to keep an eye on us and they stumbled into Mead's sentries. Mead would never have intentionally betrayed his presence."

"The big war hero can do no wrong," snapped Pierce. "How did he lose his eye?"

"What?"

"How did Parker lose his eye?"

"His wife came home from shopping one afternoon while he was on leave and found him in his parlor office examining a pretty young blondes' breasts. She hit him in the face with a shopping bag."

"Not so innocent after all, our dear Doctor."

"He swears to this day that she was worried about a lump she had found. He had been the girl's family doctor before the war."

"His wife did not believe him?"

"She never asked for an explanation. They weren't yet married."

The crew guarding the deck since before dawn was released to normal duties. The brutal sun had already turned the black painted deck of the ship into a sauna. The men watched the bay slowly empty, the receding tide flowing around the point. By late-morning, the crew felt the vibration of the ship's keel scraping bottom.

"Captain" shouted the bare-chested sentry in the crow's nest, "look yonder, toward the point. There is a small boat rowing straight south from the point." The lookout waited until the Captain looked up. "About a half a mile south of the point, probably directly east of the rebel steamer."

Chad raised his telescope and found the boat with four men aboard in less than a minute. While he watched the man in the bow set an anchor and then raised a telescope himself. Chad could feel the other man's eyeball through his eyepiece.

Five minutes later the man in the back of the boat stood and began waiving two flags.

"What do you make of that, Captain?" asked Ott Smith dabbing the sweat from his balding head with his handkerchief.

"Probably just a lookout" replied Chad. "They originally wanted to put their men on shore but ran into Mead's men. From this angle I cannot read the code from their semaphore."

Ten minutes later, a screaming whistle scorched the deck as a shell overflew the *KATARINA* landing harmlessly a half-mile beyond the ship. Chad watched as the man in the boat signaled the rebel ship with his two flags. Another shell splashed much closer; these one less than three hundred yards from the ship.

"Damn" was all that Chad could muster.

"Smart and sly our rebel Captain," uttered Doc Parker. He, Pedro Davis, Ott Smith and Pierce had made their way to the quarterdeck by the time the third shell splashed only a hundred yards from the ship. "He is using a spotter in the small boat to adjust his range. He is firing fairly flat, adjusting his powder not his barrel elevation," added Parker. "He doesn't want to put a shell through our hull to sink us."

The next two shots fell short, one to the left and the other to the right.

"I will man the boats and tow us further into the bay," offered the bosun, tugging at Chad's shirt.

"Ott," replied Captain Gritt, "we are already scraping the keel. That bastard waited for dead low tide. I doubt that we could move her a hundred feet." His telescope never left his eye.

"Then send the boat to Mr. Mead" begged Pierce. "Have him attack the rebel ship at once. With the four men manning the small boat the Rebels must be shorthanded."

Chad lowered the telescope, collapsing the three sections into one. "Mr. Pierce, two boats, crossing a mile of open water against heavy cannon would be kindling before the rowers could work up a sweat."

The next shell snapped the main mast twenty feet above the deck. The top two thirds of the mast, furled sails, rigging and spars spun backward crashing into the aft mast then tumbled toward the deck. The lookout leaped from the crow's-nest as it slammed into the aft mast. He made a desperate grab for some rigging. The bundled sail was too big around to grasp with one hand. The man bounced from the bundle and tumbled backwards.

Ott Smith and Doc Parker both hit the ladder to the main deck at the same time. Smith's two hundred pounds beat out Parker's one hundred sixty pounds. Picking himself up off from the deck the Doctor reached the crumpled young seaman moments after the bosun. The left arm folded oddly under his back and the strange tilt of the head told the Doctor all that he needed to know. Still, he gently pressed two fingers to the young man's neck. There was no pulse. The Doctor looked at Ott, kneeling across from him and shook his head. The Captain, Pedro Davis and Pierce hovered above the kneeling doctor.

"He died instantly," said Parker. "Broken neck."

"You should have given them the gold yesterday," squealed Pierce. "Now look at the results of your stubborn pride." Pierce turned away, trying to hide the spreading wet blotch on the front of his pants.

Before Chad could answer, another shell, this time a fused explosive, detonated just beyond the bow. Shell fragments ripped the sea below and swept the bow of the ship. Two men crawled back to their feet after being flattened by the shell burst.

Sixteen-year-old Brian Pennington reached up with both hands to cover the gash trickling blood into his left eye. His right hand found the wound, pressing down to suppress the bleeding. His left arm however, refused to help. Twisting to see with his clear right eye, he found no arm or hand below his left elbow. Shocked, he sat down on the raised hatch cover.

The other man, an older Marine, stumbled three steps and seated himself next to Pennington. "You go get a tourniquet on that arm and have the Doc take a look at that gash on your head" whispered the Marine corporal.

Brian heard the words, but they didn't register. He sat staring at the space in the universe that his lower arm and hand once filled. He missed the groan next to him but turned as the Corporal lay back onto the hatch cover, his feet still resting on the deck below. The front of the Corporal's shirt was crimson. His eyes stared up at the flawless blue sky. Pennington watched his eyes turn from blue to gray.

The rest of the crew was frozen in place watching the two men. Young Pennington turned and surveyed their faces, looking for his Captain, his bosun, or the Doctor. Finally, finding all three men near the stern where his friend had fallen, he rose and stumbled toward help.

Minutes later another friend, stopped the carnage by waiving a large white sheet ordered there by the bosun at the request of Captain Grit. The entre shelling episode lasted less than five minutes.

15
TEACAPAN BAY, MEXICO

IT TOOK TWO hours for a boat from the rebel ship to reach the battered *KATARINA* and another hour to deposit Gritt, Pierce and Davis on the deck of the rebel steamer.

Chad's eyes glazed; he heard nothing. The red in his face and neck were like a burning fuse. Grabbing a loose defraying pin, he turned on Pedro Davis swinging the eighteen-inch pin like a club. Davis barely shielded his head with his arms before Chad fell on him clubbing him to the deck.

Chad's shoulders were seized, and he was dragged back to his feet, his arms pinned to his sides by rebel crewmen.

"Captain Jackman," spat Pedro Davis, pulling himself to his feet. "You promised no damage to the ship and no bloodshed."

"Things change," sneered Marcus Bolton.

"Bolton," said Jackman, raising his open hand.

"While I fetched up my family you were going to threaten Captain Gritt's ship in Teacapan. With the threat of heavy cannon at close range you would take the gold then leave. That was the plan."

"Mr. Bolton is correct Lieutenant," responded the rebel captain, "things change. We need the Yankee ship."

"What the hell do you intend to do with the *KATARINA*?" asked Davis.

"Cut up her masts and spars and whatever else we can salvage for fuel."

"Why not cut timber from one of the river deltas? We've done it before."

"We tried that, Lieutenant; we ended up in a fight with a company of Juaristas. Axel was killed. We will need to supplement our coal with wood to make Chile where we can refuel."

"The war is over. You have just murdered two of my men," snapped Chad. "They were not responsible for the loss of your man."

"No Captain, the war is not over. If it makes you feel better, you should know that your sentries killed one of ours this morning. This is war, men die!"

"Captain Jackman," replied Davis, "this is no longer war. We discussed this. The South is crumbling. You promised that no one would be hurt."

Turning to Chad, he continued. "The gold was to provide a stipend for all of the Confederate officers that have lost everything in the war. It was to give the *RETRIBUTION's* crew something to start over on."

"We would have given up the gold given a chance," said Pierce.

"And who the hell are you?" asked Jackman.

"Miles Standish Pierce, Assistant Secretary of State on a mission for Secretary Seward."

"Mr. Pierce, I would suggest that you shut your mouth. Your government has wasted my country, killed at least one family member of every man on this crew. You would be well advised to shut up before you say something that provokes riotous vengeance."

"Captain" broke in Davis, "enough blood."

"Mr. Davis, you are no longer one of us. You are hereby discharged. You will be put ashore at once. If I were you, I would run for your family's place of hiding. I would guess that when Captain Gritt here is put ashore with his crew, hanging you might be high on their list of things to do," added Jackman.

Turning back to Chad, he continued. "You will be returned to your ship at once. I will send all four of our boats and eight men. You are all free to remove your personal gear and survival supplies and ferry them to shore. You will leave a work party of four men aboard to help my crew with woodcutting." Jackman wiped stinging sweat from his eyes. "We will of course remove the gold tonight. Make sure you leave behind the gold from your Alaska adventure. The rest of your crew is free to camp on the beach. When we are finished, I will put your four men ashore. You, Mr. Pierce, will do the first real work of your life. You will be the fifth man on the work detail."

"Captain Jackman!" started Pierce.

Marcus Bolton pressed a knife blade pressed against Pierce's stomach.

"May I gut this pig, Captain?"

"No Marcus, I want to watch him sweat. If he does his share, we will put him ashore with the others. If he proves a slacker, you may cut him. I'm putting you in charge of the wood cutting detail."

Pedro stood, head bowed, praying. He made the sign of the crucifix and then stepped between the two captains.

"Captain Jackman, Captain Gritt, as a way of making amends will you allow me to be part of the work crew?" asked Pedro Davis.

Chad said nothing while Jackman nodded.

"You have your gold, Captain Jackman," continued Davis. "And Captain Gritt, if you will let me, I would like to help you and your crew get home."

"Mr. Davis" snarled Chad, "what help we might accept or even if you live or die, I will leave to a vote of my crew."

Davis' eyes turned toward the deck. He mumbled a second prayer. "I accept that fate."

"Let's get started," ordered Jackman.

"The gold will be moved this afternoon and then the men you leave on board will earn your freedom, Captain Gritt," added Carlton Lee who had just joined the men on deck.

"What happened?" asked Pedro Davis noticing the sling supporting Carlton's left arm.

"Your one-armed sentry shoots well," was his reply.

The supplies already loaded in the two *KATARINA* long boats were ferried to shore and stacked on the beach. The rifles and the treasure vests had been concealed during the officer's visit to the rebel ship and other supplies had been loaded over their canvas covering. In less than an hour the boats were on their way back to the ship. Each man packed a duffle bag with his personal gear.

"There is no way I am leaving my boys, Captain," said Ott Smith. "We have already put two over the side to feed the fish. I will do what I can to keep it at only two." The Captain and the bosun huddled at the bow along with the rest of the crew while the Confederate sailors loaded the boxes of gold into their boats.

"Ott, this is not a negro thing."

"On the contrary Captain, if I was a white bosun you would order me to supervise my men in the work party."

"But you are not, Ott; these men are filled with hate."

"Chad, Captain, no man can run from his rightful place. My place for a dozen years has been leading a deck crew for your family. No group of men has a right to take that away from me. You do not have that right."

"Ott, we are not talking about right or wrong, brave or cowardly."

"I agree. This is only about duty. Mine is to the deck crew who make up the work party. Yours is to organize a plan that gets all of us home."

"All right, Ott," replied Chad. "Just watch yourself, especially what you say. The rebel officer in charge, Bolton, is mad dog mean. Now who else do you want on the work crew?"

"Gott, Wilson, and Ike have all volunteered. They will make a good crew. None of them are hot blooded."

"Fine, Ott, before I go ashore is there anything more I can do for you?"

"No Captain."

At 5 p.m., Chad stood at the rail ready to leave. "Your word then gentlemen, when my men have helped your men cut your fuel they will be put ashore safely."

Brandon Piper, the chief engineer from the *RETRIBUTION* stood next to Marcus Bolton. "You have Captain Jackman's word," answered Piper. Clutched in his hand was a writing pad with an inventory of parts of the ship to be cut into firewood.

"Your boys get the job done by the end of the day tomorrow and they are all on their way to shore tomorrow evening," added Bolton, slapping his pant leg with a riding crop he had found in Doc Parker's cabin. The man's eyes made it hard to believe the words.

"My crew will do what we promised," said Chad. "Until our men are back ashore, we will leave our boats at the shoreline and we will set our camp at least three hundred yards away as agreed."

"That's a good boy," replied Bolton. "One more thing, Captain, if there is any move to interfere with this vessel's work or with the *RETRIBUTION*, I will enjoy cutting the throat of every man in your work party starting with your family nigger. I haven't cut anybody since I killed your two men in San Francisco. Any Questions?"

Chad cringed. "No Bolton, you have made yourself quite clear."

⚘

An hour later the rest of the crew stood in front of a small pile of supplies on the beach. Doc Parker was put in charge of setting up a camp for the night while Chad slipped out of sight and trotted up the beach to find Mead, Kadzof and their men.

"Send six men with the boats to our camp, Thomas," said the Captain. "The rest of you follow me back along the shore. They know we have two boats ashore; they counted the davits. Still, we do not need to give the bastards a full count of our strength. Even a small advantage may be important tomorrow."

"We could take the *RETRIBUTION*," observed Mead. "They will be shorthanded."

"Perhaps, Thomas, but they are going to move the steamer out into the middle of the bay until daylight. They would cut down your boats with grape shot before you could get close enough to use the Henrys if they see you coming."

"Then we retake the *KATARINA* instead."

"Thomas, we would still be trapped; they still have heavy guns, and the gold is gone."

"I hate being helpless."

"Live to fight another day, Thomas. You are the military mind here. We will need you."

"Quit flattering me my friend. As it turns out, your backup plan was better than my strategy to attack the rebel ship."

"Thomas, they killed Kraus and Patrick deLaguera. The captain on that ship is the man I had dinner with in San Francisco. How could I be so wrong?"

Mead just stood staring at the shallow bay. After a day wandering along the beach, he was amazed that neither ship had run aground. "Most of us are still alive. We aren't done yet."

All four boats were pulled up on the beach and the supplies critical to what the men hoped would be a temporary camp were moved a quarter mile away. With dinner one bottle of wine was issued to every two men. The conversion to canteens was underway. With the wine some men were jocular, some melancholy and some bitter.

Mosby dragged two men to where Gritt sat making entries in the ship's log. "Stopped one of yours and one of mine from beating each other silly," offered Mosby.

Chad rose. "What the hell is this?" he asked Gary Farmer. His crewman was almost twice the size of the young marine but from his appearance he'd been getting the worst end of the fight.

"That snot-nose was mouthing off about our officers surrendering the ship, sir."

"Gary, we are all angry, frustrated. Chad turned to the young Marine. He couldn't help smiling as he studied the man, peach fuzz covering his chin. "Both of you listen. My guess is that this is the easy part. You're going to need each other. You two go gather the others, it's time for a ship's meeting/"

Mosby nodded and smiled.

"The first order of business is Pedro," pronounced the Captain. "He was a spy; we should hang him if you agree."

"Captain," replied Mead, "we are not part of the government, nor a military vessel. How can he be a spy?"

"Then he is a pirate," proclaimed Chad.

"Perhaps, Captain, but he has already helped us this day," interjected the ship's carpenter, rising to his feet.

"How so, Sig?"

"Before you left for the Reb ship he came below and directed us to refill the gold case we raided with lead and then reseal it and return it to the center hold. The Rebs think they have sixteen full cases."

"That is a true story Captain," added the ship's chef. He also suggested that we throw all of the remaining Henry rifles over the side and hide the treasure vests and our rifles in the boats."

"I still say we hang him. If it were not for his subterfuge, we would be off from the coast of Central America tomorrow," snarled Chad. "He deserves worse than hanging."

"From what I hear, Captain," Offered Mead, "he had no idea that this was anything more than a military operation."

"Then he is a spy," retorted Chad.

"So was I Captain; remember I helped the Confederacy buy that ship."

"Thomas do not try to compare your actions with his. He acknowledged that the war was over."

"Then let me change the discussion, Captain. We need him, at least for now. He is the only one who knows how to get away from here. And one more thing, Captain, he is the only one among us who speaks tolerable Spanish."

Gritt stood shaking. "Alright, Thomas, you have made your point. He may be useful. But I hold you responsible for him from here on. If he betrays us again or even spits in the wrong direction it is up to you to shoot the bastard." Two hours later, lookouts posted, the men found places on the rocky ground to sleep.

Aboard the *KATARINA* the work crews cut wood until the last light faded, then ate a meal of dried fruit, dried salmon and biscuit while watching the rebel guards devour the fresh produce in Angelo's greenhouse with fried chickens from the egg pen. While the supply of rum had been discovered by the rebel crew, only the man the ship's crew had nicknamed 'Ogre', Marcus Bolton, had gotten into the spirits. Bolton sat drunk on a stool on the quarterdeck, ordered there by the *RETRIBUTION's* engineer.

"You had best give him a wide berth tomorrow," Piper told Ott Smith. "He is mean with a hangover, and he sees slaves as one rung below snakes."

"Thank you, Mr. Piper, for the warning," responded Ott. "I take it you do not share all of his views?"

"You are correct, Bosun. I, and many like me, fought this war because we saw the northern army as invaders. Many of us believe that the South should have freed the slaves when the war began. The British and French could have been persuaded to help us and it would have increased our manpower threefold. Anyway, it is too late for the Confederacy now."

"My men are tired, Mr. Piper, we need some sleep."

"You may take the bunks in the center hold. I will have to lock you in so my men can rest. I will wake you at dawn."

16
TEACAPAN BAY, MEXICO

THE SECOND OFFICER of the rebel ship stood next to the captain of the *KATARINA*. A scorching late afternoon sun baked the two gentlemen. A worthless breeze pushed tiny waves that lapped the sand at their feet.

"Ah' feel bad, about your predicament, Captain Gritt," drawled Carlton Lee. "She was a beautiful ship, but we had no choice. Anyway, you may take off your work crew. Our engineer, Mr. Piper and gunnery officer Mr. Bolton are waiting for your boats."

"Thank you, Mr. Lee, I will send two men at once."

"Remember the rules, Captain. We send your men over the side one at a time and we will tolerate no subterfuge. Once you are back on shore you will move back to your camp until tomorrow. My men are tired, and we will not finish storing the wood in the hold of the *RETRIBUTION* until late tonight. We will depart early tomorrow. Until then do not attempt to use the boats."

"Would it be alright if we send a boat out to the ship to salvage food for our evening meal, Mr. Lee?

"That will be impossible, Captain. We will fire your ship as we depart."

"Why would you fire the *KATARINA*? Even with masts, spars, railings and covers cut up she is still seaworthy and can be rebuilt."

"Exactly, Captain. With improvised masts and new sails, she could be at sea in days. No, we will not have you on our tail."

Nick Kadzof and Gary Farmer, the huge raw-boned Welsh lad, sat at the oars of the long boat as the work party climbed down the ladder and collapsed on the seats of the boat. The exhausted men held themselves upright by bracing their feet against the ribs of the boat and holding the gunnels with their hands. Drops of blood from torn, blistered hands smudged the paint wherever they gripped. Next over the rail was Pedro Davis who collapsed onto a seat.

"I am truly sorry, Mr. Kadzof," said Davis.

"The Captain wants to shoot you, but even he might forgive if you can help us get home, Lieutenant," replied Kadzof.

A brief smile touched Pedro's lips and a faint spark shown in his blue eyes. Then he dropped his head in exhaustion. Above, the Ogre pushed an exhausted Miles Pierce against the side of the ship, knocking him to his knees.

"Get on your feet Mr. High and Mighty Secretary," snarled Bolton.

"I do not know that I have the strength left to climb down the ladder," whispered Pierce.

"I can help you, Mr. Pierce, just follow me. I will not let you fall," reassured Ott.

Pierce pulled himself back to his feet, then watched as Ott Smith swung a leg over the gunnel preparing to start down the ladder. Marcus Bolton reached out and slapped Ott Smith across the face with his riding crop, then backhanded Ott again slicing a cut first in his cheek and then across his forehead.

"Did you forget your place boy, you let the gentlemen go first."

Ott's attempt to explain was met by another lashing and a push that sent his exhausted body tumbling to the deck.

"It's alright," forced Pierce, "I can make it on my own. Mr. Smith, don't provoke him."

Kadzof caught Pierce as he stumbled entering the boat and laid his exhausted body on a seat. "Send down our bosun," commanded Kadzof.

"This boy needs to learn his place," replied Bolton. "Move your boat away from this ship. We will see if he can swim."

"I have no intention of leaving," replied Kadzof.

Marcus Bolton leaned over the rail, staring into the loaded boat. A grotesque smile gripped his mouth revealing tobacco-stained teeth. His right hand slid over the rail holding a pistol. He shot two holes through the boat bottom. "The next three all find flesh," he snarled. "Now move back a hundred yards."

Kadzof reseated himself gripping the oars. Then he and Farmer began to row. With their back to the beach, they watched the ship grow smaller with each stroke. At three hundred feet from the ships side, Nick ordered a halt. He and all of the men in the boat watched as Ott Smith climbed atop the rail, the Ogre's knife at his side. Then Bolton gave Ott a push.

Never a strong swimmer, Ott surfaced, demanding his exhausted muscles work and started for the boat. Nick turned the boat and he and Gary Farmer dipped their oars to go after Smith. A shot rang out and a bullet smacked the water next to the boat. Nick looked up to see Bolton reloading a rifle.

"Not one foot closer," screamed Bolton.

Ott had covered half of the distance using most of his reserves. He swept his hand across his eyes to clear the pink cloud from his face as the cuts on his face mixed with the water. After a few minutes' rest he struck out again.

The bump was unmistakable, but Ott plowed on. The second bump was even harder. He lifted his head and searched around him as a large dorsal fin rose from the water behind him. Only feet from the boat, Ott was dragged below the surface by a fifteen-foot shark. The men in the boat sat in stunned silence interrupted only when the screeching uncontrollable laugh of Marcus Bolton awakened them.

"Help me" came from the other side of the boat. Nick swinging his head, found Ott in a pool of pink only a few feet beyond the boat. In two strokes of the oars, they were alongside Ott. The men of the work crew pulled him into the boat just as the shark smashed into the bottom of the boat.

"My God" murmured Pierce, "he's lost both legs."

"He will never walk in front of a white man again," shouted Bolton, "now be gone."

Bolton was right, Ott blinked his eyes several times but never said a word. The stunned crew watched his life flow out in spite of their frantic efforts to tie off Ott's torn legs. The fight lasted only seconds.

The silent *KATARINA* men rowed toward shore. Behind them the last of the *RETRIBUTION's* boats pulled away from the naked hull of their ship. A moment later smoke from both fore and aft began to rise from the hull.

⚜

Brandon Piper opened a bottle of port that he had carried from the Yankee ship. He sat on one of the air scoops of the Confederate steamer and tipped the bottle to his lips. Captain Jackman watched one of his most trusted officers tip the bottle again. Jackman slipped down the ladder from the bridge and walked up to his chief engineer.

"Okay, spit it out Mr. Piper. What is so wrong that you would drink aboard ship in front of the crew?

"I guess I am just done Sir. I watched Bolton murder one of the crew from that Yankee ship today, for no reason at all. It was the nigger who supervised their crew. He did it because the man tried to help another of the woodcutters. Hell, Sir, they did exactly what we ordered them to do. We had released them to go ashore. There was no reason for what Bolton did."

Jackman considered disciplining his friend and officer for openly breaking one of his most strident rules, no liquor aboard ship. Instead, he took a seat next to the engineer.

"Bolton has his place, Brandon. He grew up fighting. His father was hung for petty theft when he was only ten. His mother supported the family as a whore until she died two years later. He's never said as much, but I think some of the johns she brought home preferred Marcus. He survived as a pickpocket until he figured out that a knife made him scary. A knife let him rob rich men.

He joined the army after he had killed one of his marks. He figured out that hiding in the army, especially in India made him impossible to find. It worked for him and gave him a new life."

"How do you know all this?"

"Bolton was in custody of the law when I recruited him. He either told me the truth, or I would have let the law hang him."

Piper tipped the port again. "Half the men on this ship come from tough families. Even they fear Bolton."

"Mr. Piper, I use that fear to run a ship with a third less crew than she was built for. I use Bolton to put the fear of God into the passengers and crew of ships we take, moments when we are outnumbered two or three to one. To a man like Bolton, a man who proves he's worthy by intimidating others, those tasks come easy. He does what we need because he likes it. Any other of the crew might do the same, but they would fight their conscience afterward."

"Captain, we promised Mr. Davis that there would be no bloodshed. Most of us were with him on that." Piper set the bottle at his feet. He turned toward his Captain. "Until Bolton joined this crew, we hadn't even hurt anyone on any of the ships we took.

Now look at us. We are all like Bolton, all but Pedro Davis, and the Yankees will probably hang him for what we just did."

Piper picked up the bottle and took another long drink, then he tossed the bottle over the rail. He rose and turned toward the stern. "I'm going below to oil something that doesn't need oiling.

※

Later that night as the drained, exhausted crew of the *KATARINA* slept with only two men on sentry duty, a boat slipped through the cloudy moonless night.

With the sound muffled by wrapping the oars in towels within the oarlocks, the boat gently touched the beach just beyond where the *KATARINA*'s four boats were pulled up on the shore. Four men came ashore: two guards and two men with cans of coal oil. Soaking the boats with oil, the men lit oil-soaked newspapers and dropped them into the boats under the covered bow seats. In moments the boats were blazing. The *RETRIBUTION*'s boat slipped away.

"They have fired our boats," yelled a sentry. The crewmen who had been spared the duty of chopping up their own ship rolled from their bedrolls, and in seconds were strung out along the beach, all running toward the burning fire. Of the five exhausted men of the work crew only Pedro Davis heard the cry and responded.

Charles Lampoc, the huge woodsman, was the first to the flaming craft. Braving the inferno, he pulled a large duffle from the first boat, throwing it out of reach of the flames. From the next boat he dragged a wooden case of ammunition and a large tin of dried food. With burns on each hand and singed eyebrows he retreated, the fire too hot for a return trip. Two other men soaked themselves in the nearby saltwater and made attempts to salvage goods left in the boats but were beaten back by the heat.

The commotion finally awakened the woodcutters, who, in spite of their exhaustion, joined their crewmates in watching the fire devour their ride out of the wilderness bay, and most of their supplies. "This changes our situation from difficult to dire," remarked Kadzof. "In the morning, we will inventory our supplies and form a new plan." He looked around, "Has anyone seen the Captain?"

"The Captain's here," slurred Chad.

The men turned to find Chad in the rear of the assemblage, a bottle of wine in one hand and a pistol in the other. The front of Chad's clothes stained red with wine, he reeked of vomit. "Nick tells it straight," continued Chad. "Already bad just got worse and you can lay it at the feet of Davis and Pierce. One is a spy, the other a coward."

Chad drained the last of the wine from the bottle in his hand, and then flipped the empty bottle into the conflagration. From his jacket he produced an unopened bottle. Unwilling to lay down his pistol he was unable to uncork the bottle.

"You two are nothing but trouble," continued Chad. "I have had enough. Come morning arm yourselves and prepare for your judgment. When I see either of you, I will start shooting."

With his speech ended and his world spinning, the Captain stumbled off down the beach in the opposite direction from camp.

"I want no trouble with our Captain," moaned Pierce.

"I am too tired to worry tonight," said Pedro Davis.

"He is just suffering from the loss of Ott. He will be alright when he sobers up," offered Nick.

"Most likely you are correct," said Doc Parker. "Still, I would advise both Pedro and Miles to walk softly around the Captain. Sorrow and anger are a recipe for a powerful blast."

"We should at least disarm the Captain and put him to bed" replied Nick.

"That would be very dangerous right now," replied Parker. "Besides the more he wallows in his grief, the more anger and frustration he will leave on this beach. No, let the Captain work this out. The captain can be a horse's ass sometimes, but he always gets us out of whatever mess we are in."

Kadzof looked at Pierce and then Davis. "Stick close to the doctor and me tomorrow and for the next few days."

It was mid-morning before two crewmen finally found the Captain curled up next to a scrub ironwood tree, more than two miles from camp. It took ten minutes to get him into a sitting position and even then, his eyes refused to focus or even work together, one eye twitching up while the other stared forward, then one darting right while the other swung left. Placing Chad's arms over their shoulders they lifted him and turned toward camp. Their journey was interrupted again and again by the retching of a sick man. The attacks continued long after he had nothing left to bring up.

The ship's company spent the day fashioning crude packs to carry the meager supplies at their disposal. Most of the food was gone; in fact, the only thing in good supply were gold and guns with ammunition but there was nowhere to buy or steal what they needed.

Doc Parker did his best to treat Lampoc's burned hands. "Charlie, that was a brave and stupid thing to do."

"I just do what needs to be done, Doc. Sometimes I get so mad that I want to forget that my faith teaches peace. Ironic, huh, I salvage three things and one is ammunition."

Davis looked over at Mead. "That's the most I have ever heard from Charlie. Later the two men huddled with Pierce and Kadzof. By evening they had a crude plan to get the company out of their predicament.

"I'll take care of our captain," offered Mead. "If he had decided to join the army, he would have been a good general. They say that General Grant's temper and drinking is directly proportional to how many men he lost."

With supplies critical, a dozen men armed with rifles scattered to hunt for dinner. By evening they returned with a dozen seabirds and three huge rattlesnakes. The birds were tough and vile tasting and did little to improve the bland cup of rice served with the meat. The snake on the other hand was fat and tasty. The good news was the palatability of the serpent. The bad news was that there was a good supply.

INTO THE HEART OF THE MEXICAN CIVIL WAR

17
MEXICAN DESERT

THEIR ROUTE WAS north and a bit east, overland through tortured terrain that flooded in the wet season. Boulder fields were covered with thick dry thorny brush that ripped at boots and clothing. The estimated forty-mile walk would take them to a rough track that Pedro thought ran from Acapuneta west to the ocean. He knew little of the place called Tecuala about halfway along the track. From there, it would be only twenty miles due east to Acapuneta near the exile home of his mother and sister. They hoped to reach Tecuala by the end of the second day.

The bearded, ragged men each carried a crude pack, a blanket and water from the now abandoned water barrel. Most carried one or two personal items, for some a pipe and tobacco, for others a book or a tintype of family.

Divided among the band were meager food rations, cooking utensils and tools. Each man carried two rifles, one slung across his back and one in his hands. All of the ammunition had been inventoried and divided equally. Four of the men carried Sharps rifles and forty rounds of the rifle's heavy ammunition in addition to their other burden.

Some carried canvas for shelters. Doc Parker's medical kit and supplies had been divided up. The ship's sextant, compass, and logbooks burdened others. The reports on the Alaska territory and negotiations summaries were added after Secretary Pierce demanded help. Backing him up was Colonel Mead who reminded the ship's party that the documentation was gathered at the request of President Lincoln.

Ten men carried the extra burden of the gold vests while others carried the packs of mineral samples gathered during Mead's cross-country expedition in Alaska. These packs had been slipped off from the ship as personal belongings. The saw filings from cutting the gold strips for the vests had been swept up, mixed with dirt from the deck, and placed in leather bags marked "Alaska" and left in the Captain's cabin as a diversion. For men who had not stretched their legs beyond the deck of a ship for weeks, the journey was hell.

Lunch was eaten around a stagnant pond, with insect larva so thick that it was impossible to scoop up a cup of water without a dozen swimmers, flippers or crawlers. A hard biscuit and a few pieces of dried fruit hardly quieted grumbling stomachs. By early afternoon, most men had consumed the water they carried.

Coarse rock tore at their feet and brush tore at their bodies while a scorching sun overhead burnt their scalps. The men traded off walking lead, others taking the extra rifles from the men in front so that they could carry a long stick, which they used to probe ahead of them into any spot that offered shelter from the sun. Over and over their probes were answered by the strike of a snake or at least a rattle.

A halt was called an hour before dusk and a quick camp was erected. The hunters brought in two scrawny rabbits and a couple of snakes. A mouthful of meat grilled over an open fire, and a handful of parched corn and a few pieces of dried fruit made up dinner. The camp was dry which meant no tea or coffee.

The absence of water meant two hard biscuits and some dried fruit replaced the oatmeal planned for breakfast. The men could barely find the moisture in their mouths to swallow. Four of the men had carried extra water bottles in their packs, the only water in camp. Doc Parker had each man lick a pinch of salt with a tiny morning water ration.

The men's exhaustion the first day had been tempered by each man's ability to drink his fill from the water barrels before their march began. There was no such luxury the second day. By eleven o'clock, Captain Gritt was forced to order a halt. Three men including Doc Parker were complaining of lightheadedness and cramping. The rotund cook Angelo collapsed in the shade of a boulder pile, gasping.

"Damn that hurts," sputtered Angelo gripping his left hand in his right.

His traveling partner knelt at his side. "What's wrong?"

"I put my hand down to catch myself," replied Gasparetti nodding toward a jagged stone. "Something stung me."

Belson carefully lifted the stone. A two-inch light brown insect scampered from beneath and disappeared into a jumble of stones only feet away.

"You dumb Italian, you have given a scorpion his fun for the day. I'll go find the Doctor; you wait here and drink your sip of water." The doctor, himself nauseous from dehydration gathered his kit from the three men who each carried a part. He tugged his prized medical book from his pack.

"Angelo, I have never treated the sting of a scorpion. Hell, I have never even seen a scorpion. The book recommends lowering your hand below your body while lying prone on a bed. Then immerse the hand in ice or cold water for two hours. Finally, a poultice over the wound of ammonia, salt and baking soda."

"I can use the rest and the ice and cold water will be very welcome."

"Perhaps tonight in your dreams, for now, just an improvised poultice and a wrap. The book says these stings are seldom fatal, but you are going to be very sore and sick by this evening."

With a cloth patch consisting of a piece of bread crust soaked in the cook's own urine, layered with salt, Gasparetti was back on his feet in half an hour. His pack was divided among his mates. A throbbing pain in the hand was joined by mild delirium an hour later.

Just before two in the afternoon the men descended into a small ravine and there found a tiny trickle of water. Like the pond the day before the water was alive with darting creatures and slime.

Chad stared at the water for a moment and then began climbing out of the gully. A shrill whistle stopped him.

"I suggest Captain, said Nick Kadzof, "that we stop here for the night and put the men to work boiling water to refill the water bottles. We will have water for tonight's meal and for hot tea and mash for breakfast."

"We need to keep moving," answered Gritt. "If I can keep going, so can they." Grit pointed at the men looking for any shade they could find.

One by one the men behind him found a place to sit. Mead smiled at the captain, which just elevated the red in Gritt's face to scarlet. "Chad, Nick's right. A few more hours without water and we begin leaving men behind."

With the cook on his blanket, Charlie Lampoc who had cooked for the exploration crew in Alaska took over. That evening's snake was cut into pieces and became the base for a stew. With the last of the dried vegetables, onion and rice, the exhausted men got their first meal in two days.

"Any man who complains about my cooking carries my pack tomorrow."

"Hell, Charlie, "as hungry as we all are you could serve rock soup and we would be singing your praises," offered Doc Parker.

Two fires were kept busy, with a kettle and metal bucket of water boiling. The small trickle ran so slowly that it took fifteen minutes of dipping a small metal cup into a shallow hole to fill a gallon pot with water. By midnight, every container that could hold water was filled.

The sentries stayed busy flipping snakes headed for the life-giving water, back into the darkness that surrounded the compact camp.

❦

A small boy herding goats ran screaming, as the mangy group of men gained the crude track between Tecuala and Acapuneta the next morning. By early afternoon, they knew that they had misjudged their march and that the village that was the goal of their trek lay behind them. Chad chose to walk on into the evening rather than make camp. Just before dark two men on horseback were stopped by the advance party, which included Pedro Davis. Pedro and one other man were sent ahead with the riders to arrange food and shelter. The ship's company stumbled into Acapuneta under a jet-black sky.

❦

"Tables have been set up in the park, Captain," said Pedro Davis pointing toward a brightly lit square only a block to the east of where the ship's company rested. "The innkeeper and his wife have organized a dinner. He and the local priest called on the congregation to help. They have arranged rooms in the local hotel for the officers. The rest of your crew can sleep in the church."

Gritt stared at Davis, then sighed. "Thank you, Mr. Davis, and please thank those who offer their help."

"You must do that yourself, Captain Gritt," replied Davis.

Chad glared at Pedro through hate filled eyes. "I am sorry, but my first priority is to find a doctor and a bed for Angelo. He is delirious and burning with fever."

"He's tough," offered Pedro.

"Tougher than Pierce. He wanted to stay with Angelo back where we first found the road. He offered to stay until we could send back a carriage."

"He may have thought that best for our cook."

"Perhaps, or perhaps he felt he should ride while the rest of us walked."

Pedro could feel the tension radiating from Chad's body. "I will arrange for your cook to be transported to my mother's house tonight. He will be well taken care of."

The men were interrupted by the approach of a tall man in a dark robe. He pulled a broad brimmed black hat from his head, revealing a head of pure white hair. A large silver crucifix hung from the sash at his waist. In a voice too soft for this giant he murmured something in Spanish to Pedro.

"Duty calls, Captain. The mayor is waiting to welcome the shipwrecked crew and the town expects an eloquent response from you. Mr. Kadzof is taking care of everything else."

18
ACAPONETA, MEXICO

SQUAWKING CHICKENS AND barking dogs were the only sounds on the walk to Acapuneta's village square. Three of the *KATARINA's* crew fought off fatigue in the early morning light. They, like the rest of the crew could have slept all day, but anything easy, anything that made common sense had become impossible. There were too many unknowns. They hoped their planned breakfast might answer some of the questions.

"You were fortunate, Señor, that it is the dry season," remarked Acapuneta's mayor. "The mangrove and thorn jungle that you passed through is often flooded. There is little dry ground and most of that is occupied by snakes and crocodiles."

"You have no shortage of snakes even when dry," replied Chad. "They taste like chicken when broiled."

"I prefer my chicken with feathers."

The mayor, a gentleman just under six feet tall and solidly built, had invited the officers of the *KATARINA* for breakfast. The night before, he and Pedro had discussed their common backgrounds, both the sons of English fathers and Mexican mothers.

Pedro Davis, Nick and Chad sat in the early morning sun on a patio surrounded by vines of red and white flowers. The mayor picked the last remnants of shell from a hard-boiled egg.

"What are your plans, Señor Gritt?"

"To move across country as quickly as possible. Then find passage to Mississippi."

"Why Mississippi, if you do not mind the question?"

"That is where the closest American navy squadron is located."

"So, you hope to intercept the rebel ship on the Atlantic coast then?"

"If we get there in time, we will even the score, Mr. Mayor."

"You know, Captain, that news of your engagement with the Confederate ship is spreading up and down the coast. By now the authorities in both the Juarez government and the court of Maximilian probably know the story."

"Really," said Chad, "I see no telegraph lines. How could our plight spread so quickly?"

"Ah, Captain, do not think us backward. The villagers at Teacapan saw the rebel ship firing its huge gun. You know, sir, that just sailing that far into the bay was a remarkable coincidence. You crossed on the highest tides of the year. The village sent a rider to Esquinapa de Hidalgo. From there horsemen took the news north and south. We knew of your plight before you began your walk out."

A visibly angry Chad tilted the heavy pottery cup, allowing the strong black coffee to lie in his mouth before swallowing. "If the villagers knew of our plight, why did they not send boats for us?"

"They were frightened by the rebel ship. The noisy beast hung on the sand bar trying to escape the estuary. It took her more than a day to find the open ocean. She reportedly dumped her big cannons and shells to lighten the ship."

"Anyway, there was no possibility of the village sending small boats past a powerful war ship. By the time a rescue party could reach your sunken ship you were gone."

"We appreciate their effort" chimed in Nick. "Please pass on our thanks."

"There is little need of that, Mr. Kadzof, the villagers have begun salvaging your ship. You will make the poor fishermen wealthy men by Mexican standards."

The mayor called for another pot of coffee. Turning back to Chad he continued. "Captain Gritt, your traverse of Mexico may be more difficult than you expect. The messenger who took word of a sea battle to the south has alerted militia units loyal to President Juarez. I am sure Royalist spies took the word to Guadalajara where the word was sent on by telegraph. The Royalists and their French and German allies will be on the lookout for you. The Royalists do not like Americans because of your country's opposition to Maximilian's rule. Even with the death of your President Lincoln they expect no change in the policy."

"What do you mean the death of President Lincoln?" asked Chad.

"I am sorry, I thought you knew. He was shot and killed while at the theater."

Chad sat stunned, as did the others.

"Won't the army of Juarez help us?" asked Nick finally.

"The Juaristas peasant armies trust no one who is not Juarista. They especially do not trust foreigners. In fact, a week ago the militia from San Reas reportedly fought a battle with French soldiers from a ship, sent ashore to cut wood. I think it was not French, more likely the rebel ship that attacked you."

"That may well be true," replied Pedro. "Captain Jackman's excuse for destroying the *KATARINA* was his inability to cut wood ashore."

"Five militiamen were killed. The Juaristas all along this coast are looking for revenge."

Chad was still processing the news on President Lincoln. "What do you suggest then?" he managed.

"You must travel with some neutral compatriots; people who are known to be non-political and who can explain your predicament. You will want them as an advance party at least an hour in front of your march."

"Are you offering your services, Mr. Mayor?" asked Kadzof.

"Be assured that many in Mexico choose not to think of me as non-political."

"If you cannot help us, Señor, can you suggest someone else?" asked Nick.

"Of course, gentlemen, I suggest the mother, sister, aunt and cousin of Señor Davis."

"Four women?" asked Nick incredulously.

"Not just four women, but four respected and honored women, and of course their escorts," replied Diego.

"Pedro, is this a good idea? Do you want to put them at risk?" asked Chad.

"Captain, I believe my mother and sister will want to accompany us anyway."

The mayor slid his chair back, brushing crumbs from his suit as he stood. "There is one concern though Captain and that is rumors of gold. Gold clouds men's minds. It can turn soldiers into bandits."

"We have made a small donation to the church and to your municipal fund as a token of gratitude for your help and hospitality," said Chad. "Beyond that we have only enough to meet the expenses of getting home."

"Captain Gritt, what is barely enough for your purposes represents a fortune in most of Mexico. Speak little about what you carry, show even less. Now gentlemen, we must arrange transport for your men to the hacienda where Pedro's mother waits."

19

FOOTHILLS OF THE SIERRA MADRE MOUNTAINS, MEXICO

THE HACIENDA WAS not what Chad expected. The house was a three-story box of local stone. The ends of massive wooden beams extended from the walls, supporting the floors of the second and third stories as well as the red tile roof. A strong stonewall surrounded the house inset with planters overflowing with fragrant roses. Tall trees provided shade for the coarse green grass.

The house sat on the southern side of a narrow canyon; a small clear stream winding its way to the sea bordered the road. Below the house two-dozen buildings, some dwellings, what looked like warehouses and workshops made up a village. Below the village, large open fields surrounded by heavy wooden fences filled the canyon as it widened. Fat cattle grazed on lush grass in most of the fields. In the narrow field across the stream closest to the house two-dozen horses pranced in the morning sun.

It had taken two hours for the men to travel from Acapuneta to the family home of Pedro's mother. The Captain had hired wagons from the townsfolk to transport his crew and their meager possessions. Along the way, the town's people stopped from time to time to place a flower on a fresh grave. "The Royalist's hang those they think are supporting the Juarista's," translated Pedro. "The Juarista's just shoot those they think favor the other side."

Doc Parker met Chad and Pedro at the door, accompanied by a tall graying woman with coal black eyes. Next to her were two young ladies.

"Captain Gritt, I would like you to meet my mother, Theresa and my sister, Anna," started Pedro.

"I am charmed to make your acquaintance," blurted Chad gently taking the hand of the elegant lady and then that of her daughter, an impish girl with green eyes and long red hair, but the third woman commanded Chad's attention.

"Captain, may I introduce my niece, Denali Bonita de la Cruz," offered Theresa Davis.

The young woman was taller with dark brown hair. Her skin was the color of suede, and her eyes were a startling soft gray. Her simple high collared white lace blouse knit vest and long black skirt somehow emphasized her beauty.

"I am pleased to meet you," stammered Chad.

Denali curtsied. "I too am pleased," she replied, a slight blush on her cheeks. "My English less than my aunt," she continued. "Please come to visit your injured man." She turned toward a huge staircase rising from the slate floor to their right.

"Cousin Denali has grown up," laughed Pedro addressing his mother.

"Up and out" replied Theresa Davis. "Remember she is five years older than your sister. By the way, did you remember that your sister's birthday was last Friday?"

"Mother, I do not even know what day it is today. The last weeks are like a blur." Turning to his sister, he continued. "How old are you sis?"

"You know I am seventeen and almost an old maid," replied Anna. "Still not as old as Denali. Twenty-three and never been kissed."

"What a loss," mumbled Chad as he turned to follow the stunning young woman. Doc Parker caught up with him halfway up the stairs.

"Her mind and her tongue have the same edge as her body Captain. I have had to remind myself that I am a happily married man, even as I bandaged my wounds."

The room was no more than twelve feet by twelve feet. A pair of large windows stood open, lace curtains rustling in the gentle breeze. Angelo lay in a narrow bed, a clean white sheet folded beneath his chin, a smile on his face. Seated next to the bed was the fourth elegant woman Chad had met in the one minute that he had been in the house.

"Captain Gritt, te presento a mi madre, Camille de la Cruz." Denali's mother was at least three inches shorter than her daughter with a darker complexion. A slightly broader face hinted at more Indian blood. Her high cheekbones and pale blue eyes left little question where her daughter had sourced her beauty.

Camille de la Cruz extended her hand, which for some reason, Chad brought to his lips.

"Mi Madre speaks only Spanish and French; no Íngles," said Denali. "Señor Gasparetti also speaks French. They have wonderful time talking cooking."

"How are you feeling, you old bottle washer?" asked Chad.

"My life passes before my eyes over and over. If I leave the care of my nurses surely, I will perish."

Denali tried to stifle a giggle with her left hand. She failed. "Señor Gasparetti will be up and dancing very soon. But only when four women do not wait on him anymore."

"It appears that Doc Parker and all of his care has worked wonders for you, Angelo."

"I take no credit Captain," replied Parker. "Young Miss de la Cruz has been Angelo's primary physician."

"How so Doc?"

"Well to begin with, she is a fine nurse. But even more she is a student of natural medicines and healing. She made a poultice of tree moss, mud and crushed berries that took down the swelling in Angelo's hand in hours. Her tea of cactus and roots broke his fever in less time than that. She has Angelo chew a leaf she gathers in the forest behind the hacienda to kill the pain. He will be fit to travel tomorrow."

"Damn it Doc, you could have stayed downstairs," laughed Angelo.

"Thank you senorita de la Cruz," offered a smiling Chad.

"I am Denali. The Indio's have practiced medicine forever, often better medicine than Europeans."

"You see what I mean by sharp tongue Captain," laughed Parker.

Denali scowled at him but laughed with her eyes.

"If all of you would kindly leave," snarled Angelo, "I will finish my recipe for dried tomato, goat cheese and garlic ravioli."

Camille de la Cruz picked up a quill pen and small writing desk and placed it in her lap. She dipped the quill into a tiny silver ink well and paused.

"Thank you, Señora, for your kindness to our shipmate," stammered Chad.

The woman, who obviously understood more English, than reported, rewarded him with a broad smile, and a slight nod of the head.

"The officers will, of course, stay in our home," offered Theresa Davis. "We have eight bedrooms plus the old nursery where Angelo recovers from the scorpion's sting."

"And what of the men?" asked Chad.

"They are at the swimming hole bathing as we speak," offered Anna. "We have moved the six vaqueros still here at the ranch to two of the small houses below the mill so your men may use the bunkhouse. Three of the women are washing their clothes as they bathe."

"It would be well for you to bathe and trim hair on faces also," added Denali.

"My cousin thinks that we stink Captain," said Pedro.

"That is true," rejoined Denali without the faintest hint of a smile. "Marietta has heated water for faces, then you use bath at spring behind house. Leave clothes on fence around bath, in the warm sun and wind, they will be clean and dry in two hours."

Chad turned to Theresa Davis who shrugged her shoulders and smiled.

"My niece knows how to take charge," was all she said.

The cool water of the pool was more than welcome in the afternoon heat. A bottle of Tequila and three crockery cups sat by the pool along with soap, and towels that would have honored the finest New York or Paris hotel. "May I buy you a drink Captain?" asked Davis, "and of course one for you as well First Officer Kadzof?"

"What are we drinking?" Nick's face twisted around puckered lips.

"It is Tequila, the national drink of Mexico. You slip a slice of lime into your mouth and sip the liquor through the lime."

"Not bad," added Chad. "I assume that Doc Parker, Mead and Pierce were out here last night sampling this poison?"

"That they were," answered Pedro. "They couldn't let Angelo travel alone."

"Well, I am happy that it is just the three of us this afternoon. We need to discuss your role in all of this Mr. Davis," growled Chad, his face flushed. He slipped a thin slice of lime into his mouth, and then tipped the class of tequila.

Pedro downed the entire cup of Tequila in a single gulp. "I said, on the beach, how sorry I was. Captain Jackman lied to me. I was honoring a direct order that was to hurt only the Yankee Treasury."

"The subterfuge still cost us two men and another maimed. We lost our ship and a cargo entrusted to us by the United States Government," snarled Chad.

"Captain," started Nick, "that is behind us. We need to focus on the challenges coming. Over the last five days, Pedro has been indispensable."

Chad glared at Nick. Rope tight muscles in his neck and arms matched the tightening in his chest. Ott's familiar face filled his head. He took a couple of deep breaths. His face slowly lost its color, and then he sighed. "I am beyond that now," he replied. "You are right. The issues now are how do we get our crew safely home and how do we bring the lying murders to justice?"

Pedro poured another drink, pondering the slowly filling glass. "I will help in any way that I can."

"Good," said Nick. "What we need to know is where will the *RETRIBUTION* make landfall."

"Captain Jackman never discussed that. But there was a meeting place, a private harbor that allowed the resupply of the Confederate raiders and blockade-runners. If I were Jackman that is where I would seek safe harbor. If we can find a chart of the Caribbean, I can show you the location."

"It will require more than a circle on a map Mr. Davis," interjected Chad. "I want you with us."

"You could not keep me away, Captain. I have been betrayed over and over since we left San Francisco. To get my mother and sister home will now put them in danger. You can count on me to see this to the bloody end."

"Do you seek vengeance Pedro, or justice?" Nick slipped another sliver of lime into his mouth.

"My vengeance will be satisfied with justice done Mr. Kadzof. I ask of you the same thing promised by Captain Jackman. I do not want my former shipmates dead."

"I worried when I heard the word bloody."

Pedro laughed. "You forget that my father was British."

Chad bit into the rind of the lime in his mouth. The bitterness mirrored the distaste he felt for the confederate officer next to him, but they needed Pedro. "Fine. All except one. I intend to personally kill that bastard that murdered Ott Smith."

"I will load your pistol for you," replied Pedro.

Chad finally smiled. "I am satisfied that we three are on the same course. There is one more issue, and that is a replacement for Ott."

"You want to appoint a bosun for a land trip?" asked Pedro.

"It is critical that we maintain the discipline and spirit of a company. I don't know what lies ahead, but we will be stronger as a company, a crew."

It took Nick only a moment. "I propose we promote Hans Got. He spent two years as a soldier in the war. I believe he was a company sergeant if my memory has not tricked me."

"The Tequila has not completely altered your brain," replied Chad. "He was a soldier. Perhaps as important he trained for the clergy in an earlier life and is respected by his peers. He is obsessed with taking care of others."

"We may yet have to fight Captain," responded Davis. "Will your man Gott lead the crew even if there might be casualties?"

It was Nick who answered, "oh Hans will fight, he loves a good fight and is almost fearless. He just wants to make sure that he is on the right side."

"He is also educated and an independent thinker" added Chad. "Between Hans, Mosby, and Mead we have solid leaders if it comes to a fight."

"How did a man like Gott ship as an ordinary seaman?" asked Davis.

"He has bounced from career to career, adventure to adventure for years, always looking but never finding," replied Kadzof. He looked over at Pedro. "It all started with a woman."

20

HACIENDA NEAR ACAPONETA, MEXICO

DINNER THAT NIGHT was under the stars. Slabs of beef ribs and corn roasted over an open fire, complemented by flat corn pancakes cooked on hot rocks around the fire. A huge iron pot of red beans completed the menu. The locals thoroughly enjoyed watching the sailors' faces as they found the chilies in the beans.

The two-dozen Mexican women who had materialized from the village laughed, danced, and sang as they stuffed the gringo sailors like Thanksgiving turkeys. The half dozen graying ranch hands played instruments and filled the air with boisterous ballads.

The women, many with small babies wrapped in long shawls on their backs, handed their bundles to friends as they stepped to the center of the group to sway, swirl and spin to the music, sometimes individually, but more often in groups.

Denali Bonita whispered something into the ear of a gnarled old vaquero whose fingers flashed across his guitar defying his age and hard life. As the song they were playing ended he huddled with the other musicians and then tapped out a gentle beat on the back of his guitar.

The fire-lit circle was mesmerized by the haunting melody of a soft trumpet joined by the other instruments in a waltz, but one with the spice of Mexico. Denali crossed the circle to where Chad sat licking the leftovers of a beef rib from his fingers. "You waltz with me Captain? I have not waltzed since Paris."

Chad wiped his hands on the linen napkin that was part of the place setting at the officer's table. He was grateful for the dark, which hid the red of his face as he led the young lady to the center of the circle. In a flash Anna Davis zeroed in on Nick Kadzof and they joined Chad and Denali.

Denali was a far better dancer than her partner, which meant that she successfully covered his leading gaffs, making the couple appear practiced and fluid. That Denali was a lady was obvious; that she was the most attractive woman that he had ever known was a fact. The couple maintained proper distance except when Denali would 'slip', brushing her warm breasts against Gritt's chest.

Nick and Anna made up for their lesser skills with energy and laughter. As the music ended Chad escorted Denali back to the lawn benches where the women of the Hacienda had reseated themselves.

"Would you sit with me?"

"Of course," replied Chad nervously. "You dance like a woman of the court."

"I studied in Paris," she responded. "My mother's father was a French diplomat here before returning to his home. When he passed away my mother's mother returned to Mexico. Our family is still very close to our French relatives."

"What did you study in France?" asked Chad.

"My father approved of music, both violin and cello. I also studied politics and nursing which he does not approve of."

"He disapproves of your nursing and yet you work as a nurse,

I am told, I mean beyond helping Angelo; I mean you help in a hospital near your home," continued Chad, his tongue growing more tangled.

Denali giggled, "My father, I love, but he does not control me. I do what I want. I have my own beliefs and dreams. I will even choose my own husband."

Chad felt as if every eye was on him, waiting for a response. Try as he might, he could not come up with one. "Would you like to go for a walk?" slipped from his lips.

"Of course."

They walked down the dirt track along the river. The special perfume of vegetation along a desert river as it cools filled the air. "Have you anyone in mind?" Chad asked weakly.

"Only very recently has there been a candidate" she replied.

Chad felt his spirit drop. "Oh."

"Yes" continued Denali, "I will have to learn all about him to make sure he is the right man. Is honest man, caring and strong. Is good provider for family and other good people. Is good lover in bedroom."

"Is good what?" thought Chad out loud.

"I learned in France that good lover starts with good kisser." Denali put her arms around Chad, her left hand tangling her fingers in his longish hair. She pulled his head down to hers and kissed him. "Test one very good," she whimpered. "Now we walk back, we have early morning. You and officers come to breakfast at 7:00 while it is still cool. We talk about trip."

"Never been kissed," mumbled Chad.

The morning air was cool and so still that Chad could hear the buzz of two silver and purple hummingbirds in the garden just below the patio where he sat. He watched the sky above the hills go from violet to orange and then yellow. He struck a match and held the flame to the end of a long thin cigar that he had found in a cedar box on the dresser in his room. The warm smoke tasted of wood, caramel and oolong tea. *Thank God,* he thought, *that the cigars available in Boston taste like burning fall leaves or I could pick up this habit.*

Chad pulled another mouthful of the rich smoke into his mouth and held it, swirling his tongue through the vapor, absorbing the taste. The patio faced the east where it caught the first morning sun and was well shaded in the heat of the afternoon. A movement on the path to the bathing spring caught his eye. Denali and her mother walked arm in arm from their morning bath. Both were impeccably groomed, Denali in a white embroidered cotton dress and her mother in a red silk blouse and long black skirt. Both women wore their long hair piled on the top of their heads, held in place with interlocking ironwood combs. Behind them one of the house servants carried two rattan baskets and two towels over her left arm.

"Buenos dias, Captain Gritt," offered Camille, noticing the glow of Chad's cigar a moment before her daughter.

"Good morning" echoed Denali.

Camille turned to the young girl following. "Theresa, coffee por favor."

"Sí, Señora de la Cruz."

Then turning to Denali, Camille conferred in Spanish.

"My mother wonders if you were not comfortable, if you could not sleep."

"Please tell her that I was most comfortable, that I am well rested. Aboard ship a Captain never gets more than five hours of sleep at a time. It becomes a habit."

"I do not understand this word habit."

"Habit, part of my daily routine, something that I do over and over."

"Ah," replied Denali, turning to translate for her mother.

The coffee arrived in a tall silver pot along with three brightly painted clay cups.

"You will join us, Captain?" asked Denali as her mother seated herself next to her daughter and began pouring.

"Muchas gracias, Sí, thank you, yes," mumbled Chad.

"Ah, you do not speak Spanish."

"Not really, except for a few words that I have picked up in the last week."

"You will learn our language more as you travel," replied Denali.

"If I can learn English and Russian, I can master Spanish," agreed Chad. Camille's eyes locked on Chad as she filled the third cup and then handed it to him.

Through her daughter, she asked, "So you speak Russian?"

"Yes, my mother was Russian and my father a Boston sea Captain."

Denali translated. Her mother answered, "Denali, Spanish, Spanish, Spanish;" none of which Chad understood.

"Denali is a very interesting name," continued Chad. "I have heard it only in Alaska where it refers to a beautiful snowcapped mountain that dominates the central part of the vast Russian America."

Camille did a second double take at the mention of Russian America. She then asked her daughter to translate.

"My mother asks if you are from Russian America. That is, you and your family."

"No, I was born in Boston, but my mother and father first met in San Francisco. Both traveled to Russian America where they fell in love."

A sly smile spread on Camille's lips and her eyes drilled a hole in Chad's forehead. Through her daughter she asked: "Your mother and father then are happy and living in Boston?"

"For years they traveled on my father's ships between Boston and New Archangel in Russian America. We have homes in both cities. They are happy. Happy enough that all that time aboard ship led to four children. They are almost retired now."

Camille continued, this time in English. "Your father owns many ships?"

"Our family shipping company owns a dozen vessels, rather we did before the loss of the *KATARINA*."

"The *KATARINA*?" asked Camille.

"That was the name of the ship we lost at Teacapan. She was named for my mother."

Denali turned to her mother whose face was flushed, a smile on her face, "Madre, le que es esta line de cuestionamiento?"

"I will tell you later, daughter," responded Camille in Spanish. "Tell Captain Gritt where your name comes from."

"My father also once traveled to Russian America. It was the great adventure of his life. My name comes from his travels although I did not know of the beautiful mountain."

Chad simply shook his head, trying to recall the whole story his mother had told of how she came to marry his father.

"Please tell me of the mountain?" asked Denali.

"It is so high that you can see it from hundreds of miles in any direction. It stands with three other mountains in a land of mountains and vast valleys, but it dominates everything around it. In fine weather it is a diamond in the vast blue sky. In foul weather its winds and rain and snow batter anyone and anything close by. It is beautiful, moody, strong and dangerous."

Both women broke into laughter, unable to stop. Finally catching her breath Denali smiled at the puzzled expression on Chad's face.

"My mother thinks I am well named," she said.

Breakfast was held up while the group waited for Pierce who arrived a half hour late.

Breakfast dishes cleared, the ten people present got down to business.

Quickly the decision was made to make the de la Cruz Hacienda near Aguacalientes the first objective of their trip. The leg would be only three hundred miles but would take at least four days, as they would cross the rugged Sierra Madre Occidental Mountains. From there they would travel through Leon, to Mexico City, and then on to Veracruz, where all agreed their best chance of finding fast passage to Louisiana would be found. The biggest surprise of the morning came from Theresa Davis.

"Pedro, I will not be traveling with you," she announced. "With your father gone, I have decided to stay here and supervise the hacienda until the issues are settled in Mexico. With my brothers split, one in Mexico City supporting the Emperor and the other raising money for President Juarez, someone needs to mind the store. When this is over, I will send word of my plans."

The group discussed the recommendation that the women travel ahead of the crew. Anna, and mother and daughter de la Cruz would escort the crew as far as the family hacienda. Pedro's cousin was due back in a day, along with four other men, who would act as escort. In the interim there was much to do.

"There are twenty-nine from the wreck of the *KATARINA*" offered Pedro. "We will need horses for each, plus two spare riding horses and three pack animals. Can the family afford to sell that many horses, mother," he asked?

"The quantity will be no problem," related his mother. "We will send Jose to the high camp today to bring fourteen older mounts in from the camp. We have more than one hundred horses, but only a handful are experienced with multiple riders."

"Captain," asked Davis, "are all of the men experienced horsemen?"

Nick Kadzof laughed. "Pedro, I would guess that half of the crew have never been in a saddle. I am a prime example. My only experience with a horse was when I was twelve. I stuck two apples in my hip pockets and went out to the hitching post to feed my uncle's horse before church one Sunday. The horse loved the first apple and pushed me with his nose, begging for the second. I tugged it from my Sunday go-to-meeting pants and the horse devoured it in seconds. Again, the horse bumped me with his nose, but I was fresh out of apples. I turned to go and the horse bit me right on my backside. It hurt like hell, pardon the language ladies, but that wasn't the worst part. The horse lifted me up by my pants and shook me until my back pocket ripped off. I fell right on my head. My father laughed like hell, but my mother was flat mad about the pants. I went to mass that day with my backside hanging out in front of God and everybody."

When the laughter at the table quieted, Chad watched Denali's mother whisper in her ear.

"Mr. Kadzof," asked Denali, "are you Catholic then?"

"I am, ma'am," replied Nick. "My father was Russian Orthodox. My Italian mother insisted we all attend Catholic Church."

"And you, Captain Gritt?" she asked.

"No, I am Lutheran. My mother was Russian Orthodox, and we would have been raised in that faith. There were no Orthodox churches in Boston, so we took the faith of my father."

A gray veil swept Camille de la Cruz's face for a moment, and then passed.

Theresa Davis used the pause to change the subject back to the trip. "We do have a problem with tack for the horses," she advised. "Here at the Hacienda, we have only about a dozen saddles that we can part with."

"Do you have a suggestion mother?" asked Pedro.

"I always have a suggestion, you know that. Anyway, each of the vaqueros owns a spare saddle. I am sure that twenty of them will be happy to sell their old saddles. That is, at a price that will buy a new one."

"And what price would that be?" asked Chad.

"Oh, I would think that ten dollars Yankee money in silver or gold would do the trick," replied Theresa Davis. "Fifty dollars for each horse would be fair."

"What about bridles and blankets?" asked Chad.

"At that price we throw in the bridles and blankets," laughed Theresa. One hundred and ten ounces of your gold, seven pounds. It is a fair price."

"Agreed," said Chad, "but how do you know of the strips of gold?"

The village priest told me," she offered. "He suggested that you convert the gold you need for your trip to coins in our blacksmith's shop. They will draw far less attention than breaking off pieces from a gold strip. It is sound advice, Captain."

"Then I will take it. My carpenter and his apprentice can work with your smithy to smelt and pour."

"We will help as we can. I will have Jose bring our foreman in from the high camp. You can arrange with him what other supplies you will need."

"Gracias, Señora," replied Chad.

"I appreciate the Spanish, but for as long as I am alive, I will be Mrs. Alistair Davis, and English will be my first language."

"No offense intended."

"And none taken, Captain. I loved Pedro's father very much but more important in this unsettled country it keeps me and this house neutral."

"Is that an issue here?"

"It is. Didn't you notice how few hands we have here, and all of those older men?"

"As a matter of fact, we were discussing that at the bath yesterday" interrupted Nick.

"It is because of the armies. The Juaristas forget that my brother Arturo travels with President Juarez and raises money for the cause. When they come, they seize our young men as soldiers. The Royalists are just as bad. My other brother Miguel was part of the Committee of Notables along with Denali's father."

"We don't know about the Committee of Notables," responded Chad.

"It was a group gathered together by the church and their Europeans and Mexican allies to create a manifesto, asking the European Kings to send a European born Monarch to rule Mexico. They wanted to drive out the liberal government with its policy of nationalizing the churches' properties. Miguel works closely with Hans Michael Fehlburg, Emperor Maximilian's European Chief of Staff. Still, when the Royalists, or their French or German allies come through, they impress our young men. We hide our young men and most of our cattle and horses in two camps in the hills."

"You were wise to take decisive action, mother," replied Pedro.

"It was your cousin's idea; Denali had watched her father strip their hacienda of young men to support the Royalists' cause. Many have died. The Hacienda de la Cruz is struggling just to maintain. We did not want the same to happen here."

Chad smiled at the young woman who had kissed him the night before, and watched as she started to speak, and then thought better of it.

"If there is nothing more then," said Theresa Davis, "I suggest that we get on with our preparations. I suggest we begin with riding lessons, which should be great fun to watch!"

21

HACIENDA NEAR ACAPONETA, MEXICO

DOC AND NICK sat on a rock, their feet soaking in the crystal waters of the stream. "Two wrist sprains, one fractured arm, a bloody nose, numerous contusions and scrapes and one ass full of cactus thorns," offered Doc Parker. "Every one of them can now sit a saddle, at least at a walk. Step it up to a trot and the bouncing heads look like a gopher colony in a dog pen. A cantor let alone a gallop and we unhorse a third of our crew."

"Since I will be one of those quickly afoot I will pre-plan organizing an infantry," replied Nick, his face serious. "I have a new appreciation of Mead, Pierce, and Sergeant Mosby after watching them ride. Were it not for their help, the ten of us who grew up as wagon jockeys would not have a prayer of getting out of Mexico in one piece."

"Pierce is the one who amazed me. He sits a horse like he was born on one. He has a gift for helping others get the hang of it," offered Parker.

"I admit, he was a great help today. It is too bad that he is a pompous ass. I close my eyes and see him sitting on a throne, looking down on the peasants expecting them to defend him."

"You judge him then?"

"You have watched him, and listened to his whining, we all have. The Captain can barely stomach the man."

"I watch, and I listen. His place of privilege certainly comes through. It irritates him to take orders from a mere sea Captain. But I think he also feels a duty to fulfill his Alaska mission for Secretary Seward and the President."

"Perhaps Doc, but his fear and pettiness make me uncomfortable. I wouldn't count on Pierce in a bind."

"Only time will tell. Me thinks, a company of foreigners crossing foreign terrain, and a land at war will test us all."

"The other one that surprised me was Señorita de la Cruz. There was no sidesaddle for her. She rides like a horse is part of her," continued Kadzof.

"She grew up in a culture that admires horsemanship. Her afternoon ride with the Captain should knock the rust off from his skills."

❧

Denali led Chad up a narrow trail on the shady side of the canyon. The stream that watered the hacienda tumbled through boulders the size of houses three hundred feet below, an indication of the force of water through the narrow canyon when the rains came. Finally breaking out on top Chad found himself in a small grotto, rock faces stretching up left and right. A hundred yards in front of him, the stream fell from a third rock face in a wispy waterfall.

From wall to wall, the grotto was filled with grass; an emerald green near the stream fading to straw next to the rock walls at left and right. Around the waterfall, where the mists, carried on the winds, irrigated everything, trees and bushes of brilliant red, white and yellow flowers blanketed the walls. Two huge mesquite trees offered shade.

From the face of the waterfall, a long narrow pool of crystal water again showed the power of the stream at high water. The surging winter rains had gouged out a basin more than a two hundred feet long and at least a third that measure wide. The depth of the pool where the falls tumbled over the cliff was more than twenty feet. From the deepest point the pool sloped up until the water, now only inches deep, narrowed and again became a stream.

Chad wiped his face with the red bandana around his neck, trying to keep sweat from his eyes. He tugged at the shirt clinging to his body, to induce a small measure of airflow, but the absolute stillness of the leaves on the surrounding trees made the task hopeless.

"It is very warm, is it not, Captain?" remarked Denali. She slid from her saddle walking her coal-black mount to the pool, letting him drink. Chad joined her while the large red gelding that he would spend the coming weeks with noisily slurped the water.

"It is very hot, not just warm," replied Chad. "I feel like a slab of beef on a broiler."

Denali led her horse away from the creek. She slipped a twenty-foot woven leather rope from her saddle; she looped it through a ring on the horse's bridle. The other end of the rope she tied to a branch of one of the mesquites, giving the horse room to graze. "You tie your horse also," she commanded.

Chad untied the small strap, dropping a similar leather rope into his left hand. His inferior skills meant that a task that had taken Denali two minutes to accomplish, took Chad five.

He turned back to the stream. Denali was standing facing the stream, her naked back as white as Alaskan snow. She reached down and pushed her silk pantaloons down over perfect hips, wiggling back and forth rather than untying the cord that fastened them. Her pantaloons at her feet, Denali took two steps, her long narrow legs stretching carefully to avoid the sharpest stones along the pool. Looking over her shoulder at Chad she smiled. "Do you come for swim or not," she asked. Then she dove into the pool, barely rippling the surface.

Surfacing in the middle of the pool Denali swept her hair from her face, dipping her head then surfacing with her face pointing straight up at the blistering afternoon sun. "Agua, water, is cool and washes away the trail," said Denali. "Come."

Chad pulled the scarf from his neck, then unbuttoned his blue cotton shirt, stripping it and hanging it on a branch. He tugged off his boots and his heavy seaman's socks. Unbuckling his belt and unbuttoning his pants he looked up to see Denali watching intently. Embarrassed, he stopped with his pants halfway to his knees, his white cotton long johns alone covering him.

"You finish undressing and join me," she coaxed.

"I will if you turn around."

"You watched me, now I watch you," was her answer. Caught by the truth he tugged off his pants and long johns and plunged into the water.

She was right; the pool was divine. The dust and sweat from two hours in the saddle, gone in an instant. He swam hard; long strokes taking him the length of the pool then back toward the waterfall. He hoped the cool water would help him with the obvious signs of his attraction. Finding a large flat rock under the surface he stood, his chest and upper torso above the water. He swam to avoid staring at the beautiful girl sharing the pool with him. He stopped swimming because his willpower failed, but the girl had disappeared.

A quick survey, by eyes trained to find the slightest irregularity in a ship's rigging a hundred feet above his head, or the smallest dot on the horizon, representing a potential threat, found not a trace of the naked beauty. The falling water splashed over his head, blurring his vision. Wiping the moisture from his eyes he searched again, nothing. The first traces of worry evaporated as he felt two hands grip his ankles then sweep up his legs. Denali's head broke the water only inches from his chest. Her hands continued to slide up his body until they reached his shoulders, then Denali wrapped her arms around his neck. She pressed her lips to his, the water cascading over their heads washing away any sound.

"You will be good lover, maybe more," she said.

The couple arrived back at the Hacienda, the afternoon sun low on the horizon. In the shade, the air had cooled substantially. The smell of tobacco reached the corral where a ranch hand waited for their horses. The ship's officers, plus Mead and Pierce sat in heavy wood and leather chairs under the trees. With them were two rugged young men, one dressed as a gentleman, the other in the rough clothing of a man who worked cattle. All held tall, heavy green glasses.

"Captain, this is my cousin Pablo," offered Pedro Davis. "And this is the ranch foreman, Carlos Rojas." Chad shook each man's hand. Pedro's cousin was tall and striking. Dressed in a brown riding suit of heavy linen with silver buttons and tall black polished boots, Pablo was perhaps six feet two, thin but strongly built with just a hint of gray in his black hair and pencil thin mustache.

Carlos Rojas looked like a bandito. Chad guessed his age at forty. His five-foot ten-inch frame carried a rock solid two hundred pounds. His gray-flecked brown hair needed a cut and his huge walrus mustache had not been trimmed in months. On his left hip he carried two knives, one a blade of six inches and the other, more the size of a small sword. His dusty work clothing topped the most worn pair of boots that Chad had ever seen. Strapped to the boots was a pair of heavy, tarnished, silver spurs. He would have been one of the most frightening men Chad had ever seen were it not for his smile. The man's warm toothy smile spread from his toes to the top of his head.

"What are you drinking there?" asked Chad. "It does not look like Tequila."

"You have that right," responded Pedro. "These are grade A, American bourbons, southern style. "Cousin Denali," he continued, "would you fetch the Captain here a drink?"

"Do I look like his maid?" answered Denali as she turned and headed for the house.

22
PACIFIC COAST ROAD, MEXICO

THE COACH DEPARTED the hacienda the moment the coach driver could discern the road from the surrounding black. The balance of the troop had intended to follow only a half hour behind, but with novice horsemen saddling and loading their own gear, it was more than an hour before they were on the road.

The troop had traveled less than a half mile before one of Sergeant Mosby's marines leaned over to reposition his foot in the stirrup. The loose cinch on his saddle gave, sliding around the ribs of his horse dumping him on his head before the saddle recovered equilibrium, hanging from the horse's belly. His was the first of five unplanned dismounts before the travelers reached the main road. It was almost noon before the men arrived in Tepic, learning that they were hours behind the coach. The plan was to meet the coach travelers at the ancient ruin of Los Toriles, for the night. The weary horsemen arrived just at dark.

Mead and Chad sat in their saddles, taking in the ancient village. Around them the moonlight threw shadows on mounds and crumbling stone buildings. "We're being watched by the ghosts of the ancient ones," whispered Denali as the two men sat next to a roaring fire where the women from the coach waited.

Denali and her cousin Pablo had hired a-half dozen locals to set up camp. Three large fires burned in a small flat plain that had once been the courtyard of the long abandoned ceremonial town. More than a dozen chickens sizzled on spits over one fire. Over another, a huge black pot of beans that had been soaking all day on the back of the coach bubbled. Camille de la Cruz interrupted one of the local women feeding roasted chilies into the bean pot. Both women laughed; the only word Chad understood was "gringos."

Over the third fire, two women grated corn using an ancient stone-on-stone grinding basin, then mixing the corn flour with water and salt, they cooked tortillas, storing the finished product in a blackened Dutch oven.

"Our trip, no problem," laughed Denali sitting next to Chad, her knife and fork now idle on her tin plate. "After we leave Tepic we meet a French patrol, eight men and a lieutenant. We tell him about *KATARINA* crew following. They ride back to Guadalajara to tell their general."

"Did the news disturb him? Do you or Pablo expect trouble?"

"No problem. He was typical French officer. A pretty girl can tell him anything."

"I see," smiled Chad.

"I tell him, we not go through Guadalajara, that we turn on small road at Tequila and go north to Aguacaliente. He says he think that is good idea, then he leaves."

The next morning was a replay of the first morning except that once the crew was on the road they managed to stay on their horses. Still, they were an hour behind the coach when the last of the fires were extinguished.

From Los Toriles, the road descended toward a broad river valley along the Río Bolaños. The hard packed road cut through brush and timber covered hills. To either side of the road, thick brush mixed with tangled vines, many climbing into the trees. At the bottom of the grade, the forest ended.

The area along the road had been cleared for more than a mile, creating a huge pasture along the river. Rounding a bend in the road, the men found Pablo Ramirez seated on a log along with a gray-haired French cavalry officer. The two men stood as Chad and Pedro reached them.

The officer was dressed in a royal blue uniform with red lapels and epaulets. He wore a billed cap, blue on top, with a shining leather bill and red band. He carried an old cap and ball revolver in a leather holster at his right, and silver handled sword at his left.

Pablo shook his head, turning to Pedro, shading his eyes from the afternoon sun.

Pedro translated. "Captain Gritt, this is Colonel leMark of his Majesty's Territorial Guard. His aide is waiting at the coach. He has heard that you have been aiding the rebels and he is here to arrest you and take you to Guadalajara for trial. He says that if you do not come peaceably, he is ready to engage and arrest the few that survive."

"I really do not know how to respond to the Colonel," replied Chad. "We have done nothing like what he accuses us of. Tell him that."

Pedro translated. The Colonel rose, untying his horse. Sliding his left foot into the stirrup of his saddle, he swung up onto his mount. Turning to Pablo he snapped something in rapid Spanish.

"The Colonel gives us thirty minutes to discuss it, then if you do not surrender, he will attack. He has a company of French lancers itching for a fight."

The Colonel turned his mount and rode back along the road to Guadalajara.

"Pablo, I really do not know what to do. I am reluctant to disarm our men especially over such a ridiculous charge."

"Captain Gritt, leMark is the worst kind of French officer. My father is a liaison between Hans Michael Fehlburg, Chief of Staff to the Emperor, and the Royalist Mexican army. Men like leMark makes his job almost impossible."

"Thank you for the political lesson, but that gives me little counsel."

"leMark is here hunting the sometime bandit, sometime Juarista Gordo Rojas, Fat Red. In Tepic yesterday we learned that leMark rounded up ten local peasants accusing them of being Rojas supporters. They were beaten and questioned for hours, then leMark ordered all ten shot."

"Were they bandits," asked Chad?

"Perhaps one or two, but certainly not all. At least three of the men are known to my family."

"Then he murdered innocent men," responded Pedro first in English, then in Spanish.

"That is what this war has become. French officers like leMark consider Mexicans little more than animals. They are here to advance their careers and nothing more. To kill Mexicans to him is like killing la cucaracha."

"I understand," replied Chad, "but where does that leave us?"

"Your late President Lincoln and your Secretary of State Seward have opposed the European involvement in Mexico for years. Your country never recognized the Emperor. That makes Americans the enemy to men like leMark."

"That may be so, I don't know. Mr. Pierce is an Assistant to Secretary Seward, perhaps he can explain our plight and innocence to the Colonel."

"Colonel leMark has already recorded in his campaign log, the presence of a spy from Secretary Seward and the presence of Americans sent to aid Juarez. He believes that it will be a big feather in his cap to destroy this foreign cancer," continued Pablo.

"So, you are saying that he does not intend to offer a fair trial."

"Oh, there will be a trial, if he cannot goad you into a fight.

Then you will be hung very publicly along with Señor Mead and Señor Pierce. Your men will be shot."

"This is the government that you and your father support?"

"There are atrocities on each side, Captain. Emperor Maximilian is an honorable man who genuinely cares about Mexico. A few men, like leMark, men who want only glory and high rank when they go home to France, surround him. President Juarez cares about Mexico, but his government is weak, inefficient and corrupt." The young Mexican aristocrat slapped his thigh with his hat. "Captain Gritt, we Mexicans are passionate people, unable to compromise."

"If we do not surrender, what happens to the women in the coach?" asked Pedro.

"We are safe. leMark knows of my father's place in the government. He has already recorded in his log that we were misled by the evil American spies."

"So where does that leave us?" asked Pierce who had heard the end of the exchange after growing bored waiting with the troop.

"You must fight; leMark must not survive, and then you must find an alternative route to Aguacaliente, away from Guadalajara. leMark's aide detests him. I will convince him to wire my father, requesting an escort from Aguacaliente."

"Señor Ramirez," moaned Pierce, "there must be a better solution. Our mission for our government is too important to risk failure because we are inept diplomats."

"Señor Secretary," replied Pablo Ramirez, "leMark will offer no place for diplomacy. He cannot leave any evidence that he has acted brashly, or his glory will be compromised or worse."

"How sad if my mission dies in a Mexican cow pasture," sighed Pierce.

"Don't you mean how sad if you die?" replied Chad.

"They are one and the same."

"Captain I must go," continued Pablo. "I will ask the Colonel to allow me to move the coach back toward Tepic so that the women can be spared any danger. By the time I return with the coach you had better be ready. The Colonel will not give you any more time to prepare."

"Mr. Pierce, would you please go back to the troop and send Mr. Mead and Sergeant Mosby forward? We will need their military expertise if we are to survive," ordered Gritt.

"This is just crazy," shot Pierce. "What can a handful of sailors due against a company of trained French troops?"

"Enough," screamed Chad. "I've just about had it with you Pierce. Now go."

Pierce mounted his horse without a word and turned toward the resting troop. Pablo Ramirez trotted his black stallion the opposite direction.

I detest a coward," said Chad aloud. Only Pedro Davis was there to hear the comment.

23
RIO BOLANOS, MEXICO

A SMALL SIDE road paralleling the Río Bolaños River ran east from the highway just before a heavy-timbered bridge. The cleared pasture stretched for more than a mile on either side of the road and continued from the main road for two miles up the river, ending where the river and a village road twisted into the foothills of the Sierra Madre Mountains.

The pasture was rolling grassland, with clumps of thorn bush and widely scattered trees. In places the grass had been grazed almost to its roots, leaving patches of reddish earth. In others, especially the hollows and shallow ravines that reached to the river, the grass was higher than a man's waist. Along the river itself the grass was still a soft gray green. The rest of the pasture was the color of straw sucked dry of all moisture by a relentless sun.

The river ran slowly through the long flat meadow. It was perhaps twenty yards wide, never more than a foot deep. In many places cattle had ground the bank away leaving little definition of where pasture ended and riverbank began. About a half mile up the river however, the river twisted through a high spot in the pasture leaving steep banks above the rocky channel. It was in this cut that Mead and Mosby positioned the crew.

A picket line had been rigged between two huge logs, partially embedded in the river bottom. The horses were tied to the line and two of the experienced horsemen were busy hobbling the horses, a strategy to keep their mounts close even if they broke away from the picket line.

The men were spread out along the banks, rifles loaded. Missing was the youngest member of the crew, sixteen-year-old Brian Pennington, who had wandered away from the troop to deal with a tough case of dysentery; the product of a chilies eating bet he won the night before. It was a testament to Doc Parker's skills that the loss of Brian's arm from the shelling of the *KATARINA* had barely slowed him down. Carlos Rojas, who could not be seen as part of the American crew had volunteered to look for the lad.

Less than ten minutes after the men had moved into their defensive position, the coach and its three guards appeared from the south. A French officer rode next to Pablo. A handful of French troops followed. Moving at a walk, it was clear that Pablo and the women were stalling, buying the Americans as much time as they could. As the coach reached the bridge, Rojas rode up out of the river bottom. Young Pennington was not with him.

The coach and its outriders continued northward, up the winding hill from the river bottom. At the top of the hill the coach stopped, Chad could see the women dismount. In less than a minute four blue-uniformed French cavalry troops took up positions behind them blocking the road. Pablo's estimate of free passage for the Ramirez and de la Cruz family appeared to be wishful thinking. Chad had little time to contemplate their fate.

Out of the woods on three sides of the meadow, lines of French lancers emerged. Along the main road, four mounted men accompanied a caisson and small brass artillery piece. The artillerymen positioned the small cannon next to the bridge and began making it ready for use.

"My God," snapped Nick, "there must be a hundred of them."

The French lancers lined up thirty abreast. Their blue uniforms with red lapels, epaulets, and pants stripes vivid against the brown and gray green of the natural background. Each trooper carried a long lance held upright; a small red flag attached below a gleaming silver blade at least eighteen inches long. In front of each troop an officer trotted his mount snapping out orders, pointing at individual soldiers with his sword. Each carried old French pistols at their sides, but none of them drew that weapon.

From the troop along the main road, Colonel leMark trotted his horse along with four lancers. They closed within a quarter mile of the *KATARINA*'s crew at which point the lancers halted and leMark continued on alone for another hundred yards. In perfect English, leMark shouted, "Remember that you were warned Captain Gritt." Turning his horse back toward the main road leMark shoved a bundle off from his horse's rump. The blanket wrapped bundle flopped onto the soft ground and began to roll. Out of the blanket sprang young Pennington, his pants around his ankles. The French troops wailed with laughter.

Pulling his pants up, Brian stood looking in every direction. Pierce scrambled up the bank to beckon him.

"Brian, we are over here."

Pennington was running before Pierce's last word left his mouth. Behind him one of the French lancers spurred his mount into a run. The French lancer caught up to Pennington in seconds, slashing his leg with his razor-sharp lance, dropping the youth, and sending him tumbling. In seconds, three more lancers were around the boy. Every time the lad would rise, a different lancer would slide in and slash at him. In seconds, Brian was bleeding from his good arm and both legs.

The crew of the *KATARINA* stood watching in stunned silence. "Captain, we have to…"

Pierce's statement was interrupted by the crash of a heavy Sharps rifle. Charles Lampoc watched with satisfaction as one of the lancers toppled from his saddle. A second shot, this one from Sergeant Mosby smashed another lancer to the ground. Chad burst from his cover, running toward the wounded boy. One of the remaining Frenchmen turned toward his own troop and spurred his horse into a gallop, but the fourth drove the opposite direction burying his blade in Brian's chest as he sat wounded on the ground. In a brilliant piece of horsemanship, he swiped the lance up and away from the dying boy, and sliding behind his horse, and lying along its side hidden from the Americans, he disappeared into one of the shallow draws.

Chad lifted Pennington's body, carrying it toward where the crew stood shocked.

"Prepare to defend cavalry," yelled Mead as he watched a platoon of lancers spur their mounts into a trot from the western road a half-mile away. The old brass cannon crashed, sending its small shell harmlessly over their heads. Less than a minute later a second shell buried itself harmlessly in the sod of the pasture fifty yards behind the men. A bugle call halted the lancers. The crew watched as the cannon crew pushed their field piece off from the hard-packed road and furiously dug a hole, to lower the towing tongue.

"They are elevating the barrel of the field gun to increase the arc and bring us into range Mr. Mead," yelled Mosby who commanded the western line.

"I see that, Sergeant. Do you think they can find the range?"

"It will be difficult," replied Mosby. "They probably have no more than thirty rounds on the caisson, they most likely will use them all before they find us."

He had underestimated the skills of the French artillery crew. The fifth shell landed only thirty yards in front of the American lines and exploded sending dirt and rocks high into the air, pelting the crew as dust and stones remembered gravity. A bugle sounded and the lancers kicked their horses into a cantor as the French crew furiously reloaded their cannon.

"Sergeant Mosby, send me your marksmen with Sharps rifles," yelled Mead.

"Mr. Lampoc, Private Rust, Mr. Gott, report to Colonel Mead." Pierce followed the men.

"Gentlemen, I make the range just over six hundred yards to the artillery crew. We must put them out of action since we have nothing to destroy the cannon itself."

The marksmen adjusted the rear sights of the buffalo guns for a third of a mile and began to line up their shots.

Before any of the four could squeeze the trigger, another shell exploded only feet in front of Private Rust. The steep trajectory of the shell drove it three feet into the ground before it exploded. That saved three of the marksmen, but nothing could help Rust whose neck was snapped instantly. Mead collapsed, a huge knot forming on his forehead. Pierce picked the Sharps from the edge of the river and began to dig the dirt out of the barrel. He rummaged through Rust's pockets and found a handful of shells for the heavy rifle.

Lampoc, Gott and Sergeant Mosby wiped the dirt from their eyes and checked the barrels of their rifles. In moments all three recovered, took aim, and fired. A moment later, Pierce pulled the stiff trigger of the Sharps. Only one Frenchman went down, but it was the most important man, the loader. One of the munitions handlers rushed to the collapsed man. The gaping hole in his chest left little doubt that the man was beyond help. Taking over the loading effort, the training and discipline of the French artilleryman proved its value. He had barely stepped away when the gun Captain sent the next shell on its way.

"Incoming" shouted Mosby to the entire crew, even as he lined up his next rifle shot. All four marksmen fired before the cannon round landed thirty yards beyond them, again burrowing deep into the earth before exploding. Two of the *KATARINA's* crew tumbled screaming from the line of men watching the tree line to the south. Doc Parker waded the stream and bent over the first man, hesitating only seconds before turning to the second. Sig Belson, the ship's carpenter lay stunned on his back, blood flowing from a gash above his right eye and wounds in his right shoulder and arm.

"How is young Procter?" gasped Belson.

"Mr. Proctor has ended his trip right here, Sig, but you will not be joining him," replied Parker. "Sit still while I bandage that eye and get your arm into a sling."

"The eye yes, but I shoot left-handed. If I can use the right arm at all to help raise this Henry pop gun, I can still man my position."

Parker smiled, "Let me help you up, and back to the bank."

The men with the Sharps rifles shrugged off the impact of the shell concussion behind them and reloaded. Rising from behind their protective riverbank they focused on the gun crew. Two more of the French were down and the remaining three were fumbling through a reload. The French artillery officer had drawn his pistol, and was waving it at his own crew, screaming at the top of his lungs. Seconds later, his body lifted completely off the ground as a heavy bullet hit him below the belly button, then jerked wildly as a second bullet crushed his chest. The remaining crew broke for the road, disappearing in seconds behind the far bank.

"Out of the trees," yelled Nick, commander of the south line. "Lancers at a gallop."

"Sergeant Mosby how far out is the French Calvary?" called Chad.

"Three hundred yards."

The sound of hundreds of hoofs echoed across the pasture. Red dust filled the air around the running horses. The ground began to vibrate.

"One more shot with the sharps, shoot at the horses; then get ready with the repeaters. Do not fire the Henry's until the French are within a hundred yards."

Two horses tumbled sending their riders crashing to the ground. The remaining French troops lowered their lances.

"The French company to the south is at three hundred yards," snapped Nick. "You heard the Captain, hold fire until they are within one hundred yards. Wait for my command." The lancers from the east and the north spurred their mounts.

The eight men facing the road reacted to Mosby's order with a volley that sounded like a single shot. Two more lancers slid from their saddles. The rest of the French howled out a challenge, knowing they were facing empty rifles. They were wrong.

In seconds, eight more lancers tumbled from their mounts and half a dozen horses were stumbling or slowing. At thirty yards six more of the French were down. The Americans dropped their empty rifles and took up their spare weapons without any let up in fire.

The French officer commanding the charge found himself in front of his wavering troops, armed only with a sword. Only ten yards from the Americans three bullets ripped him from the saddle. His surviving troops broke to the left drawing fire as they fled. Only five were still mounted as they fled out of range.

"Reload, men," ordered Mosby. "Mr. Lampoc, Mr. Gott, see if you can catch up to the stragglers with your Sharps. The rest of you lend a hand right and left."

The firing was all around now, and the results were the same. Only one lancer reached their line, skewering one of the crew between the eyes before he collapsed, four bullets ripping his body. In less than ten minutes only twenty of more than a hundred French lancers who had begun the charge were still mounted. All of them had thrown down their spears and were retreating toward the men surrounding Colonel leMark, waiting on the road.

Two of the men with leMark, realizing that the firing had

stopped, galloped to where the remaining artillery crew was hiding. In minutes they had the caisson and horses back on the road and ropes on the tongue of the cannon.

"They are salvaging the cannon," yelled Mosby. Should we try to stop them?"

"No, Sergeant," said Chad, walking up behind the west defenders.

"I agree," added Mead, pressing a wet bandanna against his forehead. "They have had enough."

"But Pablo said we needed to stop them from reporting," argued Mosby.

"We may be able to get a couple of those salvaging the cannon," replied Chad, "but those around leMark are out of range even for the Sharps."

Thomas, what are our losses?" asked Chad.

"Doc Parker says two are dead plus young Pennington and Sig Belson has a broken shoulder."

"Damn," replied Chad.

"It could have been much worse, Captain, lances against repeating rifles, old world against new," responded Mead. "They were so arrogant that they never used their pistols."

"We wait until the French gather up their wounded, then we retire to the coach and develop a new plan," ordered Gritt. "When leMark sends out a rescue party we will honor their white flag. Mr. Mead and I will stay here and keep an eye on things. Sergeant, please go help Doc Parker organize a burial party, then get the men ready to move."

Aye aye, Captain," spat Mosby. "You learn fast for a squid," he laughed.

Chad sighed. "You have the training and it showed today, but these men are still my crew."

Mosby stopped and pointed. "Look, Captain," they are leaving, abandoning their wounded."

Just over a mile away the surviving French troopers had turned south away from the carriage, leMark in the lead, and in ragged order, the balance of his soldiers. The line was just entering the trees when a volley of gunfire cut the troop from their horses like a sickle cutting hay. Then three-dozen men, most in floppy hats and white cotton pants burst from the tree line, hacking the wounded French with knives and machetes.

Moments later, firing erupted from the north. The French soldiers who had been with the carriage were cut down. A dozen more white clad men raced onto the road quickly dispatching the wounded men.

"Juaristas?" asked Mosby.

"I assume so," replied Chad.

The soldiers of Benito Juarez spread out across the battlefield, picking up French pistols and gathering loose horses. The peasant soldiers walked from body to body, kicking the Frenchmen. Again, and again the kick was answered by a moan or a scream. Rather than waste a bullet on the wounded, the victors retrieved the fifteen-foot lances dropped by the French, driving a blade through the chest of any wounded they found, pinning them to the ground.

"Do we stop them, Captain?" asked Mosby.

"One enemy is enough, Sergeant," answered Mead.

Disgusted by the carnage, Chad kicked at a line of ants winding along the water line. Dozens were crushed and dozens more were lifted into the air, landing in the water where hungry fish gulped them. In seconds the ants had re-established their line and their march continued.

Chad was grateful for the small diversion as he concentrated on blocking out the screams of the wounded French troopers.

24

ON THE RIO BOLANOS ROAD, MEXICO

WITH ONLY TWO stubby shovels, the job of burying Peter and fallen crewmates started slowly. Within minutes a dozen men had scavenged the medieval spears of the French army and were busy chipping out graves.

The men were wrapped in their blankets and lowered into the ground. "Captain, you should read from the Good Book," whispered Mosby. "If you do not have your book with you, you can use mine."

"Thank you, Sergeant, but I think The Lord's Prayer is more appropriate. Right now, solace for the living is as necessary as a blessing for those departed to a better place."

After the brief ceremony, three of the French lances were cut off, the blade end driven into the ground and the cut piece tied securely across the shaft forming a cross. A personal item from each man's pack was placed on the grave.

As the Americans buried their shipmates, a group of Juaristas rode quietly along the road toward the coach. More men in white cotton dress spread out across the battlefield, stopping to place a silver coin on the face of each French Trooper.

"I don't understand what we are watching," said Pierce.

"My mother explained it," replied Pedro Davis. "Each side will rob the dead of their valuables after each battle. The winner will then leave a coin on their enemy's body as payment for a burial. A slaughter of this magnitude will keep local villagers busy for days and represents probably a year of hard money wages. Remember, both the Mexicans and the French are Catholic, so proper reverence for the dead is observed by both sides."

"Catholic, Protestant, Buddhist, it makes no sense," said Nick.

"I assure you, Mr. Kadzof," interjected Doc Parker, "that there were no atheists on our side in this battle; but to slaughter the wounded, then honor their corpses cannot set well with God."

"Mr. Kadzof, Mr. Mead, Mr. Mosby, please gather your men and prepare them for travel," directed Chad.

"Two of the horses were wounded by the shell fire, Captain," responded Mead. "With rest they both will survive, but they are not able to travel. A bit of salve and then we will have to leave them. Chief Gott, would you take care of moving the freight saddle from the wounded gray to one of the spare horses, then turn him and the injured roan loose," ordered Mead.

Aye aye, Mr. Mead," replied Hans Gott.

It took five men to loosen the packs and saddles from the terrified animals. Within minutes the crew was busy repacking.

"Captain, a word please," asked Pierce.

"Not now, Mr. Pierce," replied an agitated Chad.

"This fight, Captain, was not necessary," continued Pierce. "We could have turned back then taken another route."

"Pierce, stop your whining. Besides, I thought you would be pleased by the outcome. Isn't it the position of the American Government that the Monarchy in Mexico is illegitimate?"

"You are correct about the policy, Captain, but we were

non-combatants, actually foreign refugees until this clash. We should be granted freedom of passage."

"Mr. Pierce, that pompous French commander was never going to allow us to pass."

"We could have reversed course, Captain. We could find passage out of Tampico to the north. Now we have taken sides in this civil war."

"Not true, Pierce," an angry Chad responded. "We were pressed into a fight and defended ourselves. Besides, all of the French are dead."

"The Juaristas will boast of this battle and our part will be revealed," retorted Pierce. "There was no need for this violence."

"Enough Pierce. Your skin is no more valuable than any man here." Chad turned his gaze on the three new graves. "Just get away from me."

"Captain, thirty years ago, in a different era, I would have demanded satisfaction for your insult…" The confrontation was interrupted by the sound of shots fired where the coach waited.

"Captain," said Nick, studying the coach through his telescope, "there is a fight at the coach. Two outriders are being dragged to the side of the road. Two more appear to be dead and one is galloping toward us."

"Mount the crew, Mr. Kadzof. Mr. Mead, Doc Parker, please come with me," directed Chad. "Nick, when you get the rest of the men ready, follow." Gritt, Parker and Mead led their horses up out of the streambed and mounted. In seconds they were trotting through the scattered French bodies toward the bridge. They reached the road just as Carlos Rojas, his hands tied behind his back flashed past the men headed south at a gallop.

Gritt, the best horseman of the three kicked his mount in the ribs. Rojas' horse had already run a mile and was tiring. Still, it took Chad almost five minutes to finally maneuver alongside the lathered horse and grab the reigns next to the bit. Sliding his hand up the reigns he grabbed tightly and pulled with his right hand while pulling his own mount to a stop with his left.

Leaping from his mount, Rojas unleashed a string of Spanish that almost lifted Chad out of the saddle. Sliding from his saddle, Chad pulled the shorter of two knives from its sheath on Rojas' belt and severed the leather cord that bound Carlos' hands. The excited string of Spanish continued unabated from the tough ranch foreman.

"No entiendo, Señor," said Chad, he then pointed toward where the *KATARINA*'s crew was just coming up onto the road. "No entiendo, Señor."

Carlos Rojas finally stopped yelling. Taking a deep breath, he remounted his horse then gestured for Chad to join him. The two men walked their tired horses back toward the bridge. Four faint shots rang out from the direction of the coach.

"That's the story Captain," translated Pedro. "Gordo Rojas, the Juarista Commander demands that you deliver ten thousand dollars in gold to him at the village of Huajimic within five days. He will take the two young women to his camp, which he calls Pajaritos. His camp is in a deep canyon with sheer walls on three sides and an entrance that a dozen men could hold against an army. He will have men waiting in Huajimic for the gold. When you deliver it, he will return the young women. Then we can go on our way with his blessing."

"Please ask Carlos if this bandit can be trusted," requested Chad.

Pedro Davis and Carlos Rojas conversed for what seemed forever to the others. Finally, Pedro turned back to Chad shaking his head. "Gordo Rojas is his half-brother," noted Pedro. "His father married, then abandoned two women, leaving families, in adjoining villages. Carlos' mother was granted an annulment by the church because Carlos' father was still married to his previous wife. She remarried a fine Catholic ranch hand. The other woman was never able to get the church to dissolve her marriage. That family and Gordo lived as beggars. Her sons turned to stealing to support the family. He learned to steal and kill at an early age. No Captain, according to Carlos we cannot trust this bandito."

The troop mounted, turning toward the north. Cresting the hill, the men were greeted by a grizzly sight. The two ranch hands, traveling as coach guards, had been tied to trees. Both had been shot through the heart, their sagging bodies kneeling in a pool of blood. The graying old coach driver struggled under the weight of a tall young French officer whose bonds to a third tree he had just cut. The French Lieutenant grimaced as he tried to support part of his two-hundred-pound weight to lighten his gnarled rescuer's burden. The Frenchman's right pants leg was soaked with blood from the knee down.

Next to the coach, Camille de la Cruz knelt over Pablo, whose right pant leg had been slit open exposing a bloody bullet wound just above his right knee. Camille was doing her best to stop the bleeding by binding the wound with the long yellow scarf she wore as a hair cover. Camille's gray hair was streaked with crimson as was her cheek and forehead. Around her head a swarm of biting flies attracted by the blood tormented the woman. There was no sign of Denali or Pedro's sister, Anna.

In moments the crew, and Carlos Rojas, were out of their saddles and assisting the old carriage driver and Camille. Doc Parker, his medical bag in hand, knelt next to the gray-haired Spanish matron, and slipping a finger inside the blood-soaked scarf, he pulled it down to examine the wound.

"Nada," cried Camille, throwing a wicked elbow that caught Chris Parker just under his right eye. Turning, ready to fight she glared at the stunned Parker. Slowly, recognition crept into her eyes, while tears cut streaks through the dust and blood spatter on her face. "Excusa me por favor, Señor Doctor," she gasped. Burying her face in her bloody hands she began to sob.

Pedro Davis knelt next to the distraught woman. Wrapping his left arm around her shoulders he slowly helped the woman to her feet and walked her to the coach where he seated her on the step. He rummaged through the food box returning with a bottle of French Brandy and uncorked it. "Tia," he said offering the bottle to his aunt.

"How is he Doc?" asked Chad.

"The bullet went clean through the leg, and nicked the femur, but the leg is not broken. The tendons are torn, but it missed the artery, thank God. He will recover, but probably will always walk with a limp." Parker finished bandaging Pablo's leg. He mixed a dose of opium in a shot of brandy and offered the sedative to the wounded man.

Gathering his kit, he moved to where the French Officer sat leaning against a wheel of the carriage. Carlos Rojas had used one of the razor-sharp blades he carried to cut the entire pants leg off at the officer's knee.

"Nick," ordered Chad, "have the men cut those two young men down." He pointed at the two executed ranch hands. "Find something to wrap the bodies in," he continued.

"This man will spend the rest of his life with a fused leg Captain," said Doc Parker. "This knee will never bend again. What kind of butcher is this Gordo Rojas? Why kill the two young vaqueros and only maim the other two men?"

"If you will give me just a touch of your pain medication I will try to explain," the French officer told a startled Doc Parker, in perfect English.

"We were surrounded and didn't even know they were here until that fool, Colonel leMark, attacked your excellent defensive position. After leMark let you slaughter my troop, and then turned to run away, the bandits came out of the woods all around us. My four troopers were mounted, and I ordered them to flee. But they were already doomed. My horse was tied too far away to do me any good. Gordo's men held us until he arrived. After he sent Carlos back to talk to you, he ordered the two young men from the ranch to join his soldiers. When they refused to leave the ladies, he had them tied up and then personally shot them from only three feet away while laughing in their faces."

"Then he had the Spanish gentleman and I tied to trees as well. We knew it was our time to die. Instead, he told Señor Ramirez that he had a lesson for his Royalist father from the Juaristas; then laughed and shot him in the knee! My role was to tell the world of Gordo Rojas' great victory over Colonel leMark and then leave Mexico. After he told me no army would want a one-legged soldier, he spat in my face and shot me in the knee."

"Well lieutenant, he probably did give you a ticket home," replied Parker.

"Doctor, my French father, a retired Bonaparte civil servant, is not a man you would travel halfway around the world to return home to. My English mother passed away years ago. I am engaged to a Mexican woman; Mexico is my home. It is not a place for leMark or Gordo Rojas."

Lieutenant, your knee needs a surgeon. The bone fragments from the kneecap and the underlying joint must be removed. A skilled surgeon might be able to give you some knee movement. How do we get you to such a physician?"

"There is a regimental surgeon in Guadalajara where the answer to such wounds is amputation," said the Frenchman wiping tears of pain from his eyes. "I would prefer to splint the leg and travel with you to Mexico."

Chad frowned, "Lieutenant, what is your name?"

"Andre, Andre Mare," replied the Lieutenant with a groan.

"Andre, we will take you with us for now, but once we form a plan to find the hostages we will be moving fast, too fast for a wounded man."

"Captain, I watched how your men sit a horse. Even with a splinted leg and in an opium stupor, I can outride all but a handful."

"Very well, Andre, I will consider your request later. For now, we must discuss our next move among the officers."

Chad used the carriage wheel behind the French Lieutenant to pull himself to his feet. "Mr. Gott, please pass the word that there will be an officer's meeting immediately."

Carlos Rojas and Camille de la Cruz joined the ship's officers, Mead, and Pierce.

"Captain, Carlos Rojas will escort the coach, Pablo and Camille, back to Tepic where the mayor, town doctor and the townspeople are all friends of the family," translated Pedro. "Camille suggests that we make camp where the road to Huajimic turns east. She thinks we need to wait for Carlos to return before turning up the road."

"Why should we not push on to Huajimic and ransom the women?" asked Chad.

"Both Carlos and Camille agree that the minute Gordo has his hands on the gold he will kill the hostages, or worse, give them to his men," answered Pedro after an animated discussion. "Carlos will send for two Indian trackers he knows who could track a breeze through the trees. He will return in no more than three days."

Chad nodded. "Until we know exactly where Anna and Denali are being held, we cannot develop a plan." Turning to the assembled officers Chad asked for any other ideas. His inquiry was met with silence.

Camille whispered something into Pedro's ear. "My aunt asks that we take the French officer with us. After what the French did at Tepic his life would be worthless there."

"I have already explained to the Lieutenant that we cannot take a wounded man," replied Chad.

"Excuse me, Captain," interjected Doc Parker, "but if I have a day in camp to work on Andre's leg, I can probably do more to help him than the local doctors. If I get the shattered bones out of the knee it will reduce the pain." Doc looked over at the young French officer. "We may be able to use his language skills."

"Alright Doc," replied Chad, "but get him out of that uniform tonight and make sure he understands that if he becomes a burden he is on his own."

An hour later, the coach departed with Camille and the wounded Pablo inside. The two murdered vaqueros, wrapped in blankets, rode in the boot. With the coach driver on top Rojas led the way.

The *KATARINA's* company followed, but lost sight of the faster coach in less than an hour. Andre, well-fortified with brandy and opium had been correct, he was not the cause of the company's slow pace.

25
ON THE HUAJIMIC ROAD, MEXICO

"IF IT WORKS," voiced Parker, "he will walk someday, if not, a French surgeon can fuse the knee later. I do not have the steel rods necessary to do it here. Maybe he will get lucky." The doctor dropped his instruments into boiling water, over an unwelcome fire in the scorching sun.

"You did what you could," replied Mead. "I have never seen such work before."

"With only minutes to work on each man after a big battle, I could not have done this kind of work. The Frenchman's good fortune is merely a result of time, nothing else. By the way, have you seen the Captain?"

"He and Pierce walked down toward the river a few minutes ago, and I haven't heard any shots," replied Mead. "Now allow me to buy you a brandy to celebrate your skills."

"We won't know whether it is a success or not for weeks."

"Okay, then let's have a brandy because I need one after watching that."

"The camp was set just south of the road junction, in another pasture along another river. With the party already two days behind schedule and perhaps a week more of non-travel in front of them, the ship's cook and Pedro had canvased three small farms and returned with a basket of vegetables and a worn one-eared sheep thrown over a saddle. Dinner that night was already simmering in two huge pots. Angelo had never made a mutton stew before, but he and his customers hoped for the best.

The afternoon breeze rattled the dull, gray-green leaves of the ironwood trees. The riverbed was strewn with boulders the size of water kegs among water ran only inches deep after weeks without rain. Chad used a stick to flip over a large flat rock in a shallow eddy. Four large crayfish scampered from their former hiding place, into the current, and with a flip of their tails disappeared down river.

Chad's boots and socks rested on a fallen log only a few feet away. The same log that Miles Standish Pierce was seated on. His fanny firmly planted on a huge boulder; Chad bathed his sweaty feet in the hole just vacated by the crayfish. The pounding sun sliced through the branches overhanging the river. Chad closed his eyes against the glare, his mind filling with thoughts of Denali and a deep river pool. He had almost pushed Pierce completely out of his consciousness. Pierce was having none of that.

"You don't like me very much," started Pierce.

Damn, I interrupt this beautiful dream for a S.O.B. like Pierce. He could not bring himself to answer.

"That's alright, you are not my favorite person either. Still, it is critical that we help one another."

"What do you want, Pierce?"

"I want to discuss our mission to Russian America. To get it right we will have to be somewhat civil. Do you not agree?"

"You were right the first time, Pierce, I don't like you."

"I'm listening."

"Well, since the trip began you have shown a selfish bent that ignores the teamwork needed on a mission like this."

"Go on," replied the Secretary.

"In for a penny, in for a pound, you're a coward Pierce. First you want to just hand the ship to the rebels. Today you want to surrender to the French, to a buffoon of a colonel, who was going to kill all of us. And you shirk the duty, the work necessary for us all to get home. You think your wealth and family make you somehow better, more important, than the rest of us. While the company pushed hard for Acapuneta, you ask to sit on your ass, waiting for us to send back a carriage. No, Mr. Secretary I do not look upon you fondly."

Pierce reached into a lapel pocket of the gray vest he wore over his filthy white shirt. His hand emerged with a flask and the Emperor's letter. He handed both to Chad.

The richness of the port in the flask was like nothing Chad had every experienced "May I have another pull?"

"Keep it, and the flask. I have the rest of the bottle in my things. I gave two bottles to Charlie Lampoc. He could keep one if he carried the other for me."

Chad tilted the flask again, shaking his head in disgust.

"Rank has its privilege, and both advantages and disadvantages. You have a taste of the privilege in your hand." Pierce paused. "I can ride with the best of men. In one day of hunting in Scotland, I shot three running stags, killing each with one shot, none under two hundred yards."

"I entered the foreign service directly from college, my family name certainly opening doors. Wealth allowed me to meet the diplomatic and social overtures of diplomats from far richer governments, when the small stipend provided by my own government would not even pay for a decent apartment in Europe. As a civil servant I have earned the confidence of both Secretary of Seward and the President," Pierce proclaimed wiping sweat from his chin.

"But I lack certain skills, Captain Gritt. I barely know the difference between a screwdriver and a hammer. I cannot prepare a decent meal. And until this trip I have never been tested in contests of survival, or endurance. I have never seen a man killed before. I have never before been frightened. I thought I had, but never like this. And I am not very good at showing my weakness or ineptitude. I have used words to diffuse tense situations both public and private, all of my life."

Chad unscrewed the cap on the flask and washed another small measure over his tongue. There was a small crack in his angry demeanor, but his tongue could form no words.

"Anyway, Captain, about my mission. I asked to travel to Russian America to counter what I suspect will be a glowing report from Mr. Mead. I make no apologies. I have felt that this whole Russian America thing was a great folly. I personally have been advocating for American intervention here in Mexico. If our huge standing army were to intervene in Mexico on the side of Benito Juarez, we could crush the Royalists in months. Once we were here, we could dictate homestead rights for Americans in Mexico. I believed that within ten years, Mexico could be persuaded to become part of the United States, just like Texas. With good government and capital this land could bloom."

Chad smiled, "You really missed the whole scene in Russian America, Pierce. There is more untapped wealth there than in all of Mexico. This place is a powder keg. You could not bring stability to Mexico in fifty years let alone ten."

"The thing is Captain; I agree with you. My counsel was colored by my feelings. The report on Russian America in my pack ignores much of what I saw and heard on our voyage. The days here in Mexico have changed me, and my thoughts. An American intervention here would be treated by much of the population the same as the European intervention, with Maximilian. An American intervention would become a quagmire. The Europeans would resent our direct replacement of their effort in a Catholic nation."

"What exactly are you saying, Mr. Secretary"?"

"I am saying that I was wrong about Russian America, and about Mexico."

"For a small sum of money, we can add great wealth through acquiring Russian America. To acquire Mexico will take tens of millions of dollars and thousands of lives, and in the end, I think we would fail. The fight here is about independence not freedom."

Gritt leaned back against the rock behind him. He practiced plucking stones from the river bottom with the bare toes off his left foot, and then switched to the right. He attempted the feat with both feet at once, a game of discipline he had learned from his father. It was easier in the warm Mexican river than Alaska's bitterly cold streams. "I'll be damned," he finally managed. "What do you want from me?"

"I will begin to rewrite my report this evening. I want you to get us all home safely so that I can deliver my report and share my observations with the Secretary and the President. I promised the Emperor that I would deliver the letter in your hand. And, if by chance I should not make it home, I would appreciate you delivering it to Secretary Seward and making my feelings known."

"Alright, Miles, stick close to me or Mead. We will do our best to get you home with all of your parts attached."

"One more thing, Captain, I have never felt this alive. Is this abnormal, that is, to feel exhilarated by danger and conflict?"

"I'm no military veteran," started Chad, then he paused. "No, Mr. Secretary. But it is dangerous. Do what needs to be done but listen to your fear. It will keep you alive."

Chad tipped the flask one last time. "Today we faced lancers, men with a long toad stickers and a small pistol. With our repeating rifles, and you and the rest with the Sharps rifles, we had the advantage. Only the field gun threatened us. Your marksmanship helped blunt the one French advantage."

"I will take that as a compliment Captain. I felt no compassion for the French soldiers that I dispatched today. They lost any right to respect with what they did to that boy. If I could have, I would have killed every one of them."

"Mr. Secretary, I wager that we have at least one more fight coming, with Gordo Rojas band. They will not line up and ride into our lead torrent. They have seen how lethal we can be."

Chad picked up a handful of stones and began flipping them into the deeper pools behind rocks in the river. Occasionally a small fish would dart away and once a larger one. The thorny shrubs across the river seemed to wilt in the sun, tilting their yellow flowers almost to the water. The beauty was offset by the smell of what was left of a large dead animal rotting on the other side of the river.

"Keep your head down, Mr. Secretary." He handed the letter back to Pierce.

26
GORDO ROJAS VALLEY, MEXICO

AT MIDDAY, TWO days later, Carlos Rojas rode into camp with two dark skinned men. Both had high cheekbones and long straight black hair. Each was dressed as a vaquero except for the soft moccasins wrapping their feet and lower legs. Through Pedro he introduced the two Yaqui Indian brothers to Chad and Nick.

"Normally Yaka and Juan keep the wolves and el tigre away from the flocks and cattle. They can track an ant across a boulder. They will help us find the banditos," said Carlos through Pedro. "Break camp leisurely tomorrow morning and move up the road toward Huajimic. Juan, Yaka and I will rest for only an hour then we will spend the afternoon and night in the saddle. We will find you tomorrow afternoon. By then we should be able to tell you exactly where the senoritas are being held. If we have not rejoined you by the time you reach Huajimic, set up camp just outside of town and we will find you overnight."

"We will move slowly and ineptly, Carlos," replied Nick through Pedro. "We will buy you a couple of days to scout." He paused for a moment. "Take Chad with you. He knows our company and our capabilities. Finding the ladies is only step one. We must develop a plan to get them back."

⁂

The four men skirted Huajimic then turned straight north following a wagon trail along a tiny stream. Yaka and Juan rode paralleling the trail left and right. Every hilltop and outcrop were scrutinized, every thicket searched but no sentinels were found. Gordo Rojas no doubt had observers in the tiny town, but he obviously felt safe in his Pajaritos hide away.

His arrogance, or stupidity, had allowed him to make a huge mistake that directed the four followers, as if he had posted signs. His band had gathered up many of the loose mounts no longer needed by the recently departed French cavalry. Unlike the Juarista horses, some unshod, others with a variety of horseshoes, all of the French horses had identical shoes. The wider shoes with their rough cleated surface painted a trail that even Chad could follow.

Chad spoke only limited Spanish, and his amigos spoke no English at all. Yet through hand signals, drawings in the dust, and common purpose they became a team. In the pre-dawn the next morning the men halted behind a thicket of silver thorn bushes. In front of them only two miles away was a cleft in a sheer rock wall, the width of two wagons. The walls on either side were sandstone faces. Behind the rock face steep ridges could be seen to the left and the right, separating enough to allow a valley no more than a half-mile wide between them.

Some ancient earth movement that split the wall like breaking glass, had created the opening between the ridges. The closest side was fronted by a mass of boulders at the foot of the wall. Through the center, a stream had worn a gap in the soft rock as cleanly as if carved with a knife. Chad retrieved his telescope from the pack on the back of his saddle. It took only moments to find the guards posted high on the top of the sandstone walls. Chad passed the telescope to Carlos who passed them on to the Yaqui brothers. The entrance to Gordo's sanctuary was a perfect defensive position. Ten men could hold the gap against an army and Rojas had, they guessed, a hundred men.

Kneeling, Carlos used the palm of his hand to smooth the surface of the dry earth. With a stick he diagramed the valley entrance and his guess as to the shape of the valley. He outlined his plan to skirt the valley to the west and then, moving his fingers like a man walking, his plan to climb the western ridge to observe. Chad stood, studying the land to the west. The ground was rugged but barren. An occasional shrub or cactus stood amongst occasional boulders. Otherwise, the land was empty sand and gullies sloping slowly down from the ridges.

How could they move without being seen he wondered?

Juan, leading his horse, traced a route through the scrub and rock using every bit of cover. Tiny ripples in the terrain, invisible from the road, crisscrossed the desert. In less than an hour they were a mile from the road, where they left the horses in a shaded spot.

The previous weeks of effort had hardened Chad after months at sea. Still, he felt like a child next to his three companions, who scampered up the steep ridge like monkeys, waiting frequently for him to catch up. The walls, like the desert, looked like sheer rock faces, but like the ground they just crossed, offered tiny creases and ledges. Nearing the top Juan chose a low spot to conceal their movement. The smooth rock made sliding on their stomachs easy. Below them was an oasis in the harsh foothills. A dozen adobe buildings stretched along the valley floor like a small town. To the east a huge green pasture held well more than a hundred horses.

A stream, running from a small cavern in the northern wall of the valley, had been dammed and a pool of five or six acres formed the northern end of the pasture. A second pool even closer to the spring carried water to the buildings in a well-planned, small rock-lined ditch. Trees and gardens filled the valley floor. Thick brush and a bed of reeds directly below the men indicated more water seeps from the western ridge where they lay. The walls around the valley were sheer drops of a hundred feet or more.

While the men watched, more than a dozen women emerged from the buildings and began to fix breakfast. The men studied the scene below as more light filtered into the shadows. Chad lifted his telescope almost getting it to his eyes before a flashing hand slapped the fragile device into the dust. Yaka pointed to the eastern ridge, then at the telescope that lay below Chad's jaw. Yaka closed his hand into a fist, then snapped his fingers open; then repeated the motion.

Chad shook his head, confused. He picked up the long glass just as the sun rising over the far ridge illuminated them with a golden glow. "Gracias," he mouthed as he slowly realized how the sun on the lens would reflect into the valley.

A bell rang from the camp below and within minutes long lines of men paraded past the cooks, and then found spots at extended tables. Chad counted one hundred and ten men, which meant that there were at least one hundred and twenty including the guards.

After the men were served, one of the women placed two plates on a platter along with a coffee pot and cups, and carried it to a tiny adobe hut, no more than four hundred yards below the ridge where the men lay. A guard at the door opened it for the woman, who entered and then exited a moment later, with Denali and Anna behind her. She led the women around behind the hut to an open-air latrine. With no cover except some brush, the facility offered little privacy. Within minutes the women were again locked in their mud brick jail.

The sun's rays crawled down the wall of the western ridge where Chad and his three Mexican companions secluded themselves, then across the valley floor. The bright light illuminated new detail. To their right, where the road and the stream slipped through the narrow gap, the walls rose almost vertically on either side of the road. At the top of the rampart on the left side was a flat mesa no more than a quarter acre across. In the front of the mesa a small adobe hut with a large, covered porch provided shelter from the blistering sun for the sentries.

The western side rose a little higher than the mesa side. There a natural overhang in the sandstone offered cover from the elements. Set well under the stone roof, a complex of walls and an ancient building of stacked rocks sheltered another group of guards. Forcing the entrance to the valley would be a suicide mission. Five men on each side, firing from positions almost invisible to any attacker below, could hold the valley.

Chad slipped back a few feet until Carlos' body sheltered him from any chance that the sun would reflect from his telescope as he studied the entrance.

From outside the valley, the position was unassailable. On the opposite side of the valley, a narrow set of steps cut into the sandstone, led from the valley to the sentries' perch. Even if the men could get into the valley, fighting up those steps would be suicide. Behind the flat mesa a tangle of boulders led to the ridge wrapping around the eastern side of the valley. Any attackers would have to scale the far ridge and attack from behind the hut to be successful.

Chad shifted his focus to the sentry position at the end of the ridge where he lay hidden. While he watched, two men emerged from the rock hut. Two other men rose from well-camouflaged positions right on the edge of the drop to the road below and waived to two men in similar holes carved into the edge of the mesa across the gap. The first men picked up a long flat box with rope handles and proceeded to walk along a low wall built up along the cliff. The men picked up more than twenty light brown sticks which lay along the top of the wall, spaced every few feet. Short cords dangled from the edge of the box, giving away the last secret of the valley's defense, dynamite.

These guys are very good, thought Chad. They prepare for an instant response at night, when an enemy could creep close under the cloak of darkness. Yet he and his companions had evaded the guards. All of the preparations assumed a mass attack from the front.

Carlos tapped Chad with his foot, pointing toward the valley floor. Four men had started up the steps to the far mesa. On their side of the valley four men led a small, loaded burro up a narrow path cut into the sandstone toward the natural overhang and the rock building to his right. The burro carried two goatskins of water. Chad watched intensely as the group with the burro reached the western lookout. They untied one of the water bags and carried it to a lean-to, where they poured it into what appeared to be a cistern carved into the rock, covering the tank with a wooden cover.

The men then carried the second bag onto a platform cut into the sandstone behind the hut and hoisted it. A moment later the dripping bag slid down a cable toward two men waiting on the mesa side. The men carried it to a similar cistern. He had missed the cable. He had seen enough and motioned for the others to retreat from their hide. Before they could move, a shot rang out from across the valley. Two more sentries stood waiving on the far ridge.

All four of the hidden men began to search around them for any sentries that they might have missed. A moment later three men on horseback emerged from a second cleft in the far wall and turned toward the camp. The men dismounted next to the only private table in the outdoor kitchen. A rotund man, with a huge mustache, and dark hair rose from the table and extended his hand toward a tall graying man in an expensive suit who had just ridden into camp. His comrades took up positions behind the gentleman who refused the hand.

Chad didn't know who the newcomer was, but he was certain that the rotund man was Gordo Rojas. It was clear from several hundred yards away that the two men were arguing. A moment later the disagreement exploded as Rojas drew his pistol and smashed it into the side of the gentleman's head. The gentleman's companions lunged toward Rojas who calmly shot each of them in the chest and then stepping over the unconscious gentleman shot each in the head.

Rojas sat down to finish his breakfast while the gentleman was dragged to the same hut that held Denali and Anna. Rojas gestured to several others of his band, who grabbed the two dead men by the legs and dragged them off toward the pasture. Four men with shovels followed.

The four watchers used the distraction to slide off from the ridge.

27
PAJARITOS HIDEOUT, MEXICO

THE TRIP BACK to where the camp was a blur to Gritt. He could recall little of the lands they passed through. His mind was fully focused on the outlaw's valley. Arriving, he tumbled from his horse, burying his face in the river between the heads of two horses. He continued to drink even as the horses backed away. Rising, he relished his water-soaked hair and shirt as he made his way to the gathering of men forming around a smoky fire remnant and a battered coffee pot.

"Jeffe," translated Pedro, "the hostage's name is Jeffe. He is the political representative of el Presidente Juarez in this district. Carlos feels that the argument was over the kidnapping of my sister and Denali." Pedro had been translating continuously since the scouts had ridden into camp. A plan had taken shape in Chad's head as he rode in the scorching afternoon sun. He just hoped that it wasn't the product of heat stroke.

Hans Gott, the ship's chief, was put to work preparing the crew. The lengths of rope that each crewman carried had been gathered and three teams were busy splicing them into long ropes. Other men were packing cold ration packages. Sergeant Mosby ordered his two remaining marines to clean the rifles of the men who would make up the rescue party.

"Their perfect fortress becomes their perfect prison," snickered Nick. "I wish I were going."

"Nick, you and Pedro are the key to the whole plan," replied Chad. "You must convince Gordo's representatives that the gold will be in Huajimic the day after tomorrow. We need two days. Carlos will send Juan and Yaka back to Pajaritos tonight, to find a route up the east-ridge and to find the entrance to the narrow passage that we saw Jeffe and his men use."

"Those men have been on their feet for days. Why not let these men eat a hot meal and get some sleep?" suggested Parker.

"They will eat," translated Pedro. "They can take turns sleeping in the saddle on their way back to the valley. They will meet us tomorrow afternoon two miles this side of the valley entrance. We wait for nightfall to climb the ridges."

Chad sat staring at the men in the circle. "Mr. Mead, you're right, it would be impossible for you to climb down the rope with one arm. Still, I wish you were leading."

"I like my part."

Chad remembered the feeling in his stomach the day he rescued Mead. He swallowed. "Then you take your men and join Yaka. Secure the east mesa and the hidden trail. Sergeant, you will take four men up the west ridge with us and seize the rock ruins. Carlos, Juan, Mr. Pierce and I will drop into the valley and find Denali and Anna, then we will slip across the valley and wait at the entrance to the hidden trail. Thomas, we will wait for your signal that the sentries watching the trail are gone."

Carlos whispered something into Pedro's ear.

"Captain," interjected Pedro, "Carlos reminds you that many of the men in Gordo Rojas band are local men whose only interest is Benito Juarez. Their only crime is being led by a bandit."

"He is right, gentlemen, we are not part of this war. We will not take revenge. Use your ammunition sparingly," ordered Chad. "The job of the men with Sharps rifles is to keep everybody's head down in the valley," continued Chad.

Mosby added, "Concentrate on the doors of the buildings. That should keep most of Rojas' men indoors."

"Finally," added Chad, "Doc you take the last two men and cover the entrance to the valley. A few men can stop anyone from getting in, but three men with repeating rifles can also stop an army from getting out."

"Captain," interjected Mosby, "we can keep their heads down until you get out, but the minute we pull off, those boys will be saddled up and on our tail. There's a whole lot more of them than us and they know the land. We won't stand a chance in open country."

"That's where the dynamite comes in," continued Chad. "While I was watching the west rim, I saw men gathering at least twenty sticks of dynamite laid out as part of their nighttime defense. Plant enough along both rims of the entrance to drop a tangle of boulders onto the road. Do the same on the hidden trail. By the time they clear enough rock to get horses out of the valley, we will be a hundred miles away."

"How do I get dynamite from the west rim to the mesa?" asked Mosby.

"You will figure it out when you get there," laughed Chad, "Gordo Rojas has built you a transport system."

"How do we get horses for ourselves and the young ladies?" asked Pierce. "We have no idea where the hidden trail comes out."

"We will take three extra horses. Pedro, please ask Carlos to have Yaka leave them at the far end of the hidden trail."

"The clock starts ticking when you blast the entrance. Everyone will meet four hours after the rock comes down. Any questions?

A half hour later Nick slipped up next to Chad. "Why are you taking Pierce down into the Valley?"

Chad shook his head and frowned. "To keep an eye on him. And the man can shoot."

28
PAJARITOS HIDEOUT, MEXICO

GRITT AND PIERCE sat side by side studying the valley. "Thank you for taking me with you today. I will try not to let you down," whispered Pierce.

"Mr. Secretary, you are going into the valley because you are the best marksman we have. If either Mosby or Mead fails to take their objectives, we should still make it to the hidden trail if we are quiet and stay hidden. I saw no guards inside the valley itself.

"If we will not need to fight, why do you need a marksman?"

"If Mead fails, we will have the two guards covering the hidden trail to contend with. They will be above us, and well hidden. A man with a rifle, shooting from below will have a very small target."

"What if both Mead and Mosby fail Captain?"

"Then a lot of good men, including the two of us, are going to die. Now if you are ready, Carlos and Juan have the rope in place. We should use this small skiff of clouds over the moon to hide our decent. We have only a half-hour to find the girls and cross the valley. First light is at 6:10; that's when Mosby and Mead will come off from the ridges and the grand show begins."

It took only ten minutes for Gritt, Pierce, Carlos and Juan to repel down the sheer rock face and conceal themselves in the thick reeds of the desert marsh below. There were tiny rivulets of water where ancient springs emptied their contents, but while the ground was damp, the warm desert air kept the springs from creating pools. The men emerged from the reeds with nothing more than wet boots.

From the reeds, it was a hundred yards across flat, rocky ground to the rear of the adobe. Juan led the way pausing first at the remains of a rock wall, then behind an old two wheeled cart, finally kneeling under a huge willow tree that marked the location of another spring. Carlos was right behind him.

Carlos motioned for Chad and Miles to wait under the drooping branches of the tree as he and Juan crept the final forty yards to the back of the hut. Both men had left their rifles under the tree. There was just enough moonlight for Chad to catch a momentary glint of moonlight on the polished steel blades that filled each man's hands. The men stopped behind the hut before separating. Both men disappeared and less than a minute later Carlos reappeared motioning for Miles and Chad to join him.

Behind the hut they found the guard crumpled, his shirt bloody, his throat cut. Juan knelt next to the grizzled, old, veteran wiping the blood from his knife on the man's cotton vest. He then tugged a narrow-bladed throwing knife from the man's ribs, wiped away the blood and handed it to Carlos.

"Remember, the man they called Jeffe is also in the adobe," whispered Pierce.

"Jeffe," said Chad quietly to Carlos, pointing toward the knife in the vaquero's right hand. Chad then made a throwing motion.

Carlos shook his head "No," then slipping the blade into a sheath at his back he stood and unlatched the crude wooden door. "Jeffe mi amigo," he whispered as he entered. "Señorita de la Cruz, es me Carlos," he added. A murmur from inside the hut was met with a sharp "silencio."

Juan dragged the dead guard around the cabin and returned wearing the dead man's broad sombrero and cradling the guard's ancient rifle in his arms. He motioned for Chad and Miles to enter the adobe.

"My dear God," whispered Denali, "where did you come from, mi Captain?" Denali leaped the three steps across the tiny hut and threw her arms around Chad's neck, kissing him wildly. In the corner, Pierce helped a stunned Anna to her feet motioning for her to put her shoes on. In the other corner Carlos and Jeffe huddled talking rapidly in Spanish.

"Captain Gritt, I am Edwardo de Harmons. I am the man the Juaristas like my friend Carlos here, and Señorita de la Cruz, call Jeffe."

Jeffe spoke flawless English with only a slight accent. He laughed, noticing Chad's expression. "I spent four years in your home town, Boston," he said. "Within the government of President Juarez, I am an Assistant Minister of State."

"Mr. Minister, may I present my compatriot in tonight's adventure, Under Secretary of State Miles Standish Pierce."

"Secretary Pierce," said Jeffe, extending his hand. "I know of you. I understand that you favor Mexico becoming part of the United States." Again, Jeffe laughed, staring at Pierce's stunned look.

"Every country has its intelligence requirements; am I not correct Mr. Secretary?"

"Rest assured Mr. Minister, that after several weeks, under difficult circumstances, any thoughts that I might have had along those lines are forever gone."

"I am pleased to hear that, Mr. Secretary. Someday we might discuss how your country with its civil war behind it, can help our young republic throw out these European interlopers."

"That of course, is a possibility Mr. Minister. You know that the United States opposes all European intervention in the hemisphere. What do you need?"

"We need repeating rifles like the ones you carry. We need modern artillery like that no longer needed by the Confederate Army."

"Gentlemen," snapped Chad, "now is not the time. We have only fifteen minutes until all hell breaks loose."

"You are right of course, Captain. Carlos here has explained the plan to me. I am sorry about the abduction. If I could stop this right now I would but the soldiers here will take orders only from Gordo Rojas as long as he lives. They live in fear of Rojas, and his girl boy, lieutenant Paco. Captain, you and Secretary Pierce take the senoritas to the trail. Juan will guide you. Carlos and I will follow in a few minutes."

Chad watched as Juan slipped his knife sheath from his belt and handed it to Jeffe.

"We have a short stop to make on the way," continued Jeffe, "to settle an account."

As the others followed a rock wall, toward the horse pasture at the far side of the valley, Carlos and Jeffe crept into the home where Gordo and Paco shared a bed. The first light of day helped them find their way, but also increased the risk of discovery.

The main group had secreted themselves for only a minute before rifle fire from the western rim shredded the quiet morning. Only four or five heavy reports interrupted the twenty sharp cracks of Mosby's repeaters. A moment later a dozen cracks from the eastern ridge were answered by only two reports from the defenders. Then almost above their heads two loud reports were answered by sharp cracks from two Henry rifles.

Lights began to flicker in the windows of a number of the buildings. A door opened in the largest barracks, silhouetting a man in the light from inside. A rifle boomed from the eastern ridge and the man slammed back through the door, lifted completely off from his feet by a heavy bullet from a Sharps rifle. A half dozen more reports from both the eastern ridge and the western ridge were answered by silence from the defenders. The crew gave the Juaristas no targets.

Carlos and Jeffe were the only men visible in the valley. They were running stooped at the waist behind the same wall that the rest of the rescue party had followed. The crash of a Sharps rifle above sent a round toward the two men. The shot slapped splinters of rock into the air behind them. A second shot missed the running men. Then the men were cloaked by the edge of the ridge itself. Minutes later they ran close to where the rescuers and rescued lay hidden. Both were puffing like locomotives.

"Over here," shouted Pierce.

Rifle shots from the buildings below began to pepper the rocks around the two men. Unable to run further they walked the last twenty feet to cover and collapsed against the rock wall that sheltered them.

"Captain," a voice carried from the ridge above. "Captain, the trail is clear."

"Gentlemen," said Chad to the two out of breath men, "gentlemen, we must go. Mr. Pierce, will you give us some covering fire while we get started down the trail?"

Pierce picked up his rifle and sighted on the closest building and proceeded to smash four windows with his first six shots. As he fed more bullets into the rifle the others slipped into a four-foot crack in the rock behind them and started down the trail.

"Did you take care of the problem back there?" asked Chad.

"Indeed, we did," replied Jeffe. "I have wanted to eliminate that garbage for years. We left the two lovers' hearts pinned together on a knife blade over their bed."

Chad shuddered but said nothing.

Pierce began a slow rhythmic series of shots again. Chad halted his trot and turned back toward the shots. Pierce stood at the entrance to the trail, the rifle this time at his left shoulder which allowed him to shoot with little of his body exposed to the Juaristas, who were working their way along the same rock wall that had sheltered the escapees. As he watched, Pierce fired the seventh shot from his rifle and stepped back into the shelter of the trail.

Beyond Pierce his shots had left a grayish blue cloud of smoke enveloping the entrance to the cleft. "*Damn*" thought Chad, "*you could not have painted a clearer sign pointing to our escape route.*"

A small pebble bounced off from Chad's head. His sharp reflexes left him staring into the grinning face of Charles. The huge Cherokee crewman was leaning out over the narrow canyon from the plateau above, waiting for orders. "You may bring down the house as soon as you see Pierce come by."

"Aye aye, Captain." "You have two minutes before Joshua blows his horn."

Chad put two fingers to his mouth, and a shrill whistle screeched down the canyon.

Pierce had just resumed firing. He squeezed off another shot, and leaving the hammer on the spent shell, he turned and sprinted toward Chad. Chad stepped aside as Pierce slid past him.

"There is no one following us. They just dragged two bodies out of Gordo's house and the entire army is just milling around arguing," said Pierce.

Chad nodded, a smile on his face. "You can slow to a trot Miles. We have friends in high places," pointing up at the rim. "Don't give yourself a heart attack."

"I am more afraid of the dynamite than the Mexicans."

The trail continued straight for another two hundred yards and then jogged to the right. Just around the bend, where the trail widened, Denali, Anna, Jeffe and Pierce stood waiting.

"Juan went ahead to scout the end of the trail," advised Denali.

"We'd better get moving," said Chad. "It is going to get noisy down here in a minute."

The four made it just past a second bend, this time to the left, when a deafening blast sent a shock wave and a cloud of dust down the canyon, knocking both women from their feet. Rising, they kept moving, their ears ringing. Three more loud explosions chased them from the mouth of the cleft. The trail dropped into a shallow ravine for a quarter mile, which itself emptied into a curved valley around the ridge.

A small stream trickled through the bottom of the valley. A thicket of ironwood offered the only cover in the barren valley where the party made their way down a short, steep track.

Seated, with his back to a large boulder was Juan, his head on his chest and his shirt covered with blood. A dead horse lay in front of him, and across the narrow stream another. There also, two Mexican banditos, both bleeding from multiple wounds, lay dead.

Denali knelt next to the injured Yaqui. Juan lifted his chin from his chest and smiled. In a labored voice he whispered something to Denali. "He caught them stealing the horses," she said. "Juan thanks you, Captain, for the rifle that shoots many times. The only problem with the gun, is that it makes small holes," she continued.

Denali carefully unbuttoned Juan's shirt. A small wound just below the clavicle seeped blood. Pulling his shirt down over the shoulder, she coaxed the weary Yaqui to sit up and ran her right hand over his upper back. "The bullet, it is high. I think it miss Juan's lung. This is good. Juan must hurt very much though; his shoulder blade is broken."

She slipped Juan's knife from its sheath and used the tip to cut a small slit at the shoulder in each sleeve of her black long-sleeved blouse. She tugged at the sleeves until each ripped away. She handed one to Chad and folded the other into a pad and pressed it against the wound. "You will please cut the cloth into long strips. We will need six pieces."

Chad enlisted the help of Anna and Pierce to stretch the cloth. Using the small sharp splicing knife that he carried, he split the sleeve lengthwise.

"Anna," commanded Denali, "you hold bandage while Captain Gritt and I tie arm and shoulder tightly." Anna knelt and pressed her hand inside Juan's blood-soaked shirt. Chad and Denali used the strips of cloth to bind Juan's left arm tightly to his chest, and then created a sling to support the arm. Finally, with the last two strips Denali bound the bandage tightly against Juan's chest. During the ordeal the tough young Indian never murmured a sound.

"You take hand away now Anna."

Chad watched, as Anna gently released the pressure on the bandage, her eyes still tightly closed as she stood. She opened her eyes and stared at her bloody hand and arm. Her knees buckled and she would have collapsed if Pierce had not wrapped an arm around her, lowering her to the ground.

"When I first become nurse, I too faint at sight of blood."

"Where is Jeffe?" asked Chad.

Pierce pointed down the trail, where Jeffe led two horses back toward the rest of the band. Ten minutes later, Pierce, cradling Anna in front of him and Jeffe supporting the wounded Juan, started down the trail toward the meeting place.

"We will send horses back as quickly as we can," said Pierce. Carlos, on foot, was already well down the trail, his eyes glued to the hard ground as he used his years of tacking skills to retrace the route. "We should not be more than an hour."

In less than five minutes the riders had disappeared. Denali took Chad's hand and pulled him toward the stream. "Come my Captain," she said, "I need a bath. Then I reward you properly for my rescue." Denali tugged the tail of her blouse from her riding pants and with her other hand unbuttoned it.

A quarter mile away, Mead watched Gordo's men loot his house. There would be no pursuit. The soldiers of Gordo Rojas would drink their breakfast. He watched two of his men slide the body of their sole casualty down toward the waiting horses.

29
SIERRA MADRE MOUNTAINS, MEXICO

"BY NOW CAPTAIN Gritt, Gordo's band will be discussing what to do now that their leader awaits judgment. The forces of President Juarez are very weak in this area, and we cannot afford for Gordo's small army to disband," said Jeffe.

"Won't Gordo's men take revenge for his death?" asked Pierce.

"No Mr. Secretary, the soldiers of Juarez will respect the strength of those who introduced the bandit to justice. His weakness as a leader was proven when your small band rescued the senoritas so easily in what should have been a fortress. It also helps that only a handful of the guards died in your attack."

Carlos and Jeffe conferred in Spanish for a moment. "Carlos extends his sympathies for the loss of your man. I am sorry as well. Gordo could never decide whether he was a soldier or a bandit. He died as a bandit, but we will sing his praises as a soldier. Our side needs heroes."

"I understand," replied Pierce. This acceptance of death was new to him.

"Perhaps," said Jeffe, "we can exchange telegrams, Mr. Secretary. When I am in the north, I cross the border regularly to purchase supplies."

"Of course, Mr. Minister. My country will be selling huge quantities of surplus military equipment at bargain prices and with excellent terms. I will be pleased to introduce you to the appropriate people."

"A sweet song for my ears, Mr. Secretary. We must go now; it is time to introduce the soldiers in the valley to their new commander, my long-time agent in the west, Carlos here. As Gordo's half-brother he will be readily accepted," finished Jeffe.

"Even if he helped kill that brother?" asked Chad.

"In Mexico, Captain, families are expected to clean up their own messes. Gordo insulted Carlos by taking the women under his protection. Carlos reclaimed his honor by taking them back and erasing the black mark on his family forever."

◈

As the crow flies it is only one hundred miles between Huajimic and Aguacalientes, but over the rough mountain trails the distance they needed to travel was tripled. The party, pushing hard, rode late into each night and were back in the saddle early. Early in the afternoon of the third day the party turned onto the road leading to the Hacienda de la Cruz.

Next to the road a small French military unit was camped. Two French guards reluctantly challenged the dirty, rugged looking party. Lieutenant Mare, his knee healing, rode forward addressing his countrymen.

"It is one hour to the house of my father," commented Denali. "Please allow me to explain what has happened."

"As you say," replied Chad.

"The bandits attacked the French, and you saved lieutenant Mare from certain death. You saved Anna and me. Do not mention Jeffe or Carlos."

"Mr. Kadzof, Mr. Davis, you heard the lady. Please pass the word."

The Hacienda de la Cruz sat on a high plateau, twenty-five miles west of Aguacalientes. The ranch was tucked into a shallow valley. The plateau was already transitioning from spring green to summer brown. Here and there blue and white wildflowers still bloomed where depressions in the land held moisture. The occasional pine trees that dotted the lands of the plateau thickened into narrow forest along the ravines, which led into the valley.

The grasslands were spotted with sturdy long-horned cattle. Most were bedded wherever they could find shade from the afternoon sun. The oppressive humid heat of the lowlands was behind them. In its place the party found cool nights and hot dry days.

From the high rim above the valley, the party gawked at miles of green fields, pastures, orchards and even vineyards. Small clusters of buildings sprouted at several places, where a matrix of farm roads intersected. Directly in the center of the valley, a large two-story home sat surrounded by vast gardens and rows of shade trees. Behind the hacienda a small green lawn stretched from the house to a small lake.

The lake was one of more than a dozen impoundments gathering water from a series of springs, feeding it into a web of irrigation ditches. Not far from the palatial home, a bell tower defined a church. Chad estimated the valley at more than six miles long and four miles across. Denali broke into song in her joy to be home. Chad was sullen and reflective.

"Why such a sad face mí Capitán?"

"I was just remembering the men who will never be going home."

"You need to think about the others, plus Anna and myself, and you cannot forget lieutenant Mare. You were our leader."

"You make me sound like a messiah."

"No Messiah, just a man."

Chad reached into his shirt pocket, retrieving the chain and cross he had taken from Peter's neck before they buried the young man. He stared at the cheap coils of silver in his hand. *It's not much, but it is all I have to give to his parents.* He dropped it back into his pocket.

The party was strung out over more than a half mile of trail. Chad and Denali halted their tired horses, waiting for the stragglers to catch up. Chad dismounted and helped Denali from her horse. Waiving his hand from one end of the valley to the other he asked; "Is this all one ranch?"

"*Si*, it all belongs to my father. Next to our hacienda is that of my uncle and there," she said pointing to a ridge more than ten miles away, "are the homes of my other uncle and my grandfather who is ninety-four years old."

"The place is enormous," observed Chad.

"I do not know this word."

"Enormous, very, very big," replied Chad.

"*Si*, it is very, very, big. When my grandfather's grandfather was granted the hacienda by the King of Spain, he was given all of the land that he could ride around in two days."

Chad stood in awe; still, he could not shake off his sadness. "I keep thinking about the men, dead in battles with three different enemies." *How many more will I lose before we are safely home?* He pondered.

"I will light candles for your fallen shipmates tomorrow," said Denali. "I will pray that your fights are over."

"That's just it, we have at least one more."

"Let your strong American army find those who sank your ship."

"I cannot do that. If there is any possible way, the *KATARINA*'s crew and I will do the job ourselves."

"You think it your duty, or do you want to kill the men who took your ship?" asked Denali, climbing back into the saddle.

"Both," replied Chad, following the beautiful young woman into the tree-lined road. The question she had asked kept rattling around his brain.

In front of the house, a woman greeted the party; two inches taller than Denali, blond, with a similar haunting beauty. The tiny creases next to her eyes told a story of a few more years and more experience.

"Where is my father, Maria?" asked Denali.

"He and your uncles are in Aguacalientes meeting with General duPre, he will be back late tonight. Are we speaking English for a reason cousin?" asked Maria.

"Yes, cousin, all of these men speak only English, except for the cute one on the black horse, that is our cousin, Pedro Davis."

"That is just like you Denali, to show up with twenty men in tow."

"They saved my life, and that of cousin Anna. Oh, I am very sorry, Maria Huarte, please allow me to introduce you to Captain Chad Gritt."

"I am honored, Captain," said Maria with a curtsy.

Chad nodded his head but said nothing.

"What brings you down from Fresnillo, Maria?" asked Denali.

A pallid shadow crept over Maria's face. "After you and Tia Camille left for the coast, the Juaristas took Fresnillo. They allowed the women to leave the next day."

"My God Maria, what of your home? What of Miguel?"

"It has been given to one of the Juarista generals."

"Maria," snapped Denali, "what of Miguel?"

"He was captured. As a Royalist officer, he was given full military honors before he and the other officers were shot."

Denali threw herself off from her horse and wrapped the now weeping Maria in her arms. "I am so sorry."

"I am alright, Denali. His is just one more useless death, in a meaningless battle, in an unnecessary war. Like your father, Miguel followed the church into this ridiculous plan to make Mexico part of Europe. If this war does not end soon, it will destroy us all."

Maria pushed away from Denali and wiped her face with a kerchief in her left hand.

"Now cousin Denali, we must arrange accommodations for our guests."

The Hacienda de la Cruz was even grander inside. The outside walls, all white stucco, were more than two feet thick. Heavy exposed pine beams resting on pine posts supported the second floor. Between the posts brick walls were covered in stucco. The inside walls, more than twelve inches deep, were tiled from the floor up more than five feet, leaving another five feet of white stucco above. Small inset shelves held sculpture and vases of flowers. Each room's tile work was unique in color and complexity creating a mosaic that represented a picture of a different industry from ranching to mining to tile making.

The floor was black tile with white grout. Here and there were bookcases and tables of varying height, constructed of cast cement faced with colored tile. The moveable furniture was all finely crafted and covered with tailored cushions and pillows. Chad guessed that every stick had been imported from Europe.

Chad was ushered into a room overlooking the huge lawn and lake behind the palatial home. The bed, wide enough for two, was extra-long and supported by four massive posts. All of the rest of the furniture had been cast in place. The dresser was cement, faced with colored tile. Instead of drawers it held tightly woven baskets. Even the chairs were cement, with massive leather covered cushions.

Chad flopped his weary body onto one of the chairs and tugged until he freed both feet from sweaty boots. The small bag at his feet held the only clothes that he possessed, two changes, either a shade or two filthier than the dusty clothes he wore. He dug out his shaving gear and the ship's log, which he had carefully kept current even after the *KATARINA's* loss and placed them atop the dresser. He poured water from a pitcher into a beautifully painted bowl. He splashed water into his eyes to wash away the irritating dust. He was about to lather his face when he was interrupted. Answering the knock at the door, he found a middle-aged maid, dressed in a simple black cotton dress. The maid handed him a card that read, *Captain Gritt, please follow Constance, your bath is drawn. Maria.* The bathroom was almost as large as his bedroom. A brass kettle of hot water sat on a small pottery stove heated by a huge candle. Into the counter next to the kettle a tiled sink was molded, and above the sink a faucet with cool water ran in a trickle.

Across the room a built-in tub awaited, filled with water heated in a huge copper tank over a wood fireplace, molded around the lower half of the tank. Faucets for cold water allowed Chad to cool the tub's water that as drawn, could be used to cook crab in Alaska or lobster in Boston.

Constance handed Chad another card. *Please undress and leave your clothes for Constance, she will arrange laundry. Enjoy your bath, but please take no more than one hour, as we have only three bathrooms with tubs. When finished, dress in the cotton pants and shirt next to the towels. On a shelf next to the tub, you will find cigars and brandy. Maria.*

An hour later Chad passed Thomas Mead in the hall on his way back to his room. Constance stood in the doorway to the bath.

"You are in for a treat, Thomas," he announced.

Mead smiled.

In his room he found a third note. *I suggest a siesta, Captain Gritt. Dinner will be served at dusk on the patio behind the house.* Chad opened the huge double windows and studied the light and the shadows on the lawn below.

"Three hours at least before sunset," he thought, "time for a nap."

EVEN DIPLOMATS CARRY A PISTOL

30
HACIENDA DE LA CRUZ, MEXICO

THREE MEN SAT in the cavernous study of the owner of the Hacienda de la Cruz.

"Tell me, Captain, of your family," requested the distinguished Spanish gentleman using Pedro as an interpreter.

Philippe de la Cruz was of medium build; and dressed all in black. His gray wavy hair was combed back emphasizing his receding hairline. A silver mustache set on dark tan skin and eyes the color of coal marked a face that neither smiled nor frowned.

"My mother was Russian and my father a sea Captain from Boston," replied Chad. "They met on a trip to Russian America."

"Are they well?"

"A year ago, when I left Boston, they were. They were leaving for the Sandwich Islands and then to our home in New Archangel, in Russian America."

"So your father's business does well, Captain Gritt?"

"Very well. We have interests in shipping, both land and sea as well as mining and retail commerce in Boston, San Francisco, and Russian America."

"And your parents, they are still active in the business?"

"Not really, they leave most of the retail oversight to my older sister and the shipping to me. We have a very loyal, very competent staff."

"That does not surprise me, Captain. Tell me, how did you come to shorten your name?"

Chad was taken aback. "You know my family?"

A faint smile crossed Philippe's face. "For a brief moment, I knew a Chad Grittenberg and a Katarina Gerhardt. I remember the night that they met at what was then called the Presidio de San Francisco."

"You must tell me more, Señor de la Cruz. Perhaps you can fill in some of the missing details that my parents do not discuss."

"I must do only what I want to do, Captain. Philippe took more than a minute to light a cigar. Ask your parents about me the next time you see them. In the interim it pleases me that they married and have prospered."

"I will pass on your thoughts, Señor de la Cruz."

"Please do that Captain," laughed Philippe, "and please tell Katarina, that at that moment, in that place, she chose correctly. Now may we shift the conversation to a more urgent matter?"

"Of course, Señor."

"I want you to take Denali and her cousin Maria with you to America."

"Of course, we will help if we can, Señor, but why?"

"I will answer your questions, young Captain, because I need your help."

Chad looked at his host, whose expression told the story of a man who was used to getting his way and who abhorred having to explain himself. The term "arrogant bastard" crossed his mind, but he said nothing.

"In 1863, when I, and the rest of the Assembly of Notables took Mexico's future into our hands and appointed the young

Hapsburg Prince, Maximilian, Emperor of Mexico, we did so because the so-called Republic was floundering.

In the short war with your country, your American Army had marched through Mexico at will. The only real resistance they found was in Mexico City, where the cadets of our military academy fought like tigers and died like men. These boys, only fourteen or fifteen, including Denali's brother, young men from the better families in Mexico, fought for the pride of Mexico, not for our weak, corrupt government. Your modern army crushed them in hours. They died for nothing in a war that could have been avoided. The Americans, finding that they had gained nothing that they did not control already, turned around and went home." Phillipe blew a long tendril of smoke into the air, watching it dissipate in the breeze from the open window behind him.

"Mexico lost more Northern Territory, but it was land already occupied by American settlers. All the war did for Mexico is bankrupt my country. There was no money to modernize, no money for trained police, no money for education. Mexico stopped paying its foreign debt obligations. Chaos and crime affected all of our citizens that could not afford to defend their families."

"Without payments on foreign debt, foreign investment stopped. Even the wealthy families do not have the hard capital to develop this country without foreign investment, technology, and expertise. The money we had invested was stranded in projects started but never finished," continued Philippe.

"The so-called Republicans blamed it on the Holy Mother Church and began to illegally seize the church's wealth. They made it clear that the holdings of all who opposed them were at risk." The aging gentleman slipped from his worn chair, stopping to gaze out the window.

"Mexico was crumbling. We invited the French, Germans, Austrians, and English to help us restore order and turn Mexico into a culturally rich, civilized country. We went back to our European roots," added de la Cruz.

"From what I can see, Señor, chaos and violence remain a problem."

"I will put a slightly less insolent slant on that statement when I translate Captain," said Pedro. "I agree Mr. Davis," replied Chad, "I was just thinking of the men we have buried in the last few weeks." Pedro translated the gist of Chad's message.

"You are unfortunately correct, Captain," spat de la Cruz, speaking halting English. "We expected the masses to recognize the need for order. We expected them to embrace a man who was making such a great sacrifice to lead them out of the darkness."

"And that did not happen?"

"No Captain, the stupid, uneducated peasants flock to their little Indian President with no pedigree. Even many landed families support Juarez. They believe that this man with no military experience will push the Europeans out."

"Señor de la Cruz, the history is very interesting," replied Chad, "but I still do not understand why you want to exile your daughter and niece."

"It is simple, Captain, the French and Royalist forces are limited and grow smaller due to attrition every day while the Republicans grow stronger. They will win many battles before the Europeans see the need to send us enough troops to end this folly."

"Have the European governments agreed then to send more troops?"

"Not yet, Captain, we are sending emissaries this summer. Even the Empress has volunteered to travel to Europe to secure more help."

"So, Denali and Maria are being sent away to protect them until the Royalists win a final victory."

The graying gentleman smiled for the first time, "well said."

"And what if they do not want to leave, Señor?"

"This is not America or France or England, Captain. My daughter will do as I say. Maria has nothing left in Mexico; besides she was very angry at Miguel for leaving his post as Ambassador to England to join the Royalists."

"Maria seems deeply hurt by his loss, Señor."

"Miguel was twice her age, Captain. They had no children. He was more a father figure than a husband, but Maria is loyal and understands duty."

"Your daughter, Señor, she seems committed to Mexico and especially to her nursing."

"Denali needs a husband like Miguel, a man who is strong and will help her overcome her impetuousness, her wildness. Do not be deceived Captain, Denali always thinks first of Denali."

"Señor de la Cruz, we have faced grave threats just to reach Aguacalientes. I've lost a quarter of my crew. The rest of our trip may well be just as dangerous. I cannot guarantee the women's safety."

"Nonsense, Captain, you would lay down your own life rather than see harm come to them. You have risked your entire crew for my beautiful daughter already. You, like your father, still believe in chivalry. Denali and Maria could not have a better shepherd."

"I will of course try to live up to your confidence."

Philippe laughed. "Do not worry, Captain, from here to Veracruz the Royalists have restored order. I will send a letter with your lieutenant Mare. You will be accorded every courtesy. Just never mention your fight with that idiot Colonel leMark."

"You know of that fight Señor?"

"Of course, Captain. Whenever we disagree, my daughter can't help discussing every transgression of our French allies. She blamed leMark for her abduction. To me, Captain, it was worthwhile. It led to the demise of that pig Gordo Rojas. I thank you for destroying this bandit."

So much for parroting the story Denali had created. Chad picked up his snifter of brandy and dipped the end of his unlit cigar into the glass. He snipped both ends from the cigar with the silver cigar trimmer in the tray in front of him. He lit the cigar rolling it in his fingers before taking several short puffs. He then changed the subject.

31
HACIENDA DE LA CRUZ, MEXICO

DENALI SMILED AT Chad. "After my mother and I bathed, she told me an old story while I braided her hair. For years, after my father returned from Russian America, he would talk of a beautiful blond Russian girl and of an American sea Captain who had disrupted a mission that the Viceroy had assigned to him My father would repeat the story every time he would drink too much. Finally at the home of grandfather, he told the story once too often. My grandfather laid down the law in front of a large dinner party. My father was told to never repeat the story again. He was told to find a wife from Mexico and start a family. My grandfather reminded him that the Spanish withdrawal from Mexico occurred while he was in Russian America, and his mission turned out to be meaningless."

"Four months later father asked for my mother's hand. It took years before my father finally told her that he felt fortunate that the Russian girl had refused his offer of marriage. It is very difficult for my father to admit that he has failed, or that he was wrong. My mother refers to that evening as the night they met me. Your mother must have been very beautiful," continued Denali.

"She still is," replied Chad, "as is your mother."

Denali and Chad had ridden for more than four hours, leaving before dawn to take advantage of the cool morning. In four hours, the couple saw just a fraction of the hacienda de la Cruz. Philippe and his two brothers had divided the huge Spanish land grant ranch of their father roughly into thirds. Chad estimated the land of Denali's father at more than two hundred thousand acres, more than three hundred square miles. That meant that the original ranch might have been a thousand square miles.

How could any one family own this much land, wondered Chad. While they rode, they passed through three villages of women, children and old people, all owned by the hacienda. "The young men are all off fighting for the Royalists," said Denali, reading Chad's mind. "If they fight my father will give them the equivalent of two acres of land up on the plateau along the river."

"That seems generous."

"In a way I suppose. The peasants have no cash, so they will be dependent on my father for seed, tools, even supplies to build a house. In the interim they will have to continue to work in the fields and factories. Even when they have crops of their own, the closest market is four hours away."

"Won't they sell their crops in the villages of the hacienda?"

"If my father approves, or if they sell first to my father at his prices."

"Still, they seem to be satisfied." Chad pulled the scarf up to cover his sunburned neck.

"They work to put food on the table. They fight for their families. If they do not fight, they and their families will be thrown off from the ranch. They leave with only the clothes on their back."

"You do not support your father then?"

"On the contrary, my Capitán, I support my father, but if he does not change his policies we will lose much if not everything. The Juaristas will drive the French out of Mexico. My cousins are split between the factions. You know that I have supported the Juarista cause by helping Jeffe. I do not worry about the Juarista government punishing our family. I worry about our peasants, our workers, taking revenge."

"You know your father is sending you out of the country?"

"I go gladly. My cousins will purchase my inheritance when the time comes. I have no interest in running the hacienda. I belong in New York, or Paris, or London. Or maybe Boston, mí Capitán, perhaps that is a good idea, no?

Denali leaned over in the saddle, running her hand along Chad's neck and cheek. The hair on Chad's neck rose and his face flushed.

"You would like Boston."

"Maybe yes, maybe no. We should go back now. We will leave tomorrow."

"One more question, your father mentioned a brother."

"My older brother died in the war with the Americans. He was a first-year cadet at the military academy. He would have been twenty-six this year."

"I am sorry, Denali, especially that he died fighting my country."

"Do not be, Capitán. Rodrigo and his fellow cadets disobeyed the orders of the Comandante to abandon the fortress. They were young and stupid and very brave. The Americans fired on them only after taking many casualties, only after trying repeatedly to get them to surrender. It is rumored that more than one American officer wept after the battle. Do not misunderstand though, mi Capitán. If the Americans come back all of Mexico will fight them. It is the one thing that could unify the Juaristas and the Royalists."

"The Americans have chosen to support your President Juarez."

"Do not say that again while you are in Mexico," counseled Denali. "The Royalists leaders are Austrian, French and Mexican sympathizers. None of them will directly oppose your travel to Veracruz. They just want you out of the country. But like the intrigue of the courts in Europe, assassination and poisoning are acceptable tools to these men. Now we must go, although I would prefer to disappear for an hour with you." She fumbled with her blouse, unfastening the top two buttons. She ran her finger down her neck and between her partially exposed breasts. Smiling at Chad, she slowly rebuttoned her blouse. "We will wait."

Maria met them at the door. "I would stay away from Pedro; he is in a foul mood."

"Why?" asked Denali.

"Anna has informed him that she is not going to Mexico or back to Estados Unidos. Nothing he says will change her mind. She will not leave her mother alone in Mexico."

Denali paused for a moment. "Pedro still sees Anna as the twelve-year-old child that fled Charleston. The week that we were captives, Anna was the strong one. Her faith and courage never failed. Pedro will never change her mind."

"Can she safely travel back to her mother's hacienda?" asked Chad.

"Everything is possible in Mexico, with mordida," replied Maria.

Chad looked puzzled. "Mordida?"

Maria smiled, "Mordida, you know bribes."

32
MEXICO CITY, MEXICO

CHAD RESTED HIS horse next to the carriage as another immaculately dressed mayor, complete with sash, presented flowers to Denali, then greeted her traveling companions. I am amazed at your father's influence everywhere we stop," said Chad.

The influence of de la Cruz was welcome on the march to Cuidad de Mexico, the nation's capital. Stops in the beautiful city of Leon and the second night in Acambaro were orchestrated by advance teams dispatched by Denali's father. Meals prepared by local restaurateurs fed the entire company, both breakfast and dinners. Denali and Maria, along with the ship's officers, were housed in the houses of the cities' elite. The men slept on feather mattresses in comfortable hotels.

In each city, the local mayor and Royalist officials greeted the company and made sure that not only their needs, but also their wants were taken care of. The bills were paid using the gold coinage minted from their gold strips. Each bill now included a ten percent 'war' tax. From Leon, a troop of fifteen French cavalrymen cleared the road ahead and cleaned up behind the ship's crew.

"I am not sure, Captain," remarked Mead, "whether the French are escorts, minders, or our jailers."

Pierce kicked his mount in the ribs and moved up next to Mead. "A bit of discretion, Mr. Mead," he offered. "Our so-called 'escorts' all speak English. My guess is that they were hand-picked by French intelligence."

"I agree, Mr. Secretary," replied Chad. "If you two will take the lead I'll swing back and pass the word to watch the chatter." The hair rose on Chad's neck. Nowhere seemed safe.

Cuidad de Mexico was a sprawling, ancient city. Massive, stone buildings lined wide, paved streets. Plazas and tree-lined walks filled every open space. The government buildings left you with the sense that you were wandering through a European capital.

The passage from their first sighting of the city had been fascinating. After passing through a ring of peasant shanties, the troop traversed a neighborhood of modest, rock and brick homes, belonging to the middle class of business and professional inhabitants of the great city. Closer to the city center, mansions of Mexico's elite and landed families stretched for blocks. Interspersed in each neighborhood were small commercial areas, offering the needs of everyday life from tortillas to zapatas.

In the outlying neighborhoods open-air markets filled with small stalls and pungent scents surrounded the buzz of voices of customers and shopkeepers debating prices. In the city center elegant stores displayed fashion, furniture and foods that one would find in Amsterdam, Berlin or Madrid.

Strangely, for a country at war, there was almost no military presence. In fact, the ship's company and their French escort brought stares and hushed conversation to the sidewalks as they passed. Clearly the sight of two-dozen heavily armed men, who were neither European soldiers, nor Mexican Nationals, was not an everyday occurrence. The French escort armed with only pistols and sabers, rode loose, laughing and joking, not like men escorting prisoners. The elegant coach of the de la Cruz family added even more intrigue to the procession.

The presidential offices were visible a block away, across a stone plaza, when the carriage turned into a street and halted in front of an elegant, rose-colored manor house. Two doormen emerged and rushed to the coach, assisting Maria and Denali from their perch. Four more men in white peasant dress began unloading bags. A moment later a tall graying man in a European-style suit dashed down the step and swept Denali into his arms, twirling her around and around like a child.

"Captain Gritt," giggled Denali, "may I introduce Juan Carlos, my father's closest advisor and associate in the city. You and your officers will stay here in the family home. Juan has arranged for the rest of your crew to take over a small hotel only a block away."

"I will have to detail my men and see to it that they are settled," replied Chad, happy to have both boots on solid land.

"Of course, Captain," said Juan in British accented English. Your French escort will also be housed with your men and have been instructed to provide them every courtesy and to act as interpreters."

"Thank you, Señor Carlos," smiled Chad. "If you give me a few minutes with my chief I will join you inside." Pointing down the line of men Chad called, "Mr. Gott, Mr. Kadzof, Sergeant Mosby, Mr. Davis, a minute please."

"Aye aye, Captain," responded Gott, while the other three simply touched the brim of their battered hats. Mosby was already walking toward Chad. "The men need new clothes," offered Chad, handing a small bag of coins to the Sergeant. "Your French escorts can help them find what they need. Divide any money left over between the men and buy the first round."

An hour later Chad was ushered into an elegant bedroom decorated in the same styles that Chad imagined a French Manor House would be. Maria met him at the door dressed in a flowing, yellow cotton dress, her hair tied back with a yellow ribbon. Her normal, gentle countenance and sparking eyes were replaced by a worried look, and her cheeks reflected the color of either hurt or anger. "Tread softly, Captain Gritt. All is not what it seems, even the walls have ears in this city. I am told we all may be in danger."

Chad started to ask a question. Maria simply put a finger upright over her lips and disappeared down the hall.

Chad carried Maria's words rattling around in his brain as the maid led him to his bath. As before, she presented a card advising him that he was to bathe and leave his clothes to be cleaned. It further advised that Juan had arranged meetings for him and Pierce and the others the next day, and that a tailor would be there later to fit him for appropriate clothing for his stay in the Capitol.

Chad shaved, and then he stripped and pulled on the heavy robe that hung on a peg next to the dry sink. He put his entire roll of clothes in a cotton drawstring bag and set them outside his door. Turning to his left he opened the door the maid had pointed to as she left the room. It opened into an enormous bath. Across the room another door stood open revealing another bedroom.

"You are so punctual Capitán," said a voice to his left. Denali sat in a huge cast iron tub filled full of white frothy bubbles, only her head and shoulders rising above the foam. "I have been waiting only five minutes. We have only two hours before the tailor arrives and we not waste it I think."

Two hours later, Chad was ushered into a drawing room just off from the main hallway. Five tailors circled and measured Pierce, Mead, Davis, Kadzof and Doc Parker, chattering, pulling and poking. A rotund, balding man with a pencil-thin mustache sat impatiently on a wooden stool rubbing some unseen material from the side of his nose. With Chad's entrance he pounced toward the door, taking Chad's arm, pulling him toward the stool. He spoke not a word as he pushed Chad's arms straight out from his side and used his instep to nudge Chad's feet apart. With each measurement he retreated to a large, folded sheet of paper with a hand-drawn outline of a man, where he recorded his figures. When he finished, he put one hand on each shoulder and pushed Chad down until he was seated on the stool behind him.

The man in front of Pedro walked the three paces across to where Chad sat and knelt before him. The man literally smelled like oiled leather. Removing the sandals that Chad had found atop the folded cotton pants and tunic he now wore, the cobbler carefully examined and then measured first Chad's left foot and then his right. A young man that Chad assumed was an apprentice carefully noted each measurement and made notes as his mentor pointed to features of Chad's feet. The clothiers, already finished with Mead, Pierce and the other officers seemed anxious to finish with him.

There was something surrealistic about the entire experience. During the process not a word had been spoken. As the artisans left, Juan Carlos closed the sliding doors and presented Chad with a bill for eighteen new suits and twelve pairs of shoes. Added to the bill was the now customary 10 percent war tax.

Unable to interpret the bill Chad unbuckled the leather coin pouch from around his waist and began counting what in the States would have been twenty-dollar gold pieces. He reached fifteen pieces before Juan swept up the coins and left the room.

Returning a minute later, Carlos announced, "The first of your new suits will be delivered in time for dinner."

33
THE OFFICES OF THE EMPEROR OF MEXICO

HANS MICHAEL FEHLBURG commanded the room. His blue eyes, partially hidden behind bushy, prematurely gray eyebrows, darted from face to face. His chiseled nose rested on a waxed handlebar mustache at least a foot wide. He wore a light gray uniform with no insignia, over a tall, trim frame. He had positioned himself next to the door, greeting each person who entered.

A summons had been delivered the night before. Fehlburg's assistant, a young French officer by the name of Zidot, arrived the next morning to escort Chad, Doc Parker, Mead and Pierce. A ten-minute walk to the Ministry of State took them directly into a large conference room already buzzing with more than a dozen men.

"Gentlemen, allow me to introduce the Chief of Staff to his Excellency, Emperor Maximilian. He will coordinate the meeting."

It surprised Chad that only Zidot and Fehlburg were European. The rest of those present were Mexican, including two men introduced as Roberto Castro, Minister of War and Arturo Peña, the Minister of Foreign Affairs. Fehlburg extended his hand, a warm smile on his face. The men talked of home and families before Fehlburg turned, walking across the room.

Fehlburg seated himself at the head of a long conference table, then opened the meeting in clipped English. "Señor Castro, I present the leaders of the American invasion that you briefed me about." The red-faced minister of war said nothing. "Gentlemen," continued Fehlburg, "when we heard of the American Army had landed on the Pacific Coast some of us prayed that a miracle had occurred. When stories of the destruction of both Royalist and Juarista armies by these forces reached the capitol, we believed."

Chad took the bait, "How are we a miracle?"

"Minister Peña," directed Fehlburg, "would you enlighten our guests."

Arturo Peña was of slight build, gray and sixty. "We are well aware that arms from the United States are reaching the forces of Juarez. Every day they grow stronger. They believe that they will triumph. Of course, they are wrong; still the one thing that would unify Mexico, and end this terrible civil war, would be a Yankee invasion. Minister Castro sent emissaries to Juarez and agents to the Royalists in the west. He wanted to document the invasion. Both sides reported a tiger. That is, a tiger that could be crushed at any time as long as one were willing to lose a lot of men. It appears now that both sides just want you out of Mexico so that we can continue to kill each other."

Roberto Castro's face had reached the color of an overheated boiler. Fehlburg rose from his chair and in three strides stood behind Castro placing his hand on the man's shoulder. "Roberto has the most difficult job in Mexico. He must defeat the army of the popular but inept ex-president of Mexico while outnumbered three to one and do it in a way that leaves one Mexico. You can understand his dream of a miracle."

A fist slammed onto the table followed an outburst by the minister of war. Rising, he continued his bitter speech, taking time between sentences to point to each of the Americans, ending with his finger almost on Pierce's nose. Finished, he stormed out of the room. Two aides gathered up his portfolio, cape and cane and quickly followed their minister through the double doors at the end of the table. For a long minute the only sound in the room was the receding click of three men's heels on the tile floor as Minister Castro and his aides left the building.

"None of the Spanish that I have learned on this trip prepared me to interpret Minister Castro's speech," remarked Pierce still watching as the departed men disappeared down the stairs at the end of the corridor.

"Thirty years before you were studying Spanish, I was working on my English at your Yale College," said Peña. "Señor Castro's speech was aimed at his Mexican compatriots, not at you," he continued. "Please let me explain. Even during your War Between the States, your President Lincoln sent arms and ammunition to Benito Juarez. The initial 3,000 muskets that allowed Juarez to field an army came from American stores in New Orleans. With your civil war over, captured Confederate arms are crossing our northern border. Some here, hoped that the pro-Juarez policy died with your President Lincoln. Your boss, Secretary of State Seward, has so far rebuffed all of my requests to discuss the matter. Minister Castro must purchase expensive arms and munitions from Europe while his enemy receives more than he can use."

"The crew of a shipwrecked, private American vessel has little influence on these policies," answered Pierce.

"Perhaps, perhaps not. Minister Castro would hold all of you as bargaining chips to get your government's attention."

"Are we your prisoners?" asked Mead.

"No, you are not," responded Fehlburg. "The Emperor is a great admirer of the United States; he would never allow it."

"Gentlemen," interjected Peña, "that is the point of our invitation to meet today. Emperor Maximilian and Benito Juarez share a very common vision for Mexico. It is a vision almost identical to the foundation of your great democracy. We hoped to convince you that instead of arming one side in our civil war, your country could play a vital role in helping overcome the stubborn resolve of two strong-willed men, men with disparate strategies to the same end."

"Secretary Pierce, as a member of Secretary Seward's staff, you would have influence. Colonel Mead, as a decorated war hero and a man versed in intelligence, you could document the military facts. Captain Gritt, Dr. Parker, you could help influence your business colleagues and even your congress," continued Peña.

Hans Michael Fehlburg walked to a table under the windows, filling a glass with water. For the first time, Chad noted that he walked with a stiff left leg. "Gentlemen, the Emperor has extended an invitation to lunch with him. The invitation is to all; however, I would propose a change. Secretary Pierce and Colonel Mead, I propose that you accept the Emperor's invitation. Captain Gritt, I personally would be happy to introduce you to members of the transportation ministry, who can arrange transport to Veracruz and on to New Orleans. And you, Dr. Parker, Lt. Mare has amazed us with his description of his wounded leg and your amazing skills in saving it." Fehlburg lifted a cane from the water table and tapped his lower left leg. "I personally lost my leg after a similar wound. I would be grateful if you could spend a day or two with our medical staff. We have hundreds of wounded. Far too many end up as amputees."

The four Americans spoke momentarily then all nodded agreement.

"Secretary Pierce, Colonel Mead, if you will follow Lt. Zidot, he will escort you to the palace," directed Peña. "Captain Gritt, Dr. Parker," continued Peña, "Hans and I would be pleased if you would join us for lunch before we escort you to your afternoon appointments."

34

THE EMPEROR'S PALACE NEAR MEXICO CITY, MEXICO

MEAD AND PIERCE were surprised by the appearance of the Royal Palace. It was a relatively plain, boxy, building of modest size, the color a cross between tan and gray. Fragrant flowers and trailing rose bushes between the windows and next to the entry doors supplied color.

An aide met the coach. He spoke in a hushed voice to Zidot. "The Emperor is in his garden," translated Zidot. "Please follow me."

The men followed him around the right side of the palace, passing through a gate in a vine covered archway, they found themselves in a huge garden of flowers, shrubs, and trees. A labyrinth of trails wound through the garden, paved in rose-colored gravel. Miguel Zidot excused himself and rushed off toward a covered pavilion across the garden. Mead and Pierce followed, noticing only one gardener in baggy white clothes and a tattered straw hat working on his hands and knees.

"One would believe they were in the garden of a European palace," said Pierce.

At the pavilion a lunch setting was laid out on a now familiar heavy wooden table surrounded by matching wood and leather chairs. The pavilion was of post and beam construction, with a tile roof. The side facing the garden was open, but walls of tightly woven vines and flowers enclosed the other three sides. A perforated copper pipe dripped water through the vines, cooling the space.

Zidot said nothing as the men mounted the steps. He was looking down the path that they had followed to the pavilion. When he spoke, it was in French. The men turned with the reply in French from just behind them. The gardener had followed them, his brown bare feet making almost no noise as he approached. Zidot and the gardener exchanged a few more sentences.

"Gentlemen," announced Zidot, "may I introduce Maximilian of the Hapsburgs, Emperor of Mexico. Before he shakes hands, he would like to wash up a bit and invites you to follow him." The only indication of luxury, at the rough outdoor sinks behind the pavilion, was lavender-scented soap and a stack of freshly laundered towels.

Maximilian was a young man of normal height with kind eyes, a neatly trimmed mustache and beard and a firm handshake. Barefoot, with stains on the knees of his simple peasant dress he plucked his straw hat from his head as he seated himself. A servant rushed from an alcove, circling the table, filling tall goblets with cold water. He looked at the emperor, who nodded, then took the emperor's straw hat from the table as he retreated.

"The Emperor does speak English, but is unpracticed," advised Zidot, "I will act as your interpreter if necessary."

For an hour, over a lunch of fresh fruit, bread, cheese and cool tea, Maximilian laid out his vision for Mexico as a constitutional democracy headed by a monarch, similar to many European states. He discussed how similar his vision was to that of Benito Juarez.

His questions about the United States indicated a great knowledge and respect. He refrained from asking for personal opinions from Pierce or Mead while making his case.

"Mexico, without strong leadership, structured government and a European export-driven economy, will flounder," Maximilian stated. "If this opportunity to stabilize Mexico is lost," he continued, "America will find extreme poverty, unrest, even banditry and revolution on its southern border for two hundred years."

The lunch closed with the Emperor handing a letter for Secretary Seward to Pierce. "I assure the Emperor that I will keep this letter on my person until I can present it to the Secretary of State," agreed Pierce.

Maximilian walked his guests to the garden gate. As their coach pulled away, he remained at the gate watching them depart. At a window on the second floor, a woman in a lavender dress turned away.

"An Emperor in peasant dress with a populist agenda," said Pierce to no one in particular. "A very different man from what I expected."

"His commitment and sense of duty come through," replied Mead. "Amazing, a European aristocrat who does his own gardening and breaks bread with commoners. A man with a warm smile but very sad eyes. I assume that the woman watching was the Empress."

Zidot ended his hundred-mile gaze out of the coach window. "Maximilian is a very different man than the savior the Supreme Council thought they were getting." The French officer paused for a moment, fussing with his coat. "As is Empress Carlotta."

Zidot stared at the two Americans sitting across from him. "His populist approach has cost him dearly with the Mexican landed rich. They expected an ironhanded monarch who would crush his opponents and govern based on their council. Instead, he promotes reform, disciplines Royalist officers who mistreat the people, and presses his so-called European allies for both development support and military help."

"You are worried about him," observed Pierce.

"We are losing this war. Juarez has painted the Emperor as a usurper, a man trying to enslave Mexico. The European allies reduce their support every month. The casualties on both sides are enormous. Sometimes I believe that he works on his hands and knees in that garden as penance."

"Why doesn't he abdicate and go home?" asked Mead.

"He believes every word he said at lunch. A weak Juarez government would cripple Mexico for centuries. As he goes back to his gardening, he will pray that your meeting can help with a negotiated settlement and a new Mexico. He is willing to die for that."

"Is the situation that desperate?" asked Mead.

Zidot turned to stare out the window, first shaking his head yes and then no.

"By the way," Zidot added after a minute of silence, "like your President Jefferson, Maximilian is a very capable botanist."

35
MEXICO CITY, MEXICO

THE SHIP'S OFFICERS were on the patio when the coach carrying Pierce and Mead pulled to a stop. The chocolate aroma of cigars and laughter led the men to the gathering. The family advisor, Juan Carlos, sent one of the servants for two chairs while a second wheeled a cart stocked with European fine wines and everything from Mexican Tequila to Kentucky Bourbon, (with a Confederate States of America Tax Stamp), toward the men. Mead and Pierce loosened their ties.

"I highly recommend the Bordeaux," quipped Pedro Davis. "Emperor Maximilian imports shiploads of European wine for sale in the city. The revenues support his court," he continued. "Señor Carlos and the de la Cruz family are among his best customers it appears."

"We leave for Veracruz in three days," Gritt advised, "on the fourth of July. The government is buying our horses. We will travel by coach and troop transport wagons."

"How many days on the road?" asked Mead.

"Four days. How did your luncheon with the Emperor fare?"

"A most interesting man," answered Pierce. "He greeted us in peasant dress complete with dirty knees from gardening. He is a student of democracy with an obvious passion for his new home."

"Sort of an Abraham Lincoln with a royal heritage?" asked Doc Parker.

"No," answered Mead. "There is nothing home spun about the man. Lt. Zidot observed that he is more like a Thomas Jefferson, and I think I agree."

"He is angry over Lincoln's support of Juarez," added Pierce. "He thinks Lincoln didn't understand what is at stake in Mexico."

"President Lincoln has been gone for more than three months," observed Chad.

"True," responded Pierce, "but since the surrender of the Confederacy, Union troops have been moving tons of supplies over the border, leaving it to be "found" by the Juaristas. Zidot estimates deliveries of more than a thousand rifles a month, plus ammunition, even medical supplies and artillery."

Grit smiled at Mead. "So, the Emperor asked for your help in halting the arms shipments?"

"He would appreciate a more balanced American policy?" replied Mead.

"If he were a poker player, that would be his jacks to open," added Pierce. "He sees both Juarez and him as democrats, with far more in common than differences. Based on our meeting, he may be right. He would really like to see the U.S. act as a mediator between Juarez and himself, toward a national unity government. When we left, he gave me a sealed letter to Secretary Seward, probably requesting his help."

"My God, Secretary Pierce," interrupted Juan Carlos, "do not mention this letter to anyone. There are men at court who would kill all of you to stop that letter."

"I don't understand," said Chad.

"We Royalists come in many flavors," replied Carlos, "some

are patriots looking only for a strong Mexico; others believe that a monarchy is the next step toward democracy; but many, especially those exiled after the earlier war of the Reform want only a return to the old system where the hacienda owners and the church have all of the power. They already question Maximilian and see him only as a means to an end."

"Where do you and the de la Cruz family stand?" asked Mead.

Juan laughed. "We are of all flavors, reportedly even Juarista flavor in one or two cases. Remember, many of your Confederates saw themselves as patriots."

"Yet, you help us, that says a lot," said Doc Parker.

Carlos nodded at the doctor. "Hide the letter well. To all of you, say nothing of it. I want none of my guests murdered, no assault on this house. I want the women to depart for Veracruz safely." Carlos eyed the two servants at the back of the patio. "Now I recommend that we dress for dinner."

"Oh, mí Capitán," whispered Denali, "you are so handsome."

Chad stood naked in the bath before his shaving mirror. Denali had slipped through the adjoining door from her bedroom wearing only a towel. "We have time before your bath is hot. Come, you can show me that you think that I am beautiful," continued Denali taking Chad's hand and leading him toward her bedroom. "Later you will tell me about what it would be like to live in Boston."

He wiped the shaving soap from his face. He was growing more accustomed to Denali, still he was speechless.

"And later at dinner," continued Denali, "you may invite me to the French Embassy party tomorrow night."

Denali wore a new gown the color of spring leaves, while her cousin Maria Huarte wore red. The six men from the *KATARINA*

wore new formal wear, delivered only hours before. Juan Carlos met the group at the hotel entrance, introducing his wife Rose, a tall woman with high cheekbones and coal black hair that fell below her waist.

Also waiting was Zidot in the Royal Blue formal uniform of a French officer. He politely brushed past the others and extended both hands to Maria addressing her in Spanish. Maria answered, taking his arm. The couple led the others through the lobby and into a huge, open-air courtyard fashioned with lanterns and decorations. A waiter in formal dinner jacket escorted them to the table directly in front of the head table.

"Lt. Zidot was a close friend of Maria's late husband," advised Denali. "I have never met him. He is very handsome."

Forty French officers hosted the affair, with one hundred couples as their guests. Seated to the right were dozens of young Mexican women, all in formal attire, some being watched over by chaperones. "Most of the officers are unmarried or their wives remain in Europe," observed Juan Carlos.

Denali giggled. "For daughters of the capitol's elite families, an invitation to this party is most sought after." Turning to her houseguests she continued, "You will find these young ladies are well educated, multilingual and excellent dancers. When the music begins, you may ask one to dance or to sit with a glass of champagne to talk, unless she is with chaperone, then you must ask for permission to talk."

The wine flowed like a river. The Americans' presence was the talk of the party and within minutes the men had been drawn away into conversations, where they were politely pummeled with questions. Miles Pierce, as a representative of the U.S. State Department, found himself cornered by a group of senior French officers and Mexican cabinet members. Minister Peña walked Pierce out of the group explaining that he needed to discuss recent developments.

Chad found himself discussing possible maritime trade with a group of businessmen. Glancing back at their table, he noted

Denali in a vigorous conversation with Zidot, while Maria Huarte sat quietly with her hands folded in front of her.

After an amazing meal that began with goose liver pate and ended with lime sorbet, an orchestra that would grace the finest Vienna concert hall began to play.

At her urging, Chad led Denali to the wooden dance floor for a waltz. They danced a second and at the beginning of the third, Chad felt a tap on his right shoulder. "May I have this one dance with Denali?" asked Zidot.

Chad seated himself next to Maria and watched one dance turn into two, then three. "He finds Denali very attractive," said Maria, and cousin Denali loves to tease. I was never able to thank you for rescuing her from Gordo Rojas. Personally, I am weary of heroes and men who would be heroes. Still, I am thankful that you were there to help Denali."

"Would you care to dance?"

"Yes," she replied. "The others will not ask me. They believe that a widow should still be in mourning. To them my red dress should be black. Denali is very young," continued Maria.

"And I am old?" asked Chad as they danced.

"Oh no, not at all. It is just that a few more years teaches us what is important, what is genuine," responded Maria. "Perhaps it takes a few years to figure out what is real."

"Experience helps to clarify responsibility." Chad looked over at Denali and Zidot.

Maria smiled up at Chad. *Men can be so foolish*, she thought.

"Responsibility teaches about duty, the foundation of success. It is also the foundation of love. Do you not agree, Capitán?"

Chad didn't answer. Instead, he watched Denali dancing with the young French officer on the other side of the dance floor and felt a twinge of jealousy.

Maria squeezed his hand. "Would a gentleman find another glass of champagne for a lady?" she asked.

Four drunks stumbled along the sidewalk outside the Manor House. One pointed down the street. A second pointed the other direction while a third seated himself on the curb, his face in his hands. Whatever they were arguing over was becoming heated. Finally, the seated man crawled to his feet. "Shut up all of you," he ordered in Spanish. "I'll ask directions."

The French sergeant guarding the front of the house couldn't stifle a laugh as he watched the drunk stagger toward the entry. Before the sergeant could react, the drunk pressed a tiny two shot derringer against the middle of his chest and pulled both triggers. The muffled shots brought the other three men running from the street.

Two of the men grabbed the dead man's collar and dragged him to the side of the house and hid him behind a hedge of rose bushes. On the steps, the murderer slipped two more bullets into his tiny gun as he scanned the area for any witnesses. Finding none, he tugged on the velvet cord next to the door, summoning the butler.

With the pistol against his forehead, the butler called to the only other person in the house, a maid. Less than a minute later, a gun at her head, she pointed out the bedrooms of the American officers. While two of the men began to ransack Mead's room the maid was escorted back to the kitchen where the fourth thief stood over the unmoving body of the Butler.

There she was tied, her hands behind her back and her ankles bound. She was pushed face down next to the butler, blood seeping from a blow on his temple. The two thieves in the kitchen raced back to the second-floor bedrooms.

The maid rolled onto her side and then her back. She braced her shoulders against a cabinet and began lifting with her hands. She worked her way to her feet. Hopping three steps to her left, she used her bound hands to tug open a drawer. In seconds she managed to slice the light cord binding her hands on the blade of a knife, then cut the cord binding her feet. She checked the butler, finding him unconscious. Quietly she slipped from the back door.

※

A very disturbed Juan Carlos met Maria and Chad at the table. "There has been a break-in at the house," he blurted. "The French sergeant who guarded the front of the house is missing. I am afraid that they only targeted the rooms of Mr. Mead, Secretary Pierce and yourself," he added. "The police investigators are there. They will need a list of what is missing."

In minutes Chad found Mead and Pierce and discreetly advised them of the problem. "Miles," he asked, "did they get the letter?" Miles smiled and tapped his lapel pocket.

Returning to the table the men found Denali and Zidot with Maria. "Juan went to find your other shipmates," said Maria. "We will all return together."

"Please give me a minute to organize a military escort," ordered Zidot as he headed for the hotel lobby.

36
MEXICO CITY, MEXICO

"ONE OF YOUR servants managed to cut the ropes around her hands and legs and slipped out the back. In less than twenty minutes we were back with the first police wagon, bells clanging," offered the policeman at the front door.

Twenty minutes had been enough. The rooms belonging to Gritt, Pierce and Mead had been ransacked. Every drawer had been emptied, every bag dumped, and every piece of clothing had the pockets pulled out. The linen had been stripped from the beds, and the mattresses had been pulled off from the bedframe. Missing was perhaps a hundred dollars' worth of gold coins left in their rooms by the men. Whoever staged the attack, left the other rooms untouched.

The police searched the house and the grounds but found no trace of the intruders. More than twenty officers were systematically searching the neighborhood with little success. The shroud wrapped body of the slain guard lay in the back of a medical wagon. Juan Carlos signed the police robbery report. The police sergeant, demonstrating little appetite for a deeper investigation, gathered his men and retreated to the police station.

Carlos and the *KATARINA*'s officers retreated to the patio, joined a few minutes later by Zidot, who had personally positioned a dozen French infantrymen around the building. Seven snifters and a bottle of brandy appeared.

"This was no robbery," commented Carlos. "They were after the letter."

"I agree with Señor Carlos," added Zidot. He closed a folder he'd been writing in.

"They walked past more valuables than they took."

"I forget the saying," continued Carlos, "someone dumped the cat from the bag."

"Close enough," commented Mead. "I will be very happy when we are on the boat, on the way home," he continued. "A night, a day, and a night."

"The Emperor and Empress Carlotta are due at the embassy party, along with Hans Fehlburg and his wife," observed Zidot. "I need to brief them on what happened here. I will offer my regards to the ladies in the drawing room on my way out."

"There's nothing more to be done here," observed Juan Carlos. "Why don't we all enjoy the rest of the night? Besides, it will take the maids I just summoned a couple of hours to tidy up the mess."

"All of you enjoy yourself," replied Chad, "I think that I will enjoy a cigar and another brandy and then make some notes on our travel security."

The full moon overhead blocked out all but the brightest stars. The quiet on the patio was interrupted only by the buzz of insects. Chad took a long narrow cigar from the onyx humidor and clipped the end. Striking a match, he rolled the cigar back and forth over the flame until a healthy glow took root. Propping his feet up on the adjoining chair he leaned back to enjoy the quiet.

"Capitán Gritt, a voice called, "I would still enjoy that glass of champagne."

Chad turned, to find Maria Huarte just inside the patio entrance. Still in her red dress, she had pulled the combs that had kept her long blond hair atop her head and allowed it to fall over one shoulder. "I relieved our waiter of an unopened bottle on my way out," she added, holding up a bottle of black-labeled champagne in her left hand.

"A glass of champagne it is, and then I have some work to do."

"Ah, that duty thing again." Maria handed the unopened bottle to Chad.

Perhaps it was the empty champagne bottle, but the two laughed for an hour.

Chad escorted Maria into the foyer, then returned to his table. He selected another cigar and moved to the edge of the patio to light it. Looking up he saw two men watching him from the balcony of another mansion. In the time it took to light the cigar they had disappeared and the light behind them was extinguished.

With the escorts from the Davis and the de la Cruz haciendas on their way home, the traveling party was discouragingly small. The entire crew including Denali and Maria gathered on the patio of the de la Cruz mansion. Angelo, the ship's cook, had taken over the kitchen and was preparing a huge New England breakfast before the day's travel. Chad sat by himself rereading the letters he had drafted to the families of his missing men.

Denali motioned to Chad from the small table where she poked at her ham and eggs and fried potatoes. "Your breakfast grows cold," she called.

Chad placed the letters into the leather writer's case that he had purchased and joined her, his mood showing on his face.

"Are you angry with me?"

"We discussed this yesterday," answered Chad, "I am pleased that you went back to the party; you seemed to be having a very good time."

"Did you enjoy your time alone with Maria?"

"Denali, we had a glass of wine, and yes it was pleasant."

"Why are your eyes so sad, mí Capitán?"

"I was remembering Ott Smith, and the others whom we have lost on this trip."

"It must be very hard to be a Captain, to sometimes lose your friends."

Chad smiled at the young woman and then dove into his favorite breakfast. He heard the sound of Denali's voice, but was inside his own head, reliving the incidents where his shipmates were lost, looking for better decisions, finding none. Denali's hand on his arm brought him back. She pointed to Lieutenants Mare and Zidot at the patio door.

Zidot motioned for Chad to join them. "Two small changes, Captain Gritt," announced Zidot. "Lt. Mare feels well enough to travel and he will command our escort. I have been asked to travel with you to New Orleans and then on to Paris with a stop in your nation's capital," he added.

"A new assignment and a promotion," commented Chad, taking his handkerchief from his pocket and dusting off a sparkling new pair of major's stars on Zidot's shoulders. "That's quite a promotion."

"Both in your country and at home, a major gets better access than a lieutenant," he laughed. "Hans Fehlburg carries the rank of general in the Austrian army, one of the allies. He and the Emperor signed the order last night."

37
ON THE ROAD TO CORDOBA, MEXICO

HANS FEHLBERG SENT three vehicles: one officer's coach and two French infantry transport wagons. The officers would ride in style. The driver's seating was in a small, covered compartment at the front of the coach with room for a driver and a guard. A second guard sat in a swiveling seat atop the back of the traveling compartment. The roof was filled with luggage.

Mead, having spent time with both sides in the American Civil War, was shocked by how French infantry traveled in style. Each of two infantry wagon was about sixteen feet long with bench seating for twenty troops. The ride was stiff, but after weeks on horseback, welcome. Like the coach, each carried a driver and a guard in a covered box, and a second guard at the rear of the wagon.

Four French cavalry soldiers rode in front of the train and two behind. The original compliment of twenty-four had been slashed to twelve mounted guards selected by Lt. Mare, who had witnessed the firepower of the Americans.

The coach led the way with the troop wagons following. Military livery stables were spaced along the road, about four hours apart, where the four-horse hitch on the coach and the six-horse hitch on each wagon could be changed. Tied behind each transport were the horses of the seated guards and at each stop those guards traded places with the mounted outriders.

A rotation of the men placed two officers in the coach with Denali and Maria at all times. The others traveled in the infantry wagons. Those wagons became the favored transportation. With only a handful of passengers in each, card games on improvised tables, reading, and music became favored means of using empty hours. The troop wagons even allowed a couple of travelers at a time to stretch out on the padded benches for a nap.

Traffic along the road was heavy in the morning and evening but almost non-existent in the heat of the day. Canvas shades were rolled down on the sunny side of the vehicles to provide relief from the scorching sun.

The routing took them up and out of the huge bowl surrounding the capitol and along broad valleys filled with gardens and livestock, watered by rivers or streams. The surrounding hills were forested with a mix of pine and hardwoods. Every few miles a small road would snake out of an adjoining valley, connecting one or a dozen small villages to the highway. At almost every intersection, local villagers offered fruits, vegetables and cheese or meat-filled tortillas.

Knowing the route and having suffered from choosing the wrong refreshment stands in the past, most stops were at locations where clear, cold spring water was available. No stop except lunch lasted more than fifteen minutes; just enough time to stretch weary legs, dewater the travelers and water the horses.

Each night the train stopped in one of the larger towns where hotel rooms were waiting. After twelve hours on the road chilled beer and white wine flowed at dinner, happily served by restaurant owners delighted to be paid in gold rather than Royalist paper currency. Each evening Lt. Mare arranged for the local army garrison to supply sentries for the hotel, allowing his troop a good night's sleep. Stable hands from the local livery left with the wagons and horses each night, and each morning the wagons and coach were returned cleaned and with well-fed and rested horses.

The French, from the elite palace guard regiment, were all either a corporal or a sergeant. They spoke fluent Spanish as well as their French, even a little English. The travelers were surprised to find that among the twelve troopers, two were Austrian, one was Basque, and one was English. With the Spanish that the crew had picked up, conversation was relatively easy, and friendships were established.

The French were all armed with single shot British carbines, a heavy saber, and two new Samuel Colt six shot pistols, one in a holster and a second in their saddle bags.

A friendly contest after lunch the first afternoon pitted Sgt. Mosby and the senior French Sergeant in a shooting contest. The Henry proved vastly superior to the single shot carbines of the French. The metallic cartridge Colt pistols proved superior to any of the small collection of pistols owned by the Americans. By the time the wagons again rolled, each of the French including the two officers owned a Henry and boxes of shells and twelve of the Americans owned a Colt and a box of cartridges. The combined company could have taken on a small army and held their own.

The road was so heavily used, and so hard packed that it gave off no dust. The hot dry heat of the first day, slowly gave way to hot humid heat the third day of travel. By the time the travelers reached the beautiful town of Cordoba, a bath, not a beer was on their minds. The company halted travel at the small French army post at the edge of town. Lt. Mare, who had ridden ahead, met them at the gate.

"Maria, Denali," he announced, "the Comandante's wife has invited you to her home to bathe. The officers will follow me to the officer's quarters where they have showers." Pointing to a graying man in a working uniform he continued, "the rest of you please follow Sgt. Folk here to the enlisted bath house. Clean clothes are in order, if you have them, as the Comandante has arranged dinner with the Mayor. Please meet me here in an hour for transport."

Detailing two enlisted men to carry the women's trunks he turned his attention back to the men. "Take what you need but leave your bags on the wagons."

⚜

The mayor, the son of a French mining engineer and a Mexican architect's daughter, was still in his twenties. He was an ardent Royalist, and if Denali's perceptions were correct, probably the most available bachelor in town. He also owned one of the hotels where the travelers were lodged, and the restaurant that catered a dinner for more than fifty.

At each stop, Secretary Pierce presented an envelope bearing the Royal Seal of the Emperor to the Mayor. It contained a letter of introduction and a request for safe passage and every courtesy to "friends of the emperor!"

The mayor welcomed the travelers and their military escorts, in the name of himself and ten notable guests included the Comandante and his wife, the local Catholic Bishop and the head of the Banco de Cordoba.

"…Rebuilding the ties of friendship between the United States and Mexico," translated Major Zidot; "…securing Mexico through strength, the church, and stability," he continued. "…The children of the villages in the hills guided by wise, strict parents using teachings of the church and those selected to lead," ended the twenty-minute speech.

"I have not heard such a defense of the landed elite's destiny to rule in years," whispered Zidot to Chad, Denali and the others seated at the table of six. "The British would label that as over the top." Neither Chad nor Denali showed any sign that they heard him.

"The meal is called Mole Poblano," replied Pedro Davis to a question from the crew's chef. "I will see what I can do to get you the recipe."

"It is the favored meal of special events in Central Mexico," added Maria.

Angelo Gasparetti's eyes danced. "Chicken, onion, tomatoes, chilies, raisins, almonds, cinnamon, chocolate, what a combination," he spewed. "This meal would make a restaurant in New York or Boston famous."

"Shouldn't we be wrapping up?" asked Chad of Zidot. "We have a full day on the road again tomorrow."

"Tomorrow is shorter and all downhill. We can enjoy ourselves."

The evening continued with a custard type desert and was followed by a local favorite, brandy with a touch of chocolate, followed by another short speech. Then the music of a string quartet was followed by more chocolate brandy.

Well after midnight the French troopers were excused, and the ship's crew followed them to the hotel on the west of the plaza. Mead, Mare, Kadzof and Doc Parker excused themselves, escorting Maria to her room in the mayor's Hotel.

Denali sat quietly, her hand on Chad's arm. "Denali, if you will excuse us for a few minutes, I need to discuss security with Major Zidot, and the Mayor," requested Chad. "I will be along in a few minutes."

"If you will allow me Señorita de la Cruz," offered Pierce, "I would be honored to escort you to your room." Denali rose and took his arm, stopping to offer her thanks to the mayor.

Chad's first question was about night security for the travelers.

"Your Lt. Mare approved the arrangement," offered the Mayor. "We have no garrison troops here, only service forces. I personally added two police patrols and believe that sufficient." It took a moment for Zidot to translate.

"Each of you arrived safely and will depart safely," added the Mayor.

"There are no absolutes in Mexico, Captain Gritt," commented Zidot. "There are no troops available to guard the hotel. I have learned to accept the best possible from others and to add a bit more preparation myself. I note that you share my philosophy, Capitan," he added tapping the leather writer's folder that Chad carried in his left hand. "Your folder appears to have increased in weight by about one Colt pistol."

The men stopped at the front of the hotel, finishing a cigar presented to them by the mayor. Chad laughed, "was it that obvious?"

"Only if you wonder why one would take their writer's case to a dinner."

Chad's response was interrupted by two sharp cracks and a seconds later a woman's scream from the third floor of the open-air hotel. "This cannot be good," snapped Zidot, reaching for the pistol in the covered holster at his side. "If you will go in the front, I will cover the grounds," he continued. Chad watched Zidot start into the garden as he fumbled in his writer's case for the Colt. Then he bolted for the stairs.

The stairways were well lighted with oil lamps on each landing, but the hallways poorly lit. Still, it took only seconds to see that the second-floor hallway was empty. Continuing to the third floor Chad cocked the big Colt and turned down the hall. Two men stood at the far end, one holding a table lamp.

The door on his right swung open. Chad dropped to a knee and found he was pointing the Colt at Doc Parker. "God, Doc," he blurted, "I could have turned you into a eunuch."

"What's going on?" asked Parker.

"I don't have a clue."

"Chad, Doc, come quick," came Nick's voice from the end of the hall.

"Tell it quickly now, Mr. Pierce," continued Nick as Chad and Parker arrived.

"I was walking Ms. de la Cruz to her room when two men appeared from the back stairs. We turned to run, only to find that two men were blocking the other end of the hall. One of them demanded the Emperor's letter and told us that no one would get hurt if I gave it to them. I told them it was in my room and that I would get it. One man followed me in.

I wasn't going to give them the letter, so I reached into my case for the pocket gun that I always carry there. As I turned the man was raising a pistol, so I shot him with both barrels. He stumbled out of the room and a moment later Denali screamed."

"The wounded man's partner demanded the letter and my pistol, or he would shoot Denali. I threw both of them out the door and the three men disappeared toward the back stairs with Miss de la Cruz."

Below, Zidot crept through the open-air hotel lobby, where oddly no one was at the front desk. He slipped into the rear courtyard just as two men dragged Denali from the stairs. He couldn't shoot without risking hitting the woman. Sliding his Colt into his holster he bolted toward the abductors, tackling the larger of the men. The two men tumbled to the ground, Zidot landing on top. He swung at the huge man's head with all his strength, his fist landing just below the man's left ear. The attacker turned his face up at Zidot and smiled, shaking his head.

Denali's scream and the sound of men yelling brought the men in the third-floor hallway to the rear landing. Below Zidot, and a much larger man were fighting. The larger man smashed Zidot's cheek with a pistol, then pushed the French officer off and scrambled to his feet. He pointed his pistol at Zidot's head. Chad squeezed the trigger of the Colt resting on the railing of the stairs.

The man assaulting Zidot melted onto the ground like hot wax running down a candle. A second released Denali and ran.

In the moonlight, Chad noted two men stumbling along the alley in front of the running man. As the runner caught up, he pushed one of the men to the ground, pulled a pistol from his coat pocket and calmly shot the fallen man in the head. Bolting from the moonlit alley, the remaining two men ran into the trees and a moment later the clatter of horses' hooves could be heard on the adjoining street.

Chad lowered the big Colt, not even realizing that he had pointed it down the alley.

"Where are they?" called a voice from below. Chad looked down to see Zidot helping Denali from a tangle of bushes.

"One is face down in the brush just about ten feet in front of you," said Pierce.

"I saw Señorita de la Cruz putting up a fight as two men dragged her down the stairs. I couldn't risk shooting," said Zidot.

"Pierce shot another one, and unless I miss my guess, one of his comrades just finished the job at the end of the alley," continued Chad. "The other two are gone." Three men on the balcony headed down the stairs, Nick and Doc each carrying a bedside lamp, while Pierce ran back into his room for two more bullets for the double barrel gun he had picked up from the floor.

"Pierce gave them the letter," blurted Nick.

Zidot quickly searched the dead man. "It's not here."

"Doc, stay with Denali," ordered Chad. "Major, Nick, let's check the man down the alley." It took only minutes to determine that the letter was gone. Returning they found Pierce standing next to Doc, who had seated Denali on the steps holding her trembling hands.

"I will write to the Emperor. I will advise him that the letter is gone," said Zidot. "Lt. Mare can carry my note back when he returns."

"That will not be necessary," answered Pierce. "I threw out my pistol as demanded, but the letter they got was our letter of introduction." Producing an envelope from his right lapel he continued, "the Emperor's letter is right here."

"Why did the robbers kill their friend?" asked Denali.

"He could not go far with two bullets in his gut," surmised Pierce. "They didn't want to leave a witness."

"Will they be back?"

"Probably not tonight, Miss," replied Parker.

In the distance the clanging bell of a police carriage could be heard. "Where are Mr. Mead and Lieutenant Mare?" asked Zidot.

"When Mare told us of the security problem for the night, he and Mead walked back to the troops hotel to organize a security detail," replied Doc Parker. "They should be here about the time that the police arrive. Both appear to be a bit late."

"Gentlemen," directed Zidot, "we should meet them in front."

"I'll be right with you," said Chad. Taking Denali's trembling hands in his he asked, "are you hurt, are you alright?"

Denali rose; slapping him she started up the stairs. "Now you finally ask," she screamed.

Chad watched her go, and then at the top of his vision, caught a glimpse of a blond woman in a white robe turning from the third-floor balcony.

JUSTICE IS COMPLICATED

38
ON THE ROAD TO VERACRUZ, MEXICO

NIGHT WAS BECOMING morning when the men finally wrapped up with the local police. Each managed three hours of restless sleep. The French troopers who had volunteered to guard the hotel got none.

The bleary-eyed travelers picked at a simple breakfast. At precisely at 8:00 a.m. the wagons arrived. Within an hour they were on the road.

"Do you believe that the mayor was involved?" asked Mead riding next to Gritt and Zidot well in front of the coach. Lt. Mare trailed by only a few feet, trying to stay awake.

"Perhaps," responded Zidot. "You would never find firm evidence if he was and politically you could never even ask the question."

"I found it strange that neither the police chief nor the mayor put in an appearance," added Mead. "The police didn't seem surprised by the attack."

"There wasn't even an effort to search the premises or the dead men for evidence," added Chad.

"I will ensure that the governor gets an army request to investigate," volunteered Mare.

"Nothing will come of it," responded Zidot. "The failure to make any progress in solving the case will be explained away; inexperienced investigators, late at night, foreign language problems."

"They did not even interview Señorita de la Cruz; perhaps she could have provided a description of her attackers," complained Mare.

Zidot sighed and shrugged his shoulders. "Sometimes I envy the Juaristas, Lieutenant." They have one enemy and a singular goal of pushing the Europeans out of Mexico. What will happen if they win is not even discussed. The Emperor wrestles with arguing partners all day. The church, the hacienda owners, the vested rich and the Europeans all have a different view of the war and what Mexico will be after they consolidate power. It is better for the coalition that no one is found responsible for the attack. They can't even blame it on the Juaristas; Cordoba has been declared safe."

Machiavelli would appreciate this," sighed Chad, "I do not. A final act of the War Between the States lands me, and my crew in the middle of your civil war. I can't figure out who to trust; maybe no one. All I want is to bring the pirates who sunk my ship to justice, and then go back to running my shipping company. I am a weary man."

"Captain Gritt, you volunteered to ride point, but I am sure that I can get one of my troopers to relieve you," offered Mare.

"No, I'm sorry," answered Chad. "Let your troopers sleep; they were on duty for more than twenty-four hours."

"The Captain and I are happy to be riding with you, Lieutenant," added Mead. "The first sign of a fine officer is how he takes care of his men."

The men rode on in silence. The forest turned to jungle, the shrill calls of its birds filling the air. Mead stopped at a stand of what looked like tall reeds next to a poor stick and mud farm and opened his pocketknife. He cut four long stems and stripped off the leaves. Handing a piece to each of the men he explained; "sugar cane, chew on it, it will pump up your energy. It was a favorite treat of mine when I was in the south. Tell me, Major, about Veracruz."

"Dirty, a port town, poorly administered, surrounded by swamp. Did I mention the mosquitos and biting flies?" continued Zidot. In 1862, when the allies first occupied Veracruz, with 8,000 men, more than ten percent were downed by disease in the first two months. The locals call the jungle the Tierra Caliente. To those who were not born there it is the land of malaria and vomito-negro, what our English allies call Yellow Fever. I thank the Holy Mother that we will only be there a day or two."

By the time the group stopped to exchange horses, the riders delighted in exchanging their saddles for seats in the wagons where window screens kept most of the insects at bay.

The group stopped for lunch at Lattuja, the highway intersection that connected Tabasco, Campeche and southwestern Mexico with the rest of the country. The fields of sugar cane and coffee plantations were welcome compared to the dense jungle, where any breeze was lost in the treetops. The road was raised above the level of fields of crops on either side.

The track was crowded with farm traffic, which slowed their progress, especially where the road narrowed over a single lane bridge crossing yet another dark jungle stream. The men in the first troop wagon were all sleeping when one of the guards from the coach banged on the door. Lt. Mare listened for a few seconds and then climbed from the coach. A moment later he stuck his head back inside.

"You might want to alert the rest of the crew; tell them to find their rifles."

Chad jumped from the wagon, the leather folder with his Colt in his hand. "What is going on?"

At a small bridge only fifty yards from the front of the coach, a wagon was twisted, blocking the bridge. A huge black bull stood bellowing, tethered in the wagon. The wagon rocked as the bull twisted its head violently trying to free itself from the ropes. Behind the wagon stood two heavily armed men and behind them three empty farm wagons waited. Chad scanned each side of the road. The fields could conceal hundreds of attackers.

"I have a really bad feeling about this," he offered to Mare.

"So did the guard on the coach. The front left wheel of the wagon is off the axel, but the axel itself doesn't seem to be broken."

"Sergeant Mosby, could you get our crew armed and out of the wagons," called Chad. "Do it quietly."

"I have already ordered my troops to set up a skirmish line in front of the coach," said Mare.

Chad chanced a glance into the second troop wagon. Mead lay stretched out on one of the benches, snoring. He shrugged his shoulders and turned to Mosby. "Sergeant, have your men spread out beside and behind the wagons. Tell them to be ready to get down on the ground if someone starts shooting. They will be easy targets on this raised roadway."

Across the bridge, the drivers of the three empty wagons tied off their reins and jumped to the ground. They started toward where men dressed like farmers stood near the stranded wagon.

"They men from the wagons don't look like they are armed," observed Mare, "only the guards behind them."

"There could be rifles in the wagon with that bellowing beast," replied Chad, who now had the Colt in his hand.

Behind the stalled wagon the four heavily armed men stopped talking and began walking toward the bridge. "I like this less every second, Lt. Mare."

Two of the armed men handed their rifles to their friends and joined the wagon drivers and the farmers in placing their shoulders under the left front of the wagon and lifting. The last farmer muscled the huge wheel back onto the axel and then retrieved a replacement nut from a box under the wagon seat and a huge wrench. A moment later, the wheel secured, the same man walked to the head of the team of four oxen and began leading them.

Mare, cradling his rifle, made his way to the wagon, striking up a conversation, as the wagon cleared the bridge. The armed guards walked their horses close behind. Mare turned and called, "these men are transporting a prize bull, that just came off a ship from Spain. The animal is worth a small fortune," he called. "The rest of the wagons just delivered a load of sugar cane to Veracruz."

Chad glanced at his shipmates. All were kneeling, rifles at ready except Pierce who stood in the open, waving his pistol at the fields.

"Take it easy," called Chad. "Mount up, the bridge is clear, we're on our way."

It was early evening when the group passed through the fishing village of Boca del Rio and a short time later rolled into Veracruz. Zidot's description of the city had been harsh but accurate. The central community was a collection of mismatched buildings set on poorly maintained streets. But the primary impression came from the nose. The smell of mustiness and mold, and rotting fish, seemed to come from every direction.

Chad studied the community and the harbor. There was a lot to do in Mexico when the war ended, but there was a lot to work with. He remembered what Pierce had repeated after his lunch with the emperor. With stability even his small company could be interested in investing in a port with this potential. He ran his hand down the back of his neck, smoothing the hair that gave away his nervousness. Stability was not coming soon.

※

The white stucco hotel sat on a hilly point overlooking the port and an old Spanish fort on an island just offshore. The travelers were greeted by two negro doormen in crisp starched uniforms and were escorted to a registration desk in a lobby filled with fresh flowers. A graying woman in a white linen dress greeted them.

"Welcome," she gushed in English with a southern drawl. "We have had few American visitors in the last few years, almost none from the north. Ah' have moved some of the guests around to give yawl the entire south wing. You have twenty rooms, eight on the ground floor and twelve upstairs," she continued. "Your enlisted men will have to double up."

"And you are?" asked Denali.

"Mrs. Russell Stowell, Margaret to my friends," answered the woman. "Originally from Mobile, but Russell and I moved here ten years ago. It saved our marriage, him being from New York and my family all plantation folk from Alabama," she laughed. "After ya'll freshen up a bit, the bar will be serving libations on the terrace over the bay. There are two cold water baths on each floor, and you may use the two on the ground floor of the south wing," she added.

An hour later, Chad watched as four freshly showered French troopers in light gray fatigues relieved four of their comrades who had taken up positions at the hotel entrances. He was pleased to see one of Mosby's marines, also in French fatigues, was with them.

He seated himself at a table for six, where Lt. Mare was chatting with Margaret and a heavy-set man, with almost no hair, and sparkling blue eyes. "Captain Chad Gritt, Mr. Russell Stowell," announced Mare.

"New guest," called Margaret to a waiter, "a mint julep for the Captain. Captain Gritt, there is positively nothing more refreshing after a day in the heat." One by one, the other travelers arrived, with Mead and Pedro Davis seating themselves with Chad.

"I was a railroad engineer with a small investment in two southern railroads," said Stowell. Margaret and I owned a hotel in Mobile. Like Mr. Mead here, I graduated from West Point, but left the army after eight years. I fell in love with Margaret and the south.

"We saw the war coming," added Margaret, "Russell believed in the Union with all of his heart. My family and friends were all for southern independence; we both knew that the north would win, but the south would fight. We simply could not be a part of that."

"So, we sold our stock, and the hotel, and I accepted a job to help design a railroad from Veracruz to Mexico City," continued Russell.

"There is a railroad?" asked Mead.

"No," laughed Stowell, "The government granted a concession ten years ago, but it was a pipe dream, no capital."

"So instead we built the hotel," continued Margaret. "It has been very good to us. With the Mexican war we have a constant stream of officers and diplomats. Men from the Southern blockade-runners, and the British and French ships that they trade with, stay here. And now that the civil war is over, perhaps my boys will join us."

Now, Margaret, they are grown and gone," interjected her husband, "Michael will probably make the army a career and Calvin is going to be tied up a while; then he's the only one left to help your mother and father get Marian Wood back in business."

"Your son was in the army?" asked Mead.

"Both of them, Sir," answered Margaret.

"Michael graduated from West Point just before the war. He's now a major with General Sherman in Texas. Calvin was a cadet at the Virginia Military Institute when Alabama seceded. He took a Captain's commission with General Beauregard and was with him and Joseph Johnson when they tried to stop Sherman's March on Atlanta. By then he was also a major. He is a proud, passionate romantic, and the Confederacy is his cause."

"Michael wrote us that his brother had been captured trying to cross into Texas where he believed the war was continuing," added Margaret. "The army of Texas had surrendered days before, so he was arrested as a common criminal. It is not fair."

"Margaret, he knew the cause was lost," replied Stowell. "His brother is working on his release."

"But his only crime was his love of Marian Wood, and the southern life."

"Marian Wood, gentlemen, is Margaret's parents' plantation on the Alabama River north of Mobile," advised her husband. "It is now largely in ruin as is most of the South."

"Shall I light them pots now, Ms. Margaret?" asked a tall black man in a white uniform.

"Yes," answered Margaret. "And then bring another tray of juleps. We will be ready for dinner in one hour."

"Most of our staff was with us at Stowell House in Mobile," continued Russell. "They were all free men, raised at Marian Wood. After we built the hotel here, Margaret went home for three months and when she returned, they came with her."

"Please excuse the smell of the fire pots," begged Margaret. "The ocean breeze keeps the flies at bay almost all day and all night; all except sunset when the air cools in the mountains and flows downhill and brings the flies from the swamps. The pots use an old slave recipe of minerals, flowers, herbs and cattle dung to keep them at bay. The breeze will turn around before dinner."

"Mrs. Stowell, my family is from the South," declared Pedro Davis who up until then had been a silent listener. "I was, until a few weeks ago, an officer in the Confederate Navy. Your son sounds a great deal like my shipmates. Most of the officers lost everything. They knew the war was over when they attacked Captain Gritt's ship in order to steal gold for a fresh start for them and other Confederate officers."

"But you now serve with Captain Gritt," observed Stowell.

"It is a long story. My mother is from a well-to-do Mexican family. They helped us get to Mexico City. The bloodshed during the taking of the *KATARINA* and the destruction of the ship were not part of the plan. With Captain Gritt's blessing I am now making amends."

"You sound like a good Catholic boy," responded Margaret, "making amends an' all. Ma' family, like most southern families of French descent, is also Catholic."

"Perhaps you could escort this sinner to morning mass, ma'am," requested Pedro. "That is, if we have time and Captain Gritt approves."

"Time should not be a problem," interjected Stowell. "You see that side wheeler anchored north of the harbor? That is your ride back to the States and right now she is waiting for a berth to unload. Our port can only handle three ships at a time, and the dock is full. She will not have a berth until tomorrow evening. Her master, Captain Kelley, will be joining us for dinner."

Margaret rose to check on dinner. Touching Chad's arm, she whispered, "When you catch those boys who sunk your ship, I pray you will be merciful."

The dinner of steamed shrimp, crab, grilled fish and a variety of salads was served buffet style on the patio. As Margaret predicted, the wind had reversed itself again and now flowed gently over the patio. "You have ignored me all day and all evening," whimpered Denali as Chad took a seat next to her, almost spilling a mountain of shrimp on his plate.

"Last night you were angry at me," responded Chad, "and today was very busy."

"What does my Capitán expect? Last night was very difficult and I am a woman." Denali ran a finger across his cheek.

Chad just started to eat as Russell Stowell walked a well-dressed man of medium height and build to the table. The man tightened his ribbon tie, and then buttoned his coat. His most identifiable feature was a shock of curly bright red hair that exploded out from under a small-billed cap. "Captain Chad Gritt, I am pleased to introduce Captain Patrick Kelley," announced Stowell.

It was after eleven when the dinner service was cleared, and the majority of the party moved to the small hotel bar in the lobby.

Gritt, Mead, Pierce and Pedro Davis seated themselves next to Zidot and Captain Kelley. "I earned my pay the last five years running back and forth to Cuba for the French and running the Union blockade for the Confederates. We were based in New Orleans but slipped out of the Mississippi the day before Admiral Farragut blockaded the mouth of the river. Me and the boys represent the entire maritime presence of the Free State of Jones."

"The Free State of what?" queried Chad.

"Our entire crew is made up of farm boys from Jones County Mississippi. None of the small farmers in Jones County wanted to fight a war to protect the planters, so in 1861 we seceded from the Confederacy," answered Kelley.

"Jones raiders attacked supply depots of both North and South, didn't they?" asked Mead.

"So it is said. We consider ourselves neutrals. Still, I am told that both North and South had warrants out for what they call 'gangs from Jones County.' We did well over the last five years. The winnings are all in a bank in Cuba. Now all we want is to go home," he continued, adding something from a flask to the drink in front of him.

"Here is my offer, based on the rumors about your predicament. We will run you and your party to New Orleans. Your Secretary Pierce will provide a letter of safe passage for the river. Four of us, myself, my first officer, my engineer and his assistant will stay on board. My other hands will jump ship in New Orleans and head home. You hire a new crew to avenge the loss of your ship and we will take you to Cuba. We won't fight but we will get you there."

"Then what?" asked Pierce.

"We make one stop, in Havana, to make a bank withdrawal on the way home. When we get to the North, you arrange a pardon with your signature, and we head for home. Captain Gritt, we will sell you the *MOLLY K* for a song."

"Do I want your ship?"

"Captain, the *MOLLY* was built for passengers, with twenty private cabins and a lounge. She's a little under the weather from hauling wartime passengers and contraband, but she will spruce up just fine. She is also the fastest steamer in North America. She can outrun anything on the water. Even in peace time, speed is money."

"And if we fail in Cuba?" asked Mead. "Where does that leave you?"

"Then, Mr. Mead, we are exactly where we are today, trying to find a way to go home as rich men," answered Kelley.

"Let us sleep on it, Captain," requested Pierce.

"Fine Mr. Secretary. I'll meet you for breakfast. I'm staying in the hotel. Now if you will excuse me, I'm off to find Russell to arrange sale of that portion of cargo not on my manifest. I trust Major Zidot, that your mission is more important than getting involved in a black-market investigation." Kelley turned from the table before Zidot answered.

A few minutes later Chad opened the door to his room to find Denali curled up on the bed wearing one of his shirts.

"I forgive you for ignoring me," she said.

"Maybe we should talk more about Boston."

"Tomorrow."

39
THE GULF OF MEXICO

THE BRIDGE OF Kelley's ship resembled that of a river steamboat, not an open ocean ship. Kelley maneuvered the *MOLLY K.* out of the harbor on a flat calm day. The rain shower as they departed Veracruz made clear the advantage of a pilothouse over a sailing ship's open bridge. Chad bolted through the door just as the rain ended, wiping water from his face and head with the sleeve of his coat.

"Welcome aboard Captain Gritt," said Kelley. "We are at a fast cruise speed of 17 knots, with the current, almost 20 knots across the globe. If the weather holds, and the bar crossing at the mouth of the river goes well, dinner in New Orleans the night after tomorrow."

"How much will a little wind slow you?"

"Ten knots from the front or rear will not affect us. More than that, it depends on the wind direction."

"Gritt RusAm Trading does almost all long-range shipping," continued Chad. "Boston to California, Alaska and China as well as routes to Europe, make up most of our business. We also have the Rum Run, from New England to the Caribbean and back, all under sail. I know little about steam powered ships."

"There is not much difference, except different things break," laughed Kelley. "You watch wind patterns as well as sea currents while we chart only by current. Because we don't have to tack with the different wind directions, we can generally sail a straight line. That makes us much faster. Would you like a tour of the *MOLLY*?"

The tour was an eye opener. Designed in 1850 the *MOLLY K* had third generation, steam power, rocking-arm engines. A separate engine drove each of the huge side paddle wheels, and two fireboxes fueled each engine. The noise was deafening and the six men on duty all had huge wads of cotton stuffed in their ears. Six large air scoops on the fore and mid deck pushed a steady breeze through the engine room and out two large vents at the rear of the ship.

"You said that you were at fast cruise," began Chad, "how much faster can she go?"

"Another five knots or even a bit more, but that extra five knots chews up more than fifty percent more fuel. Still when you need it, it's nice to know she has wings."

Chad pointed to the stern of the ship. "What flag are you flying?"

"That sir is the Jones' flag; we fly it on the open seas. What flag would you prefer? We have American, Confederate, Mexican, French Tricolor and Spanish with appropriate documentation to match. All five countries use Irish crews," he laughed. "We prefer speed over guile, but sometimes quick thinking beats hard steaming."

"Would you mind if Nick Kadzof, my first officer, and Hans Gott, my chief, understudy your crew for the voyage. It's time we learn about steam."

"It would be our pleasure."

The morning of the third day dawned gray with a light rain

falling. The sea beneath the ship was brown with silt from the Mississippi, even though they were six hours from the dreaded bar crossing. "Our last star sighting was about three hours ago," offered Nick, "we were right on course."

"Great news Mr. Kadzof," responded Chad. "Get some rest, I want the officers fresh for a planning session after we cross the bar. This ship will require more crew than we have, and we will need more men who know how to fight."

There were no picket ships at the mouth of the river. The *MOLLY*'s shallow draft made the run over the bar uneventful and in less than an hour they were steaming up the south passage.

"You may use the forward cargo storage for your meeting," offered Kelley. "It is set up for group transport, with folding chairs and large tables." Mead, Sergeant Mosby, Chad, Kadzof, Pierce and Doc Parker had invited Zidot and Captain Kelley to their confab. Zidot had excused himself, not wanting to be part of any action in Cuban waters with Spain a close ally; Kelley accepted.

"You will need eight stokers for the boilers," advised Kelley. "The trip to Cuba will be less than two days. Each crew change will work no more than four six-hour shifts to get us there. Once we leave Cuba, we will stoke only one boiler on each side for the trip north. The economy cruise will give us about ten knots. The other stokers can transfer to the rebel ship when you make her your prize. You do plan on keeping her do you not?"

"We have not discussed it," answered Chad, "but unless she is damaged, I believe we will."

"Sergeant Mosby, what will you need?" asked Mead.

"I would like Lieutenant Mare and his twelve Frenchies," quipped Mosby as the room erupted with laughter.

"Not possible, I am afraid," answered Doc Parker. "By now they are on their way back to Mexico City, probably with giant hangovers. That twenty dollars in gold our Captain paid each of them was probably a month's salary," he continued.

"We have plenty of light arms firepower, with the Sharps and the Henrys," drawled Mosby. "I will need about eight marines armed with Colts and sabers to clear the decks. We will want to secure the below decks first to keep them from scuttling her, then the main deck and the half deck on top."

"Mr. Mead, Mr. Pierce, you two are leaving directly for Washington, with Miss de la Cruz, Mrs. Huerta and Major Zidot, is that correct?" asked Doc Parker.

"Our mission to Alaska is our first priority," replied Mead. "No matter what happens in Cuba, the Alaska report and our individual summaries of what we observed in Mexico need to get to the new President and Secretary Seward. Your captain is the right man to lead the recovery."

Pierce looked over at Gritt, "I would prefer to go with you, I feel there is unfinished business."

"Let us finish it Mr. Secretary," replied Nick. "You have more important things to do."

"That makes me very uncomfortable, kind of like I am deserting."

"Not at all Mr. Secretary. Our primary purpose for this trip was the Alaska study. That is your mission."

"Besides there are no more than thirty Rebs on that ship. Pedro said they sailed with a skeleton crew. A number of her crew disserted in San Francisco and started home. There are already plenty of us plus whatever marines Sergeant Mosby rustles up, and we have better weapons and surprise," voiced Doc Parker.

"Hopefully you can hit them at night, right after they arrive, maybe even while the officers are ashore. Hit them hard and fast and maybe not a shot will be fired," added Mead.

"If we can take her before her boilers are cold, we can move the ship," said Pedro. "If not, it takes more than an hour to get up steam. We may need to hold off an armada of small boats filled with desperate former soldiers. We need a plan to tow the *RETRI-BUTION* or a plan on how to defend her."

"Alright gentlemen, we need two lists. One of what we need if everything goes right and the second with what we would like to have." The meeting was interrupted by a lookout reporting to Kelley.

"Gentlemen, we are approaching Fort Jackson. A Union ironclad has signaled us to stop."

The ship dropped anchor about one hundred yards from the *USS PORTLAND*, a heavy river gunboat and only a quarter mile below the guns of Fort Jackson. The Mississippi ran a half-mile wide where it wrapped around the old stone fort. Beyond the riverbanks the delta seemed to go on forever. Nothing rose above the low swamps.

"The absence of any land features and the sodden sky makes this really dreary," observed Chad. He and Kelley stood on the wing of the bridge as flag messages were exchanged.

"Not if it's home," answered Kelley. Even a hundred miles upriver the land is flat, swampy. For us southern boys, up and down just wastes energy that could be better used going farther. Maybe that's what I love about the sea."

Chad began to laugh. "I love a flat sea and land that stretches my neck muscles up and down."

※

On the bridge of the *PORTLAND*, a tall gray-haired man surveyed the *MOLLY K* through an old-fashioned brass telescope. The red veins showing in the dark tanned face told a story of heavy drink and a hard life. "Sergeant Ross, I want you to bring the men on the bridge of that steamer to the ship's mess after you inspect her papers," he directed.

A half hour later he watched the small steam launch pull away from the side-wheeler. Ten minutes later Chad, Mead, Zidot, Pierce and Kelley were escorted into the *PORTLAND's* dining room.

"Buy you a cup of coffee little brother?" asked the Captain of the iron clad.

"My God, Carl, how are you?" responded Chad as he rushed across the room and embraced the older man.

"The Captain of a Man-O-War should not be seen hugging another man," laughed the Captain holding his younger brother at arm's length. "It's good to see you, Chad."

"Gentlemen, my big brother," announced Chad, looking the older man up and down; "Commander Carl Gerhardt Gritt."

"I can offer you real coffee from Venezuela and fresh biscuits and honey," offered Carl, pointing to a linen covered table. He picked up a coffee pot and poured a cup for himself.

"Chad, that's not a RusAm ship, what in the hell are you doing here?" asked the *PORTLAND*'s skipper.

"A long story Carl, one worth listening to, but first let me introduce my friends. On the left is Captain Patrick Kelley, master of the *MOLLY K*; next to him Under Secretary of State Miles Standish Pierce; then Major Miguel Zidot of Emperor Maximilian's staff in Mexico and Colonel Thomas Jefferson Mead of the War Office."

"Welcome gentlemen, will you please be seated?" asked Carl motioning to another linen covered corner table; "I have to hear this story. Sergeant Ross, would you please ask Lt. Polk to join us?" The astonished sergeant said not a word but spun and headed out the door. "Before my second in command gets here, how about the short version?"

"Clandestine survey of Alaska, secret transport of Treasury Gold, attack by a Confederate raider, the loss of the *KATARINA*, shipwreck, fights with both sides on a forced march across Mexico and a plan," replied Chad.

An hour later the story and the missions to Washington and

to Cuba were on the table. "An amazing tale little brother, and the next chapters all key on finding what you need in New Orleans," smiled the *PORTLAND*'s Captain.

"Lt. Polk, you will take command for three or four days. Please enter into the ship's log that I will personally be escorting Secretary Pierce and a ship of questionable documentation to New Orleans," ordered Carl. "Chad, I am coming with you, I think that I can help keep the occupation bureaucrats at bay. If you will give me ten minutes to pack a sea bag, I'll meet you at the launch."

"I haven't seen Carl in years, since I bought out most of his share of the company. He was always the wild one, the rebel of the family; too much drink, disappear for days, women of questionable reputation," remarked Chad.

"All here enjoy too much wine from time to time," replied Kelley, "and who does not appreciate a woman who spits in the eye of her church choir once in a while?"

The five men waiting on the deck laughed. "But Carl would bring them home for the holidays," offered Chad, shaking his head. "He was a good Captain, that is until he lost his ship on the outer banks, along with half of his crew. After that, he walked away from the family and all of his old friends except rum. A year later he walked into the office and asked me to buy him out."

The ship was underway minutes after the six men were safely aboard. Captain Kelley set the ship racing to beat the coming darkness, feeling uncomfortable on the unfamiliar lower river on an overcast night.

"That young Irish captain, with the Mississippi accent, has a very fast ship," offered Carl. "She would have made a great blockade runner," he added with a smile.

Chad changed the topic. "How in the hell did you end up in the Navy?"

Carl pulled a pouch of tobacco from his pocket and a roll of tobacco wrap and tore off a piece. He sprinkled a large pinch of tobacco on the paper, rolled his cigarette and struck a match. "Care for one little brother?"

"No thanks."

"After the loss of The *VALHALLA* nothing seemed important," started Carl. "You know that our father and I never got along. I hated his proper approach to everything. I loved being the black sheep of the family. Why he kept me around I will never know." Carl pulled the cigarette from the corner of his mouth, wiping away bits of disintegrating paper.

"After dragging myself ashore on that Carolina island, with the cries of drowning men on the wind I reached the end," continued Carl. "I would never measure up; I couldn't even save my crew."

"You were fighting a hurricane. Both of your arms were broken."

"I could have done something. Every night for years I would relive that storm and second-guess every decision. Then I would reinforce my drink from the previous evening until I would pass out. I hated the sea and my lack of fitness."

"I've lost a third of my crew in three months," stuttered Chad, "I could have done things differently."

"Let it go little brother; you appear to have done your normal amazing job. Men, mission, mostly intact. You have the possibility of righting the wrong. You even have two beautiful Latin women following your every move."

"What do you mean two?"

"You will figure it out, everything always becomes clear with time. Three years ago, I woke up one morning with the worst headache that I ever had. Worst, my mouth felt like a chimney from dozens of cigarettes the night before. I decided that either tobacco or rum had to go, I couldn't survive both."

"Must have been a bad morning," Chad responded with no effort to control his smirk.

"I still smoke, but I haven't had a drink since March of 1862," announced Carl. "That summer I asked our father to write a letter of introduction to the Navy Department and on August 1, was commissioned a First Lieutenant. I was in on the fight at Vicksburg and since then I have enforced the blockade, the last two years as Captain of the *PORTLAND*. Nothing is more boring than the life of a brown water sailor on picket duty. I miss the purity of blue water."

"Neither father nor mother ever told me."

"I asked them not to," replied his brother. "Now I have a request. My tour ends in a couple of weeks, I want to go with you. You can't avenge the loss of a ship to the sea's fury. But you can undo the manifestations of brutal men. Besides I want to be there when they hang the man who killed Ott Smith."

"We can't wait weeks Carl. The rebel ship could reach Cuba any day now. We hope to be on our way in a couple of days."

"Chad, I have months of leave coming, I have nowhere to go. Well, there is this widow woman. Anyway, with peace breaking out the academy guys are happy to see those of us with wartime commission's leave. They will be happy to cut the orders tonight."

"We can use your help." Chad extended his hand.

"Which one are you sleeping with little brother? I know, a gentleman would never tell, but I would bet on the wild-eyed girl with black hair. Doesn't her temperament remind you of someone from your past?"

"Who?" asked Chad.

"Me."

40
NEW ORLEANS

KELLEY NEEDN'T HAVE worried about navigating into the night. He'd signaled his engine room for maximum power, trading fuel for speed. The ship approached the city well before dark.

"I suggest that you tie up at the old keelboat landing across from Algiers Point," advised Carl Gritt. "It is just past the center of the city."

"I know the spot," replied Kelley.

"You will need to leave a guard on board. The city is in chaos."

The officers, Zidot and Mosby were in the wheelhouse, as the ship chugged past the plaza de Armas, at the center of the city. "The blockade destroyed the economy. Perhaps a quarter of the business district is boarded up, but you can still find shops filled with merchandise shipped from St. Louis around the St. Charles Hotel. We will all take rooms there."

"Chad, Secretary Pierce, Colonel Mead, you will please accompany me, oh, and you as well Sergeant. If the rest of you can handle the luggage, you will find a dozen cabs lined up by the time we tie up," added Carl. The five men piled into a coach at the top of the levy. "The Governor General's office," commanded Carl.

"The General be down at the St. Charles by now," replied the driver.

"Let's check his office first."

They arrived at the Military Commander's offices just as the General and a Navy Captain were boarding a buggy driven by an army corporal. Carl darted out of the coach. "One moment Sir," he called, jogging toward the buggy.

"Carl, you old rumrunner, I thought you were on picket duty at Fort Jackson?" replied the Navy Captain.

"I was, and I am," replied Carl, to a puzzled Captain Black. "I brought four men with me, including Undersecretary of State Miles Standish Pierce and Colonel Thomas Mead of the War Department. They have a story you and the General need to hear."

General Fuller, who was already seated in the buggy, leaned out and extended his hand toward Commander Gritt. "Nice to see you again Commander. Is this important, I mean right now important?"

"I believe so sir. I left the *PORTLAND* to bring them directly here."

"Can we discuss it at the bar?"

"At least initially, it would be better in private."

"All right Commander, please have your coach follow us. We can chat at my residence," directed the General. "Change of plans Mitchell, we will be going home."

The General's residence was an ornate, two-story home just above Canal Street. The end of the street had a military police checkpoint, which of course waived them through. Loping up the stairs in front of the six other men, the General snapped a Military salute to the Police Sergeant at his front door; "Go find my butler and tell him we will be in the parlor."

"A truly remarkable story," said General Fuller. "I'm the former

Governor of Rhode Island and only here as a politician; Captain Black here is the military mind in our office. I'll let him speak to the military issues, but the politician in me sees two major problems. First, I doubt that the President of these United States is going to send a military mission into action, for any reason, in Cuba. Nor will the government allow serving U.S. Military to personnel participate in a mission in a sovereign foreign country. A dozen powerful Senators are already pushing to use the standing army to seize Cuba and the President is pushing back.

Second, if you are going to do this yourselves, how will the venture be financed? If I go through proper channels, diplomatic channels, it will take months just to present a demand to the officials in Cuba. Do you not agree Mr. Secretary?"

"I agree," mumbled Pierce. The men from the *KATARINA* sat in silence.

"Getting Colonel Mead, the French Major, Secretary Pierce and the two ladies to St. Louis will be easy. I do not recommend a military transport. After four years of heavy work, they would find the boats quite worn, and the presence of two Latin ladies might just cause a riot," contributed Captain Black. "Operations on the Mississippi are still under martial law. Commercial steamboats depart for the North every two days. We will commandeer five staterooms and I will send along an escort. Is your man, Lampoc, going or staying?"

"Charles will remain with Captain Gritt, the younger Gritt that is," answered Mead.

"So, five state rooms is what we need. Sergeant Mosby, are you and your two men going to Washington?" asked Black.

"We were ordered to guard the gold Sir. It was taken on my watch, and I lost two nice young Marines; we would all like to finish our mission."

"I knew the answer before I asked," laughed Black. "What about you, Carl?"

"My tour is almost up, and I have months of leave coming. I would like to tag along, you know, look after my kid brother."

"If there is going to be a mission to Cuba at all, I can arrange that," agreed Black. "Sergeant Mosby, you and your two privates will have to request an emergency three-month leave; that too can be arranged."

"Which gets us back to the bigger issue," harped Pierce. "How do we do this without military help?"

A huge smile appeared on General Fuller's face. "Mr. Pierce, lets you and I work on a Rhode Island solution."

There was no shortage of blank stares around the room.

"As late as fifty years ago, this country had a minimal military. In the war of 1812, private ships sailed as privateers with "Letters of Marques" from the government, supplementing our tiny Navy. They were in effect authorized pirates, who preyed on the British, and most were from Rhode Island."

"I propose that Secretary Pierce send a comprehensive telegram to Secretary Seward explaining what you have just told me. We will suggest that Captain Gritt is willing to attempt a recovery and that we recommend a single mission letter of Marque, including a 30% reward of the treasure recovered. We will copy the President and I will send a personal telegram to Andy recommending that he approve this. Jack, I suggest you do the same. What do you think?"

"We really shouldn't advertise this in a telegram," suggested Chad, finally figuring out that Andy was the new President.

"Oh, we will send it coded through the War Department, for addressee only, over Secretary Pierce's signature."

"Let's try it. Can we send the messages tonight?" asked Pierce.

"As soon as we are done here. Now, what will this cost?"

"Our estimate is about $12,000," answered Mead. "If we have to hire mercenaries instead of using Marines, perhaps another $4,000. A budget of $16,000 should do it."

"How much do you have?"

"After our costs to get here, and after providing for enough to get the party to Washington, about $6,000," replied Chad. "I can wire our bank in Boston and have them send the balance."

"That will take at least two weeks, because we are still under Martial Law, it will have to go through the War Department. How much was the shipment worth?"

"Sergeant?" asked Mead.

"Sirs, I was told the original shipment was about a million dollars, but I think it might have been more."

"Well 30 percent would be $300,000, but there will be less. We can deduct what you used to get here and what the rebels used to make it to Cuba. Still, 30 percent should be over $250,000."

"Probably about right," responded Chad.

"How about a business deal. I'll back the other ten thousand dollars for twenty-five percent of the reward," offered Fuller, "unless you want part of this Jack, or someone has another plan?"

"I'm career Navy, and we are prohibited from taking prize money."

"I see this as a simple investment. Does anybody have another idea?" Fuller looked around the room but heard nothing but silence.

"Fine, the money will be available tomorrow. Let's go send some telegrams. Secretary Pierce, Captain Black and I will meet the rest of you at the St. Charles in two hours."

"You just got a good look at the North's management of the Confederate States," offered Carl "Lincoln and Grant wanted a full reconciliation with the south. That's not happening."

Chad stopped walking, staring out at the Mississippi. "Are all of the Governors as greedy as Fuller?"

"From what I am told, most are worse. They and their friends are basically stealing everything of value down here." He paused to light a cigarette. "We will leave that problem for the folks in D.C."

The St. Charles rivaled any hotel in the world. Hundreds of rooms with private baths, all with hot and cold water, powered by a steam engine in the rear of the ground floor that literally made the building vibrate. The bar off from the lobby could seat hundreds, although it was only half full when the Gritt brothers, Mead and Mosby walked in.

Their travel companions were all seated at a long table next to the windows. "Sergeant Mosby," started Kelley, "I hope you don't mind, but I used your two privates as part of the guard on the *MOLLY K.* I thought that having a uniform visible would deter the petty thieves."

"Agreed," replied Mosby, "Although I would like to give them some R and R tomorrow."

Carl Gritt seated himself and gave his drink order to the tan skinned girl that hovered behind him. "The usual Emily," he directed. "Now Sergeant, I believe that we can arrange for a Marine guard early tomorrow morning if that would help."

"It sure would, and Captain Gritt," continued Mosby, looking at Chad, "if those two boys could get a room here for tomorrow night and just a bit of spending money for their pockets you would make their entire year. They have never been in a place like this. Hell, I have never been in a place like this."

"They have earned it," replied Chad. "Carl," he continued, "we will need to convert about fifteen pounds of gold to currency in the morning."

"I don't want to know any more. It will take an order from the quartermaster's office to the Bank of New Orleans, but General Fuller can get that done first thing."

Chad had taken a seat next to Denali. "Mí Capitán" she whispered, placing her hand on top of his, "this evening is for all and tomorrow you will be busy with plans, I know this. But tomorrow night dinner is for only us. You agree, yes?"

"You can plan on it," responded Chad. "After tomorrow we go different directions."

"I know this," whimpered Denali, wiping a tear from her cheek. "My room is next to your room and there is a door," she whispered.

"Tomorrow we can talk about Boston," whispered Chad.

"I do not want this, not until we meet again in your Capitol City."

The next day started too early. A young army captain escorted Pierce and Mead to the telegraph office before their visit with the Transportation Office.

The Gritt brothers and Mosby remained in Captain Black's office. "General Fuller dropped this bank draft on my desk before his political briefing at seven. His buggy, driver and his aide are at your disposal."

"Here is an authorization for Captain Kelley to top off his coal bins at the collier just down river from where his ship is berthed." Black passed a gray sheet of paper across the table. "Have you thought about what the fuel supply might be on the Reb ship?"

"I gave it some thought last night," responded Carl. "Since Cuba is her destination, she may limp into port on coal dust."

"I agree. Here is a second authorization for six tons of sacked coal. Make sure Kelley stores it where it stays dry; once you get aboard the Reb ship you are going to want to get up steam in a hurry."

"I've been thinking about quick steam," responded Carl. "If we had a cord of dry split pine and a drum of coal oil, we should be able to make steam in less than an hour even if the boilers are cold."

"I'll add the coal oil to your fuel allocation." Black slid a second authorization across the table and added a note. "The pine you can buy on the open market. Fuller's driver is an expert scrounger. He will find it for you and even get it delivered. Please no more than a five-dollar tip, he will already be getting a kickback and we don't want to ruin the young man," laughed Black. "You will need to pay for the fuel with cash."

"As to men to complement your three Marines, Sergeant, and crews for the *MOLLY K* and the rebel ship, here is my idea. Every day we cut orders to send as many as two hundred sailors and twenty Marines home. Like you, Carl, they have finished their enlistments. They muster for inspection at nine every morning at the enlisted barracks across the street. Some have seen action; some would like to before they go back to the family grocery. I sent a message to the officer in charge to break out a group of sailors with engine room experience and Marines with either experience, or training, in boarding and clearing. They will be waiting for you in a half hour. A hundred dollars apiece for two weeks' work and a chance for a bonus should get you any man you want. Just bring their names and service numbers back here and I will arrange an early release. Sergeant, we will need the same from you and your two men to cut temporary separation orders. Which gets me to you, Carl, just get the same to personnel on the second floor and I will personally sign off early separation."

"What about my command, Jack?" asked Commander Gritt.

"I'll have a replacement by tomorrow, I would appreciate you dropping him at the *PORTLAND* on your way down river. You will want to say goodbye to your command anyway."

"Thanks Jack," replied Carl, "for the thoughtful send off and all your help."

"Forget it. The peacetime Navy can be a very boring place. I may be knocking on your door in a year looking for a job."

"We could use you right now," offered Chad.

"Maybe later, I'm too busy. Now one more thing. How are you fixed for arms and boarding boats?"

"We will need six ten-man cutters," offered Carl, "four for the boarding and two more to move the fuel."

"We just sold fifty to a surplus outfit. The General's driver can take you there. And arms," he asked?

"We have Henry repeaters, four Sharps rifles and about a dozen Colts," responded Mosby. "We could use a dozen Cutlasses."

"We will arrange to surplus twelve from the stores. You will have them tomorrow."

"From what you say there is a risk of a boat assault, to try to take back the ship after you seize her," added Black. "How do you intend to repel that?"

"We'll do our best," was Mosby's answer.

"I have a better idea. You take care of your banking, recruiting and paperwork. Then we will take a two-hour lunch. There is a demonstration that I would like you to see."

41
THE CARIBBEAN

THE *RETRIBUTION* LOOKED as tired as her crew felt. Routines to keep the vessel ship-shape were ignored. In their place, the crew used their remaining energy just to keep the ship moving north and west. There was no unnecessary conversation.

"Carlton, prepare to get underway," ordered Captain Jackman. The small steam launch that served as a harbor tug at Port of Spain, pushed the heavy ship away from the coaling dock.

The slow pace of the trip grated on everyone. They ran at only eight knots from Mexico all the way to Chile in order to stretch the inefficient wood fuel. There the restless crew had been confined to the ship to minimize risk of someone getting drunk and spilling the beans about their cargo. That decision left the already overworked crew in a foul mood as the ship pushed hard for Cape Horn.

The cape itself matched the crew's mood. It was dark and sullen with showers and a blustery wind. They negotiated the southern tip of South America, and the ship was northbound for a full day when the storm hit. Force four winds from the Northwest had pounded the *RETRIBUTION*. All Jackman could do was hold the bow into thirty-foot waves as the ship was pushed eastward for two days. The ship limped to the Falkland Islands to repair cracks in the wooden deck opened by the twisting hull.

The steam powered bilge pumps had been more than a match for the leakage as wave after wave swept over the deck, but saltwater rained through the split seams. Brandon Piper had refused to release his black gang to deck repairs, instead they had worked for days cleaning and lubricating every moving part that they could reach. It took days for the stench of whale oil to dissipate.

A small steamer had interrupted their departure from their quiet Falklands anchorage. It's signals to stop had been ignored. They assumed that it was a British customs boat, after it fired a small cannon mounted on the bow. The customs boat was gaining on them until a warning shot from the *RETRIBUTION's* stern chaser reminded the Brits that they would have to be alive to collect their pensions.

Of the eight cannons aboard the ship when she left San Francisco, only the bow and small stern guns remained. Six heavy cannons were dumped into the sea, as the ship struggled to free herself from the shallow water of the inlet, where they left the *KATARINA* burning. The same bilge pumps that saved the ship after rounding the Cape had been harnessed to escape. Fire hoses had been rigged to allow the pumps to pick up seawater and send it to crews at the bow of the ship. High pressure water blasted a narrow passage through the sand, but it took two days.

They fueled again in Porto Alegre. The officers faced down a minor mutiny from crew confined to the ship.

The *RETRIBUTION* pushed northeast to Ponta de Calcanhar, the most eastern point in Brazil, where they could finally set a northwest course for Cuba. At Port of Spain, they had taken on enough coal for ten days of hard steaming even though the last leg of their journey would only take half that long. The officers knew that the patriarchs of Palmo's Inlet tolerated no ship in port for more than five days.

"Rudder hard left, all ahead, dead show," ordered the Captain.

"Aye aye," replied the quartermaster. Elim Beershieu was a small lad of twenty-three who had grown up on the water. Originally from Natchez, Mississippi he had been working riverboats since he was twelve. When the war started, he had been in Charleston visiting kin. He had enlisted in the Confederate Navy, and had found himself in England, part of Barkston Jackman's original crew.

Elim brushed his tangle of sandy hair from his eyes and braced his feet as he swung the spoked wheel in front of him. He absent-mindedly wiped the sweat from his hands on his pants. The hot, humid day reminded him of home. Home. When he reached home, he would pick a lemon from his mother's prized lemon tree and eat it, peel and all. He'd always wondered how she grew lemons that had just a touch of sweetness.

"Carlton, please secure the ship," ordered Jackman. "You may haul those empty crates from the hold and strap them down on the deck. I want to look like any other freighter. When we are well out to sea and away from prying eyes you may uncover and dismount the fore and aft cannon. We will not make landfall again until Cuba. I do not want any confrontation with the Spanish authorities, now that we know that they are disarming Confederate ships."

"You believe what we heard this morning?" asked Lee.

"I do; the Spanish have a right to be worried about the Yankees. The Yankee Navy has at least two hundred ships, and there must be at least a half-million blue coat soldiers, and neither have much to do. The Spanish have refused at least three offers to sell Cuba. If the North wants it, now would be the time to take it. They could sweep the Spanish aside like drunkards from a rum punch. The Cuban officials are stepping on eggs."

"Captain Jackman, may I ask a question?" inquired the quartermaster.

Of course, Elim, what is it?"

"You know Mr. Bolton came back to the ship drunk as a fiddler's hitch last night, and you ordered him to his bunk and all."

"Be careful how you speak of officers," snapped Lee, from the chart table.

"It's alright, Number Two," offered Jackman, "let him speak. If I've learned anything about Elim, it's that what he says is seldom a waste of breath."

"Thank ya' sir," continued Elim, "well, Mr. Bolton came down to where the boys are grousin' about havin' to stay on board. He says the word is the Yanks are givin' all the Confederate soldiers forgiveness and a free pass home. Is that true?"

"That is the rumor. If they want one country again, that would be a good start," answered Jackman. "Your course from here Mr. Lee?" he continued.

"Through the channel, stay in the middle," replied the navigator. "Then steer three-four-zero degrees until midnight, then we turn west, two-seven zero until we turn toward Palmo's Inlet."

"You have that, Elim?"

"Yes Sa'," replied the quartermaster. He continued, "We Creole are water folk. I miss Lo'osiana and Mississip'. Will I get to go home like the soldiers Captain?"

"Mr. Beershieu, I guarantee it. We may need to make up a story to cover the last year. The Yankees are not going to be happy about us taking the *KATARINA*. You will go home with your portion of the crew's share," assured Jackman.

"Ah don' care about that," replied Elim. "I jus' need enough jingle in the pocket to get home on. Besides Mr. Bolton says the Spanish are gonna' take the gold and throw us all in jail."

Captain Jackman exchanged worried looks with Lee and his third officer, Peerless Johanson. "Elim," he said, "all of the officers except Mr. Bolton and Mr. Piper down in the engine room are listening and no one else. What else did Mr. Bolton have to say?"

"I do not need no trouble with Mr. Bolton Sa'."

"The Captain asked you a direct question Elim," snapped Lee.

"Well, he was sayin' to the boys that it might be better to go to Haiti or Venezuela where there ain't no Spanish. He figured we could cut a deal with some guv'nor who won't Arkansas us."

"For now, Elim, we stick to the plan, let Mr. Lee and Mr. Peerless and I worry about who might cheat us and how to deal with the Spanish," responded Jackman. "Elim, you are the best quartermaster that it has been my pleasure to serve with. Just do your job and everything will be fine."

"And Elim," added the Peerless, "do not tell anyone that you discussed this with us, but make sure that you keep us posted if you hear any more wild talk."

"Ah' will not tell a soul," quipped the quartermaster. "If Mr. Bolton found out, he'd gut me like a hog."

"Mr. Peerless," asked the Captain, "how long to Palmo's Inlet?"

"We should be there about dusk, five days from now."

THE FINAL BATTLE OF THE CIVIL WAR

42
NEW ORLEANS

THE MOLLY K idled with her bow resting in the mud of the Mississippi, her decks buzzing with old and new hands. On shore, a dozen people wrestled with an uncomfortable goodbye.

"Mr. Pierce sends his apologies," said Mead, "he scheduled breakfast with the Creole Mayor and plans to visit the Anglo Mayor. He wishes you success in your mission, as do I."

Major Zidot stepped forward offering his hand to the officers waiting at the head of the gangway. "I too offer you my prayers for a safe and successful voyage. Remember Mrs. Stowell's prayer for mercy," he continued.

A slightly irritated Chad took the French officer's hand but said nothing. Turning to Maria and Denali he extended a package wrapped in oilcloth. "Ladies, I wish you a safe trip to Saint Louis, where the army has reserved a private coach on the train east for you. That should get you into Washington by Sunday. If you would be so kind, I would appreciate you carrying the *KATARINA's* ship's log with you. There will be an inquiry into her loss and the log will be important evidence; I wouldn't want anything to happen to it."

"Allow me," offered Maria. "It would be safe with you on the *MOLLY K.*, but I am happy to help. Now Capitán Gritt, to your duty." Maria gently kissed Chad's cheek then passed down the line of officers, smiling and touching their hands with her rosary wrapped in her fingers.

Denali grabbed Chad's arm and pulled him away from the others. "Mi Capitán, I do not want you to go to Cuba. I know you will go. I will wait for you in Washington then we will speak of Boston."

"Denali, I should be there in less than three weeks. Colonel Mead will take good care of you and Maria. Remember we have a dinner date at the Howard House," whispered Chad.

Denali kissed him on the cheek then turned, wiping tears away with a yellow kerchief.

※

"One stop, gentlemen," said Kelley, then on to another grand adventure."

"How long to our destination, Captain?" asked Carl.

"I make it two days to Cabo San Antonio, Cuba's western most point, and then a few hours to the small inlet on the southwest coast that Mr. Davis marked on the map. I wish we had a better chart of that coast. It may be difficult to find."

"Pedro doesn't think so," replied Chad. "The inlet is only about a mile and a half deep and no more than a half mile wide. It is the only inlet along that coast with a village at the head of the bay."

"Sounds like a perfect little hide-away," offered his brother.

"According to Pedro, it was built as a pirate village for Spanish privateers, who prayed on English and Dutch shipping. There is no road connection to the rest of Cuba. For three hundred years the Spanish complained about piracy by their northern European neighbors. They wanted their own pirates hidden from prying eyes."

"How large is the village?" asked Carl.

"Pedro remembers two or three restaurants and taverns. There are at least two rooming houses, as well as warehouses and stores full of staples and luxuries that have never seen a custom's stamp. A long narrow dock runs from the village, just far enough into the deep water to allow an ocean-going ship to tie up on either side. A large boom at the end allows easy movement of freight between ships."

"It sounds like the kind of place a Confederate blockade runner would know well." Carl Gritt smiled at Kelley.

"You know gentlemen, it does sound like a place that is discussed in certain circles. Run by the same family for generations. Very hostile to ships that are not there to do business, or to people who may disrupt such trade."

"What if we were to anchor right in the mouth of the bay?"

"Well, I don't know, but if I were them, I would send a fleet of small fishing boats with red sails into the approaches to the inlet. You know; if red sails appear, get the hell out of here."

"Then we shall have to find a place to watch the mouth of the inlet, where we will not turn the waters red." Chad was enjoying the jousting between Kelley and his brother.

"I am sure we will."

Carl pointed at Kelley. "Someday, sir, you will be Senator Kelley from Mississippi."

"I just hope, gentlemen, that the *RETRIBUTION* is not in port as we speak. Her cargo will be easy to unload," offered Kelley. "We will be there on the nineteenth. You had better be ready."

The ship, loaded with fuel, reached the *PORTLAND* in three hours. The change in command, and Carl Gritt's goodbyes took only a half hour and by mid-afternoon the ship was well clear of north pass, although it would be after dark before they reached blue water.

Among the small mountain of supplies delivered the night before, were landing boats, crates of food, and several drums of lubricating oil. Early the morning of departure, a flat bottom scow just over thirty feet long, was towed to the side of the ship. A wooden platform had been erected on the decked over scow. On the platform, were two large wooden crates, and on the deck were a dozen smaller crates. The *MOLLY* towed the scow, still fully loaded until she stopped at the *PORTLAND*. While Carl Gritt said his goodbyes, the crew unloaded the scow. It now rode high in the water on a line behind the ship.

The two crates were labeled 'The Richard J. Gatling Farm Implement Co.' Inside each was a brass and steel, ten barreled gun on a carriage. Ready to mount were two large wheels and a host of small attachments. Sergeant Mosby, assisted by a Gunnery Sergeant, recently on his way home to Pennsylvania, but now in route to Cuba, supervised six former Marines as they cleaned the grease from the barrels and the action of the Gatling guns.

"Save the crates," directed Carl. "We will use them for target practice."

The officers stood watching the marines, along with almost everyone not in the engine room or on the bridge. "Did you notice Dr. Gatling's southern accent?" asked Chad.

"Jack Black told me that he was from North Carolina, but lives in St. Louis. His machines for sowing cotton, wheat and rice seed made him a rich man," continued Carl. "When the war shut off sales of farm equipment to the South, he devoted his time to his automatic loading gun. If the Ordinance Department had adopted that weapon in 1862, when he offered it, the war would have been over the next year."

"I thank the good Lord that he was a Union man," quipped Mosby. "What was he a doin' in New Orleans?"

"He was trying to get his farm equipment business going again," answered Chad. "He brought four of his automatic guns with him to demonstrate for the Army and the Navy as well as the local police. He believes that just the threat of his gun can maintain the peace."

"Sergeant Mosby, are you two about ready?"

"We are, Mr. Kadzof," came the answer. "First a little instruction. The brass shells are loaded into these long metal magazines, which are inserted into the top of the action," advised Mosby demonstrating the process. "The shells feed into the action by gravity, with the shells loaded on the first half of the barrel rotation and the spent brass ejected on the second half. The weapon swivels and moves up and down on its mount, allowing the gun crew to cover a great deal of area. You fire it by turning this crank."

"Let's brace the gun against the stern rail," suggested Carl. "Block the wheels. Set one up starboard and the other port. When you are ready you may fire."

"Before you fire," interjected Kadzof, "let me warn the bridge and the engine room. We don't want them to think a new war has broken out on the stern."

Ten minutes later, the rumble of two Gatling guns, each pouring out more than fifty rounds per minute, shook the ship. "These things take a lot of strength to aim and fire especially when you compensate for the pitch and roll of the ship," observed Mosby.

"I agree," added the other sergeant. "These weapons would be well served by the biggest men we have."

"And a full-time loader, to replace the magazines, would greatly increase the rate of fire," added Mosby. "Captain Gritt, you have two big men on your crew, Charlie Lampoc and Gary Farmer."

Chad turned, looking for the two men. He found them standing at the rail of the promenade deck above him. "Charlie, Gary, would you be willing to man these guns?"

"Looks like fun" replied Gary Farmer. "How about it, Charlie?" he asked the older man.

"I'll do it Captain," answered Lampoc. "I'll man it, but I hope that Dr. Gatling is right about his gun being a deterrent, I'd hate to turn that thing loose on a group of men."

Chad stared at the darkening sky above the men's heads. "Gentlemen we all hope that this goes smoothly."

By dark both shipping crates had been reduced to kindling behind the ship, and the platform on the scow in tow was in need of repair. Four of the eight ammunition crates lay empty. Two of the crew, were now loaders.

Dinner that night was interrupted by one of the new marines, who barreled through the saloon door dragging a man by the arm. "Look what I found climbing out of the forward chain locker."

"Miles Standish Pierce," gasped Chad, "what in the hell are you doing here?"

"You could not keep me from this fight. I left all of my reports, my samples and detailed letters to Secretary Seward for Mr. Mead. I sent a commercial telegram to the Secretary telling him that I would arrive with the captured boat. This will probably be the last fight of my life; I didn't want any of you to waste your breath trying to talk me out of coming."

"Mr. Pierce," said Chad, "for a really smart man, you make some really stupid decisions. If everything goes well, there will be nothing to see and if it doesn't a lot of us may be dead."

43
THE CARIBBEAN

THE OFFICERS OF the Confederate raider sat glaring at one of their own.

"I told you; it was just the liquor talking," answered Marcus Bolton. "I admit it makes me angry, we do all the work, take all the risks; all for our share of only ten percent. We could be rich, all of us and still have plenty for the Gray Coat Officers you are so worried about."

"Mr. Bolton," replied Peerless with a snarl, "your views were clear in the officer's meeting back in May. The vote was five to one. Even the bosun, representing the crew voted against you."

"Bo Tanner had only been bosun for two weeks. He's not educated like Axel was. He thought three or four thousand dollars was a lot of money."

"Enough Marcus," spat Jackman. "Your argument is like winter up north. You never look forward to it, but it comes every year, over and over. That's why I stay in the south, so I don't have to put up with winter and I am not putting up with you anymore.

One more word on the subject and we will hold another meeting and you will get nothing."

"No need for that, Captain. It's the enlisted boys I'm thinking about. The enlisted share split eleven ways ain't much."

"It will be split twenty ways; one share somehow, to the families of the crew we buried at sea. Even after we pay the piper to convert the gold, it is more than most corn crackers will see in five years," offered Jackman.

The *RETRIBUTION*'s officers sat on either side of the small galley table. Bolton stood at the end, nervously twisting a length of hair in his left hand. He was relieved as those seated turned their gaze toward each other.

"What do you think it will cost to convert the gold to currency?"

"Carlton, I really don't know."

"I've been conjuring on that Captain," said the ship's engineer. "The Palmo family will want their normal twenty percent if they help us. With so much cash money at stake, maybe we can do a deal for fifteen percent." Brandon Piper relit his pipe.

"Brandon, the Palmo's won't have a million in currency," offered Peerless. "If they go to Havana to broker a deal, we run the risk of the authorities finding out."

"Then we get nothing, except maybe a cell," said Bolton.

"Let me finish," argued Brandon Piper. "The Palmos have a small foundry at the boat yard. Suppose we melt the bars and pour five-ounce gold coins, you know like hundred-dollar gold pieces."

"We can't turn them into actual coins, Brandon," replied Lee. "We don't have hydraulic strikers like they have in a mint."

"True" replied Piper, "but we do have a crewman whose father was a tool and die maker. He could fashion cast iron strikers, not like from a mint, but hand strikers. We can make coins that look just like the hand struck coins they make in Peru."

"That's a great idea Brandon, but will they pass muster?" asked Peerless.

"Gold is gold," answered Piper. "As long as they are presented a few thousand dollars' worth at a time, even a reputable bank will convert them to currency for a five or ten percent exchange fee."

"All right then, at least we have a plan," offered Peerless Johanson. "When we get to Palmo's Inlet we will anchor at the mouth of the inlet. All incoming ships have to hold there until a deal is done with the Palmos. Unless you accept their standard fee, you can count on hard bargaining for at least a day."

Mr. Johanson, you have lots of experience with the Palmos, right?" asked Lee.

"More than thirty years. After the American's broke up Jean Lafitte's pirate band, his officers scattered. I sailed with Gambi on the voyage before he was killed. It got into my blood, that's how I ended up running slaves. It makes no difference what contraband you are running; the Palmo's can do the deal. They are the most honest thieves you will ever meet."

"What do you recommend, Mr. Johanson?" asked Jackman.

"After we secure the ship, a few of us will take a boat to the village. We will take a half dozen of the bars with us. We take a table at the Black Rooster and wait. The old man or his son will find us. Remember no more than ten men ashore until the deal is made."

"I have only been there twice," offered Lee. "I have never seen harbor defenses or militia or even armed guards. How do the Palmo's enforce their rules?"

"When you have been running their type of business for generations; when you have paid off grandfather, father and son, you minimize trouble. Their business works for everybody in the Caribbean. It all works on an honor system."

44
CUBA

THE MOLLY K rounded Cabo San Antonio at dark, anchoring in Hugbay at the south of the Cape. The crew practiced making the landing boats ready on the starboard side of the ship while on the other side, the ship's carpenter rigged railings around the platform on the scow, and hold-downs for the wheels of the Gatling guns. The guns were swung into place and secured, allowing the gun crews to practice loading and aiming their fast-firing weapons, but not a shot was fired.

They found that by lashing one of the longboats to either side of the scow, six oarsmen could row the awkward craft at a reasonable pace. With directions from the men on the platform, they could maneuver the craft or hold it in position for firing. In less than two hours the practice was deemed adequate, and the scow was once again tied along the ships side.

While the crew worked on the gun platform, Mosby led two boats in the dark toward the starboard side. As the boats bumped against the fore and aft ends of the huge shield that housed the paddle wheel, four marines scrambled up the shield from each end.

Four men armed with Henry rifles and pistols practiced clearing the lower deck, while two more headed for the ladder and the wheelhouse. The final two, each armed with only pistols and a short saber raced for the door to the engine room.

While the crew finished strapping the scow just in front of the starboard paddle wheel, the marines practiced their boarding a second time. With everything secured the ship resumed its course for the small inlet that Pedro Davis had marked on their charts. The ship slowed to five knots, steaming close to shore in the dark while the crew ate one of Angelo's gourmet dinners.

"Thank you, Mr. Davis, for the drawings of the RETRIBUTION. They really helped," said Mosby. "The *RETRIBUTION* is longer and wider but has the same general layout as the *MOLLY*. The passageway between the paddles will allow us to clear both sides of the ship from the center aft and then move forward. Two men should work to take the engine room and two for the bridge."

"Those automatic guns will have to keep the bow and stern clear until we are aboard, also the second deck, aft of the bridge," added Mosby. "We are going to need more men right away. If we take ten or fifteen prisoners, we will need to guard them while we clear the second deck."

"One more thing," he continued, "with no light on the port side of the *MOLLY* here, it was damned dark. It will be difficult to tell friend from foe on the deck, and impossible from a hundred yards away on that scow. I don't want my men in the middle of fifty rounds a minute from those guns. We need to be invisible getting to that ship, and impossible to miss once we are aboard."

"Painting the boats black helped," offered Carl. "If you wear your old blue uniforms and black your faces, you will be hard to see as long as the moon is neither directly in front, nor behind you. Maybe you could fight butt naked once aboard. That alone should get Johnny Reb to surrender," he laughed.

"A little navy humor," observed Mosby.

"How about cutting white flour sacks into tunics, that you can slip over your heads just before you board," suggested Kelley? "We have a stack of them in the engine room. We cut them up for rags."

"Should work," stammered the new sergeant, Murphy, "if they don't have cannon like you heard, or a strong guard, and they are anchored; and the gold is still aboard and the damned ship hasn't come and gone, or never shows up."

Kelley's timing was perfect. The *MOLLY K* crossed the narrow entrance of Palmo's Inlet at first light. From two miles offshore, four telescopes trained on the inlet. "She's not there," observed Chad. "There are some small boats at the head of the bay, but no ships at all."

"We dust off Plan B," offered Kadzof.

Once clear of prying eyes from the village, the ship started a slow left turn back toward the mouth of the bay. It had surprised no one, when the red-haired captain, produced a detailed chart of the Western half of Cuba. A small bay only three miles east of the inlet was marked in black pencil.

"All stop," Kelley signaled the engine room.

The lines holding the scow to the ship's side were untied. Within ten minutes, the longboats were lashed to its sides and the scow, and its crew pulled away from the ship.

"We will be back early this afternoon," yelled Chad. "Tie up to the mangroves just inside the bay and camouflage the scow."

"And watch out for things along the shore that will bite you or eat you," warned Kelley. "We're going to check up on the missing ship."

A half hour later the ship rounded the east headland of Palmo's Inlet and dropped anchor well beyond the long dock that stretched from the center of the village. Three men, Kelley, his chief engineer, and Chad climbed into the ship's boat, where four briefed crewmen waited to row them to shore. "Let's run through it one more time" barked Kelley as the boat pulled away."

"We are replacements for the men who jumped ship in Texas when the war ended," answered Hans Gott. "You are here looking for dishonest work to keep your ship and crew busy until things settle down along the gulf coast, and you can go home. And you are curious as to what other ships in the same predicament are doing. We are supposed to use words like 'affeared,' 'the cause,' and 'get shed of' in any conversation."

"If I can teach you to speak a little slower, Hans, you could become a prideful son of the south," quipped Kelley.

Four hours later, after an amazing breakfast at the Black Rooster, courtesy of Alejandro Palmo V, the boat was back on its davits and the ship was ready to weigh anchor.

"Clear the bay by a mile or two and then set a northerly course that will hide us from the village," ordered Kelley. "When we are out of sight, we will turn back toward where we hid the scow."

By four in the afternoon the ship lay anchored fore and aft along a mangrove covered point. The *MOLLY K* was hidden from any craft that passed, except one from the north, and there was little chance of that. A lookout was posted on top of the bridge where a man could look over the tops of the mangroves all the way to the mouth of Palmo's Inlet and far out to sea.

Only the lookouts were missing from a meeting in the main saloon. "That village, it is an amazing place. It is a small city with almost every amenity, even a doctor. The fifty or so men that live there, are all skilled tradesmen, from accountants to metal smiths and ship rites," began Chad. "There's a school and a church and five times more buildings than you can see from the head of the bay. Every building is green with brown trim or brown with green trim. Every window is set so it won't reflect the sun out to sea. There must be a hundred and fifty people living there."

"With all due respect Captain Gritt, we appreciate the travel lecture, but what did you find out?" asked Mosby.

"The *RETRIBUTION* has not been there," replied Kelley.

"Within days of General Lee's surrender and for the next six weeks there was a steady flow of Confederate vessels, everything from ocean schooners to fishing boats. At one time there were thirty craft in the inlet. Since then, the flood has turned to a trickle, with only one small coaster in the last week."

"Where did they all go?" asked Nick

"Alejandro was summoned to Havana, where he was reminded of the Spanish concerns over the U.S. Military. The Spanish are disarming Confederate ships and soldiers. They allow disarmed Confederates to remain in Cuba if they have the resources to pay their way. Alejandro estimates that three or four thousand have come through Palmo's Inlet," offered Kelley.

"Alejandro was not pleased about the number of people who were directed to his village," added Chad. "Pedro, I am happy that you didn't go ashore, he may have recognized you. He embraced Patrick and the Chief Engineer like long lost friends. He seems willing to help his long-time clients."

"You said there were thirty boats at one time, Captain Kelley," said Kadzof, "where did they all go?"

"They are scattered all over the island, and probably all the way from Honduras to Venezuela. The Spanish are encouraging them toward the east end of the island, away from Havana and the American Consulate. Alejandro directed most of the larger craft toward Guantanamo Bay."

"Then we may be at the wrong end of the island," continued Murphy, "or even in the wrong country. Feels like we are chasing our tails."

"Could be," replied Carl, "but we can't be everywhere at once, and we can't just barge into a busy harbor like Caracas or Port of Prince and seize a ship."

"I agree," said his brother, "I still think Pedro's first guess is our best bet. This seems to be the first stop for refuge Confederate ships, especially those that have a history with the place."

"We have food and water for seven days, plus our trip home. Let's give it a week. If she doesn't show up, we go home," proposed Carl. "I wouldn't know where else to search for her."

45
THE CARIBBEAN

THE CREW OF the *RETRIBUTION* was anxious, like spirited horses that had just caught a glimpse of their stable after returning from a long ride. It could be that they were only a day away from their final trip as a crew, but that explanation didn't feel right to Captain Jackman.

"I make our position just about a hundred miles south of Jamaica, Elim," voiced Jackman. "Sunup in about a half-hour, that puts us into Palmo's Inlet just before dark tomorrow."

"I declare Cap'n," offered Elim, "I'm ready. I'm ta-red' man, and plumb ta-red' of the good ole *RETRIBUTION*. Afta' twelve hours on the wheel, at night, I'm always worried that I'll drop my cookies."

"Elim, nobody rides a compass and feels the wind and current at night like you do. I don't worry about mistakes with you," continued Jackman. "I am tired too, but Chase should be here in a half hour to relieve you, and Mr. Bolton will have the bridge."

"That don't make you comfortable does it Cap'n?"

Jackman shook his head.

The first beam of sunlight crept through the starboard window as the assistant quartermaster and Bolton relieved the two men. After a five-minute briefing Jackman announced, "You have the bridge, Mr. Bolton." He and Elim started down the ladder, looking for a cold breakfast and sleep.

Bolton watched the two men until they disappeared below. He walked to the opposite side of the bridge and opened and closed the door three times. A few minutes later Chase's brother Benny and the tall Texas stoker, Juan Bacon slipped onto the bridge. "Listen up," commanded Bolton. "Chase, you continue to steer a straight course. Benny, you and Juan go open up the armory and fetch up the ready pistols and bring them back here. We will take the officers first and lock them in the forward hold. Then we will gather the crew in the mess, and give the others a chance to join us, or the Captain. Caleb is on watch aft; he will need a pistol. Now get," he concluded.

"Mr. Bolton, what about the engine room?" asked Juan.

"After we gather up the officers, you and Caleb go round up Scottie and the stoker and march them to the mess."

"Mr. Bolton," continued Juan, "we're outnumbered two to one. What if they all don't want to join us; I don't want to shoot my shipmates."

"Tell them I will shoot the Captain and Mr. Lee if they put up a fight," answered Bolton. "Now get you two."

The two men headed for the door to the starboard walkway.

"Not that way you idiots," barked Bolton, "not where you can be seen. Go through the ready cabin." He pointed to the door at the back of the bridge. Two nervous men leaped for the door, their shoulders colliding as they passed through.

A moment later they backed out of the door. "Mr. Bolton," Benny called to the officer now studying a chart at the navigation table. Bolton turned to find Juan and Benny standing with their hands above their heads, facing Carlton Lee and the third officer each cradling a double barrel shotgun.

"Chase," ordered Lee, "five rings please."

Chase reached up and tugged on the heavy cord above his head five times, the bell signal for, "Captain to the Bridge."

The Captain stuffed the last of a cold honey biscuit into his mouth as he leaped to his feet. "Damn," he mumbled through the biscuit, and raced for the galley door. Turning the corner, he collided with the ship's bosun.

"Bo," he mumbled, "we have a problem on the bridge." Jackman pulled a heavy caliber two-shot pocket pistol from his coat.

"I don't know nothing about no trouble, Captain," stammered Tanner.

"Follow me Bo," called the Captain running for the ladder. They barged into the already crowded bridge.

Carlton reached behind his back and retrieved an old pistol. He handed it to the bosun.

"Bo," he ordered, "go find Caleb, and march him to the forward hold while the Captain and I heard these four down there."

"What the hell?" responded Tanner.

"Caleb and these men, including Mr. Bolton, were plotting a mutiny." He nodded toward the third officer. "We heard it all," answered Lee. Turning to the Captain he continued, "It was almost exactly what we guessed."

"Where were you going to go Marcus?" asked Jackman.

"I figured on Cartagena. With all of the gold coming from the mines, and every bank buying, I figured that it would be easy to convert the gold."

"Then what?" snapped Lee.

"I was going to take my share in gold coin and convert a bunch of it to emeralds; then I was off to the Pacific. I hear that the Sandwich Islands are nice."

"You can dream about the Sandwich Islands from inside the

hold with these men," replied Jackman. "You can look into their eyes and watch the hatred build as it dawns on them that you have probably talked them into a noose."

"You can't hang us, Captain. The war is over; this is no longer a military vessel."

"When we get to Palmo's Inlet, there will be enough general officers to convene a court-martial. I doubt that there will be a single officer who will defend you. Remember the oath; an officer does not lie, cheat or steal let alone mutiny. Now move Mr. Bolton or feel a fifty-caliber ball in your gut."

The captain pointed to his third officer. You will take the helm until we get these five locked up," directed the Captain. "As soon as the hatch is locked signal all stop to the engine room; it's time for a company meeting."

"Bolton, I should have left you on the beach with Captain Gritt and the *KATARINA*'s crew. It would have saved me a lot of trouble," commented Jackman pushing the man toward the forward hold.

"Captain Jackman, you should have killed all of them."

The ship rocked on a gentle easterly swell, the soft vibration from the powerful steam engine, now at idle, the only indication that the ship was alive. Not even a lookout was posted, as the members of the crew not locked in the hold stood silently. "I give down Cap'n," blurted one of the men, "we heard talk. I thought it was jus' talk, you know the kind you hear after two months out of sight of a gal or a sip."

The general nodding of heads told the Captain all he needed to know. "We will have to trust one another," he started. "We are shorthanded, and every man will have to cover more than one job. We will all pitch in. The good news is, it's only for a day."

"What's going to happ'n' to Juan and Benny and the boys?" asked Scottie the engine room chief who had just started his shift.

"They grabbed the wrong end of the poker," answered Lee.

"You know Mr. Bolton can hector a man terrible," replied Scottie. "You can't contradict the man directly. Most just smile, and nod, and hope he walks away. If he comes back harping on something, you just piddle-diddle. Some of the younger boys never learned how, Mr. Lee."

"Scottie, there will be a court-martial when we get to Palmo's Inlet, a regular trial among fair officers. I suspect that Mr. Bolton will meet the hangman, maybe the others too. It will not be up to the Captain or me," answered Lee. "What they did was ugly, just plain wrong."

"We need to get to work men," ordered Jackman. "I promise that you will all be given time to speak your mind at the trial. Keep your dobbers up and things normally work out."

"We have three long shifts, and then for us the war is finally over," offered the engineer. "Mike, you keep the food coming. Captain, the bosun and I will keep the engines moving forward," continued Brandon Piper. "My wife has been a grass widow too long."

"I agree," smiled the Captain. "Mr. Lee, Mr. Johanson, Elim and I will steer a straight line. Once we have a deal with the Palmos, there will be liberty for all."

Within minutes the ship was under way. The stern faces of the crew reflecting both worry and resolve. At noon the following afternoon the ship rounded the eastern end of Isla de la Juventud, only a hundred miles from their destination.

46

CUBA

MANGROVES HID THE *MOLLY K.* "Captain Grittenberg, if I ever decide to go back to sea I will be knocking on your door," advised Patrick Kelley. "Your chef, Gasparetti, should be on a recruiting poster. I grew up on pork and potatoes. After two weeks of Angelo's meals, I declare I am a convert."

"Our father taught Carl and me that a happy crew starts in the galley," responded Chad. "The chef on a RusAm ship is paid the same as a third officer."

"Even at times like these, just sitting for two days, it gives the crew something to look forward to," added Carl. "Another card please." Pierce dealt Carl one card, then two to Chad. He took three. All three of the *MOLLY's* officers stood pat. The card game had been going since lunch and not more than thirty dollars had changed hands.

"Two dollars," said Chad throwing two chips into the center of the table.

"If you row as bad as you deal Pierce, we probably won't find the *RETRIBUTION*," drawled Carl Gritt. "I fold."

"I'll get you and Pedro to the side of that ship; you can count on that," answered Pierce. "I'll get the boat tied securely and I will be right behind you. I'll also raise two dollars."

The port door flew open, two marines burst into the saloon. "Hands in the air Johnny Reb," one yelled while the other moved quickly toward the seated men.

"On the floor, face down, hands and feet wide apart," he commanded.

"That's okay gentlemen," said the first Marine, just another practice run. In a moment both were gone.

"Mosby and that new sergeant are working their men hard," commented Nick from a chair next to an open window, book in hand.

"They want their men ready without stopping to think," responded Carl. "A marine may train for years for one hour of action. They want it right. Besides it keeps them from getting nervous while they wait."

"I'd be a lot less nervous, if just one hand would go to someone other than one of *MOLLY*'s triplets sitting here," laughed Pierce. He stared at the deck of cards on the table.

The game continued until the clock on the wall struck five, and then after a break resumed. The readers continued reading. Those working on hobbies or playing checkers and chess continued to play. The guitar that had been strumming from the stern continued to entertain the entire company. In the galley, Angelo filleted five fat Redfish the crew had caught that afternoon. The activities chosen by each crewmember to burn time over the last two days continued, all except for one man.

The sentry almost missed a step on the ladder from the roof of the bridge, and then raced down the second ladder to the main deck, bursting through the door of the saloon. "There's a smoke smudge way out on the southeast horizon" he blared. "I've been watching it for ten minutes. It's definitely smoke."

"There is no question, it's the *RETRIBUTION*," called Pedro Davis. "We painted the spokes on the paddle wheels red, white and blue to make the old girl less of a risk from a distance. Captain Jackman will anchor with the bow out to sea. With the breeze building from that cloud buildup inland he will need to drop a stern hook as well."

Chad turned to the small group of men on the wing of the bridge, just below where Pedro continued to peer through a powerful telescope. "It will be dark in an hour. From then we will have an hour before the moon lights up that inlet like a sailor's saloon."

"Gentlemen, she has begun to back down. Her anchors will be set in ten minutes," continued Pedro. "All I see are crates where they mount the bow and stern guns. Except for small arms she appears to be unarmed."

"How long until you have steam to move, Mr. Kelley?" asked Carl.

"We've been slowly stoking since we first saw the ship, no sparks and no smoke. With the sun setting, the dusk will hide any smoke. We're ready to move."

ஃ

With the *RETRIBUTION*'s huge paddle wheels stopped, the Captain made a short notation in the ship's log and followed his first officer and navigator from the bridge.

"Cap'n," came the bosun's voice out of the dusk, "I have assigned Caswell and Cain to lower your boat. They will take you and Mr. Lee ashore."

"Change in plans, Bo," responded the Captain, "the third officer will be joining us. He will buy up some fresh meat and vegetables and a couple of bottles of Tennessee Mash for your men and bring them back to the boat. It's not as good as shore leave but at least you 'all will have a good meal and a drink or two."

"Is Mr. Piper going ashore too?" asked Tanner.

"You know how he is with his engines; it will take him a couple of hours to put his babies to bed. I suspect that he will want to come ashore after dinner," answered Jackman.

"Cap'n, there are no other boats here," continued Tanner.

"Old Man Palmo will know where they are. We will send word back. An aft watch should be adequate. If you need an officer's help, go find Mr. Piper. You will have the deck Bo."

"Cap'n," continued Bo, "if there are no other officers here, what will we do with them boys in the hold?"

"For tonight bosun, just feed them and let them be. We may have to deal with them ourselves, but not tonight. Darken the ship, all except for a lantern at the stern. I'll see you in the morning," continued Jackman.

Their small boat ground onto a gravel beach, where a boy with a lantern met them. The men were led to the Black Rooster where they ordered old-fashioned grog while they waited. On the floor next to Jackman and Lee, were two canvas bags, each containing three gold bars.

Aboard the *RETRIBUTION*, Bo Tanner stopped by the galley and poured himself a cup of hours' old coffee. "Mike, you could tar the deck with this," commented the bosun.

"I been thinkin' instead of workin' Bo. It ain't fittin' that the Girods and Juan and Caleb get hung, or even Mr. Bolton, just for lookin' out for us," replied the cook.

"I agree Cookie, I ain't gonna be any part of hanging those boys," replied Tanner. "When Mr. Bolton first whispered the idea, I almost signed on. It could be me in that hold."

"I'm worse Bo, I rue back on my word. But the Cap'n has been a good officer. He got us through the war safe. We only lost a few men. By God that's amazing."

"If we add the five locked up, that would be almost a third of our crew. As I see it, we got a hangman's choice. Either we cut them boys loose and run and face the Cap'n later or we help hang our shipmates," offered Bo.

"We hadn't ought to buck the Cap'n Bo, but we have no choice. Mr. Bolton will have a plan," argued the cook. "With thievery impossible, he will want to fix this." The man stared at the floor for a moment and then up at Tanner. "We will make sure that this is made right, won't we Mr. Tanner?"

⚓

The *MOLLY K* turned straight out to sea, just before the point that marked the northeast entrance to Palmo's Inlet. The string of craft that she was towing watched the darkened ship swing left and one at a time, each released the rope of the boat behind them. As the scow with the Gatling Guns was cut loose, three oars on either side of the scow bit into water and the craft started the final leg to its covering position fifty yards off from the rebel ship's beam. Behind the scow two boats with four marines each started for the paddle wheel. The Gritt brothers, Pedro and Pierce began a steady stroke allowing the marines to extend the gap in front of them.

It would take the scow twenty minutes to travel the distance needed to reach its position. The other boats would be only seconds behind. The *MOLLY K* made a second turn after moving another mile offshore, and increased her speed to six knots, still cruising as silently as possible. She would cross the mouth of the inlet and then continue on to a rendezvous that only Kelley and the Gritt brothers knew about. The boarding team was on its own. Their ride home lay anchored less than a mile in front of them.

⚓

On the bridge of the *RETRIBUTION*, Elim Beershieu finished stowing the last of the maps from the chart table. Taking one more look around, to make sure everything on the bridge was secured, he turned down the oil lamp above the table and dropped the metal shield that blocked its light. He pulled open the heavy blackout curtains around the bridge. In the distance he though he a faint light. With a trained eye he continued to scan the ocean for another five minutes. He never noticed the cover to the forward hold propped open.

"Mr. Bolton, you're the big dog here, what do we do?" asked the cook.

"There's only fourteen on board," added Bo Tanner.

"There are seven of us here. Who else is aboard, besides the loaders and stokers?"

"Mr. Piper is shutting down his engines, and Elim is clearing the bridge. Scottie is asleep and Paco is on the watch aft," answered Tanner. "We grabbed seven pistols."

"Obviously, Piper is not with us. What about the others?"

"Paco will help," replied Juan. I don't know about Scottie or Elim."

"We will need either Piper or Scottie in the engine room. Whether they like it or not, one of them will be with us," directed Bolton. "Mr. Tanner, go get Elim, and Mike you find Scottie. Caleb you and Juan go fetch up Paco. I want you three to dig the stern chaser out of the rear hold, get it mounted as fast as you can. Ready a-half dozen rounds of hail-shot. If someone tries to stop us, a round or two of shot should buy us time to get under way. Bring Elim and Scottie to my cabin."

Elim was just descending the ladder from the bridge when Tanner found him. "That was an odling," voiced Elim. "I thought I saw some light, like from the stack of a steamer or a partially covered window about five minutes ago, but nothing since."

Tanner shrugged, "Elim, come with me, we need to talk."

Scottie was just backing out of Bolton's cabin when they arrived. "I'll tell Mr. Piper that you will kill Elim unless he cooperates," he said to someone inside. "I'll send him up. You promise not to harm him right, Mr. Bolton?"

"You have my word don't you," answered the voice from the cabin. "Come in, Elim."

"It's about saving your shipmates, Elim, jus' listen to Mr. Bolton," offered Tanner.

"I don' need no lecture from no bushwhacker, Bo. I warned the Cap'n' bout Mr. Bolton. I warned him to lick his flint. I ain't no mutineer."

"So, it was you, Elim, that spilled his guts to the Captain. Grab his arms Bo, we'll take care of him right now." Bolton pushed Elim out the door of his cabin.

"Mr. Bolton, I have Mr. Piper here," came Juan's voice from behind him.

Bolton turned to face the engineering officer. "Piper, I hope you can swim. Tell the Captain that he can find his ship in Cartagena." Bolton stepped forward and pushed Piper over the rail. The ships engineer surfaced, screaming. Bolton leaned over the rail. "Swim straight out, out of rifle range before you turn to the beach, or you will end up shark food. Back in Mexico you saw what they do to a wounded man."

The light from inside Bolton's cabin showed directly on Elim's face and lit up the sea on the port side of the ship. Sweat dribbled down Elim's forehead as Bolton drew one of the knives that he had taken from his cabin. "Spill your guts to the Captain; almost get me hung; Bo, turn him loose. I want to see him fight before I gut him," screamed Bolton.

Bo stepped back, pulling Elim with him. "Leave him be, Mr. Bolton" said Juan from behind. Elim was just doing his duty, like we all did a long time ago."

"Juan's right, Elim jus' runs his mouth," added Bo, pushing a startled Elim over the rail. "Now let's get out of her Mr. Bolton."

Bolton took a step toward Tanner but stopped when he heard a pistol cock behind him. "Your right of course," he responded, slipping the twelve-inch blade back into its sheath.

"When Paco and Caleb have the gun mounted, they are going for shells," offered Juan carefully releasing the hammer of the old pistol in his hand.

"Fine Juan, have them load a round and then practice swinging the gun. I expect that the Captain will try right or left rather than coming directly at the stern, if he takes a notion to interfere," ordered Bolton, then paused. "No, Bo, you go talk to Paco and Caleb. Juan, I need you and Scottie to get us underway."

Bo turned to leave, "take a fire-axe with you Mr. Tanner, when the wheels start to turn cut the stern anchor free," continued Bolton. He closed his cabin door, plunging the deck into darkness. "I'll go find Benny and Mike and put them on the forward anchor, you can find me on the bridge when we are underway."

"Mr. Piper," called Elim, treading water about twenty yards from the ship, "where are you?"

"Is that you Elim?" came a response.

"It is Mr. Piper."

"I'm about ten yards in front of you and I'm about give out son."

"You jus' tread water sir, he'p' is on the way."

⚓

The scow was holding its position with all three boats bobbing alongside. Gary and Charlie stood on the platform, loaders at their side, and watched the spectacle at Bolton's cabin unfold. As long as the port side of the ship was bathed in light the marines couldn't move. The moment that the cabin door closed eight oars bit the water for the dash to the side of the ship.

"What the hell is going on?" whispered Chad.

"They just threw two men overboard," responded Charlie. "They are also trying to get their stern gun ready. We can't have that, one round of canister shot would clean out a boat."

"We're going to check out the voices in the water," whispered Chad, "Pedro thinks he knows who they are."

Elim reached the tired engineer and took him in tow just as the bow of a boat appeared out of the dark. "Who is that?" whispered Elim.

"Let me help," came a reply and four strong hands pulled Piper from his grasp and into the boat.

"Now you, son," came a familiar voice. "Be quiet now."

A moment later Elim looked up into the face of Pedro Davis. "Mista' Davis" he stammered, "what y'all doing hea'?"

"They are taking the *RETRIBUTION*," whispered Piper.

"Brandon has it right," replied Pedro, "and if you aren't very quiet, we will have to gag you."

"Gag us, no need Pedro," said the older man now sitting up.

The two boats with the marines were only yards from the ship when the two men at the stern slipped a shell into the small, short barreled, cannon and pivoted it toward where the boats approached, still cloaked in darkness.

"Damn," cried Charlie. "Gary spray the stern, try to shoot over their heads."

The big farm boy's adrenaline surged, and he cranked the handle of the gatling gun. A stream of bullets ripped into the window in the aft saloon, and then continued aft shredding the railings, boat davits and the aft loading boom. The gun fired for no more than fifteen seconds and when it stopped there was no one manning the stern gun.

The marines climbed the wheel fender from each direction and then stopped for only seconds to pull on their white vests. As the boat carrying those who had volunteered to guard prisoners approached, they could hear the marines calling. "Clear aft starboard, clear aft port, moving forward starboard." Now and then a shot rang out but there was no consistent firing until the marines tried to clear the bow. There they were met with pistol fire.

The guard's boat thumped into the side of the ship just aft of the paddle wheel. Carl, Chad and Pedro clambered out of the boat, pistols in hand. "Let us come with you, we can stop this," offered Brandon Piper. Come on Elim, let's talk to the boys."

Chad started to object but was cut off by his older brother. "Let them save their shipmates," was all he said. He extended a hand to Piper and pulled him up behind him. "Stay very close you two, you do not have vests."

They crossed to the other side of the ship where they met Mosby. "There's two of them hold up in some crates on the bow. They keep saying they would rather be shot than hung. They wounded one of my men. Once we clear the top deck, we will send a couple of men to the bridge with rifles to see if they can clean them out."

"Where are the rest of them?" asked Chad

"Those we already captured are in the saloon. The marine watching them can use some help," he suggested looking at Carl.

"Pedro, take these water rats up to the bow and see if they can talk those two into throwing in the towel," directed Chad. "How many of you were there?" he asked the soaking men.

"Only twelve still on board, Captain Gritt," answered Piper. "The man who started this was the same bastard that killed your man Ott."

"Do I know you?"

"We met on the *KATARINA*."

"Twelve minus six in the saloon, and two on the bow and two dead in the stern, we still need to find two," said Mosby. "Let's get to work."

Chad and Mosby charged up the ladder toward the bridge. Bullets fired wildly sent splinters flying from the rails along the ladder. Mosby stopped to return fire, as Chad raced to the top of the ladder. He kicked in the door to the bridge, slipped inside and dropped to a knee. Two shots from the back of the bridge shattered the window above his head. Chad fired the heavy Colt twice, not bothering to aim. Another shot came from the dark as the shadow of a man tumbled forward, landing on top of Gritt. Behind the falling man, a door slammed. Chad crawled from under the body just as Sergeant Mosby stepped over him and crossed the bridge, turning up the lamp. Chad scrambled to his feet and stumbled out the door that Mosby had just entered. "There is one more, headed toward the stern," he yelled.

Pierce finished tying up his boat and clambered up toward the deck. Swinging one leg over the railing he was startled by a man dropping from the deck above directly in front of him. "Secretary Pierce, how surprising to find you here," sneered Bolton. "I'm going to need your boat," he continued, pointing his pistol at Pierce. "Now be a good boy and get back in the boat."

"Bolton, I'm not going anywhere with you. This is over."

"Mr. Secretary you have a short memory. I am a man who likes his orders followed." Bolton squeezed the trigger, catching Pierce in the chest and knocking him backward, his body pitching over the rail. Bolton leaned forward to shoot again as Pierce slid toward the water.

Chad dove from the deck above, knocking Bolton from his feet, his gun flying into the water. He rolled to his feet just as Bolton tugged a knife from his belt and lunged. Chad swept the arm with the knife into the rail and smashed Bolton with his fist. Chad's hand felt like he'd just slammed it into an anvil. Bolton just grinned.

Bolton slashed at Chad, ripping the front of his shirt and opening a gash across his chest.

Chad kneed the heavier man in the groin and then hit him again.

Bolton doubled over, lunging with his knife. The blade bit Chad in the hip, glancing off from bone.

Chad pushed the heavier man's head down and then brought

his knee up catching Bolton under the chin, a blow that would have killed most men. Bolton toppled over the rail, sliding down the paddle wheel shield, landing in the boat that Pierce had tied to the ship. Somehow, he had held onto his knife. He reached out and cut the line securing the boat to the ship and grabbed the oars.

Chad searched the darkened deck for the pistol he lost when he tackled Bolton. His hip hurt like hell, especially when he knelt to pick up the Colt. Mosby helped him to his feet.

As Bolton pulled away from the ship, Pierce pushed to the surface and twisted his arm into the rope holding the Marine's boat.

"Captain Gritt," called Pierce, "I'm down here and I am shot. It was Bolton."

Mosby was over the rail and had Pierce by the coat before Chad could react. "I've got Pierce, get that bastard."

Chad searched the darkened sea. Bolton's boat had disappeared. "Charlie, Gary, that same swine that killed Ott Smith has just shot Pierce. He stole a boat. Can you see him?"

"There's a boat about thirty yards off from your bow, but we can't see who's in it," replied Charlie.

"Everybody else is aboard ship, it has to be Bolton."

Two Gatling guns swung toward the boat. The first huge slow-moving bullet shattered Bolton's left leg, toppling him onto the seat behind him. No more than five of the thirty rounds from the Gatling guns missed the boat, half finding Bolton's body.

The guns stopped firing as the shattered boat sank to the water line.

"How is Mr. Pierce, Sergeant?" asked Chad.

"He's dead, I'm really sorry sir. He turned out to be damned tough for a college boy. Give me a hand getting him on the deck."

"Sergeant, Bolton cut me a couple of times. I'll have to find someone else to help."

"We've found one dead on the upper deck," came a call from the now lighted bridge above. "That's all of them. I know you shot, but it looks like he was killed by one of his own. This man was shot in the back."

"Is that you, Pedro?" asked Chad. Can you help the sergeant down where the boats are tied? We need to get Pierce's body out of the water."

Pedro pushed past Chad as he climbed down to help Mosby. "How bad are you hurt?"

"Not too bad, there is just a lot of blood. My hands are slick. I'll get doc to sew it up. Where's my brother, how fast can we get underway?" asked Chad.

"The boat with the split pine and coal oil is already unloading at the stern. Your brother and that Piper guy are in the engine room now. You can trust the other water rat on the bridge. You should have a little steam in ten minutes."

"Sergeant, get the scow tied astern along with these boats? As soon as you're finished, we're underway," directed Chad.

"None too soon, there's a line of lanterns coming down the hill from that village Captain," replied Mosby.

"Get that scow over here or row home," yelled the marine. He couldn't see the barge, but he heard a desperate rhythm as oars splashed the water from where the scow should have been.

The ship pushed the sinking boat with Bolton's torn body out of the way as it crawled from Palmo's Hope.

In the saloon, Parker stitched Chad's wounds before going to work on one of the Marines who had accidentally shot himself in the foot.

47

THE CARIBBEAN

THE SMALLER SHIP rode at anchor in a channel between two small islands, every lantern lit.

It had taken the *RETRIBUTION* hours to cover the thirty miles to the rendezvous. A dozen lengths of oil-soaked pine went into the firebox. The coal oil ignited in seconds and the dry wood built a roaring fire that would have taken a half hour with coal. As the steam increased, they were able to coax more speed out of the engine, still it took an hour to reach a ten-knot cruise.

Using only a hand drawn chart provided by Kelley, Carl took the larger and heavier ship into the channel slowly, two men on the bow taking depth soundings every two minutes. He nudged the bow of the *RETRIBUTION* alongside the stern of the smaller ship, and then signaled for engine stop. Four men lashed the two ships together.

While the marines and the crew of both ships lugged hundred-pound coal bags from *MOLLY*, onto the bow of the *RETRIBUTION* a short meeting got underway in the saloon of the captured rebel raider.

"Mr. Piper," asked Carl, "why did you and Elim offer your help?"

"I see by your coat that you, Sir, are a serving officer," started Piper. "I watched that automatic gun clear the stern of the *RETRIBUTION* before those men could even find a target. I knew the men on the bow, protected only by empty crates would be next.

Worse, I know my Captain, Sir, once there were shots fired; he and the men ashore would do everything they could to get back to the ship. Your gun would have cut them to pieces just like it did that scum Bolton. Those men are my friends, and the war is over."

"What now, Mr. Piper?" asked Pedro. "There are only a few of you left, and what; four or five back at Palmo's Inlet?"

"I will only speak for myself; I would like to go back. Someone needs to help Captain Jackman understand that the war is over."

"We should all go back," added Juan; "even those of us that will face the music."

"Juan, that may be a bad idea," worried Piper. "You and Benny and Chase are on the Captain's blacklist. After losing the ship his mood will be foul. It would not be a good idea to darken his door, at least not now."

"Mr. Piper, in one way or another we all were in on this, everyone but Elim. We got Bo and Paco and Caleb killed," continued Juan. "Maybe we got it cummin' or maybe the Cap'n will figure we ain't worth hanging."

"I'm with Juan," added Scottie. "I wasn't part of the mutiny, but I was part of what happened tonight. If we had been a crew, the kind of crew we have been for three years we might have saved the ship."

A wry smile swept Pedro's face. "Scottie, until three months ago I was part of this crew. This crew started to come apart when we started killing and stealing and lying, instead of fighting a war." Pedro filled a mug with coffee and slid it across the table to his former shipmate.

"And there is no way that you could have defended this ship, not with twice the men. Did you see how the Yankees are armed; rifles that shoot fifteen times before reloading, pistols that reload in seconds, not minutes, and guns that shoot more than fifty rounds a minute? That's what our brothers in the trenches faced in the last months of the war. It's time to go home. It's time for Captain Jackman to accept that he is responsible for what happened to his crew."

"Mr. Davis," asked Juan Bacon, "are you now with the blue bellies or are you still one of us?"

"Juan, there is no more them and us. I am going home. I'm hitching a ride with these men who have treated me fairly. You can go with us, or you can go help your Captain. All Confederate commissions have been canceled. You are all of equal rank now."

Brandon Piper looked around the room, then up at Chad. "Captain Gritt, I'm real sorry about your bosun. I've served at sea with free black men for twenty years. Most of them were damn fine sailors. Some went back to the South, a few even owned slaves; I never understood that The South is changed forever. It will need our help. It's time for us to go home, but we need to take our Captain and Mr. Lee and the others with us. We're going back."

"You may take two of the cutters Mr. Piper. You will have oars and oar locks for three rowers, and each boat has a sail. We will make sure you have water and rations for a couple of days, but my crew could get me back to Palmo's Bay by evening tomorrow," ribbed Chad.

"Thank you, sir, we are grateful," replied Piper. "Do you suppose that we could find some of those rations now? We haven't eaten since coffee and biscuits this mornin'."

"Neither have we, Mr. Piper," snarled Carl, "and I personally get nasty when I am hungry. If I have your word that war is over, you and your men can join us on the *MOLLY K*. Our chef has a late dinner ready. We're not moving until first light so you can all use your old bunks for one more night."

After a meal and moving the rest of the crew and freight to the captured ship, the *MOLLY* weighed anchor and crept out of the channel in the moonlight. Sergeant Murphy and four marines went with them. "We should be in Havana by the end of siesta," yelled Kelley from the stern. "We will meet you ten miles off from Freeport in the morning, three days' time."

"If we miss you, don't wait," replied Chad. "I'll see you in Norfolk in ten days."

"I'm not taking your new ship anywhere close to a Yankee naval base without your brother," screamed Kelley over the clatter of two huge paddles churning the water.

Chad awoke with a start and was, for a moment, totally disoriented. The knock came again. "Come," moaned Chad.

Soft morning light flooded Captain Jackman's cabin as the door opened. "It's seven, Captain," said Pedro. "Brandon wants to know if it's alright to pack the personal belongings of the men who are ashore at Palmo's Inlet?"

"Ya, sure, of course," stammered Chad sitting up.

"He will need access to Captain Jackman's outfit in this cabin."

"Just let me get my boots on and it's all his. I need some coffee."

Chad found Piper, Pedro and his brother outside the cabin. "I'll follow my nose to the coffee." Carl Gritt stayed with Piper while Pedro knocked on the next door, then waived at Benny and Chase Giroud who were waiting by the saloon. Each carried an empty flour sack.

Piper quickly packed his Captain's sea trunk with personal gear and clothing. Finally, he removed a painting from a hook above the small desk. "The Captain's family in better times," commented Piper. "I'll try to get it to him dry."

"We'll find some canvas to wrap it," offered Carl. "Do you have a key for the lock on the safe?" He pointed to the gray steel door behind the painting.

"He never locks it."

Carl pulled the door open. Inside were four stacks of bills, and behind those four small sacks of gold and silver coins. "Here," said Carl, handing a six-inch stack of Confederate bills to Piper. "Someday you can paper your library with these," he laughed.

"Keep it. I have my share of Confederate States of America memories already."

"Do you, and your men have any traveling money, Brandon?"

"Captain Jackman has six bars of your gold."

"Here," offered Carl, counting out twelve hundred dollars, "when you get back to the States, that should get you home." He opened a small leather sack of coins. 'Hand struck from Peru,' he said to himself. Returning the gold coins to the bag, he handed it to Piper. "There's probably five hundred dollars in gold. That should get you boat tickets home."

"The Captain will take care of us," offered Piper. "We have government gold straight from the California gold fields. We don't need charity."

"Brandon, I've served with a lot of officers in New Orleans, men who fought a lot of battles, men who will never get over the war, mean, irrational men. Your Captain sounds a lot like them. Take this, give it to a church if you don't need it."

Each boat was heavily loaded as it pulled away. "The barometer is steady, you should have an onshore breeze all day," called Carl.

Piper waived. "Someday I'll be in Boston to buy you a drink."

Minutes later, with the Gatling Guns and ammunition stowed aboard the *RETRIBUTION*, Charlie poured five gallons of coal oil over the deck of the scow and pushed it away from the ship. He then lit an oil-soaked rag and flipped it onto scows deck.

At the exact same moment, the paddle wheels began to turn, pulling away from the flaming scow. "That may be the last act of the war," commented Chad, standing next to Charlie.

Charlie nodded. "Kind of ironic isn't it, the final act of a war that killed thousands, done by an orphan Indian raised by a Quaker family who abhorred violence and taught only love.

Chad felt a tap on his shoulder. "I need to show you something," whispered Doc Parker. "Down in the hold where we are wrapping Secretary Pierce's body in lime and canvas."

With the cover off, the hatch was bathed in light. On the deck was a roll of canvas tied at each end, next to an open cask of powdered limestone. Doc Parker picked up a blood-soaked coat and retrieved something from the lapel pocket. He handed it to Chad.

"It's the letter, Chad, the one from Emperor Maximilian to Secretary Seward. The bullet went right through the Royal seal."

"Damn," moaned Chad. "Did the blood make it hard to read?"

"Worse," replied Parker, "it was written in water soluble ink."

48
WASHINGTON

THERE WAS NO wind with the rain that thundered onto the decks of the two ships as they crept into the Norfolk Harbor. A harbor tug led each ship to mooring buoys only a hundred yards apart. A small harbor boat approached the ship. A graying ensign clambered over the rail carrying a message pouch.

"Witness the effects of the peace time Navy, little brother," commented Carl watching the officer climb the ladder to the bridge. "A few months ago, that man probably commanded his own ship, now he's a message boy."

"I'm looking for Commander Carl Gritt, Retired," puffed the winded the ensign as he was ushered to the bridge.

"That would be me ensign," said Carl taking the message pouch from an outstretched hand and reading the communiqué inside.

"We have been summoned, little brother; you, me, Doctor Parker, Nick Kadzof, Secretary Pierce and Patrick Kelley. All others are confined to the ships," announced Carl.

"What the hell is this about?" Chad gripped the edge of the

chart table fighting off an urge to beat the hell out of the messenger. "Well?" he continued.

"Six months ago, I might have known," said the ensign, "now I deliver messages and probably will until I retire. Are all of you aboard this ship or do we have to go over to the *MOLLY K*?"

"Four here and one on the *MOLLY*," answered Carl.

"I am to bring six of you to the harbormaster's conference room."

"When we reach the beach, ensign, you can send a corpsman and a coffin for the sixth. Make it formal, like you were transporting a flag rank officer; trust me," answered Carl.

"Thank God we had enough water to clean up this morning," quipped Kelley as they stepped into a no-frills black coach flanked by two marines. Ten minutes later they were ushered into a large gray room with a huge gray table and a dozen gray chairs. The room reeked of stale coffee and tobacco. The curtains were drawn. A moment later a door across the room swung open.

"Thomas, is that a star on your shoulder?" asked a surprised Chad, gripping the hand extended by Thomas Mead. "How did you know we would be here?"

"We intelligence types have our ways. You were observed passing Freeport by one of several patrol ships looking for you. They shadowed you to Charleston and then went ashore and sent a telegraph."

"Thomas, why are the crews confined?" asked Doc Parker.

"In a minute Doc," replied Mead. "First, where is Secretary Pierce?"

"Miles was our only casualty," answered Chad.

There was a gasp from a tall, slight, man in a plain brown suit standing at the table. His scared face held stern eyes. Finally, he forced a smile.

Mead walked down the line of men introducing each to Secretary of State, William Seward. Seward grasped each man's hand in a firm handshake. Seward then introduced them to the third man in the room.

"This is Assistant Secretary of the Treasury Stephen Gartlin," he offered. "Now please sit with us while we explain. Thomas, it would come best from you."

Mead remained standing. He opened a leather briefcase and extracted three stacks of papers, and a folder with his notes. "Tomorrow afternoon this group will leave for the Capitol. We will travel by rail in a private car, and we will have no discussions with any other passengers or crew. The remaining crew will be ferried ashore this afternoon and will be housed in a hotel that the navy has taken over just about a mile from here."

"Are we prisoners or something?" asked Nick.

"No, Nick, but there will be some precautions. The voyage of the *KATARINA*, our exploration of Alaska, the diplomatic contacts in Mexico and the Cuban trip have all been declared national security issues. Some of it never happened. The rest happened as outlined in these reports." He picked up a document from several stacks and handed each to the men. "Every man will read, and sign a report for that portion of the adventure that they participated in. They will swear not to discuss anything that is not in these reports."

"I don't get it; you want us to lie?" asked Chad.

Seward stepped up next to Mead, placing a hand on his shoulder. "Let me help, Thomas." "First Alaska; there have been informal talks between Russia and the U.S. since 1843 over Alaska. In the next couple of months, Ambassador Stoeckel, will be returning to Russia for consultation with his government. The Russians need money, and their government is discussing selling Alaska. They don't know what Mead found in his exploration and we don't want them to know. It will only drive the price up."

"Now Mexico. Major Zidot has been very busy trying to sell the Emperor as a peacemaker. This government sees Maximilian as an agent of European intervention in the Western Hemisphere. We have championed independent democracies all over the Americas, and we don't want to be intervening across the hemisphere to keep the Europeans out. I'm looking forward to reading the letter the Emperor sent with Secretary Pierce. Maybe there is something we can do, but for now, all we will offer is to help him leave."

Chad reached into the leather writing folder he carried and extracted the letter. He handed it to Seward. "Pierce carried the letter to his grave," he commented, "you can see that it was destroyed."

A tear appeared on Seward's face, as he turned the letter over in his hands. "It is probably for the best," he said. "Since it is illegible, it is of no use diplomatically. Perhaps Miles' parents will want it as a memento."

"Now, this part applies to all of you," continued Seward. "This wild tale about a Confederate raider that no one knew existed, stealing gold that was never shipped, and a private recovery venture into the waters of a sovereign nation must stop. This country is tired of war. Some in the government are urging military intervention against Spain and in Mexico. The President and I want no trouble with Spain. Our official policy is to support Juarez in Mexico. Are there any questions?"

"How long before the whole story can be told?" asked Parker.

"Someday someone will fill in the blanks," replied Seward, "a story will be written. It will be fiction."

Kelley raised his hand like he was still in school.

"Yes Patrick," responded Mead.

"The crew of the *MOLLY K* only provided transport. Why are we under your thumb?"

It was Gartlin's turn to answer. "Captain Kelley, there is no record of the *MOLLY K* ever being registered. There is no record of the *RETRIBUTION* anywhere. There are plenty of wild tales of the exploits of some Jones County pirates and raiders. Those tales led to warrants for the arrest of anyone connected. Now if those two ships had been properly documented, before the war, let's say to you; and they had been impounded here in Norfolk for the last five years, well then, those tales would obviously be wrong. The warrants would be dismissed, and you would be free to sell both ships to the RusAm Trading Company."

Kelley smiled, "I could have used you over the last four years."

"I am authorized to settle the recovery fee for the treasury gold, that never shipped for a flat two-hundred thousand dollars," continued Gartlin. "I know the going rate is thirty percent and thirty percent may be more or less, but this will allow you to settle with your men tonight before we leave for Washington. It will also make it easier for them to see why protecting their government's diplomatic secrets is a grand idea," laughed Gartlin.

"Let me guess, Thomas," smiled Carl. "We aren't going to get a drink and the crews are staying put until we work out the details."

"Carl, you don't drink," replied Mead.

Carl smiled. "Give us a couple of hours. Do you have a room where we can hold a crew meeting after that?"

"It's set for 4 p.m. in the hotel ballroom," said Mead.

By six that evening, the deal was done. A tutoring session was set for the next day to help teach the crew how to handle questions. Secretary Seward hosted a final crew dinner.

Chad was the last to toast his shipmates, but there was little left to say. "Thank you. I have been proud to serve with all of you. Good Luck. Oh, by the way, Carl and I will be back here one week from today and we will need crews for both ships. We need to get them to Boston and then everyone will have three months off. The pay is good and the food better."

There was a laugh in the hall. Carl continued, "Hans Gott will be bosun of the *RETRIBUTION*, I mean the *WILLIAM SEWARD*, and Gary Farmer has agreed to accept the position of bosun on the *KATARINA III*. Please see them if you are interested."

Chad met General Mead in the hotel bar just before it closed.

"Thomas" he asked, "what will we be doing in Washington?"

"You will brief a presidential committee on what you know about Alaska and what you personally saw in Mexico."

"Will Zidot be there?"

Mead smiled, "No, he and the young ladies went to New York. They plan to meet you in Boston."

***

Twelve days later, the *KATARINA III* tied up to the RusAm dock in Boston harbor.

Chad crossed the wharf and stepped into the office. A proper lady sat waiting for him.

"Maria, it is good to see you."

"Captain Gritt, may we walk, I have things to tell you."

Chad held the door for Maria.

"Denali left for France three days ago. She is with Major Zidot. She said you will understand that she needs to keep an eye on what is happening. She has asked that I relay messages from Boston to a contact in Texas so that they can get to President Juarez. She hopes to be back next year," relayed Maria.

"I see," said Chad.

"You are disappointed Captain," continued Maria, "you are sad?"

"Neither surprised nor disappointed. Perhaps you could have dinner with me tonight?"

"Would it be for duty or for pleasure?" she asked.

"Pleasure, I hope."

"I accept."

APPENDIX

Meeting Minutes of the Committee for Manifest Destiny submitted to President Andrew Johnson:

August 5, 1866
Informal Meeting Minutes
Committee for Manifest Destiny
Confidential Report to President Andrew Johnson, Roster:

Sen. Reid McCarthy (R) N.Y
Sen. Marshal Bobby (R) Penn.
Sen. Sollis Taft (D) Maine
Rep. Paul Gifford (D) Ohio
Rep. Carson Peterson (R) Indiana
Rep. Chuck Barnett (R) N.J.
Sen. (Ret.) Marston Brook (D) Virginia
Gov. (Ret.) Clifford Thorp (R) Missouri
Lyle Barrston Jr. Pres. Astor & Bylan Trust Co. N.Y.
Mica Mills Pres. Mills Capital Syndicate Boston MA.
Hon. William H. Seward, Secretary of State

Subject:

A hearing on the validity of the conclusions of three reports filed by the late Assistant Secretary of State, Miles Standish Pierce:

Witness List:

Gen. Thomas J. Mead - leader Alaska Exploratory Expedition 1965
Chad Gritt: Chmn., Gritt RusAm Trading

Nicholas Kadjoff, First Officer *KATARINA* (wrecked) in Mexico

Christopher Parker M.D., Physician, *KATARINA* across Mexico March

Patrick Kelley - Commercial Marine Captain between Mexico and Cuba

Report 1 (desirability of U.S. intervention (and annexation) of Mexico)

Conclusion: Mexico is, has been, and will continue to be a territory more than an organized nation with deep class and political divides which consume all needed internally accumulated capital and drive off potential outside investors. These divides have led to four major civil conflicts in the last half century and can be expected to spawn continued conflict for decades to come.

The only thing that could unite the country (although only for a period of conflict) would be an intervention by the U.S.A. The cost of any such intervention would be enormous and would be dwarfed by the cost of occupying the land which is in need of everything and would be then torn not by a two-way conflict, but a three-way conflict where the existing polarized Mexican parties each demand services of the U.S. Treasury and make hidden war on the occupiers.

Discussion:

Witnesses: Gen. Mead, Capt. Chad Gritt, Nicholas Kadzof, Christopher Parker, M.D.

The witnesses found themselves shipwrecked on the Pacific Coast of Mexico and then had to make their way across war torn Mexico to the Gulf Port of Veracruz. During the trip they were embroiled in conflict with regular and irregular forces of both Royalist and Democratic factions and were invited to council with political factions of each side. The rules of war were that there are no rules. Murder, kidnaping, robbery and brutal execution of foes including wounded were part of the tactics of each side. There seemed to be a fatalist attitude by both factions that if they don't win this war, they will win the next one.

All witnesses support the conclusions of Secretary Pierces report.

Report 2 (potential U.S. intervention in or purchase of Cuba)

Conclusion: While Secretary Pierce did not travel extensively in Cuba, he was murdered there during a brief visit. Prior to that he talked to numerous officials and generated a report from Mexico with the following conclusions.

The class conflict of Mexico is as great or greater in Cuba, but the Spanish authorities have suppressed any conflict, which will only cause a greater explosion when the conflict starts.

The use of slavery for sugar cultivation represents the majority of the Cuban economy and the same forces that opposed emancipation in the Confederacy exist in Cuba, however in Cuba there is a real risk of a slave rebellion resulting in both sides fighting for their very lives.

Any U.S. involvement must include a heavy military hand and potentially devastating and costly conflict. The reward would be primarily agricultural and with more than half of the agricultural lands of the southern states lying fallow, a smaller investment in rebuilding southern agriculture would yield vastly greater reward.

If the U.S. is determined to push Spain out of the hemisphere it should wait until the Cubans themselves take action, which they inevitably will, and support their independence effort.

Discussion:

Witnesses: Capt. Patrick Kelley, Chad Gritt, Nick Kadzof

Captain Kelley was the primary witness on the theoretical conclusions of Secretary Pierce's report and related from personal experience their accuracy. While the use of slave labor remains legal in Cuba, the importation has been illegal for more than a decade, yet hundreds of slaves are landed illegally in Cuba every year.

This trade feeds a culture of piracy, smuggling and corruption that may be impossible to stamp out. The other witnesses concurred and added that this culture played a part in Secretary Pierce's demise.

Report 3 (The potential value of the Purchase of Alaska)

Conclusion: Secretary Pierce traveled to Alaska to meet then Colonel Mead at the conclusion of his expedition with a prejudice against any involvement. He favored annexation of Mexico over any expenditure for the vast "icehouse of Alaska."

Mead's reports and evidence as briefed to Secretary Seward began to change Mr. Pierce's mind. His experience in Mexico as noted in that report finished the job. Secretary Pierce was simply amazed by the vastness of Alaska. Alaska has more timber resources and fisheries and fur resources than have been developed in all of North America in three hundred years. Now with clear evidence of real mineral wealth the anticipated price of $10,000,000 seems a bargain.

Including Indians, there are probably fewer than twenty-five thousand people in the land and no political, class, or military conflicts. Pierce recommended immediate action to acquire this territory.

Discussion:

Witnesses: Gen. Mead, Chad Gritt, Nick Kadzoff

General Mead indicated that Secretary Pierce's summary was accurate and added detail not included in his report. He suggested reviewing other reports such as the telegraph survey of 1864 and the immediate funding of other surveys that can be "on the record" to bolster the momentum to acquire Alaska.

Captain Gritt and Nicholas Kadzof both have extensive experience in Alaska and Gritt's family operates the only open trading company between Boston, San Francisco and Alaska. He agrees with the report's conclusions but added three precautions:

1. It will be very easy to concentrate only on the fur seal industry, which is well developed, and miss the real opportunities outside of the one hundred square miles of the Seal Islands;

2. There is almost no infrastructure in Alaska and the country must be willing to invest in order to unlock its vast resources;

3. Alaska is like nowhere else in the country. A logger in Minnesota could not fathom the timber resources in Alaska. A fisherman on the grand banks could never imagine the quantities of fish in Alaskan waters. A railroad engineer building across the continent could scarcely imagine the distances and terrain difficulties of Alaska.

"Congress supports development where Americans live and promote their land. Alaska is empty with no self-promoters. Congress needs to learn about Alaska, about its vastness, because Congress itself will have to promote Alaska," offered Gritt in a handwritten note to all present.

Meeting Result:

All agreed to pursue Secretary Pierce's recommendations. It was agreed that the source materials and this report of the findings may be used for discussion purposes, and those present may represent the facts as accurate, but the sources themselves shall remain confidential until the documentation is released by order of the President.

W. H. Harrison, Confidential Recorder

AUTHOR'S NOTE

This story is fiction, but the conflicts presented in the United States and in Mexico are largely consistent with those wars, and traces of historical findings. The people, except for the few historical figures presented, are all fiction. They too are representative of the men and women who fought in, died, or survived those conflicts, and went on to influence their governments.

The scenes and locations in the book are all real, but in order to make the stories work, I have taken liberties with some of the detail. The same is true with the timelines in the book.

Alaska's purchase diffused a political movement at the end of the Civil War, to use America's newfound might to expand its borders.

While there is no evidence that the Emperor Maximilian ever warned the United States about coming instability in Mexico, there is a great deal of evidence that he was a transplanted patriot who desperately wanted a stable country. If he did not pass on the warning in this book, he should have. Unlike the American Civil War, which unified the country, the Maximilian-Juarez civil war did the opposite. It could be argued, that while there is progress in Mexico, many of the divides still exist. The political conflicts remain much the same and the banditry and corruption still challenge permanent progress. It seems that far too many friendly and industrious people of Mexico are still born to suffer.

And as to Alaska, there are now more than a century and a half of stories to tell. My GRITT BOOK SERIES finds snippets of problems and failures covered up by the powerful when something they wanted went all to hell. I then create fiction that just might offer a more accurate picture of what really happened than what is written in the history books. All of these stories have roots in Alaska. –Rodger Carlyle

ABOUT THE AUTHOR

RODGER CARLYLE *is a storyteller who draws on an enormous personal library of experiences. An adventurer, political strategist, and ghostwriter whose love of flying began in the Navy, his experiences stretch from New York to Los Angeles, from Amsterdam to Khabarovsk in the Russian Far East, and from Canada into Latin America.*

Through his passion for research, he treasures finding those events that are ignored or covered up by the powerful when some strategy or plan goes completely to hell. From there, he creates a fictional adventure narrative that tells a more complete story.

Rodger is comfortable in black tie urban settings, but he is never happier than in the wilderness. He has faced down muggers in San Francisco, intimidation by the Russian Mafia, and charging grizzly bears. Most of his stories take his readers to places they will never visit. He likes to think that he is there with them.

www.rodgercarlyle.com
Goodreads Author Rodger Carlyle
Amazon Author Rodger Carlyle

Made in the USA
Middletown, DE
25 July 2024